The Wolf Banner

Sons *of the* Wolf
Series
Book Two
by

Paula Lofting

LONGSHIP
Publishing

About the Author

Paula Lofting was born in Middlesex and grew up in South Australia where she nurtured a love of history as a child and adolescent. She returned to England in the late 1970s and now lives in West Sussex with her family. A psychiatric nurse by day, she spends as much of her spare time writing as she can. She is currently working on Book Three in the *Sons of the Wolf* series, *Wolf's Bane,* and a few other projects, such as her blog commemorating the year of 1066. Also a reenactor with Regia Anglorum, Paula can be found on her website - 1066: The Road to Hastings.

www.paulaloftinghistoricalnovelist.wordpress.com

ACKNOWLEDGEMENTS

Firstly, let me thank those of you who have waited patiently and impatiently for me to finish *The Wolf Banner*. I must apologise that it has taken so long to finish and make ready for publication. Originally, *The Wolf Banner* and *Sons of the Wolf,* had been written as one book, but when I came to publish, it was suggested that 250,000 words was a little ambitious for a first novel. So, I decided to make the cut off point for the end of Book One, Freyda's rescue. Four years on from 2012, when the first edition of *Sons* was published, the last half of the original manuscript has been completed with an addition of around 80,000 more words. I had decided to add more content, as the original felt more like the second half of a novel than an entire book, and this meant more research. Long story short, it took four years to get the thing done, edited, proofed and so on.

There are many people I want to thank for their help in getting this book published. They all know who they are. Thank you massively guys. I also want to thank Mike Harris and Richard Price for advising me on the siege of Scrobbesbyrig, and my friends in Regia Anglorum re-enactment society, especially Kim Siddorn, founder and Eolder of Regia, who sadly passed away in 2015. If not for him and his creation, I would not have this wonderful insight into the lives of the people of the late Anglo-Saxon age.

Lastly, thank you to fellow author and most wonderful friend, Louise Rule, for her encouragement and providing me with a tranquil place to write: The Cabin.

Dedicated to my wonderful children
Ron, Catherine
and
Connor

PLACE NAMES

Andredeswald – Forest of Anderida
Cantwarabyrig – Canterbury
Ceaster – Chester
Cofantreo – Coventry
Dyfflin – Dublin
Englalond – England
Ergyng – Welsh Archenfield
Glæsbyrig – Glasbury
Gleawecestre – Gloucester
Iralond – Ireland
Ircingafeld – English for Archenfield
Lundenburh – London
Northymbralond – Northumberland
Norwæg – Norway
Sæfren – River Severn
Scrobbesbyrig – Shrewsbury
Sumorsæte – Somerset
Súþrigaweorc – Southwark
Súþ Seaxa – Sussex
Súþseaxan – South Saxon
Pefensea – Pevensey
Wæg – River Wey
Westmynstre – Westminster
Y-Clas-ar-Wy – Welsh for Glasbury

THE LANGUAGE
of
SONS OF THE WOLF

Áwæcnan: To wake up, revive, spring from

Braies: For this period, braies are referred to as being a type of underwear that men wore. They might wear trousers over them or 'hose' legging-type garments held up by a belt looped into holes at the top of the hose.

Burgh/Burh: Referred to as towns with a walled enclosure.

Candelmæsse: A religious festival in February.

Ceorl: Pronounced 'churl': a man of the lower classes, though some ceorls could be substantial land-owners of reasonable affluence. There were different classes of ceorl within the social system, the lowest classes being slaves, then cottars or bordars.

Cniht/Cnihthad: A youth that serves, perhaps on horse. Forerunner of the later medieval knight.

Cýþþ ond Cýnn: 'Kith and kin', friends and relations.

Déaþscufa: (Dey-ath-shoo-va) Death's Shadow.

Dēorling: A term of endearment: dear or darling.

Dux Anglorum: An honorary title bestowed upon Harold Godwinson as the leading man in the kingdom, second only to the king. The Latin term for duke is d*ux*. Harold appears to have been the only earl who was given this title, such was his prestige in his time.

Earl: The term earl, or eorl, was formulated with the coming of the Danish king, Cnut, who introduced his *jarls* into a role like that of the English ealdorman, the magnates who governed the shires. They were largely responsible for administering justice within their lands. These men were second to the king, perhaps third after the *Dux Anglorum.*

Englisc - English

Fæderswica: Betrayer of fathers.

Fleóswín/Swínfylking: Battle formation, commonly known as the wedge, or boarsnout.

Géolatad: Yuletide.

Geoluhread: The colour of orange.

Handfastened/Handfasted: In this period, the eleventh century, this term mainly refers to a union between a man and woman that was not officiated by the church, therefore, although official in the eyes of the secular law, could be dissolved later, allowing both parties to marry elsewhere. Seems to have been more customary in these times, where a highborn man marries a woman who is of lower status. Also termed as *more danico,* the latinised version.

Heofonlice: Heavenly.

Heorþwerod: (heor-th-werod) Hearthmen. A lord's retainers.

Hide: a land-holding that was considered sufficient to support a family. This was equivalent to between sixty and 120 old acres (approximately thirty modern acres [120,000 square metres]) depending on the quality of the land. A thegn would need to hold a minimum of five hides.

Hlaford: Old English for 'lord', derived from *loaf giver*.

Hundred: The term, *hundred,* is first recorded in the laws of King Edmund I (939-46) as a measure of land and the area served by a *hundred* court. In the Midlands, this usually referred to a hundred hides within the boundary of the *hundred*; in the south, the number of hides in a *hundred* was variable.

Hundred moot: The meeting place at which the hundred court was due to meet monthly, as provided by the *Hundred Ordinances*. It was here that any man, of whatever status (except those who were slaves) could bring his suit to be heard. Criminals would be pursued and brought to justice by the leading men of the district.

Ísernwyrhta: Blacksmith, or one who works with iron.

Min leoftost/lufestre: Terms of endearment: my love, my lovely/lover .

Morgengifu: Directly translated to morning gift

Nihtgengan: Malevolent spirits that walk the night.

Níðing: (nithing) Someone who has been outcast – a person of no honour, no lord, no home.

Onbæc: Go back. Used in battle to command men to withdraw from engagement.

Pintel: Penis.

Scīr/Scīra: In the eleventh century England was made up of large units of land, shires, that were then divided into *hundreds*. Shires made up an earldom, of which the earl was in charge. The earl had his own thegns and officials to help run the *hundreds*. They also had a *scīrgerefa*, shire-reeve, who would help the earl run things in his earldom and deputise when he was away attending to the king.

Swica: Traitor.

Thegn: (Pronounced 'thane') A landholding servant of the king owing military and other duties in return for his land. A thegn is lower in status than an earl, but there are different levels of status within a thegnship. For example, a thegn might hold his land from an earl and not the king; therefore, he is lower in importance than a king's thegn. A thegn must own a minimum of five hides. Some thegns were very wealthy, holding hundreds of hides. The complexity of landholdings was not straight forward, with some thegns owning land from multiple lords, including other thegns.

Unwyrd: Misfortune, as opposed to *wyrd*, which means fate, good or bad.

Wéalas/ Wéalisc: Of the Welsh or Welsh language.

Wimple: A woman's garment, covering her hair, neck, and shoulders.

Wæpenwyrhta: Weapon smith

Witan/ Witenagemót: witan: council of the 'wise'; witenagemót: the meeting of the council, whose main duties were to advise the king. The witan was made up of earls, important thegns, and ecclesiastical clergy; some of these might also be women of high status - or abbesses. The king was expected to seek the Witan's counsel when choosing an heir.

Wyrmlicin: Meaning like a serpent. To call someone a *wyrmlicin* would be to insult someone.

THE FORTUNES OF MEN
(Old English poem)

Very often it occurs, with the power of God,
that man and woman conceive in the world
a child from their union, and prepare its form,
coaxing and cheering it, until the time comes,
going into the count of years, so that these young limbs,
these life-fast members, come to be burdened.
So they carry him and go forth on foot,
the father and mother, giving him much
and preparing him. God alone knows
what the winter will bring him in growing up!

For some that go forth with youthful spirits,
the conclusion will come woefully to the sufferer.
A wolf must devour him, a hoary heath-stepper—
then the mother will mourn his going-forth.
Such is not within the control of any man!

Hunger must despoil one. The tempest must drive away another.
The spear must spill out one, and warfare destroy another.
One must eke out existence without legs,
groping with hands—another feeble in the feet,
sickened with sinew's bane, bewailing his injuries,
mourning his measured destiny, afflicted in his mind.
Another must from the lofty tree fall featherless
in the forest, nevertheless he flies—
bouncing on the breeze, until he flies no longer,
a fruit from the woody tree. Then he upon the root
descends dejected, deprived of his soul,
fallen upon the earth, his spirit venturing forth.

One must on foot go forth onto the far-ways
by constraint, bearing his provisions,
treading the earth boldly, leaving behind him
only damp tracks, a stranger—he keeps
few living caretakers—hatred will be everywhere
due to his bleak fate, the friendless warrior.

One must ride upon the spacious gallows,
swinging in death, until his soul-hoard,
his bloody bone-coffer is broken.
There the raven seizes his eyeballs,
dusky plumed, tearing him open, soulless—
he can neither defend himself hatefully
with his hands against that breeze-reaver,
his life is departed, and he insensible,
despairing of spirit, waits for the outcome
pallid upon the pole, covered by deadly mist.
His very name is miserable!

Another must be in burning, afflicted with brands,
devoured by the wicked flame, a man fated to die.
There his life-parting is sudden,
the reddened fierce coals—a woman mourning,
who sees her child covered with torches.

The edge of the sword deprives another of life,
there on the mead-bench, by an angry ale-sot,
a man replete with wine—he was too nimble of words.

One must be in his beer by the butler's hand
a mead-flown warrior—then he does not know
moderation in restraining his mouth
in his own mind, but must yield up his life very sadly,
endure great sorrow, be shorn of all pleasures,
and men call him a self-killer—
bemourning by mouth the drinking of the inebriate.

Another must in his youth by the might of God
entirely ruin his misfortunate itinerary,
but in his old age soon become blessed,
dwelling in days of joy and partaking of prosperity,
treasures and mead-horns in kin-city,
which any human should be able to hold from here.

So variously, the Mighty Lord deals to all
throughout the four corners of the earth,
arranging and allotting, and holding onto his decrees:
for some prosperous weal, for others a share of woes,
for some gladness in youth, for others war and its fruits,
wielding the war-play, for some a throw or a shot,
and the brightest of glory, for others the skill at dice,
the weaving of chess-boards. Some are scholars,
becoming fast in wisdom. For others, wondrous gifts
through goldsmiths are prepared—very often he obeyed,
and he adorned the warrior of the generous king well,
and so he grants him broad lands as a reward—
and he accepts them graciously.

One must serve in the throng of heroes,
exulting at beer among the bench-sitters—
there is a great joy of drinkers there!
Another must sit at the foot of his lord
with a harp, accepting payment,
and always promptly twanging its strings,
letting the plectrum loudly resound that leaps,
the nails singing sweetly—his is a great longing.

One must tame the proud wild fowl,
the hawk in hand, until the blood-swallow
becomes pliable—he attaches the jesses,
feeds it in those fetters, exultant in its wings.
He feeds the wind-swift with little morsels
until the servant, with dress and deeds,
becomes manageable to his feeder
and used to the bachelor's hands.

And so elaborately the Preserver of Armies
throughout middle-earth shaped and shared
the crafts of men, and ferried their fate
to every one of the widest race upon the earth.
Therefore now must all say thanks to him,
because he allotted these to humanity by his mercy.

Translated from the Old English by Dr Aaron K Hostetter with his permission.

http://anglosaxonpoetry.camden.rutgers.edu/the-fortunes-of-men/

Part One

Secrets

1056

Chapter One

The Aftermath

Horstede, March 1056

Ealdgytha placed flowers against the wooden cross that marked the little grave of her daughter. Drusilda, who'd only seen two summers in her short life, had passed away four weeks previously, when winter's hard frost had lain upon the ground. Now the frost was gone, and as Ealdgytha raised her face in prayer, clouds assembled like guardians protecting the frail sunshine. She whispered the words for her daughter's soul and felt an ache in her heart at the reminder of its emptiness.

A hand touched her shoulder. "We will have more children, Ealdgytha."

She acknowledged her husband's presence with a wry smile. He knelt beside her and wound his around her waist. She rested her head against his shoulder. "God has given me more than I can bear. I pray there will be no more heartache for us."

"She was a beautiful little thing, but we will have many other children," Wulfhere said. "And we are not the only ones to have lost their children this winter. We will have more little girls."

Ealdgytha began to sob. She did not want more children. She wanted the baby she'd lost. But Drusilda's death had not been the only heartache that winter. For the fever had taken both the old and young in the village of Horstede.

It had been one thing after another starting with Esegar's death before *Crístesmæsse,* caused by the abduction of their eldest daughter, Freyda. The murder of Wulfhere's right hand man at the hands of

1

the abductor, had also caused a pall of depression over the village. Then there was that other problem: Freyda had bolted herself in her bower and refused to come out.

Ealdgytha had hoped that Æmund, her daughter's newly betrothed, would be able to coax the girl out of her despair, but he and his father, Leofnoth, left soon after the girl's rescue. When questioned as to their intentions regarding the coming wedding, Leofnoth shrugged apologetically, saying his son needed time to think about what had happened. Whatever that meant exactly, Ealdgytha had been uncertain.

She didn't voice her fears to Wulfhere, but intuition gave her an idea of what they might be thinking – that with Freyda came trouble. And the inevitable whispers and gossip that his wife had been kidnapped and abused by a lowly ceorl was too hard a thing for a young man to accept. And although Freyda vehemently denied Edgar molested her during the kidnapping, there would still be those who would doubt her words saying that there was no smoke without fire.

So, the young thegn left Horstede without word for Freyda, leaving the girl bereft, miserable, and listless.

After some days languishing in her self-imposed prison, Freyda emerged, much changed. She was not the same, and most likely would never be.

As for Wulfhere, he was not indifferent to his daughter's suffering; he simply felt powerless to help in any way. He avoided her as though she were contagious, believing the womenfolk would comfort her. Esegar's loss, however, plagued him more than Freyda's distress. The man had been his closest companion and the one upon whom he'd always relied on when in need of counsel.

With all this strife in his heart, and Ealdgytha too immersed in her own grief to give him comfort, Wulfhere longed for the warmth of his mistress, the dark, beautiful Ælfgyva. His need was a constant nag, intensified by grief, knowing also that soon a new child would be born to his lover. *His* child.

But, as fortune would have it, heavy snowfall that winter meant riding over to Waldron was impossible and the separation from Ælfgyva left him reeling with frustration.

In a way, Wulfhere was grateful for the obstruction, for he'd promised his wife, and himself, he would never see Ælfgyva again. So, the snow was a godsend, an answer to his prayers that he would not break the vow. At least not for now.

*

Sigfrith bent down to gather her little boy into her arms. His hair shone yellow in the sunshine making no mistake whose loins he had sprung from. Affectionately, she scolded him for having his hands everywhere and in everything. It seemed only yesterday she'd learned of her condition and now Leofweard was crawling as fast as a mouse, making it difficult to watch him whilst she worked.

As she beat the dust from the wall hangings, she thought about how grateful she was for his boisterousness. It meant he was alive and *hæl*, for she'd nearly lost him when the sickness came.

Sigfrith took the gurgling boy in her arms and a vision of his handsome father entered her mind. He'd visited his son for the first time only recently, displaying the exuberance of a little boy greatly taken with a new plaything. The smile that filled his face had lasted for days.

"He looks just like me. Another little Tigfi. And it *is* true what Lord Wulfhere said about his hair," the huscarle observed proudly as he cradled the boy, parading about the steading, displaying his pride like a peacock.

The sound of a horn blowing and a commotion at the gates brought Sigfrith out of her musing. Looking across the yard, she saw Yrmenlaf, the *isernwyrhta's* nephew, running down from the wooden rampart that bordered the palisade.

Shielding her eyes from the winter sun, she held her breath as the gates were opened to admit the visitors.

"Leofnoth..."

She watched them enter through Horstede's double gates. In came the twins, Wulfwin and Wulfric, fourteen winters old now and much grown in height and body since she'd last seen them. She clapped with excitement. Her master had sent them to live with Leofnoth to learn the disciplines of men, though Lord Wulfhere had another reason to send them from Horstede.

Their boyish unruliness had become more threatening, causing more harm to their younger siblings than light-hearted pranks should. In exchange for taking the boys in, Wulfhere had promised Leofnoth that he would give his daughter, Freyda, as a wife for Leofnoth's son, Æmund.

This was done despite her being already betrothed. Sigfrith may

3

have been a lowborn cottar's daughter, but there was little that went on in the master's household that she did not know.

Sigfrith knew her master and his friend Lord Leofnoth, had concocted the plan to wed Freyda to Æmund, to prevent her from marrying Edgar, the son of Wulfhere's long-time enemy, Helghi of Gorde. But the plan had gone awry, because now, it seemed, Æmund might have changed his mind.

Sigfrith strained to see who else was entering the gate and hoped that Æmund was among them, for she'd seen how gravely unhappy Freyda had been. Then, as she was almost giving up hope, there he was, last to enter, leading his horse into the compound. She gave a squeal of delight and ran inside to inform her master and mistress. They were going to be so pleased.

Wulfhere rose early that morning and busied himself with greasing and polishing his mail. Keeping himself occupied was the best way to cope with his grief. Esegar would have been doing this and thinking of Esegar made him bitter. If Freyda hadn't embarked on that reckless affair, his fyrdsman would still be alive and with him now. Esegar's wife's angry words still resonated with him, blaming the feud with Helghi for her husband's death. Wulfhere had given her Esegar's *wergild* but this had not eased her anger toward him. She still hated him.... And it had been little comfort to know Edgar was now declared *niðing* for Freyda's abduction and for shooting the arrow that killed Esegar. Edgar was not present at the sentencing. He was gone, no one knew where, but his life was now forfeit. Anyone was free to kill him with impunity, should they ever come across him.

As Wulfhere worked on his armour, Ealdgytha and her daughters were in the process of clearing out the old and cleaning away the cobwebs of winter. Wulfhere sighed as his wife rebuked Freyda for not paying attention to her work. "You are about as useful as a hunting bow without arrows," she'd scolded.

A flurry of excitement over by the hall doors caught his attention and he looked up to see Sigfrith wittering animatedly. "Lady! My lord!" she cried. "Your sons are here! They ride with Lords Leofnoth and Æmund."

Wulfhere shared a look of curiosity with his wife and hurried outside. To his delight, Wulfric and Wulfwin leapt from their horses and hastened to them, taking a parent each in turn, embracing them with hearty laughter.

"Wulfhere, *Wæs hæl!* I bid you good day," Leofnoth said as he dismounted. Wulfhere went to him and clasped his hand. "I hope we are not imposing?" Leofnoth smiled, showing his toothless gums.

"Not at all, my friend. You and Æmund are most welcome, most welcome indeed. Come inside and have some refreshments." Wulfhere felt a surge of hope that his friend had come to tell them good news.

"What do you think of your boys? Are they not growing into good strong men?" Leofnoth grinned, throwing his arms around the twins.

"Aye, they are indeed. No doubt you have been working them hard," Wulfhere replied, ruffling their hair. He noted the thickness of their upper arms and necks and was impressed.

"Their spear and sword work improve daily," Leofnoth said. "Soon they will be ready to stand in the shieldwall."

The boys beamed at the praise.

Wulfhere, his hand on Leofnoth's back, walked him into the hall with Æmund following quietly behind barely having said a word. Once inside, Wulfhere drew his friend away from the others so they could speak privately in his workspace.

"So, you have come to arrange the wedding?" he asked, glancing at Æmund who did not join them. Instead the boy leant against the lime-plastered wall as Wulfhere directed Leofnoth to sit at a bench where he had been working.

Leofnoth shrugged. "To tell you the truth, I don't know. Æmund is still unsure about having Freyda for his wife, and after what happened can you blame him?"

Wulfhere sat upright and frowned, curling his lips together and folding his arms across his chest. He was disappointed. "Yet Freyda is hardly at fault. She was taken against her will, as you and your son know."

"Nay, it was not her fault, but all men have a right to a wife with an unsullied reputation."

Wulfhere sighed and blew out his cheeks. "Granted, Freyda has always had a mind of her own, but she was young and foolish when she started the thing with Edgar. She could not have known how it would turn out. None of us could have known the evil in Edgar's mind. If truth be told, I always thought the lad a far better man than his father." Wulfhere paused, looking once more at Leofnoth's son,

5

who stood passively. "And Æmund knew she had been promised to Edgar before him. Nonetheless, he still insisted on having her – you did, too. You persuaded me to break my oath to Helghi and risk the earl's wrath for your son to wed my daughter. I lost a good man because of it – and now – now you tell me your son may change his mind?"

"It is one thing for a girl to have been promised to another man, but for that man to have carnal knowledge of her when she is promised to another…" Leofnoth hesitated, "well, that is a different matter."

"For Christ's sake, Leofnoth! Freyda insists he did not touch her!" Wulfhere banged his fist on the table. He was not fool enough to think his daughter was the innocent in all this. Freyda as good as admitted to him once that she'd lain with Edgar. There was no point in arguing Freyda's cause when he'd little faith in her himself. Instead, frustrated, he asked, "So what happens now?"

"It is for my son to decide." Leofnoth nodded towards Æmund. "I have told him it is his choice and I will stand by him whatever he does." He leant across and put a hand on Wulfhere's shoulder. "I have known you since you were born, your father was my friend, as are you. I would not want this to harm our friendship."

"Can you not make him keep to his side of the bargain?" Wulfhere jerked his head at the lad. "Think what this would mean for Freyda. If Æmund rejects her, all will think it was because she was raped and then no one will want her. Can your conscience allow that to happen? She might as well join a nunnery." He gave Æmund another sidelong glance, then turned back to the boy's father, saying in a gruff whisper, "I'm counting on you, Leofnoth, to make sure he doesn't go back on his word."

His friend looked sympathetic. "Before you and I come to blows over this, let Æmund see her and make up his own mind. Then you and I can thrash it out with an arm wrestle. Best of five, eh?"

Wulfhere nodded reluctantly. "You know I would win." It was a half-hearted attempt to indulge Leofnoth, but he was not really in the mood for jests.

"Then, where is she, this daughter of yours?" Leofnoth looked around the hall.

Over by the hearth, Ealdgytha and his other daughter, Winflæd, were being happily regaled with the twins' amusing tales. There was no sign of Freyda.

6

"She is not in the hall, lord," Sigfrith said, arriving with a jug of ale.

"Then find her and fetch her if you will," Wulfhere said.

"Nay, don't..." Æmund, emerging from the shadows, said, "I would speak with her alone if I may, Lord Wulfhere, if I have your permission?"

"You have my permission," Wulfhere replied. "Sigfrith, fetch her if you will."

"If you would pardon me, lord," Æmund interrupted, "I would rather find her myself, if I may."

Freyda all but collapsed. *Æmund! Here?* Darting this way and that, her heart pounded until she found a quiet spot in the kitchen. She set about the milk churn as though she wanted to beat the life out of it, reasoning that it would stop her shaking.

"So - here you are. I looked for you in the hayloft... but...."

Startled by his sudden appearance, her hand flew to her face. Over the milk churn went, the creamy contents spilling out onto the bottom of her dress. Freyda's gaze jerked to where Æmund stood in the doorway, framed by the sunlight. He still took her breath away.

She said with a weak smile, "You came. I thought you would not. It's been so long."

Freyda wiped her hands on her apron, then touched her cap to make sure it was in place.

"I am sorry." Æmund's eyes went to the mess on her hem.

"Look at me, I'm such a sight," Freyda said, self-consciously trying to tackle the dripping cream with her apron.

"Sorry, it was my fault, I frightened you."

"No, it was..." Freyda clammed up, could not speak.

"I... I... I wanted to see if. . . if there. . . there was to be a child," he stammered, his brown eyes flitting here and there.

Stunned, and refusing to look at him, she removed her apron and lifted her mantle, revealing a flat stomach. "As you can see, there is no babe. I told the truth when I said I was not raped."

"You are thinner..." Æmund said after a while, sheepishly.

She let go her mantle.

In a voice filled with guilt, Æmund said, "If I had not wanted you so much, I would not have waited to see. I would have looked for another."

Anger now replaced her nervousness. "And I am supposed to feel, what – honoured?" She wiped a tear that rolled down her cheek.

His lips twitched and he looked down at his feet.

"You think it was my fault, don't you? Look at me, damn you!"

He shifted awkwardly, one foot to another.

"You *do*, don't you? You *do* think it my fault. I can see it in your face."

Eyes flickering, he looked at her again. "Freyda I … You're not the same. You have changed."

"'Tis not *I* who have changed, but *you*. If I seem different it is because my heart… is broken." She retrieved the churn from the floor, stopping it from emptying itself, holding it like a talisman. She moved toward him, shaking. "I was powerless to stop him from taking me, and yet you look at me as if I gave permission. And yes, he did try to rape me, but he could not go through with it, because I begged him not to."

"You convinced him?" Æmund looked at her askance.

"Edgar may be many things, but a monster he is not. I said if he truly loved me, then he would let me be with you."

"And he agreed?"

"You don't want to believe me, do you? Why can't you just tell me? Do you want me or not? Is it so hard for you to say?"

"I *do!* I want you." She was before him. He touched her face tenderly and she inclined her head, trapping his hand between her shoulder and cheek. She momentarily kept him there until he withdrew and rubbed an escaped strand of her hair between his fingers, saying in a barely audible voice, "I remember how your hair shone like gold that day in the barn. Like a waterfall it was, flowing over your shoulders and down your back. That day it was for me – and only me, I hate to think he has touched you, laid his eyes over your body…"

She started to protest, and he touched her lips with his fingers. "I thought you were going to hit me with that thing," he said with a sensuous smile that sent a shiver down her spine. He took the churn from her, dropping it to one side. She closed and opened her eyes, tears of hope pooling in them. *Please, God, make him want me again.*

He tugged at the ties of her cap, pulling it free. Then he undid the clasp that held her hair in a knot. Its silky strands tumbled through his fingers, and he held it to his face, breathing in its fragrance.

"I have always imagined myself immersed in your hair," he whispered, his forehead resting against hers. "I still stir at the thought of you, my little Freyda. Nothing matters anymore, I still want you and I would like you to be my wife – if you will have me."

Leaning back, she stared at him, and he thumbed away a tear that ran down her cheek. "I *will* wed you, my Lord Æmund."

"Then we will forget all that has happened." Æmund drew her into an embrace and a strangled sob emanated from her throat.

He found her mouth and kissed her for some moments. Relief and tears poured from her. They withdrew and she cried unashamedly.

"Don't cry," he said pulling her close. "I am sorry I doubted you."

"I thought you believed it was my fault, that I had lost you forever," she sobbed.

"Nay, little Freyda I know it was not your fault. Not now…"

She lay her head against his chest and felt joy at the warmth of his body as he stroked her hair. It made her happy. But would things ever be the same between them? Could the past ever be forgotten? She wanted to believe it would and pushed such thoughts aside to concentrate only that he had come back to her.

Chapter Two

The Emptiness

"You must eat, girl!" It was the eve of the wedding and Ealdgytha was frantically making alterations to her daughter's gown. "It hangs on you like a clothes pole! You're nothing but a bag of bones. Your husband will chafe himself when he lies with you."

"It is not my fault, Mother. I have been unwell."

"Unwell, my foot. There was nothing wrong with you. Nothing that was not your own making. Sigfrith, give me some more of those pins." Ealdgytha snatched them as a hand came around the side of the partition, then knelt to tack the hem.

"Why must you always think everything my fault?" Freyda snapped.

Ealdgytha looked up and glared at her daughter, catching the girl's leg with the needle. Freyda cried out.

"Honestly, Freyda! Can you not see your own behaviour in any of this at all? If you had not been running wild in the forest, meeting secretly with that Edgar Helghison, that *thing* would not have happened in the first place!"

Rubbing her leg, Freyda retorted, "Perhaps *you* should have cared more about what I was doing. After all, is that not a mother's duty? Perhaps it is you who is at fault."

Ealdgytha got to her feet. "How dare you speak to me in this manner? You are most fortunate we have not disowned you and cast you out like a *niðing* for the trouble you've brought upon this family. Esegar lost his life because of the mischief you caused. His poor wife is still beside herself with grief. You have no consideration for others. You should be grateful that Æmund still wants to wed you."

Freyda gave a haughty laugh, then said, smiling, "Oh yes mother, I know the trouble *I* have brought upon this family. If it was not for me, it would be *you* who stood shamefully in judgement before everyone. It would be *your* shame they would see... *yours!*"

"Just what do you mean?"

"You treat Father like a servant and no wonder he runs off to be with that woman, bringing shame on you – shame on us all! Yes, Mother! If not for me, the black sheep of the flock, then it would be *you* everyone would be talking about. It is *you* who should be grateful to *me* -"

Ealdgytha shut her up with a slap. Freyda gasped and held her hand to her face, already starting to glow.

Ealdgytha's hand smarted. "How dare you? I've had enough of your impudence! You are selfish to the core, young lady. Sigfrith, fetch Gunnhild and tell her to bring the stick from the kitchen."

"You're not going to beat her are you, my lady?" gasped Sigfrith.

"I certainly am, and I'll thank you to run along and do as you're told without question. I should've done this a long time ago!"

"But my lady!" Sigfrith protested.

"Sigfrith, you will fetch Gunnhild and the punishment stick, and you will return quickly. That stick has not been used for years. It's about time it was!"

"Nay, my lady, please don't. Would you have her go to her husband black and blue on her wedding night?"

"No doubt Æmund will thank me for it when he hears of this behaviour. Now, if you value your position in this house, Sigfrith, you will do as I say – *and quickly!*"

Gunnhild had always criticised her for allowing the children to be so unruly. At last she would silence the fat troll once and for all.

Freyda quivered like a newly sprung arrow. "Please, Mama, I am sorry. Do not beat me, *please*. I am truly sorry for-for everything – really!"

"I have suffered your insolence for long enough, daughter. My mother would never allow me to conduct myself with such disrespect. You've had far too much independence, and it has spoiled you. What your husband is going to do with you, I do not know."

Freyda threw herself at Ealdgytha's feet.

"*Please*, I am truly repentant! There is no need for this! I will never again be insolent - or rude, I swear! I will be your good obedient daughter, Mother, if you will just let me!"

11

"Stop being hysterical and stand up! Have you no dignity? You have never understood the meaning of obedience! It seems it must be beaten into you!"

"About time too!" The wicker partition was suddenly thrust aside, revealing the indomitable sister-in-law, Gunnhild. The widow of Wulfhere's brother stood tapping the punishment stick against the palm of her hand.

"I've always said that girl needs a good beating! Anybody would have thought the little minx royalty the way she swans around the place, pleasing herself as to what she says and does without a care in the world!"

"Aunt Gunnhild is right," Freyda sobbed, "I should not have been given so much liberty to do as I please. You should have locked me in my bower, Mother, and not let me out – ever!"

"Ealdgytha, don't just stand there, *do* something," Gunnhild said, shoving the stick into Ealdgytha's hand. She grabbed one of Freyda's arms and called to Sigfrith to take the other. "Well, what are you waiting for, woman? Remove the dress from her and let's get on with it!"

Stripped to her shift and held by her aunt, Freyda stood sobbing whilst Ealdgytha trembled, waiting for Sigfrith to appear, but there was no sign of her.

"Sigfrith? Oh, confound that girl. Ealdgytha, just get on with it, I will hold the girl myself."

Her determination fading, Ealdgytha stood reluctantly with the rod in her hand. Facing her, Gunnhild held Freyda by her bone thin arms, nodding encouragement. Freyda whimpered and Ealdgytha shivered at the sight of the knobbly spine showing through the girls shift.

"Sister, get on with it! Oh, by the wings of the blessed wood-sprites, you are a feeble woman! You take over here and I will do the deed."

Gunnhild thrust Freyda forward and they swapped places. Ealdgytha looked away, unable to look at her daughter's eyes as her sister-in-law wasted no time in commencing the procedure. At the first strike, Ealdgytha let out a cry and Freyda screamed. Freyda cried out again as the next blow struck, and the next, and the next, and with every crack of the stick, Ealdgytha recoiled.

"Papa! I want my papa!" Freyda called out.

After the fifth blow, Ealdgytha could no longer stand it. "Stop! God have mercy on me! Gunnhild! It is enough!"

12

Suddenly the door flew open and Wulfhere stormed inside.

"What in Hell's name is going on in here? I can hear the screaming outside and so can everyone over at Gorde I would imagine! Gunnhild! Put away that damned rod. Wife, would you have our daughter spoiled for her wedding night? Leave her be. God's bones, woman, what are you doing?"

"She is already spoiled!" Ealdgytha raged at him amidst her tears. "And you did nothing to stop it!"

Wulfhere grabbed the stick as Gunnhild, determined to get another strike in, raised it once more. The woman's puffing, sweaty face glowed with effort as she wrestled with Wulfhere to retrieve it, but not before Wulfhere snapped it across his knee and threw it at her feet.

"What are you two old hags thinking of, for the love of Christ?" Wulfhere demanded, staring at each of them in turn. "Look at her," Freyda, a sobbing heap on the floor, was bleeding through her linen undershift. "Do you think her husband will want to see her marked like this when he beds her?"

Freyda crawled to him and he gathered her in his arms. Watching them, Ealdgytha teemed with jealousy. Chin trembling, she said, "This is your fault, Wulfhere, you've done nothing but indulge her since the day she was born. She has always been your favourite, even before me or any of the others!"

"Don't be ridiculous, woman. Why were you beating her? What has she done?" He gathered Freyda in his arms and carried her, still sobbing, to the cot. Sitting beside her he lifted the bloody shift to examine the wounds. Ealdgytha's heart sank, hearing him draw breath.

"She said some things… discourteous things, and I snapped. Perhaps I should not have," Ealdgytha said, her bitterness tinged with regret.

"She has needed a beating for a long time now, that one."

Wulfhere, his face lined with disgust, turned on his sister-in-law. "Get out, Gunnhild. This is nothing to do with you!"

"I was only doing what your wife didn't have the courage to do! And in all due respect, Wulfhere, Ealdgytha is right. You *have* indulged the girl far too much for what is natural. She needed to learn a lesson."

Wulfhere got up off the bed sharply. "The only lessons to be learned in my household are the ones *I* see fit to teach. I'll thank you to remember that."

"If you did your duty as a father should, then your children would not be so wild and unruly. *Someone* has to teach them!"

"Get out of my sight, Gunnhild. You're lucky I haven't rammed that stick up your fat backside! If you touch any of my children again, I will dispossess you and you will have nothing! You and that idiot son of yours can starve to death in the woods for all I care. Now get out of here!"

Gunnhild gasped, hands going to her hips. Ealdgytha would have laughed had she not been so upset. With flared nostrils, puckered lips and thick, caterpillar brows crumpled together, the woman resembled an angry ox. Wulfhere stamped his foot and feigned a lunge. She gasped again, turned on her heel, and hurried to the door where she hesitated for a moment, looking Wulfhere up and down, her mouth pursed indignantly. "Well, we all know where *that* little madam gets her behaviour from. Obviously from her father!"

The door slammed behind the she-bear and Ealdgytha, filled with remorse, burst into sobbing.

Looking at her in disbelief Wulfhere said, "Why is it that *you* cry? Your daughter is the one who should be crying."

Through her tears she replied, "I know I did wrong... I am too late. It should have been done before now. Lessons like these should be done long before the age of sixteen."

Her husband took her by the shoulders and shook her. "Ealdgytha! She is to be married tomorrow, and you would beat her black and blue for her husband to see what a bad daughter she is?"

In his eyes there was such contempt. She had not noticed the change in him until that moment. He seemed older, more strained, hair thinning on top, grey strands replacing the fair. The lines around his eyes, less blue than before, were more noticeable. Once those eyes had sparkled vibrantly for her; now, they seemed so lifeless.

"What have we become, Wulfhere?" she asked.

Wulfhere blinked and bowed his head. "We?" He let go of her. "I do not know," he said quietly, his eyes downcast.

She wanted him to comfort her yet lacked the courage to ask. To do so would be to invite rejection and she could not bear that.

Through his silence, she sobbed until he said at last, "Take care of her, Ealdgytha."

Ealdgytha nodded and mumbled as Wulfhere rose to his feet to leave, "Wulfhere, I am sorry..."

14

"No, Ealdgytha, be sorry for Freyda's sake, not mine."

Ealdgytha, wiping away the tears, went and sat by the curled figure of the weeping girl. She stroked her face but Freyda pushed her hand away.

"Papa, I want my papa."

Accepting the rebuff, she stood, looking at Wulfhere for guidance. His hand was on the door latch as though waiting for her permission.

Ealdgytha nodded. "I will get a honey poultice and some water. I have to alter the gown, so you stay with her." With that, she picked up the garment and made for the door, looking back once as Wulfhere sat stroking his daughter's hair. The image burned deep into her soul: the girl on the bed, her life just beginning. She remembered how happy she'd been on the eve of her own wedding. Ealdgytha would never feel like that again, for Wulfhere's heart no longer belonged to her. The thought was like a stab wound in the chest and with nothing left but jealousy, lost love, and an ebbing marriage, she moved through the doorway, a silent prayer on her lips that God would take her soon, for she no longer wished to live with the emptiness.

Chapter Three

The Wedding

The grass was cool beneath Freyda's bare feet as she made her way to the little stone chapel where Æmund and Father would be waiting. Behind her a trail of giggling maidens skipped and sang as they scattered petals in their wake. A slight wind harried her finely woven veil, bringing with it a sensation that she was floating, such was her joy.

Outside the chapel, surrounded by his friends, Æmund stood, the lovely sunshine shining on his brown hair, giving the illusion it was the colour of chestnuts. The air was infused with the spirited banter of youth and it sent a thrill of enjoyment through her. Acknowledging first the well-wishers on either side of the path, Freyda's nervous gaze then wandered over to her betrothed. His smile, reassuring, exposed the attractive dimples that she'd found so charming the day they'd met in the hay barn.

Æmund's companions laughed and administered him with congratulatory backslaps and whispered encouragements. Freyda imagined the nature of these jests, and the smile slipped from his lips, coyly, when she caught his embarrassed eyes.

His gaze wandered over her, and as she came to stand by him, her eyes met his. He grinned and took her arm in his as they walked in through the archway of joined hands. Father Paul was waiting with a garland of violets and primroses. When they stood before him, he placed it on her head, to signify her virginity, and she thought she heard people sniggering. She brushed it off, laughing gaily. *Let them think what they like.* Nothing was going to ruin this day.

Mother had advised her to keep her gaze low and humble, but she was unable to stop herself from sneaking a peek at him now and then.

16

His hair was smartly combed, his face shaved, and she could not help the tiniest of smiles at the razor nicks on his chin and jaw.

He was dressed neatly in a reddish tunic, and hose of dark madder, overwrapped with finely woven *winningas,* secured with silver hooks. A leather belt encircled his slim waist, buckled with gold plating, a wedding present bestowed on him by her father.

From this he hung the bridal gift she had given him, a *seax* in a patterned leather sheath. For a passing moment, she thought of Edgar, doubting that he would have evoked the same pride in her that Æmund did. It was a heartening thought, for it meant that she'd no regrets.

The contract and bride-price were agreed and recorded, and it was time for Wulfhere to step forward with Freyda's shoes, presenting them to his new son-in-law as a token of his acceptance and his transfer of her care. Her bridesmaids giggled making Freyda laugh as Æmund gingerly took the shoes from Wulfhere, passing them to one of his friends. The rest of them guffawed as the friend pinched his nose humorously.

Wulfhere then took both hers and Æmund's hands for the handfasting, wrapping a silk ribbon around both.

"I give to you in honour, Æmund, son of Leofnoth, this woman, Freyda, my daughter, to be your wife, with a right to half your bed and your keys, and to a third of your goods acquired, or to be acquired, according to the law of the land and the Lord God in Heaven," Wulfhere said.

Freyda and her groom were then ushered inside the chapel to hear the wedding mass. Father Paul stood at the altar. The young couple knelt before him, as he spoke the mass, alternating between Latin and Englisc. After this, Æmund's friend, Redwald, handed him the marriage ring, and he placed it over Freyda's left thumb, saying, "I take this woman Freyda, daughter of Wulfhere, to be my wife, according to the law of this land, and in the name of the Father." Then he placed the ring on the next finger saying, "And of the Son." He moved it to the next finger. "And of the Holy Ghost." Until finally he left it on her fourth digit. "Amen."

Father Paul blessed their union with a benediction, beseeching them to treat each other well and be true and faithful, forsaking all others, or forever to suffer the displeasure of the Heavenly Father should they not. He made the sign of the cross, and the congregation joined by saying, "Amen."

Freyda's shoes were once again the object of mirth as they were passed to Æmund. He looked at them momentarily, then with a look of amusement, lightly tapped them on Freyda's head as cringing, she tried to duck out of the way of them.

Æmund giggled and said, "I accept you, Freyda, daughter of Wulfhere, as my wife."

That over, and to cries of "Kiss the bride!" a great cheer went up as Æmund leant forward and brushed both her cheeks with his lips before kissing her mouth to applause. Happiness overrode any hurt or discomfort from her punishment the day before and as she and her groom walked outside, it seemed that the sun was shining for her at last.

*

His daughter stood on her tiptoes to whisper into Wulfhere's ear. "Thank you for this, Papa."

They watched the whirling wheel of dancers spin by, stamping their feet in time with the music. "It has been a wonderful day."

"Don't thank me, thank your mother. She is the one who organised it, I just shed the silver for it."

Wulfhere followed Freyda's stare to where Ealdgytha sat alone.

Her face is so sour it would curdle a bucket of milk if she looked at it long enough," Freyda muttered.

"Now daughter, you should not speak so of your mother, even if she can churn milk into butter with just one look." They both laughed and she gave a small cry, grimacing as he embraced her. "I hope you do not hurt too much today, sweeting?" he asked her.

"Just a little, Father, but I will not let it spoil the day."

"I'm glad. You look beautiful, daughter. Your husband is a lucky man, but I hope you learn to curb your wilful ways. Don't give him cause to spurn you!" He gave her a smile to lighten his words.

"I won't, Father. You will be proud of me. And soon you will have a grandson to play with."

A voice behind them made him turn. "Lord Wulfhere? Might I speak with you."

Wulfhere stared. *No, it can't be, not today of all days!* It was Ælfgyva's woodsman. "What are you doing here?"

"My lord, I wish not to trouble you, but I need you to see something," Welan replied.

Wulfhere ushered the man away to a quiet corner and leant over him, his hand against the lime-plastered wall.

"Why are you here, woodcutter?" he demanded, as he hid Welan from the rest of the guests. "If you have come to tell me Lady Ælfgyva has had the child, then you have picked the wrong day to do it. Today is my daughter's wedding."

"Then come with me to your stables, my lord, where we can speak in private."

Wulfhere relaxed his arm and glanced slyly over his shoulder. He nodded, and took the man's elbow, leading him through the crowd and through the adjoining kitchen to an outside door. The noise from the hall rang out as Wulfhere hurried Welan across the courtyard.

The stables were crowded with guests' horses, and Welan led Wulfhere to where Ælfgyva's servant, Fritha, was nursing a bundle as she sat on a pile of hay. A young man whom Wulfhere knew to be Fritha's son, Morcar, stood by her, arms folded.

Wulfhere's heart missed a beat when he saw the swaddle in the woman's arms. *Ælfgyva's child. His child... his secret.* The woman stood, held out her arms and frowned when he did not take it. Instead Wulfhere gazed mutely at the little bundle.

"How did you all get in? I gave strict instructions for the gates to be locked."

Welan said, "I climbed them, my lord, and opened them for the others. There was a problem with the ditch, but I am used to wading through water in the marshes. Do not fear that anyone saw us. I made sure we were not seen."

Wulfhere turned again to look at the child held in the woman's arms. The tiny head with a smattering of downy black hair and little rosy cheeks appeared as unfamiliar as any strange babe would. It was nothing like his other child, Rowena, whose death had reunited him with Ælfgyva almost year ago. She had been as blonde as he, unlike this one who was dark like its mother. How could he be sure it was really his?

Wulfhere turned to scowl at Welan. "Why do you bring the child here on such a day? You must know we celebrate my daughter's wedding today."

"My lady asked that we bring your daughter to you. It is her dying wish she be with you, my lord," Welan said.

"*Dying*? Did you say – *dying* – wish?"

Welan nodded, his crinkled old eyes filled with sadness. Wulfhere had always known that like himself, the woodcutter also loved the black-haired enchantress. But unlike Wulfhere's, the woodcutter's love had been unrequited.

"By now, she might be gone already," Fritha said, drawing the bundle back to her.

"But what happened?"

"The babe came late," the scornful Fritha said. "The labour was not a good one and there was much blood loss. Lady Ælfgyva was much weakened by it."

"Is there no hope at all?" Wulfhere found no comfort in her stony face. He turned to Welan whose eyes refused meet his. "What of a healer? Has one not been sent for? Is she alone?" It tore at him to think of Ælfgyva by herself and suffering.

"The midwife was with my lady when we left. I would not have left her, weak as she was, but she was strong enough to insist we bring the littl'un to you," Welan's voice cracked. "My lady said you would see to it the babe is looked after and… that you would trust me to take care of her property until the time the child can take care of it herself."

"Ælfgyva, she still lived when you left her?"

"Aye," nodded Welan. "Barely."

"Did she not call for me?" Wulfhere asked.

"She thought only of her daughter. She knew you would not come again – not now."

Fritha held his daughter out to him again. "Take her, my lord."

'Her daughter' – another girl, then. Reluctantly, he took the bearn in his arms, but he could not look at her. He looked away from this reminder of the woman he'd lost. "I cannot do this. I am sorry, but I cannot."

Fritha looked at him disdainfully.

The child gave a little mew.

Welan said, "Do this one thing for my lady, by the light of God, you owe her something!"

Then Fritha spoke, this time with a gentleness that surprised him. "She is *your* bearn, my lord."

Another mewing sound and Wulfhere at last met the babe's eyes. The little dark pupils seemed so full of knowing as they gazed intently at him. *She knows who I am.* He was at once filled with joy and sadness as he held her. Any doubts she was not his melted away in the warmth of her little body. With her screwed up face and fine black hair, she *was* his daughter – and Ælfgyva's – born of their love. Soon her mother would be no more. How could he turn his back on her?

The bearn began to cry. "Ssh, little one." He gently rocked her and a moment later looked up to see Fritha, her son, and Welan disappearing through the doors of the stable. He called to them, "What do I call her?" But they hurried away and did not look back.

The little bundle vibrated as a shrill cry rang. He searched his mind for a credible plan. He could not walk into the hall in the middle of his daughter's wedding, a newborn child in his arms.

As he tried to comfort her, a thought came. Sigfrith. She was still feeding her own little boy… That was it! He would pretend the bearn was a foundling, unwanted and left in the stables. Such things happened he'd heard. It was a feasible story. Wulfhere placed the child in the basket and went to find Sigfrith.

As he explained the tale of a babe he'd found in the stables, Sigfrith's eyes narrowed as she looked at the child, then back at Wulfhere.

"She needs feeding," Wulfhere said, feeling uncomfortable. Sigfrith picked up the squalling babe, cooing as she held the little mite.

"She? How do you know it is a girl, lord?" Sigfrith asked.

"It looks like a she," he blundered. *Damn!* The woman was a hard set of eyes to pull the wool over.

Sigfrith rifled through the child's swaddling. "Oh, you are mistaken, my lord. 'Tis a little boy."

"No, Sigfrith, it is a girl, I tell you!"

Sigfrith smiled and Wulfhere felt like a fool as he scratched his head.

"Of course, lord, so she is. It is I who am mistaken." Sigfrith turned with the bearn in her arms. "Come then, little foundling, let's get some of Sigfrith's milk into you."

"Sigfrith! Don't let the mistress see her just yet!" Wulfhere called to her. "Not until today is over, at least."

"What is she to be called, lord?"

"I-I have no idea."

Sigfrith tutted and walked away, and Wulfhere sank down on a pile of packed straw, head in his hands. If only Esegar was here... *he* would know what to do. But Esegar was dead, and Ælfgyva was dying. Wulfhere pushed away images of his lover on her deathbed. He must pull himself together and get back to the wedding. After a few moments, he breathed deeply and rose to join the others in the hall.

21

The newlywed couple burst through the wooden doors of the stables. Freyda's laughter rang out as Æmund darted here and there, panicking, and looking for his horse. Any moment, Æmund's friends would be on their trail like wild cats chasing mice.

Æmund scratched his head. "Now, where did I secure my damned horse?"

"Do you think they saw us leave?"

Æmund chuckled. "No doubt, my little Freyda. I bribed Redwald to allow us a head start. But knowing my dear friend as I do, he won't be able to restrain himself or the others for long. Now, where is that animal?"

"Here, let's take my father's horse," Freyda suggested, leading him to Hwitegast's stall.

"That great thing? The brute will kill us both!" There was a glint in Æmund's eye. Hwitegast snorted as Æmund patted the white horse's neck. "He must be at least fifteen hands! I have only ever seen one bigger, a horse that belonged to a Norman cniht in the king's household," Æmund said, sighing. "Mind you, we will need a strong, fast mount if we are to get away at speed."

"Hwitegast is indeed strong and fast."

Freyda smiled and shrugged like a mischievous child. Æmund's arms went around her and he groaned, his mouth warm on hers, tongue ardent and exploring. She shivered as his kiss sent sparks running down her spine. He felt her breasts, one to the other, stroking, squeezing, as the heat stirred in her groin. Nothing would ever make her feel as happy as she did at that moment.

"You're shaking," she said when they drew apart. "And blushing." Freyda touched his cheek.

"It is you, my little Freyda, I could take you here, right now." Grabbing her buttocks, he lifted her to him.

"Nay, Æmund there will be time later for that, but for now, we must make haste," she said, "or they'll catch us!"

Together they readied Hwitegast. Æmund swung first into the saddle. He leant, extending his hand with a sensuous smile. She took it and their fingers melded, eyes locking for a moment. He pulled her up behind him in the saddle and she pressed against him, enjoying the sensation of his nearness. Within minutes they were out of the gates, tossing a coin to the boy who'd opened them, and galloping away down the sloping village track, leaping over the low boundary hedge and into the fields that skirted the village. Æmund turned his head to look at her and she laughed and clasped tighter around his waist as he spurred Hwitegast on to a gallop.

Æmund allowed Hwitegast to have his head, impressing Freyda with his horsemanship. They reached the road and she caught a glimpse of something up ahead. "Æmund? Is there someone in the road?"

"It looks like Edgar Helghison!" Æmund muttered, slowing the horse down.

"It *is* Edgar!" Freyda cried.

Freyda peered at the figure as they came to a halt just a few feet away. A man stood like a stone statue, blocking their path.

Æmund stiffened. "What does the Goddamned fool think he is up to?" Hwitegast pranced and snorted nervously.

Freyda looked to the left. Too muddy and there was a watery ditch. To the right it was bounded by trees.

"Why doesn't the idiot move out of the way?" Amund growled.

Edgar's eyes stared at them. His face was expressionless, and Freyda barely recognised the young man she'd secretly met with in the woods. He stood, like a soul in torment, barefoot, dressed in pitiful, filthy rags. What could be seen of his dark hair was wild, and his beard, like uncarded wool, reached down to his chest. He was much leaner than before, making him appear taller. Her stomach churned; it did not sit well that she was the cause of his descent from vibrant youth to a mere human shell.

Æmund shifted in the saddle and Freyda feared he would dismount to confront Edgar. She tightened her grip on Æmund's waist and tugged him closer to her. Edgar's demeanour unnerved her.

Freyda whispered in Æmund's ear, "Leave him. He is already a *niðing*."

Æmund ignored her warning. "What are you trying to do, man?" he barked at Edgar, "Do you want to get yourself killed?"

Edgar said nothing. He continued to stare blankly at them.

"He is mad," Freyda whispered. "Living in the forest has made a lunatic of him."

She shivered as Edgar's gaze met hers and for a moment there was a spark of recognition in Edgar's eyes, then it was gone and there was nothing again.

"He is lucky he has not been hunted down and killed like the outlaw

23

that he is!" Æmund said. "I do not wish to be reminded of what I have taken so long to forget, today of all days."

"Please, my love, don't let anything spoil this for us. Let him be."

"I do not wish to spill blood, *min deorling*, rest assured." Æmund turned to speak to Edgar. "Stand aside, man, and let us pass!"

Edgar did not move.

Hwitegast appeared to sense something was amiss, and Æmund fought with the animal as he tried to take off. "If you do not move, you low-born *wédehund*, then I will ride you down!"

Still Edgar did not move. Æmund shifted again in the saddle, his hand feeling for his *seax*. Hwitegast circled uneasily. Edgar's gaze seemed aimed at the sheath on Æmund's belt and Freyda feared the worst. Then he moved slowly to one side so they could pass, and she breathed a sigh of relief.

"He is letting us go," Freyda said, putting a hand on Æmund's wrist as he unsheathed his weapon.

"I could kill him, damn him!"

"What would that achieve? He is already a ghost."

"Aye, but he is also an outlaw, to be killed on sight. You want that Edgar should get away with what he did to you? Do you still care for him?"

"Nay, Æmund, I care not for him. Remember what you said to me that day in my father's orchard, 'The past is no more than a whisper, faded into the air on the wind of time'. He is dead to me. I beseech you, let us leave him be."

Æmund smiled at her over his shoulder. "Aye, I did say that, didn't I? Are you sure you feel nothing now?"

"Nay, nothing. You are my husband and 'tis you that I want."

Æmund nudged the horse's flanks and Hwitegast walked forward.

Looking away, Freyda felt Edgar's eyes boring into her as they passed by him. She risked a last peek at him as Æmund urged Hwitegast into a canter. Edgar was no longer there. He was gone, leaving nothing but the rustling of bushes. But further behind them on the road, she saw a party of riders come galloping around a bend.

"Æmund! Faster! They're coming!"

"Damn!" Æmund replied and spurred their horse on. "We'll never escape them now! Damn Edgar! Just one more reason to hate him!"

He kicked Hwitegast into a gallop, but the hunters were catching up with them. There was an abundance of whooping and fighting among themselves to be the newlyweds' captors. As Æmund rattled the reins and shouted, "Yah! Yah!" Freyda's brothers rode alongside them, grinning, voices ringing out above the pounding of hooves, calling instructions to each other.

Freyda squealed as their horses collided. Wulfric, who was riding pillion, reached out to grab their halter and Æmund failed to swat his hands away. Laughter rang out and a horn blew as Æmund was compelled to be captured.

"Ha! It is fitting that the maiden's brothers should rescue her from this insolent abduction!" Wulfwin cried triumphantly as he and his brother slowed them down, eventually forcing them to a halt.

"I let you win," cried Æmund.

There were cheers from the others as they gathered around them and Freyda, infected by their laughter joined in. Then it was time for Freyda and her abductor to be brought back to Horstede now that their escape had been thwarted.

They stood like thieves, hands bound together, barely able to contain their giggles as Father glared at them, feigning displeasure. Mock accusations of having captured her unlawfully were levelled at Æmund. Freyda caught a remark made from someone in the crowd that it was the second time she'd been kidnapped in a year. She shrugged it off, ignored the snorts of hilarity and murmurings of agreement, even finding humour in it herself. She was unsure if Father had heard them, for he carried on the charade and demanded Æmund state his offer for his bride. Æmund declared that Freyda would receive, upon his satisfaction on the morning after their wedding night, land and livestock for her own use to dispose of as she would; the keys to his house; and the clothing, bed linen, and household furnishings that once belonged to his mother.

"And what do you gift me, her father, the man who has raised her and provided for her since birth?" He stood, feet apart, hands on hips, his expression grim.

"For you, my lord, if you would accept me as your son, I would give you the price of a woman's wergild, to hold for her until such time your daughter needs it."

"Is this man to your liking, daughter?"

She looked up, smiling. "Aye, Father, this man is to my liking."

"Then unbind them, for they shall have each other."

A cheer rose from the crowd. Redwald untied the bindings and they crowded into the hall for the celebrations to continue into the evening.

*

"I must go, Leofnoth. I could not bear it if she died without me seeing her one last time."

Shaking his head, Leofnoth rested a comforting hand on Wulfhere's back. "Such a tangled web – but if it shall not let you rest, then mayhap you should go."

"I cannot leave my daughter's wedding – I cannot. Ealdgytha would never forgive me for that."

Wulfhere followed his friend's eyes to where his wife sat, staring vacantly as Gunnhild chatted incessantly at her.

"Your wife has company to keep her occupied. And seeing how you two have behaved with each other today, I don't think she will miss you. Besides you would more likely get away with it."

"She will for certain. She never misses a thing these days."

"But she always forgives you, Wulfhere, whatever you do."

"I should go?"

"You know it will always haunt you if you don't. I can tell her something for you if it comes to it."

Feeling absolved by Leofnoth's encouragement, Wulfhere stole away into the dusk and rode with haste to Waldron.

Chapter Four

Morgengifu

Æmund yawned, stretched, and rolled over, his arm brushing against Freyda's warm skin. He reached out and lightly stroked her cheek. She was deep in sleep, face snuggled into the crook of an elbow. Lifting a handful of her curls, he inhaled the aroma. The night before, it had smelt of honeysuckle and now it was infused by the distinctive tang of hearth smoke. He liked the scent, it felt familiar and comforting, like the childhood memories of his now deceased mother.

Caressing his bride's head, he marvelled to think that only a few hours ago, this vision of innocence had fulfilled his every desire until he was thoroughly exhausted. There was something alluring about a woman who whilst wanton and desirable, could still retain an air of uncorrupted virtue. He recalled a conversation with a friend, newly wedded, who bitterly complained that his bride lay like a sack of manure on their first night. 'Might as well have been swiving a hole in a mattress!' the friend had said. Æmund had no desire to wed a whore, but a wife who knew how to pleasure a man would most likely take pleasure from the act herself. And a woman who took pleasure from her husband was one to be cherished.

He leant over, pushed the hair away from her face so he could caress her cheek with his lips. Sliding in close, he pulled her to him, making her shudder unexpectedly, crying out in pain.

"Wh-what? What ails you, my love?" he asked.

"My back..."

He brushed aside her tresses to examine the welts and grazes that decorated the skin of her back. "Oh, Freyda... *deórling.*" He took a deep breath. "Did I do this? Last night... I may have been a little overzealous, but..."

"Nay, 'twas not you, dear husband." She turned to face him on her side and rested her chin on her palm. "It happened the day before our wedding."

"I didn't notice… How did you keep them from me?"

"I don't think that either of us noticed anything much last night," she said, smiling. She snaked an arm around his neck.

"Who did it?" he asked, body stiffening in her arms.

"It matters not, my love. Not now."

She stroked his groin and he removed her hand from him. "Don't think you can distract me with your guile, my lady, I want to know."

Freyda sat up gingerly and pulled the bedcover over her naked breasts. "'Tis nothing. I caught myself on branches whilst in the forest collecting berries, it is just a bit sore, that is all. Did you sleep well, my husband?"

"You're not a good liar, *luflic*." He sat, his legs folded beneath him and leant against the bedstead.

Freyda giggled nervously. "It is nothing, as I said."

"You have been beaten, Freyda. I know the signs of a good thrashing when I see them. Who has done this to you?" Æmund studied her intensely. "Tell me, Freyda, and tell me why – and don't think that you can lie to me. I will not have a dishonest wife."

"I-I… it-it w —"

"Was it your father? By God if it was I will —"

"No, it was not my father!"

"Then was it those devils, Wulfwin and Wulfric?" Æmund leapt out of bed and paced the chamber.

"No, no it was my… It was my fault, actually. I insulted my mother and she had me beaten."

"Your mother?"

"Well, she couldn't do it, so my Aunt Gunnhild did it. But my father stopped her before she half-killed me."

"That beast? That bloody ogre did *that* to you?" Æmund shook his head furiously.

She threw back her head and laughed as he paced the room in his nakedness.

"What are you cackling about?"

"You, calling my Aunt Gunnhild a beast and an ogre." Freyda tried to supress her giggles. "And – well, you do look amusing, marching around like *that*."

28

"Well, she *is* an ogre. My father calls her the 'she-bear'."

Both fell about laughing and Æmund bounced onto the bed like an over-eager child. He straddled her lap and said, "So, what did you do to deserve this beating? Wait, do not tell me – you were refusing to marry me, and they beat you into submission?"

Freyda smiled. "You know that they would not have to. But no, I said something to my mother that I should not have."

"What did you say?"

"I cannot say. Please do not ask, Æmund."

Fingering her hair, he said, "Well, whatever it was it could not have been that bad, for I know that you are nothing less than a sweet angel." He leant forward and they kissed for a long time, his lips melting against her mouth, their tongues entwined. Withdrawing he said, "I shall never let anyone beat you again, my lady Freyda. You are mine now, and no one will ever lay a hand on you in anger again." She moulded herself to him and he stroked her hair. "We will protect you, I promise."

"We?" she asked, massaging his smooth, hairless chest.

"Aye. Myself, and Lord Alfgar."

Æmund took her hand and placed it against his hardness. "See how he swells with anger! He is very displeased that you have been hurt."

Freyda sniggered. "Do all men give names for their *pintel*?"

"Nay, I think not, but I have a friend who calls his –"

"Do not tell, me," she interrupted, putting a hand over his mouth. "So, is Lord Alfgar displeased with me after last night?"

"He is not displeased at all. In fact, he is much pleased." Æmund leaned forward and nuzzled her neck and she inhaled deeply. Stimulated by her little mewlings of pleasure, he squeezed a breast and nipple through the sheet that covered her. His fingers teased as he played with her, and as he held back, the sensation in his groin hovered between pleasure and pain until he could no longer hold it. He wanted her so much.

He rolled onto his back and she slid across him, the sheet slipping from her to reveal pink nipples adorning her milk-white breasts. The little gasp as she lowered herself onto him triggered sparks of pleasure from his head to toes. He groaned loudly and immersed himself inside her, gripping her gyrating hips. His hands went to the soft flesh of her backside, squeezing.

Then he touched her secret place, felt her muscles throb as they

29

enclosed around him until he could no longer contain the need to expel his seed. Reaching mutual climax, where grunting, groaning, and crying out, they both let go, and her beautiful lithe body collapsed against him, bathed in sweat. His arms went around her, wanting to lie like that inside her forever. He loved her. How he loved her.

When they parted, it was reluctantly, and they lay side by side, catching their breath and looking at each other smiling. She was breathing heavily, her limbs outstretched, an arm reaching out to him. He drew her to him, entwined their arms and legs and before sleep took him, he realised that there could never be anyone else for him but her from that day on.

"Freyda! Freyda, my love, come and see what I have for you!"

His young wife, clutching a bed sheet to cover her nakedness, looked out of the unshuttered window, face alight with mirth, as a grinning Æmund, bare-foot and clad only in his braies, stood in the middle of the courtyard, holding the halter of a beautiful golden mare. It was early morning still, and there was little other movement in the yard apart from the clucking of hens, snorting of pigs – and Aunt Gunnhild – who was sweeping the debris from the previous day's feasting.

"Look, my love, do you like her? Her name is Heafonlice, she is *min morgengifu*. A heavenly creature, for a heavenly beauty!"

"Oh, Æmund!"

"Do you weep, Lady Freyda? You do not like her?"

"Of course, she is beautiful! Thank you," Freyda replied, beaming.

Just then Aunt Gunnhild called out, "Just look at you, prancing around half naked in another man's yard! Get yourself made respectable, young sir! Is this the way your father allows you to behave in the household of your in-laws?"

"Oh, I *am* sorry," Æmund began, turning to face Gunnhild's unwelcome intrusion. "Are *you* the lady of this establishment," he looked at the broom in her hands, "or merely one of the *servants*? Or, are you indeed one of the animals?"

Gunnhild waved the broom at him. "You know perfectly well who I am. I am the sister-in-law of the thegn, and you, young man, are a disgrace!"

"And *you*, dear lady, must be either blind or drunk, for I am far from a disgrace. I have it on good authority that I am both handsome and charming, so my bride tells me. Is that not so, my love?"

Freyda giggled. "You are indeed most definitely handsome and charming!" She cupped her hands to her mouth to shout, letting the bed sheet fall and exposing her breasts, "Also extremely skilful in the bed chamber."

Gunnhild put a hand to her forehead, and her jowls shook as she raged, "Christ preserve us, how my head boils! Wait until your father hears about this, you little harlot!"

"Your head can explode for all I care, it worries me not, old hag." Freyda laughed.

Gunnhild's eyes sprang open, a look of outrage on her face. "How dare you, trollop! And *you*, young man, are you going to allow your wife to behave like a slut? I should have beaten her twice as hard when I'd the chance!" She levelled the broom at him.

Æmund lunged and whisked the broom out of her hands. He hefted it aloft as though it were a spear, ready to strike. "It is *you*, who should be beaten, you great ugly troll. Look at you, picking on little girls half your size! What did she do to you to deserve such a thrashing?"

"How dare you! I have been in this family longer than you have been a member of it. I'll show *you* who does *what* to *whom*!"

The woman's chins wobbled as she lumbered forward. No wonder his father called her the she-bear. The murderous look in her eyes hinted at her intentions and Æmund was terrified of what she might do to him. He thrust the broom, brush end into her face and gasped when he saw that she stood fiercely, hands on hips, largely unaffected by the assault apart from spitting out bits of hazel. *Why was she not on the floor?*

The she-monster's nostrils flared. There was more viciousness about the woman than Æmund had ever seen in a tavern brawl.

Freyda shouted from the window. "Run, she'll kill you!"

"Never fear, my love! I shall defeat this monster, just as Beowulf defeated the Grendl!"

He retreated, the broom keeping her at bay. She spat out more hazel and stalked toward him, her eyes bulging. "Come here, boy! I am going to tear your arms from their sockets and rip your head off with my bare hands!" The pitch of her voice rose to a crescendo and she demonstrated with her hands what she would do to his head.

Æmund circumvented her.

"Behind you!" Freyda squealed.

Looking over his shoulder, Æmund glimpsed a wooden bucket and lost his balance dodging it.

"Ahhhhh!" he cried, hopping on one leg, arms flapping.

Gunnhild came at him. The she-bear's determined expression brought him to mind of an enraged boar. Grunting and snorting, she stormed forward, stepped in the bucket, and ploughed headfirst, cursing, into the pigswill.

Barely able to control his mirth, Æmund crept up behind, placed his foot on her substantial buttocks, and gave an almighty push. She rolled. The wooden trough went over and for a moment, her fleshy, flailing limbs were all he could see. Then she was under the container, immersed in an oozing mess.

Æmund gasped, then offered a hand to her, stepping as close as courage would allow. "Let me help you, dear Aunt Gunnhild."

"Get this thing off me, you idiot," she demanded. And when he had moved the heavy wooden trough from her, she slopped a filthy hand into his and he cringed as the swill squelched between their enclosed palms. He stood back as she wiped a sleeve over the muck on her face, revealing glowing red cheeks.

Laughter had been growing in the background and now it echoed around the yard. "Just what are you giggling ninnies laughing at?" Gunnhild roared, eyes blazing at the gathered children. Looking at Æmund, she roared, "Just look at what you've done to me. My clothes are ruined. You'll pay for this, you may mark my words, young man!"

"My lady, I fail to see that your current state has anything to do with me. If you choose to throw yourself into the pigswill, how is it the fault of mine?"

"You kicked me, you little devil!"

"I thought it would help you to enjoy your refreshment better!" Æmund could not contain his laughter. He was bent double with it.

Nearby, the twins were beside themselves also. Æmund threw the bucket and mouthed the word 'water' at them.

Gunnhild, swinging the broom that Æmund had discarded, threatened, "First, I am going to beat you with this, and then you are going to scrub these clothes until they are spotless!"

"Why, my lady, and leave you to run around naked? Think of the offence it would cause."

Æmund looked down, saw the filth-ridden ground and grinned. He glanced up in time to see Gunnhild's legs in the air as she slipped and landed on her backside in the slush, swatting at the piglets licking her face.

Æmund laughed. "Of course I will be happy to help with the cleaning process," he said as the twins passed him the bucket of water. "There, this should help," he said, throwing the contents over her.

Gunnhild, shrieked, and squawked like an enraged goose, sliding in the mess as she scrambled to her knees.

His audience cheered, and he bowed. Freyda hooted from the window.

He looked up and blew a kiss. "See, fair maid, I have avenged you! The beast is now dead!"

Ealdgytha raised her throbbing head from the pillow, groaning. With blurred vision and a tongue like wood shavings she sat up slowly. She had a vague recollection of Sigfrith and someone else – she hoped it was not Tigfi - putting her to bed. Beside her, the bed was empty and there was no sign that Wulfhere had been there last night. As Ealdgytha stared at the vacant space, the emptiness inside her heart returned.

Bile rose in her throat and she lurched out of bed. She made it to the piss pot just in time to vomit. Steadying herself against the wall of the chamber, Ealdgytha felt miserable and weak. If only she had eaten more and drunk less.

Hearing a racket outside, she opened the shutter. The sunlight streamed bright through the window and she squinted. There was a commotion in the yard, the sounds of laughter mingled with raised voices and unpleasant oaths. Trying to ignore the ache in her head, Ealdgytha straightened her clothing, groomed her hair, fixed on her wimple, and steeled herself to go to the hall. There would be more celebrations later, and more work to be done.

Ealdgytha stared in astonishment as she stepped into the yard and a grimy Gunnhild, leaning on Sigfrith, limped toward her.

"Just look what your daughter's ruffian has done to me," Gunnhild complained bitterly. Sigfrith grimaced as she tried to keep up with her.

Hand covering her mouth and nose, Ealdgytha said, "What an earth has happened? You look as if you have fallen in the pigs' trough." Turning to the maid, she said, "Have you seen Lord Wulfhere this morning, Sigfrith?"

"Nay, my lady, not since last night," Sigfrith replied.

Inside the hall, Ealdgytha had expected her husband to be reloading timber for the hearth. The villagers were clearing away the debris of the evening's feasting, but Wulfhere was nowhere to be seen. She caught the sound of an infant's cries and her gaze settled on a young village girl who cradled a little bundle.

"Is that *your* bearn?" she asked.

Ealdgytha tutted. It seemed that all the village girls were following in Sigfrith's footsteps of late; it would be the third child to be conceived out of wedlock in a year.

The girl gasped, "Oh no, my lady!"

"Lord Wulfhere found the bearn, mistress," Sigfrith explained. "He asked me to take care of her."

"What do you mean *found* her?" Ealdgytha asked. "*Where* did he find her?"

She went to investigate and removed the child from the girl and rocked the little mite in her arms. The babe stopped crying and looked up, staring at Ealdgytha with inquiring eyes. The little lips formed soundless shapes, and Ealdgytha imagined a smile. She touched the baby's cheek tenderly and smiled back.

Glancing up at Sigfrith, she said, "You say my husband *found* her?"

The maid nodded, looking for a stool for the complaining Gunnhild. "He found her in the stables, mistress. 'Twas yesterday it happened," Sigfrith replied.

"During the wedding? Who is her mother?" Ealdgytha asked.

"She has been abandoned it would seem, my lady."

"Most likely she is the child of an unwed mother who is too ashamed to claim her," said Ealdgytha. "I wonder who she is?"

"Perhaps her mother is married after all, and the father is a secret lover," Sigfrith said, and Ealdgytha noted the maid's indignant air. "Or perhaps the *father* is a married man, and the mother has left her here for her father to take care of her."

Gunnhild, interrupting, bellowed, "Never mind about the blessed creature. Find me something to sit upon – and I shall need clean water too! Doesn't anyone care I have been assaulted by that oaf, Æmund? Just look at me!"

Ealdgytha, ignoring her sister-in-law, barely registered Sigfrith's comments. She was drawn to the little bundle whose eyes, seemed to follow her every move.

"You poor little mite, who on earth could have abandoned such a beauty like you? Well, it is obvious the Lord in heaven wishes us to look after you. And so we will. I will be your mother now, little one. And as the Lord has sent you to us, I shall call you Godfrida, God's peace."

*

On his return around late morning, Wulfhere crept quietly into the antechamber. Lifting the latch, he pulled the interior door open no more than a finger's width, and resting there, listened. His heart raced. He'd not made it home last night, and Ealdgytha would be curious to know where he'd been. What should he say to her?

From inside the hall echoed the sound of chatter and laughter. He heard children's voices, trestle boards and benches being scraped over the floor in preparation for the coming feasting. He heard a baby crying and broke out in a sweat. He couldn't push the door, he just couldn't.

Then the door flew open, "Ugh!" Wulfhere exclaimed.

In the frame, stood Sigfrith.

The maid's expression transitioned from surprise to a cynical smile. "Lord Wulfhere! There you are at last. The mistress has been wondering where you were!" She pulled him inside and shut the door.

"Sigfrith, does the mistress…"

"Lady Ealdgytha thinks she's a child from God, so taken with the little mite, she is."

Wulfhere looked across the hall. People were milling about, setting up the boards for the feasting, and in the middle of it all stood Ealdgytha, wearing her best tunic and wimple, his child in her arms.

Wulfhere trembled, feeling all eyes on him. Ealdgytha, swaying with the babe, looked up, saw him, and smiled, her face radiant and beaming. "Wulfhere, where have you been? Well no matter, you're here now. Come see the child. She must have been sent to us. A gift from God."

Wulfhere glanced at Leofnoth. His friend merely shrugged.

Approaching his wife slowly Wulfhere realised that Sigfrith had been right when she said Ealdgytha was taken with the bearn. Gone were the dark circles and lines around her face. She was young again.

Wulfhere was contrite. "I'm s-sorry, I - there was a problem with one of the horses last night… and I fell asleep in the barn." He knew it was a bad lie when he saw Leofnoth's eyebrows rise.

Ealdgytha said, "Leofnoth told me you had been to look for the parents," she gave a little chuckle, "there's no need to make such a story up…"

Wulfhere gave Leofnoth a look of annoyance and said "I - had gone…to look for them, but it was no use, there didn't seem to be anyone… Then one of the horses was ill and I –"

"Oh well, 'tis no need for me not to know, I think we can safely say that we have been truly blessed, Wulfhere. God has sent us this little thing to replace the children we have lost. Why you could not tell me last night I'll never know – but no mind. We are calling her Godfrida."

He'd intended to tell her the truth, but not until a plausible story had been thought of. How could he tell her the child she was so charmed with was Ælfgyva's and his, and that her real name was Wulfhild. And that he'd ridden over to Waldron last night to be at his dying lover's bedside and promised Ælfgyva that he would love and care for their daughter without even thinking how he was going to explain it to Ealdgytha. But now the solution had been given him and he need not, it appeared. The happiness in Ealdgytha's eyes was fair consolation for the guilt added to his pile of mounting sins.

Ælfgyva lay deathly pale as Wulfhere arrived. The stink of blood pervaded the room and a pile of dirty linen in a corner sat in blotched clots of scarlet. Her lips were chapped and had lost their colour; cheeks pinched and hollow.

The tears had crept into his eyes, thinking she was already gone.

He was weeping when she woke, his head bowed, a hand to his forehead. He'd looked up to find her eyes glazed and upon him.

"Wulfhere…" she whispered almost inaudibly.

"I'm here, *min luflic*." He kissed her forehead, her frozen, bloodless hand in his. At times her eyes closed, then she would open them again, sharply, as though startled.

His voice choked as he said the words he should have said long before this. "I have always loved you, please know that…. I… will always love you. Please forgive me for leaving you."

Her nod of acknowledgement was almost imperceptible. Wheezing, speaking in barely a whisper, she said, halting, "I will forgive you, Wulfhere, but… if you abandon her too… I will haunt you for the rest of your days, and…"

He kissed her hand, "You will always haunt me my…" Her smile was weak and feeble. "No, Wulfhere, you do not get off so easily…"

He shook his head, "I will not abandon her, I promise."

Reluctantly, Wulfhere dragged himself away from her in the early hours of that morning. Ælfgyva had not wanted him to see her die and had beseeched him to go.

He rode back to Horstede, slowly, knowing he would never see her again. This time it was not because he did not wish to, or Ealdgytha had forbidden it, but because she would be gone for ever.

The marriage festivities over, Freyda could hardly contain her excitement as Sigfrith helped comb and braid her hair ready for the journey. She was going to her new home – a place that would be hers. She was to be the mistress now.

"What are we going to do without you, Lady Freyda?" Sigfrith said and finished off the braid, winding it into Freyda's nape. The maid laughed, adding, "Life will certainly be dull without your mischief!"

"It will be a lot more peaceful without me, of that I'm certain! Mother will have no one to mither."

Sigfrith secured the ties to her cap and ensured it covered the knot of hair neatly pressed into her neck.

"But in truth, my little mistress, 'twill be much less colourful," Sigfrith said, and sighed. She placed the snood Ealdgytha had made over Freyda's head and straightened it before pinning it with clasps made of silver, gifts from her new husband. Sigfrith stepped back to make sure that every strand of Freyda's golden hair was covered, as befitted her married status.

"There, now you truly look a chaste and married lady." Sigfrith smiled and hugged Freyda to her.

"Oh, Sigfrith, I wish you could come with me, you and your little one. I should ask Mother."

"You know she would never allow it; I am too valuable to her. Besides, you will have a woman waiting for you at your new home, I'm sure."

Sigfrith kissed her forehead. "You must visit us – and often. I will miss you, Lady Freyda."

Ealdgytha kissed her daughter on both cheeks. Freyda hardly responded, not even a smile passed her lips. Ealdgytha smiled regardless and kissed her new son-in-law. She bade them both farewell as they climbed onto the cart's seat.

"Remember what I told you, my girl, be good to your husband. Love him and treat him well, even above yourself," Ealdgytha whispered to her daughter.

"As well as you have treated my father, Mother?" Freyda replied with a glint of contempt. "I think I can manage better than that – much better."

Her daughter's words stung her. Ealdgytha leaned in closer and hissed, "You think you know everything, yet you know nothing at all. You will never make this marriage work, Freyda. You see, to men, women are either too wanton, or not wanton enough. He will tire of you, mark my words. That's what he will do in the end."

"You are wrong, Mother. For I know how to love - and I will value my husband. My husband will never seek out another, you mark *my* words."

Chapter Five

Ranulf

May 1056

Winflæd would have much preferred to be running through the woods, or soaring over the rockpool on the rope swing, or even practicing her sword play with Tovi than sitting on an itchy rush mat spinning endless reams of wool. Instead, she was forced to listen as Mother exulted the charms of the little foundling to the village women, each of whom had an opinion on how the child had come to be in their lord's household.

The little babe was tired, and having been generously supplied with Sigfrith's milk, was being rocked to sleep in Mother's adoring arms. This was a relief as prior to that, the child had screamed until it seemed its lungs would burst, along with Winflæd's eardrums. Mother seemed to have forgotten her other children. Wherever Mother went so did the bearn, and if Mother had possessed milk of her own Godfrida would have been at her breast, too, most like.

"There, she sleeps like an angel now," Mother murmured.

"Such a noisy little thing," Sigfrith remarked, tossing a recently spun skein of wool into the basket. She took up another unworked batch and teased out the fibres, meshing it together with the wool on the spindle. "No wonder her mama sought to be rid of her."

"Nonsense, I cannot imagine how anyone could abandon such a beautiful child. She has been sent to us from God. She is a miracle."

"I for one am certain she is not a miracle but has come from the devil himself. The noise is too much to bear sometimes." Sigfrith sighed and looked at her own infant, happily playing in a wicker pen nearby. "Thankfully, Leofweard is nothing like that screaming brat."

Winflæd sucked in her breath. It always amazed her how Sigfrith could say whatever she wished with impunity. Sigfrith's imposing manner resembled Aunt Gunnhild's, except Sigfrith was generally right in her assumptions, and it seemed to serve her better than it did Gunnhild.

Eanflæd and Ælswith, wives of the miller and the wood smith, were speculating on the origin of the babe. "I wonder whence she came?" remarked one of them.

"Do you think the mother could be one of our village girls?" asked the other.

Ælswith's daughter-in-law, Cuthburga, studied the child looking over Ealdgytha's shoulder. "Obviously, the child has been fathered on some poor girl out of wedlock and she is ashamed, as she should be, so she has left her somewhere for someone else to bring up," the young woman said.

Looking casually at Sigfrith, Mother said, "If anyone would know, Sigfrith would. What do you think, Sigfrith? Could the mother be one of our village girls?"

"Of course, Sigfrith knows everything, but Sigfrith has *not* noticed any swollen bellies of late," replied the maid with equal sarcasm.

"Perhaps the daughter of the one of the charcoalers, the girls are little strumpets, I hear," Eanflæd said.

Sigfrith rolled her eyes as Ælswith asked inquisitively of her companion, "How do you know, Eanflæd?"

Cuthburga interjected, nodding her head at Eanflæd. "Ask that son of *hers*, he would know."

"What do you mean?" asked the miller's wife. "My son does not associate with such girls."

Sniffing indignantly, Sigfrith said, "Why do folk always blame the girl? Why is it that men are never taken to task for *their* conduct? They take a girl's maidenhead without so much as a word said against them, but the girl who has had it taken from her is constantly spoken ill of."

Winflæd could tell by the way Sigfrith lips bunched together that the maid was seething.

"Mayhap the mother left the child where the father might find her," Sigfrith added sharply, throwing a ball of wool into the basket with a tad more effort than was needed.

Mother glanced warily at Sigfrith and seemed uneasy for a moment. "Nonsense!" she said and lowered the sleeping child into her cot.

"Why would she leave her in *my* husband's stables? *He* is not the father."

Sigfrith, a hint of a contented smile on her lips, continued to spin.

A thought came to Winflæd, and she ventured, "Perhaps the baby's mother knew the father would be attending the wedding."

Instantly, heads turned in her direction and Mother's sour expression burned Winflæd's ears.

"Such talk is not for little girls, Winflæd, so I would ask you to keep your mouth, and your ears shut, and mind your own business!"

Winflæd lowered her head and welcomed the diversion of helping Gerda to re-thread her spindle. She was now relegated lower than the village women in her mother's eyes.

She missed Freyda. Unlike Mother, Freyda would not have treated her like a worrisome insect. Her sister and she had never been close when they were younger, but in the weeks leading up to the wedding, their relationship had grown. Winflæd never really understood what had caused all the fuss surrounding Freyda, her kidnap, and the uncertainty afterwards. One moment Freyda and Edgar seemed happy, always together, and the next *he* was banished, and *she* was to wed another. No one deigned to inform a little girl what exactly happened, or why. But to Winflæd, it was clear that Freyda was much changed by that business, whatever it had been.

In the past, the young men had gazed at her sister; hung on her every word and waited with longing eyes for a glance their way. There had never been such looks in Winflæd's direction. Where Freyda was petite and graceful, Winflæd was skinny and awkward. Once, she'd overheard Grandmother and Mother comparing them over their sewing. As usual, Freyda emerged more favourably. Winflæd would always remember how it hurt to be spoken about as if she were a poor lady's trinket to Freyda's precious jewel.

She tried to busy herself with her work, but it was no good; she could not stay in the hall listening to everyone prattle away and not be permitted to speak. Putting down the spindle, she rose from the rush mat and stole quietly from the hall. Gerda skipped along beside her, grabbing Winflæd's skirts as they walked in the sunshine. It irritated Winflæd that the child followed her everywhere.

"Go back inside, Gerda!" But her sister continued to trail after her, undaunted.

After she repeated the order a few more times, Winflæd stooped to

41

grab her little sister's shoulders and shook her. "What is the matter with you? Have you not heard a single word I have said? Go back to the hall! I do not want you to follow me everywhere!"

The smile vanished from the little girl's face. Gerda's bottom lip rolled, and she knuckled an eye, as she held up her spindle.

"What? You want to spin? Go then, go spin. Go back to the hall and spin with the others and leave me be!"

Gerda made a gurgling noise, one of the only sounds she could make, and shook the spindle again, determination upon her little features.

"No, Gerda. I am not spinning now. Go back to the hall."

Gerda's sad blue gaze filled Winflæd with regret. "Why do you never speak, little sister?" Tears pooled in the corners of Gerda's eyes and Winflæd bent down to hug her. "Oh dear, Gerda, if only we knew why you are so silent. Come with me then, if you must."

A wave of intense heat seared Tovi's face as he pumped the bellows to maintain the forge. It had to be kept hot enough for Ælfstan to hammer the iron into the shape of a horse's shoe.

It had not been Tovi's choice to replace the blacksmith's nephew, Yrmenlaf, as Ælfstan's apprentice. He'd hoped that Father would take *him* as Esegar's replacement. Instead, Tovi, now consigned to the smithy, resented the eager young Yrmenlaf.

Father had said, "'Tis a man I need, not a boy, Tovi. When you are older, then I shall have need of you. In the meantime, you can help Ælfstan. Learn the skills of the *isernwyrhta* and you will be much sought after. With such a craft and skill, any lord would prize you in his household."

But Tovi did not want to be a weapon smith. He wanted to feel the grip of an axe or a sword, a spear in one hand and a shield in the other. He wanted to crush skulls with them, rip the guts out of men's stomachs. He wanted to be a fighting man.

Lifting his head momentarily, Tovi gazed straight into the staring faces of his sisters.

"What do *you* want, Froggy?" Tovi asked, gingerly removing the horseshoe from the anvil.

"Little mistresses!" Ælfstan greeted the girls smiling, wiping his soot blackened face with a grimy apron. He was a big brawny man with the typical strong build of a hardworking smith.

"*Wæs thu hæl*, Ælfstan," Winflæd replied. "I want Tovi to fight with me." She held up the wooden practice weapons made by her father. Gerda held up her spindle.

"Can't you see I am busy?"

"I can carry on without you for a bit, Master Tovi, if you want to go with your sisters. Anyway, 'tis to where a man must go in times of need, if you'll excuse me, master and mistresses," Ælfstan said, with a wink at Tovi.

"Well, are you coming?" Winflæd's eyes were wide and hopeful.

"I said I was busy, Froggy. Haven't you got some spinning or sewing to do?" He put Ælfstan's tongs in a bucket of water to cool off.

Winflæd shook her head. "I want to fight. Please? Mother has had me spinning all morning, and well, we hardly ever practice anymore."

"I have work to do. How many times must I tell you?"

"But Ælfstan said –"

"I don't care what Ælfstan said, do you really think I want to play childish games with you?" Her chin quivered, and her eyes watered, but he didn't care. "I am no longer a child to play with, Winflæd. I am going to be a warrior. I fight with men now, not little girls like you. And you should be doing what Mother tells you, not playing at being a boy!"

Winflæd looked about her. "What men? I don't see any here."

Tovi ignored her and carried on cleaning the tools.

"Why are you angry with me? 'Tis no fault of mine that Father has chosen Yrmenlaf instead of you to take Esegar's place. If you are such a big man now, why did he not choose you?"

Tovi snatched the wooden sword from her and threw it spinning in the air with all the force of his anger behind it. "G-go back to your s-s-s... s-spinning, little girl, and - and leave me be!"

He turned his back to examine a previously forged adze and a painful thud between his shoulder blades rocked him. As he reached around to rub the spot, something bounced on his heel. "Aagh!" Winflæd's shield. He picked it up and swung around to see his sister biting her lip and looking scared.

"Why, you little...!"

"I'm sorry. Are you all right? I-I'm sorry. I didn't mean..."

"Take this thing," he thrust the shield at her, "and go away!"

He'd not meant to her push her so hard, but she picked herself up as quickly as she had gone down, rolling over and leaping up off her

43

knees to her feet. Then, with a rage she'd never before displayed, she tore her cap off and stamped on it. "Nobody wants me! I am nothing to anyone, just a-a thing! A-a fly to be swatted! An ant to be crushed underfoot! I-I am... *níðing!* That is what I am! *Níðing!*"

In a gust of tears and sobs, she ran.

Shame crept over Tovi as he watched her. "Win, wait!"

She did not turn but kept running.

Angry with himself, he picked up the shield and rolled it along the ground. It drifted for a bit and then collapsed on its side.

"Winflæd! Wait! *Wait!*"

He sighed. Thinking to go after her, he felt a tugging. Gerda held up her spindle. Crouching down he put a hand on her shoulder and in turn she put her palm on his forehead to soothe him.

"I know, I should not have done that," he said. "I am a *bad* brother."

"Tovi, is it *you* picking on your little sister these days? I thought that was usually your older brothers."

Tovi looked round and saw a pair of legs. *Who did the russet hose and expensive leather boots belong to?* He stood to his feet.

"Ranulf!" he exclaimed and grinned like a fool. "Is-is it really you?"

"Yes, Master Tovi, indeed it is," replied the smiling newcomer, who seemed much taller and deeper voiced in the two years Tovi had not seen him.

*

Winflæd ran across the yard to her bower. The smell of supper made her nostrils twitch and stomach rumble, but before attending supper, she would have to get out of her dirty clothes, lest Mother see and have a fit.

She threw open the lid of a coffer, tossing the garments everywhere, and searched for a clean woollen dress. Finding one, she pulled it over her grubby linen tunic and groaned at the muddy splodges made by her hands. Winflæd grabbed a water jug and tipped the remains down the skirt to wash out the stains.

That will do, she thought and rubbed at the last of the dirty prints. She tugged at the knots in her hair and braided it clumsily. Then covered it with a clean cap and the hooded wimple that lately Mother insisted on her wearing.

"There you are, young lady," said Sigfrith, as Winflæd stepped out into the yard. "It's supper time. Where have you been all day? Your mother has been spitting feathers because you are missing."

"Oh, has she?"

"Yes indeed. We have guests and she was most annoyed that you were nowhere to be found."

"Guests? Who?"

"Who, indeed." Sigfrith seized Winflæd's hands and turned them over with a disgusted sniff. "Just *wait* until you see who. But first you will need to wash these paws. Look at you, girl. Your face! I expect you have been in those woods again. I can see the dirt beneath your nails. Nought but mischief will come to you there, young lady; look what happened to your sister!"

Winflæd shrugged off Sigfrith's berating and hurried to the longhall, curious to find out who the visitor was. It was busy inside with helpers from the village hurrying about, carrying crockery and extracting table linen from chests. As she crept stealthily across the hall to the wash area, Winflæd wondered who the guest might be. It *had* to be someone important for all the fuss.

She drew back the curtain and her eyes bulged when they landed on a tall, handsome, bare-chested youth, lathering himself with goose-fat soap, care of a large tub of water.

"Winflæd? Do you not know me?" The boy grinned; his dark eyes creased at the corners.

"Ranulf..." she breathed. "I thought we'd never see you again." She threw her arms around his neck, then sprang back, feeling awkward. When she dared look at him again, he was laughing. *He must think me so silly!*

He looked different. The thick chestnut curls that once graced his head were gone, leaving a hairstyle so short, it put her in mind of a monk. Her eyes rested on the smoothness of his chest as he picked up a linen towel to dry himself. He showed no shyness as her eyes hovered over him. He must have seen at least fifteen summers now. He'd been tall those two years ago, but now seemed taller. His trunk was lean and tanned and she found his young, muscular frame appealing.

"Goodness!" she exclaimed, realising he was clad only in his braies. Winflæd was suddenly mortified.

Seeing that Ranulf was occupied, head buried in his tunic, Winflæd hurried out through the curtain, wondering how she was ever going to face him again.

*

"So, Master Ranulf, what brings you back to Englalond?" Ealdgytha asked and ladled stew from a pot into her young guest's bowl. "It is indeed a delight to see you, especially after we thought we would never have the pleasure again."

"It is like this, my lady, since my father's recent demise, his properties and title have passed to my older brother, however he has left me the lands that were my mother's; nothing grand, just some small holdings. But there is enough to see me comfortable and will support me in my quest to make my way in the world and become a mounted cniht."

"Lord bless you, Ranulf, I am sorry to hear of your father's passing," Ealdgytha said. "He was a good and Godfearing man, I believe. Does this mean that you will be returning to reside here?"

"No, my lady. I wish I could, but I have a place in Lord FitzOsbern's household in Normandy as his squire."

"Lord FitzOsbern?" Ealdgytha asked, not familiar with the names of foreign notables. "Is he an important man in Normandy?"

"Aye, my lady," Ranulf replied with a little smile. "I should say so. He is cousin to the duke; also his steward."

"You have done well, Master Ranulf, very well indeed. And who have you brought with you?" Ealdgytha looked across the hearth to where Ranulf's retinue were sat at another eating board. She had already met his father's chamberlain, a sour old man, tasked with escorting his young charge on the journey to his Englisc estates. Leon de Havre, seated next to Ranulf at her table, had said barely a word to her since having arrived.

"Those are some of my brother's men," Ranulf nodded to where they sat. "They are to see me safely to my estates and back to Normandy."

Ranulf's young escorts seemed to enjoy the hospitality of their Englisc hosts, unlike de Havre who picked at his food as if it was slop instead of the tasty stew that Ealdgytha had concocted with Herewulf.

Ealdgytha caught the gaze of one of the young men as he stared at her across the flames. Even in the dim atmosphere of the hall, she could see he was attractive. The young man took a sip, and she blushed as their eyes met. His smile was beautiful, lighting the dim glow with it. Something inside her quickened and she felt a thrill flush her body.

Ealdgytha looked away quickly, despite enjoying the attention. She returned to Ranulf. "It is so good of you to think of us - to come and visit. I am sorry that Wulfhere is not home, he is away at court as usual, performing his duties for the king."

"I am sorry to have missed him, I hope he is in good health," Ranulf replied. "If the truth be told, my lady, we were passing from our landing point at Pefensea along the great road to Lundenburh and I recognised the area. I insisted, of course, on calling here. I have never forgotten the time I spent here two years ago with you and your family. I have such fond memories."

Ealdgytha smiled, flattered by his charm. "We are so happy to have you stay, Master Ranulf."

"The stew is delicious, and your hospitality well received. I am looking forward to spending time with Winflæd and Tovi." He nodded toward her son and daughter as they served the other table. Winflæd turned and smiled at him like an adoring pup. She had been the perfect little hostess, thought Ealdgytha, proudly.

Tovi, however was somewhat sullen this evening, about as welcoming as a barn with holes in the roof. Perhaps it was because he had to serve and had not been permitted to sit at table.

As for the twins, Ranulf had barely acknowledged them. Ealdgytha recalled that there may have been some trouble between them when he had stayed at Horstede before. Ranulf's foster father, the Earl of Wessex, had made arrangements for Ranulf to go home to his father in Normandy, but the boat coming for him had been delayed and so Wulfhere was asked to look after the boy and escort him to the boat when the time came. As she recalled, the trouble between Ranulf and the twins had been something to do with them tying Winflæd to a fence by her hair and throwing food at her. She shook her head as if to rid herself of the memory. She did not want to think of such embarrassing things and she surveyed the hall with pride. It was not often they were in receipt of visits from important personages.

The hearth that burned between the two groups, sent out just the right amount of heat to reduce the smoke. Earlier, Ealdgytha had arranged for bedding to be aired and brought to the hall, ready for when it was time for the guests to retire. She had the feeling that Ranulf's guardian, de Havre, was not impressed at having to spend the night in a draughty Englisc longhall. He had an apparent eagerness to get the business here over and done with so they could return home to Normandy as soon as possible.

The sound of Godfrida's crying interrupted Ealdgytha's thoughts and she looked over to where Sigfrith had been feeding the little foundling babe. The child rested in Sigfrith's arms as she rocked her to sleep after a feed. Ealdgytha felt envious. How she wished she could feed the child herself.

"Sigfrith, you may bring the child to me," Ealdgytha called to her maid.

As Sigfrith handed her the bundle, Ealdgytha turned to Ranulf once more. "So, will you be visiting your cousin, the Earl of Wessex?"

"Yes, he has promised to assist me in my land claims with the king." He looked at the babe in the crook of Ealdgytha's arm. "I see you have a new addition to the family."

"Yes, is she not beautiful? I lost my youngest child to the winter sickness this year, and this *lytling* has been sent to us from the good Lord in Heaven to replace her."

Winflæd leant over with the jug of mead and filled Ranulf's cup. "She is a foundling, not our true sister," she said.

Ealdgytha shot her daughter a censorious look. "Of course she is ours." She forced a chuckle from her throat. "By the angels, I swear, she is truly a gift from God. She has been sent to us in place of the child the Lord God took from us. 'The Lord taketh and he giveth', is that not right, Father Paul?"

"Something like that, my lady." Father Paul had been about to spoon a large amount of stew into his mouth.

"Run along, Winflæd, and serve our guests," Ealdgytha said.

"You are truly blessed to be given such a gift," Ranulf said kindly.

"Yes, she was left in our stables, just as the Christ infant was." Ealdgytha looked down at the child asleep in her lap and smiled wistfully. "She will bring our village luck. Why, already we have seen an improvement in the weather and the ploughing and sowing has all gone very smoothly so far this year."

Ealdgytha continued to chatter about Godfrida's portentous qualities, until she was satisfied her guest had heard all of them. "It has been such a terrible winter and goodness knows we have need of better luck in this village, but enough of such talk. Master Ranulf, how long do you plan to visit with us?"

Ranulf opened his mouth to reply but the stern-faced guardian answered instead: "We will be spending as short a time as we must, Madam," he said in thickly accented Englisc. He then said something

48

to Ranulf in Francisc. Ranulf replied in their shared language. He sounded irritated by de Havre's words, whatever they were. Ranulf then turned to Ealdgytha and continued in a less prickly tone: "I should like to stay for a couple of days, my lady, if your hospitality permits. I regret it cannot be longer, but my liege, Duke William, still has troubles within his realm, and my Lord FitzOsbern may have need of me."

"Of course, Master Ranulf, you are most welcome to stay as long as you want to. Our homestead is humble, but our hospitality is not meagre. I am sure we can accommodate you *and* your servants." Ealdgytha flashed a derisory look at de Havre.

De Havre did not offer any retort but gazed into his drinking horn with a look of absolute disgust, as if its contents were utterly distasteful. The Norman put the horn aside on the table and turned to Ranulf and spoke again. Ranulf's reply to him was once again curt. Then he looked at Ealdgytha and politely asked if she would permit her guest to take leave of them.

Ealdgytha, pleased to be rid of de Havre's brusque presence, instructed Tovi to show the man to the curtained area of the hall where the sleeping quarters had been made ready. Not for the likes of that horrid man would she grant her best guest's chambers away from the hall. The odious man could sleep with the other of his companions.

"I apologise for my guardian's impropriety. I am afraid he does not travel well," Ranulf said when de Havre was out of earshot.

"I do hope he will find it comfortable sleeping in the hall. I have given him my best sleeping pallet and bed linen. Such a miserable man, Ranulf. I fear he has no liking for our Englisc customs," Ealdgytha said dryly. "More stew?" she offered, rising to her feet.

Ranulf nodded and held his bowl out to her. "I would be foolish to refuse; this supper is most gratifying." His handsome face was lit with a charm.

Ealdgytha bestowed him with her warmest of smiles and dished more food to each of the others in turn, still cradling the child in her left arm.

"Coincidentally, the same complaint about my guardian was often made by my mother, God rest her," Ranulf said with a little laugh. Ealdgytha was content to hear this, knowing that Ranulf's mother had been Englisc and a kinswoman of Earl Harold. "I cannot say that the rest of my retinue are as averse to Englisc hospitality as my Lord de

Havre." He waved and called to the men across the hall, and they raised their horns to Ealdgytha.

The handsome young man she'd been sharing looks with earlier flashed her a brilliant smile. She tilted her head slightly and returned it modestly. She was drawn to him as a moth drawn to a flame, captivated by the beguiling gaze that seemed only for her. Ealdgytha blushed again and distracted herself by signalling to Tovi and Winflæd to replenish the drinking vessels.

"So, Master Ranulf, had your father chosen a bride for you before he died?" Ealdgytha asked. She glanced absent-mindedly at the young Franc, who acknowledged her with a smile and a raised cup. Her heart fluttered. She sensed his gaze was upon her, even when not looking at him. Every now and then she stole a glimpse and found him staring at her, and she felt a warm stirring within.

Ranulf's voice brought her back. "He had ideas, but no arrangements were ever made. My brother may have someone in mind for me, though, a girl from a good family," he grinned broadly, "hopefully an heiress with lots of lands. But he has yet to find a bride of his own, so he will take the best for himself." Ranulf laughed. "But I think I am too young to think of such things yet."

Ealdgytha rested discerning eyes on her daughter. *Nay*, she thought. *The girl is too plain, too silly and by the saints, she looks such a mess!* In the dark she had not noticed how unkempt she is. *No one would ever consider her in that state! Certainly not a lord as important as Ranulf.*

Ealdgytha resolved to do something about her daughter's shoddy appearance on the morrow and pushed it to the back of her mind. For now she wanted to focus on being the good hostess.

"...and nor am I such a grand match for anyone just yet," Ranulf was saying. "I plan to gain favour in the household of my master, continue my training, and when I am given my *cnihthad,* make my fortune. *Then* I might have something worth offering my prospective bride, whoever she may be."

"What is it like to be a cniht?" asked the twins in unison, their attention captured for the first time.

Ranulf indulged them. "First, you have to train as an *esquiere* to a highborn lord. You must be tested and only if you have acquired all the skills that are requisite, may you then receive the honour of a *chevalier*."

"*Chevalier?*" Wulfric asked.

Ranulf nodded. "Here you might say, cniht. A mounted soldier who serves his master." He went on to describe how he practiced on a device known as the *quintain,* and how those who excelled at it could win prizes at tournaments, emphasising how dangerous and fearsome the tournaments could be.

Ealdgytha left them to it, leaving her place at the table to put the child to bed. *Let the boys prattle for a while about things that boys liked.* The babe was tired, and she enjoyed putting her to bed, but if truth be told, she was finding herself far too interested in the young man sitting opposite than was decent and thought it best she divert herself elsewhere for a time.

Resting his elbow on the table and cupping his chin in his palm, Tovi had taken the opportunity of his mother's disappearance to join the conversation with Ranulf. Wulfwin reached across and poked Tovi's elbow and it slipped. His chin hit the table with a jolt. Wulfwin and Wulfric laughed, just as Ranulf was in the middle of reciting one of his tales. Tovi scowled and moved out of his brothers' reach. Ranulf seemed to take no notice and continued his stories about the famous *chevaliers* in Normandy. He told them about a fierce warrior, a Franc called Pepin le Stampede, who, because of his size and agility, could take down a horse and its rider, on foot.

Winflæd, inserting herself into the discourse, said, "Ranulf, you must help me practice my swordplay tomorrow. I am much improved since you were here last; I cannot wait to show you how good I am now. I can even beat Tovi in a fight," she said.

"Anyone could best Tovi in a fight," Wulfwin laughed.

Tovi sneered, but said nothing, preferring not to draw more insults from his siblings. He hated them all at that moment, even Winflæd.

Ranulf turned to Winflæd and said, "Aren't you too old to be playing boys' games? I thought you'd be quite the little lady now; after all you must nearly be ten… eleven?"

Tovi smiled inwardly as the grin on Winflæd's face evaporated.

"Perhaps tomorrow, then, if you are not too busy."

Winflæd's face lit up once more and she gave Tovi a look of triumph. "Thank you, Ranulf!" Tovi pulled her away and she called over her shoulder, "And I can show you what I can do with my bow, too."

"Frog Spawn, Ranulf is no more interested in playing games with you than I am," Tovi said to her when he'd got her on his own. "He is a man grown now; can you not see? He has better things to do than play foolish games with little girls."

"A man? Oh, you mean like you, brother? You cannot even count twelve winters yet, hardly a man!" Winflæd said.

Tovi grimaced. "'Tis your bedtime, little sister." He pushed her toward the doors.

"Tovi is right, run along now, Winflæd," Ealdgytha called out. Winflæd shrugged, bade them a brusque goodnight and Tovi watched her, making sure she left swiftly.

Sometime after, Mother came back from putting the babe to sleep and brought out her harp to entertain her guests. Ranulf, sleepy from the effects of the potent honey-flavoured mead, retired to the guest chamber outside in the yard, and seemed content to leave his miserable guardian asleep in the hall. Sigfrith had also gone to her bed, while the twins, having drunk their fair share of mead, slunk behind the curtained quarters of their sleeping area. Awake in the hall was Tovi, his mother and the Francisc guests.

Fighting the urge to sleep, Tovi straddled himself over a bench by the hearth, playing himself at *hnaftafl*. He'd rudely refused the offer of an opponent from one of the visitors. Inside he seethed and was determined not to leave his mother unsupervised. The attention the men gave her, and their over familiarity irked him. Much to his chagrin, Mother appeared to enjoy them far more than was decent for a wedded woman. Their amusement at her attempts to speak their language chafed him and he felt for his *seax*. It was a comfort to know it was with him just in case he'd need of it.

One of the Francs had taken Mother's harp and was regaling them with a Norman *chanson* that he boasted rivalled any Englisc or Danish saga. Tovi wanted to believe that his mother was not flirting with the men, that she was merely playing the good hostess. But, if it had been possible for his father to betray his mother so willingly and his sister could so easily discard her betrothed for another, then was it not possible that his mother could do so too? As the night wore on, the noise subsided into hushed, murmured tones. Tovi stared at the boardgame in a daze. He hadn't moved any
of the pieces for what had most likely been an age and was completely lost as to which piece's turn it was. He yawned and struggled to keep

his heavy lids open as he looked around him with blurred vision. Illuminated by the orange glow of the hearth, Mother had engaged with the young dark-eyed warrior in a game of their own. He was teaching her to dice explaining that each side had a mark on it to signify a gain or a forfeit. Mother's girlish squeals made Tovi squirm uncomfortably. Curiously, she did not appear to be conscious of Tovi's presence, so absorbed with the man's company was she.

Eventually, Tovi's head nodded until he could hold it up no more. When he awoke, slumped over the boardgame, the pieces scattered, the hearth no longer burned but smoked, crackled and spat. The hall was still, apart from the harmonised wheezing and snoring of drunken men. He looked about him, disoriented, then remembered that the last thing he'd seen was Mother laughing with the stranger as they huddled together in a corner. He froze, seeing neither of them.

He tried to count the individual snores and remembered there'd been about six men in Ranulf's retinue all together. Or… were there five...? He could barely make them out in the dark. He got to his feet and stumbled forward; head heavy like lead. Mother was not the only one who'd consumed too much. As he steadied himself, he heard the stairs creak in the ante chamber.

Footsteps.

He froze. A tall dark figure moved in through the doorway.

Tovi stared at the man's outline, in the darkness. Instantly, he knew it was him, the dark-eyed warrior. Tovi bristled. The man had come down from Mother's chamber upstairs. His heart beat fiercely in his chest, like a smith hammering an anvil. As the man approached the hearth, Tovi could see him more clearly.

The cniht held up a lantern, ominously illuminating his beardless mouth, leaving his eyes in darkness.

Tovi was rooted to the floor. *He knows what I am thinking. He knows that I know he has been with my mother.*

"*Je suis désolé de t'avoir dérangé,*" the stranger said softly, with a charming smile and a bow of his head. "I am sorry to disturb you."

Tovi, unable to speak, shook his head. He pushed past the young Franc and made for the door; felt dizzy, and nauseous. He needed to get outside. As the chill of the night air hit him, he vomited and when he had finished spewing his guts, he made for one of the empty burgh-houses.

Crashing through the door, head spinning with Mother's laughter

53

and the image of her smiling companion touching her face, Tovi threw himself onto an empty cot. The image of Mother and the cniht did not leave until unconsciousness overcame him and he slept.

Ranulf stayed two more days. Ealdgytha grudgingly allowed a happy Tovi and Winflæd time off from stone picking in the fields so that they could spend more time with their guest. The old alliance from two years ago was reformed. Arrows were shot through apples, fortresses assembled from tree branches, and they hunted for fish and swam in the old rock pool where Tovi had saved Earl Harold's daughter. Now and then they would take their practice swords to the sward, and Ranulf would show them how to fight one on one. Ranulf enjoyed being a boy again. There'd been no time for games since he'd returned to his father's estate in Normandy.

At night, with Tovi curled up on the end of Ranulf's mattress, they would talk and talk about anything from horses to girls, swords to spears, *hnaftafl* to dicing, and from mead to wine, before drifting off to sleep.

One night, as Ranulf was about to float into a deep slumber, Tovi spoke out in into the darkness. "Ranulf? Did your father ever – did he ever go with another w-woman?"

Ranulf forced himself alert to answer. "I never knew my father to take up with other women when my mother was alive, but he has fathered some bastards that I know of, since her death."

"And your mother?" Tovi asked. "Was she ever disloyal with another man?"

"Nay, I doubt very much that many women would do such a thing. In Normandy, if a woman dared to cuckold her husband, she would be cast out if caught."

"Cast out?"

"Aye. Why do you ask?"

"I just wondered... What is 'cuckold'?"

"For a woman to betray her husband with another man."

"Oh."

Tovi said no more after that and Ranulf preferred not to broach the subject. He had noticed that Lady Ealdgytha seemed to be very taken with Thierry, and although the lady made some attempt to be cautious, it was plain to see the attraction between them.

On the morning of his departure, Ranulf went to look for Winflaed and found her in the woodshed exchanging pleasantries with Ælfstan as he chopped logs for the hearth.

"Winflæd, here you are. I come to make my farewell with you."

Winflæd put down the heavy basket of firewood. "I did not think you would be going so soon."

"I must, I am afraid. *Faran þe wel*, Lady Winflæd," he said, giving her a little bow.

Winflæd smiled uneasily. *"Faran þe wel*, Ranulf."

"So, aren't you going to embrace me or something?" Ranulf asked. His arms spread wide, he laughed at her awkwardness.

She encircled his waist, put her head against his chest for a few moments, then pulled away, and said, "Will you come back soon?"

"Would you like me to?"

"Aye, I would." She dug her shoes into the dirt like an ill-at-ease child.

"I dare say I shall return, someday."

"When will you come?"

"Oh, some day when I am a *chevalier* with a fortune of my own," he laughed. "Do not look so sad, little Winflæd, the next time I see you, you'll most likely be wed to some local thegn."

"I wish I could be *your* wife!" She shifted, looking shocked at her outburst. "I...."

She made to leave, and he stayed her. "I can think of no other girl I would like to have as my wife." His smile was genuine. "But both of us, we are young, and our worlds and paths lie in different directions."

She averted her eyes. "Of course, it was a silly thing to say. You will go home across the sea, and I shall not see you again."

"One day our paths may cross, little Winflæd. Who knows what the *norns* might weave for us?" Ranulf said. "And who knows what lies beyond our own imagining? We did not think it possible last time, did we? And here we are."

Instinctively he knew that she cared for him in more ways than friendship would dictate and did not want to hurt her. She was a much-loved 'sister', a childhood playmate to be fond of. Beyond that there was no more. When she withdrew from him, he took the silver cross and chain from around his neck and placed it about hers. "To bring you luck and keep you safe," he said. Winflæd removed her own little iron cross, the one that Edgar had made for her. "Then you must have one to keep you safe too. It is not silver like yours, but..."

55

"I will keep it forever." He smiled and bent down so that she could garland it around his neck. "And I will remember you always."

Ealdgytha watched as Ranulf's entourage gathered at the gates to leave. A cool wind tugged gently at her wimple and she sighed. She was going to miss them. The young *chevalier's* dark eyes caught hers as he turned to smile and wave. His look sent her body aquiver, thinking about what had gone between them. It had been sinful, but Ealdgytha didn't care; if her husband could take a lover and get away with it, why not she? It felt good to be wanted again instead of playing bed-mate to a man who loved another. They'd been discreet, or so she thought, but that little weasel de Havre's sidelong glances of condemnation hadn't gone unnoticed – not by *her* anyway. Ealdgytha had paid no heed to his reproaches. It was *her* household, *she* was the lady here, and what happened in it was *her* business alone. The man could go to hell and take his disdain with him.

When the last horse passed through, Ælfstan and Tovi pushed the gates shut.

Ealdgytha walked back to the hall, recalling with pleasure what she and Thierry had done in her bed. That a married woman in her thirties could lure a man so much younger than she, was the most exhilarating aspect of the affair. And that the arrogant, pompous de Havre knew of it, pleased her even more.

She was not sad to see Thierry leave, for it was a liaison that could not last. But she would miss his company, especially in the lonely evenings.

"S-so, Mother, your bed will be empty now until Father comes home."

She spun to face him. the boy must have crept up behind her. "I don't know what you are talking about," she lied.

"You know what I speak of, M-Mother, you and your F-Francisc lover."

"Tovi, are you suggesting that a lady entertaining guests in her husband's hall would dare to do anything improper?" Ealdgytha hurried on.

"Your b-behaviour was less than p-proper, M-Mother," Tovi called after her.

Ealdgytha stepped onto the porch and turned to glare at him. "What would a mere boy know of such things?"

"I have seen en-nough of w-women to know that they - they can be w-wicked... and evil."

She laughed and moved off the porch toward him. "My poor boy, you are sadly mistaken if you think the faults of women outweigh the faults of men. I could speak a hundredfold of the wickedness of your father."

Tovi stepped back as if in fear of her and said, "Without s-such women, m-men would not be at fault." There was no mistaking the spite in his voice.

"So, what are you going to do?" she hissed, *"Tell him?"*

Tovi said nothing, and Ealdgytha stared at him defiantly. "Don't you know by now, dear boy, that your precious father and I have no reason to be loyal to each other? He has been sleeping with that whore in Waldron for years. Why, you caught them at it, didn't you? You found them together in her bed! Believe me, taking a man to *my* bed could never match what he has done over and over again. Do you think he would even care if I –"

Suddenly she reeled, clutching her face. The slap had caught her off guard and she was outraged but also mortified at the words that had spilled from her mouth without thought.

They stood silent. Tovi's narrowed eyes were filled with hate. Ealdgytha's face pulsed, but it was nothing to the pain she felt in her heart. *Dear God, what have I done?*

Ealdgytha stood, stunned. She did not know what to say next. But just then, Wulfhere's voice could be heard, "What in the name of Loki has gotten into you both?"

They spun around. There he stood with a grim look on his face, arms folded.

In unison, Ealdgytha and Tovi cried, "Wulfhere!" "Father!"

"Yes, 'tis I. Will someone tell me, why must I always come home to trouble?"

Chapter Six

A Sense of Foreboding

Earl Harold's estate near Súþrigaweorc
Two weeks later
Stooping to avoid the lintel, Ranulf entered the hall through the dark red doors, now common practice since he had grown so tall. The last time he'd been measured he was just below six foot.

Harold welcomed him into the hall and made a jest about having to build a taller doorway.

"I am well, my lord, I have a place in the household of Lord William FitzOsbern, but he has graciously released me before I start so that I might venture here to claim my inheritance."

A servant helped him remove his boots, caked in sludge from the pathways encountered on the journey. "Ah, Englisc mud, still as thick and cloying – glad to see it never changes," he joked.

"It is still a veritable swamp out here at times," Harold replied with a chuckle. "The weather is unfortunately chill for the month of May. I hope you were not caught in the awful storm the other day during your travel."

"The mud does not evade me in Normandy either, but here it seems so... so comforting; like home." Ranulf smiled and looked around at the familiar furnishings. The earl's personal bodyguards were scattered around in groups that huddled together, engaged in various activities, polishing their war gear or playing dice.

With smiles and warm gestures, they acknowledged Ranulf's presence as Harold directed him to a private chamber partitioned from the rest of the hall. The earl motioned him to take a seat in a comfortable chair by a small trestle, its board laden with a jug of what smelled like wine and vessels for drinking the refreshment.

"It gladdens my heart to see you, Ranulf – so tall, and strong. Is it good to be back in the old country?"

"Aye, my lord, it is my home, after all I *was* born here."

"Home? Such words please my ears. I was worried you would forget us and the household you grew up in. Eadgyth will be pleased to see you again, you know."

"Ah, I have missed my foster mother – and Waltham. Is the Lady Eadgyth here?"

"I regret, but she is not. You remember how Eadgyth loathes leaving Waltham. It is as if her very soul is embedded in its foundations. Now she loathes to leave it even more, and since we commissioned the new church, she sees it as her duty to supervise the work. It is her excuse not to come to court or anywhere else I go of late. Waltham is her nest and she barely leaves it."

Harold smiled and Ranulf recognised the old gleam that appeared in his cousin's eyes whenever he spoke of his beloved Eadgyth. "She will be more than glad to see you, though; Eadgyth always talks of you. I shall take you to Waltham after we have sorted out your business with the king. You can see for yourself how she misses you." Harold looked at him with a glint of amusement. "Eadgyth will not like it that you no longer have your curls."

Ranulf ran a hand over his shorn head. "I shall be delighted to see the Lady Eadgyth again, sir. Speaking truthfully, my lord, I rather hanker after my longer locks. I preferred them to this monkish style. It kept my head warmer in the winter months."

"I have heard a tale that our Norman friends keep their hair closely cropped so they cannot be caught as they run from their enemy." Harold laughed.

"I haven't been caught yet, my lord, so it must be true. Not that I would ever have cause to run; I am as good a fighter as any boy my age."

"Of course. You always were, Cousin."

A servant entered with a jug of wine and a platter of food laden with bread, cheese, cold meats, berries, and lettuce leaves drenched in spiced vinegar. Harold poured the wine into a vessel made of the finest glass Ranulf had ever seen and he took it and examined its beautiful detail before taking a sip.

"So, Ranulf, what can you tell me about my brother and my nephew?"

Ranulf had anticipated that Harold would ask this question. "That they are safe and well in Normandy, my lord. I have seen Hakon. He is a page in the duke's own household."

Harold offered Ranulf a plate piled with food. "So, it is true. The king said as much last year when he finally deigned to break his silence on the issue. It was the only thing I could get out of him on the matter. We've not had word of the boys' whereabouts, or their safety, till now."

"They are safe, my lord, and well looked after." Ranulf took the plate. "Thank you, lord. I am grateful for the refreshment and so is my rumbling stomach."

"A growing lad needs to eat well! Judging by your size, they must be feeding you horses in Normandy."

Ranulf and Harold shared some laughter for a few moments before Harold continued. "Tell me, what does a page's duty entail?" He filled a trencher with food and sat back in his chair.

"In Normandy, boys are taken into a lord's household at seven, placed under the care of the lady and taught to serve table, wait on the lord, and other such skills. I would be here all day to list them, but it is not unlike how things are done here."

"What are these 'other such' skills?"

"Singing, music, dancing…"

Harold was animated. "Good! Good! I like the sound of Hakon dancing and singing, he was always a boisterous lad as I recall." Harold smiled broadly. "You spoke with him?"

"No, sir. I wanted to, but there was never the chance. He seems well, though. And the duchess, Lady Matilda, I am told, adores Hakon."

"She does?"

Ranulf nodded. "She calls him her *petit chiot Anglais*."

Harold's smile widened. "I think of Hakon often, Ranulf. He was always bouncing with life. I'm glad to hear he is still the young pup he always was, but... what of my brother, Wulfnoth? He was the studious one amongst us. He loved nothing more than to pray and help with mass. Not long before I last saw him, he expressed hopes to follow a career in the church. Mother said he'd got his heart set on wearing a bishop's pallium. Wulfnoth was never the fighting type, much more interested in his books."

"Then you will be pleased to know, lord, Wulfnoth is cloistered in the Abbey of Jumièges." He shook his head, pre-empting Harold's next question. "I have not seen him, I am sorry to say, but my father told me this before he died. And I believe it to be true."

Harold stroked his chin. "I am glad no ill has befallen the boys. It puts my mind at ease to know they are being treated with the respect they are due. I'm grateful to you, Cousin, for the knowledge of them."

Neither spoke for a few minutes while they ate.

After a while, Harold continued. "So, tell me, how does the duke regard them? Wulfnoth and Hakon, that is."

"I do believe he regards them very well. It is believed by many, and certainly the duke himself, that the boys were sent by King Edward as a gesture of his goodwill and as surety of his intention to name William as his heir."

"So, the duke believes that this is how they came to be in Normandy," Harold murmured. "Of course, Champart would not dare admit that he kidnapped them to spite my father."

"It certainly seems that way, lord. But it is a good thing because it means that they will be well-treated."

"Aye, but the duke will not return them – not on that premise. I had hoped your father might have spoken up for them on my behalf, so the duke might send them home to us. Neither William nor your father has ever replied to our letters."

"If my father ever spoke to the duke, he did not tell me of it."

Harold became quite sombre, and Ranulf felt guilty, as if by being half Norman it made him complicit in the Godwin boys' plight. After all, they were his kinsmen too.

Harold sat forward in his chair, clasping his glass. "So, Bishop Ealdred was right. That *is* why Edward evades the subject at every twist and turn. That bastard Champart was always whispering in Edward's ear, scheming and trying to manipulate the king into naming William as his successor – and the stupid old fool fell prey to his wicked machinations!"

Alarmed at the venom in Harold's voice, Ranulf said, "My lord, should you speak thus of the king?"

His cousin turned glazed eyes toward him and Ranulf realised that this was not the first glass of wine that Harold had drunk that day.

"I am only concerned with my brother and my nephew's welfare. As hostages, they were given in good faith by my father and brother to the king – and only to the king. They were not meant to end up in Champart's hands to do whatever the swine wanted with them."

Harold stood, began to pace. "I can hear the scheming *horningsunu* now, convincing the king to let him take them to Normandy. Edward

61

Edward had no right...."

As Ranulf's gaze followed him, he noticed that Harold's face had become hard as the earl continued, "My father, he always blamed himself for threatening Champart, but he is not here now, so I must do what I can to get them back – and one day I will. It is good for that rancid archbishop he is dead - if I were to see him again, I would rip his guts out."

Remembering the events of four years ago when the whole Godwin family were forced into to exile, and he with them, Ranulf said, "Is it certain that Champart took them with the king's fore-knowledge?" Ranulf swivelled to be better able to see Harold behind him. His cousin had stopped pacing and stood, arms crossed, head bent, in deep thought. "Would the archbishop not have taken them anyway? With or without Edward's permission."

Harold's head snapped up sharply. "Oh, he took them all right, so he did – for protection, threatening to harm them if anyone tried to stop him. That was how he was able to leave these shores unmolested. No one dared risk my father's wrath to go after him, should anything happen to the boys."

Ranulf could see the predicament. In the silence that followed, he considered the matter of the succession which seemed to be a sticking point in all this.

"My lord, if Duke William, was to be king here in Englalond, would that be such a bad thing?" Ranulf was careful to sound non-judgemental.

Harold placed his hands on the back of Ranulf's shoulders, "I forget that you see things with Norman eyes now. And of course, it is only natural that you should be loyal to Duke William. But when the time comes, the Englisc people will decide who will be their king. Who knows? They may well select the duke for their king, but it will be the choice of the Englisc, not that of the Normans, with their greedy eyes on our lands."

"Of course, Cousin, I am forgetting myself."

"Forgive me, Ranulf, it is *I* who am forgetting myself. You have lost your father recently and I have not given you my condolences. He was a good man."

"Thank you, Lord."

"Your elder brother, William, he fares well?"

"Yes, lord, he does indeed, he is entering tourneys and is making a name for himself."

Harold smiled. "You must tell me about these tourneys, I know nothing about such things. So there is nothing of your father's lands for you?"

Ranulf shrugged. "It is the way in Normandy. Father thought I would be comfortable with my Englisc lands."

"But you said they are nothing more than hovels."

"'Tis true, but they will do. I will employ a reeve to collect the revenue, oversee their maintenance, and make any improvements that need to be made."

"Why not stay here, and see to their management yourself? I have a vacancy for another lad in my household guard."

He was stunned by his cousin's offer. He replied, faltering, "I... I am happy with my place in Sir William FitzOsbern's household, my lord. He is a great, important man, a close advisor, kin, and friend of the duke. He has promised me that when I am given my *cnihthad*, I will have hearth space amongst his retainers."

"In that case, I understand fully. FitzOsbern will be of great value to you."

Ranulf had been content with his place in FitzOsbern's household, but now Harold was dangling the carrot, he felt drawn to the idea. Not wanting to reject the earl's offer out of hand, Ranulf mentally weighed up the good and bad. Should he leave Normandy, where he might be able to make his name and become one of the fiercest warriors on horseback to ever ride the tourneys? He loved the *quintain* and the contests, loved the feel of his horse beneath him when charging at the target, javelin held aloft, waiting for the right moment to release it. In Englalond they rarely fought like that. As one of Harold's huscarles, the expectation would be to dismount and fight on foot, a great, broad-bladed axe in one's hands, a magnificent and fearsome weapon – but it could not compare with horse warfare, the most exhilarating form of fighting.

Harold's face was hopeful, and Ranulf felt guilty. "Cousin, I am honoured, more honoured than I can tell you, but I have sworn to serve my Lord FitzOsbern, and I –"

"No, lad, don't feel guilty, I should not have mentioned it."

"But I *am* honoured, sir. If you had asked before the arrangements were made I–"

"It's all right, lad, I'll not hold it against you." Harold grinned. "An oath is an oath, and I would not ask you to break it. But I would ask a favour from you."

Harold went to a small wooden box and fetched out a piece of parchment, rolled and enclosed with his wax seal, the Fighting Man.

"It's a letter from my mother, for my brother, Wulfnoth. I had one prepared for the duke, but I do not trust that he will pay any heed to it. He will not want to let Wulfnoth and Hakon go, not without some sort of bargain. I always thought that was the way of it, but now you have confirmed it." He held the letter out but as Ranulf's fingers closed over the missive, Harold hung on to it. "Can I trust you, my Norman cousin?"

There was an edge to Harold's voice when he said the word, 'Norman'. Ranulf met his eyes. "Aye, you can trust me." Still, Harold hung on to the letter, and they were locked together, awkwardly, both holding it as though it were a piece of treasure neither desired to relinquish.

"It would seem I am powerless to help the boys for the time being. But I am satisfied that they are not in any harm. What troubles me is what may come if the duke is impeded in his plans. I have heard of his ruthless acts of revenge. Now that there is a mission to find the king's exiled nephew, I worry what might happen if the duke gets wind of it."

"He will hear of it, but I do not think that…"

"What? That William the Bastard does not harm hostages, even if it suits his purpose? You know him well, then?"

Ranulf dropped his hold on the letter and Harold put down his hand.

Ranulf said, "'Tis true what you say, but he has also been known to show fairness and…"

"Compassion? The kind of compassion he showed the people of that town, what was it called? Alen something... Alençon, when he cut off the hands and feet of its people!"

Ranulf was silent, unsure of what to say next and unnerved by Harold's switch of temperament. *Perhaps it is the wine.*

"I cannot in truth assure you of the boys' safety, but you can trust me to speak for them if need be. After all, they are *my* kin, too, and I will see to it Wulfnoth gets the letter from his mother… *and* that none but you and I will know of this conversation. Of this I give you my word."

Harold stayed his hand for a few moments, then held out the letter once more and let go this time when Ranulf took it.

In a complete change of humour, Harold clapped him around the shoulder and said, "How about we go hawking, Ranulf? I have a new gerfalcon that I long to take out on her first hunt. You used to enjoy the birds if I remember right. And you showed some skill with them too. Is this still so?"

Ranulf grinned and nodded. His loyalties lay with Normandy, now, but it did not mean he should forget the years he spent in Harold's care.

As Harold guided him to the birds, he felt an uncomfortable foreboding that one day he might have to face his cousin on opposite sides of the battlefield. He said a quick prayer that it was no more than a feeling.

Chapter Seven

Constant Heart

Waltham, June 1056

Eadgyth sighed as she pulled the comb through her daughter's hair. Such a pretty head, with hair that shone like silk. She examined the comb and it was just as suspected. Riddled with lice.

Eight-year-old Gytha's itching and scratching had driven Eadgyth to distraction for days.

"Sit still, little fish!" she chided, as Gytha squirmed in the chair.

"It hurts, Mama!" Gytha wailed.

"Yes, my sweeting, but it must be done," Eadgyth insisted. "And quietly, for you will wake your father."

"Alas, 'tis too late for that. What is all the howling about? Anyone would think that some foul murder was occurring." Harold raised his head from the pillow where only a few moments ago he'd been snoring loudly, buried beneath the coverlet. The first Eadgyth had known of his arrival was late last night, when he'd slid into bed with all the stealth of a *nihtgenga*. Drowsy with sleep, she'd allowed him to rest his head on her breast, content in the knowledge that tomorrow when she woke, he would be beside her.

"Mama is killing me, Father!"

"Her ladyship has a plague of lice and her poor lady mother is trying to remove them, but of course, her ladyship must fidget and squirm and make the task *very* difficult." Eadgyth winked and smiled at her husband.

"A plague, you say. I fear I may have fallen prey to them myself."

Harold was bare-chested and very attractive with his tousled, shoulder-length hair… until he scratched his head with such vigour that she thought he would make it bleed.

66

"Then you, dear husband, will also have to submit to my treatment." Eadgyth brandished her comb threateningly.

Harold made a sound of mock terror and hid under the bed clothes.

She laughed and turned to finish searching through her daughter's hair. She bound it in a coil and replaced the linen cap on the little girl's dainty head, binding the ribbons until it was firmly secured. "There! That should keep the horrors out!" Eadgyth said. "Now, kiss your father, and run along. Go find your nurse."

"But I don't want to go! I want to stay here with Father!" protested the child. She leapt on to the bed and clung to Harold's neck as if caught in a raging current and he a fallen branch to hold on to.

"Do as your mother told you, little one," he said and removed Gytha's arms from his neck. "I will come play with you soon. Now, your mother and I have business to attend to."

Eadgyth returned his look with a smile, her longing beginning to stir.

With Gytha now gone, they were at last alone.

Harold threw off the covers and came across the room, naked. She watched him from the wash basin as she dried her hands, revelling in his obvious desire. He still took her breath away after all these years: the muscular arms she loved to stroke, the flat stomach she loved to kiss, and the firm backside she loved to knead beneath her palms.

Harold groaned as she threw off the pale night shift, and reached for her, sinking his mouth onto hers. Eadgyth pushed into him, desperate to feel him close. He held her, stroking her hair, head against his chest. *If only it could be like this forever.* Lifting her chin, he brought her mouth to his once more, then moved to the soft, still pert breasts, his tongue flicking over them. She massaged him, wanting to pass on the sensations she felt. Making appreciative noises, he arched his neck, her nipples between his thumb and forefinger, rubbing. Eadgyth worked him harder, pouring the love she felt for him into the act. She brought him close to climax, and he put a hand over hers. "Stop," he said, "I need this to last."

Gathering her to him, he carried her to the bed, laid over her and slid with ease inside her. Harold looked down at her lovingly. "Faith, but it is good to be with you again."

Staring into the blueness of his gaze, she whispered, "I have missed you so much." She wrapped her legs around his thighs. All hers – he was all hers.

Floods of ecstasy shuddered through her as he kissed her slender white neck, breasts, and eager mouth. Consumed by love for him, Eadgyth pressed herself closer, their hips joining and moving together. It had always been so with them since the first time they'd shared one another. Now, more than ten years on, nothing had changed. And she knew, as he had told her many times, it was the same for him as it was for her.

When they had both had their fill of each other, they lay naked in each other's arms, and fell into a contented sleep. Later, a breeze blowing through the window, gently rattled the shutters, stirring her from slumber. She felt too warm to rouse, lying against Harold's hot skin, but knew they could not lie abed all day. She had a toddler to feed, children to care for, and the midday meal to oversee. Harold was snoring loudly.

She gave him a nudge. He stirred, then continued to snore.

"Harold, my love, we should wake ourselves."

He murmured incoherently, and Eadgyth harried him until he opened his eyes. "Greetings, my Lady Swannehæls."

"Greetings, Harold Godwinson, Lord of all Wessex," she smiled. "Come, let us see what food awaits us. I am so hungry."

As Eadgyth and Harold walked arm in arm across the sward, the children were playing a game, the youngest child, Gunhildr, bouncing and squealing with laughter in her nurse's arms. A tall, slim boy at the centre was blindfolded. Long, slender arms stretched and flailed at the air, trying to catch the younger ones as they ran around him. He looked so comical, a tall willow amongst shrubs.

The children's laughter was infectious, and Eadgyth and her husband looked at each other and grinned as the blindfolded stooge lunged aimlessly here and there.

"Who is he?" Eadgyth asked, curiously. Her husband was known to being home waifs and strays that he saw potential in.

"Do you not recognise him? 'Tis Ranulf! Come back from across the sea to visit," replied Harold brightly.

Ranulf whipped off the blindfold and stood there smiling at her.

"By all that is Holy! Is that really you, Ranulf?" Eadgyth beamed. "Look at you – grown so tall."

She laughed and cried at the same time and held her arms to him. She let him go after some moments and kissed his cheeks. "Oh, if ever there was a sight for sore eyes, 'tis you. When did you arrive? Harold, why did you not tell me?" She brushed a hand over the boy's head. "And what *have* you done to your lovely curls?"

Before either of them could reply to any of her questions, she grabbed Ranulf's arm in hers and walked away toward the longhall, drowning the boy with a further stream of questions. Behind her, Harold followed with the children in tow, singing loud enough to wake the bees, "Papa is home! Ranulf is home!"

The midday meal was an informal affair, with a variety of bread loaves, butter, and soft cheeses to spread, diced raw carrots and lettuce leaves mixed with onions in a light dressing. There were also boiled eggs and griddled oatcakes and berries. Harold was telling Eadgyth he'd insisted Ranulf left his entourage behind in London, at Harold's own expense, of course, except for Thierry, whose amiable, nonchalant manner Harold liked immensely. The earl had not been keen to let the Normans come to his home. There was something about de Havre's demeanour that Harold found suspicious, though Ranulf laughed at this, advising them that although his guardian was unpleasant, he was harmless enough.

Learning that Ranulf had been in Horstede, Eadgyth was keen to know how things were there, asking of Ealdgytha's welfare and of her family.

"Lady Ealdgytha appears to be in good health. Lord Wulfhere was away serving the king. Their eldest daughter Freyda has just been married."

"Ah yes," Harold recalled. "Let's hope the young maid will not cause any more trouble there." He laughed and went on to say, "The little minx has caused her father a headache with her unruly ways, promising herself to one lover and then another. I hope you keep our daughters in check, dear lady."

Eadgyth shot her husband a quelling look, before turning back to address their guest, "Take no heed of him, Ranulf, 'tis just gossip and should not be spoken of."

"Speaking of gossip, I have a tale of my dear sister I have been longing to tell you of," Harold said and amused them all with the latest scandal at court involving his sister, the queen.

When Harold had finished regaling them, Eadgyth said, "I simply cannot believe it. Did Edith really deny the poor abbot his gift, just because he refused to allow her to greet him with a kiss?"

"I am afraid it is so. The abbot turned his head in horror, and my sister saw it as a great personal slight against her," replied Harold.

"But surely it is understandable that a holy man should not accept kisses from a lady, is it not? Even if the lady *is* the queen."

"I do not have much opinion on that, but Edith's pride *was* hurt. Abbot Gervin has been visiting court for many years and he had become one of Edith's favourites. I suppose Edith felt she was entitled to take such a liberty, especially since she had gone to a lot of trouble to make him an amice, rather beautifully made, too, and adorned with orphrey and jewels." Harold broke off some bread and was spreading some cheese on it.

"What did she do?" Eadgyth asked.

"She called him an ungrateful little wretch, grabbed the amice from his neck – just having placed it there – and flounced off to her chambers," Harold said, giving them a rendition of his sister's behaviour.

"*Oh my*! What did the king say?" Eadgyth giggled.

"Edward was furious with her and fell over himself to apologise to the man. He stormed to Edith's apartments with an entourage, including myself. I was not going to miss that scene. Anyway, he chastised her in front of her women. Of course, this only served to throw more fuel upon her fiery temper, and she refused to attend supper that evening in order to slight the abbot further."

"Goodness! Only a queen could get away with such terrible behaviour," Eadgyth said as she laughed.

"Actually, she didn't really get away with it. Edward was enraged with her. You know how he is with his holy men." Harold paused and took a sip from his horn. "If the truth be known, it was one time that I could sympathise with my sister. In my opinion, the abbot was being a pompous little Francisc upstart, but Edward was horrified. Abbot Gervin's abbey in Ponthieu holds many estates here, and Edward receives a quarter of their annuity. They regard Edward as a pious and virtuous benefactor. Edward was not inclined to have his reputation sullied with his wife's unqueenly behaviour."

"So, what happened next?" Ranulf asked.

"Edward made her apologise, and the next day she went before all the court and humbled herself to Abbot Gervin, begging his forgiveness, claiming she now understood his scruples. Then she announced that the kissing of all men of holy orders by women was to be forbidden, and that from thence onwards, any woman found doing so would be banished from court!"

Eadgyth paused with her spoon about to enter her mouth. "By all the saints, was that not too harsh?"

"I am afraid it goes for you, too, my darling Eadgyth, for your kisses should only belong to me."

Eadgyth felt herself blush. "That shall not be such a hard task for me, husband dearest," she replied, "for you shall not find me anywhere near the court."

"All the better, my love, for I would have you all to myself here, at Waltham."

As the afternoon's feasting blended into supper, Harold and Eadgyth took leave of their guests and sought the privacy of the bedchamber. With Eadgyth settled between his thighs, Harold ran a comb through the soft waves of her hair and watched the strands fall to pool in his lap like windblown corn. This was what he dreamed of when he was away from her; warmth, peace, comfort.... The delights of her body to come in the wee small hours, and the chance to forget the troubles his position brought. But it was not just his responsibilities to worry about, sometimes there were matters of a more personal nature that plagued him.

His wife had been wittering away in her usual loquacious fashion, but wallowing in sensuous thoughts, he'd barely been listening.

She turned to face him. "Harold?"

"Aye, sweeting. What is it?"

"Have you heard anything I've said? I was talking about how wonderfully Ranulf has grown to manhood, don't you think?"

"Of course. I have been listening, *deorling*. What else do you think I've been doing?"

"Day-dreaming, judging by the expression on your face. Tell me what ails you?"

"Nothing, my sweeting. When I am home with you, there is nothing that could possibly ail me." He put his arms around her and squeezed.

"Your eyes belie your words, dear husband," she said sweetly. "I know when you are false with me."

He moved her gently back into her previous position and she moulded into his body once more. The warmth of her skin against his as she reclined against him was comforting. He covered her

71

hands with his, resting them on the slight plumpness of her belly, caused by many years of bearing his children.

"Perhaps you know me better than myself." His voice was low and soft.

"So, are you going to tell me, then?"

Harold did not want anything to mar his time with her, but now she'd mentioned it, he needed to admit, even to himself, that he was feeling out of sorts. "I'd not realised I looked so melancholy. I was thinking of Wulfnoth and Hakon. You reminded me when you spoke of Ranulf and Normandy..."

"Oh, Harold. The thought of them makes me sad also. But we must take heart that they are well, as Ranulf has confirmed to us. Surely the Duke of Normandy is a man of honour and will not harm them." She reached up to stroke his face. He in turn, brushed his fingertips lightly between her breasts. He felt her relax, her tension gone.

"How the man treats them is not the point. They belong here, in Englalond, not in Normandy to be used as pieces in a board game between Edward and William. For that is all they are to the king, little pieces in the game he plays with us all," he said bitterly.

She turned his head towards her and brushed his lips with hers. "I wish I could kiss away your pain, Harold."

"I should have protected them. If I do nothing for Wulfnoth and Hakon, then I've failed them, failed my father, failed my mother... and failed myself."

He pulled away slightly. He felt her relax and resume her position against his chest and he kissed the top of her head by way of apology.

"You have done all you can, *min leoftost,*" she said.

Harold shook his head. "I have done nothing for them. I made a promise to my dead father's soul that I would get them back. I need – I *must* do more."

But what he could do, Harold did not know.

"You have written enough letters to the duke to make a whole goat. Are you at fault if he chooses not to answer them? You appealed to Ranulf's father for help and he failed you. And from what you tell me, if you push for their release, it will most likely bring troublesome winds our way. *You've done all you can.*"

"I should go to Normandy and speak with the duke in person. Take a ship and a crew to bring them back – by force if need be."

"And risk your life, and theirs too?"

72

"I'm failing the boys and my parents, for the sake of keeping that Norman bastard off the Englisc throne."

"And there's the rub, isn't it?" she sighed. "For one compromises the other and leaves you stuck between two rocks."

"I dream, sometimes, the boys are looking for me and I cannot get to them. I hear Wulfnoth's voice when I am falling asleep at night, asking me why I have abandoned him. I should go..."

"All we can do is trust in God, that He will bring them home in His good time. It is out of our hands now. Let go and trust in our Heavenly Father that when the time is right, they will be restored to us."

*

"Now it is your turn to be pensive, *min deore*," Harold whispered to Eadgyth as they emerged from the cool darkness of the old church into the morning sunshine. The mass had been given in honour of Harold, to welcome him home. Everyone in Waltham had been present.

"If I am thoughtful it is because I'm thinking about how happy I am to have you here," Eadgyth replied. The times when her husband came home were precious few.

One of the local landowners stopped to pay his respects to Harold, proudly introducing his wife and new-born daughter. Harold graciously shook his hand and both Eadgyth and Harold congratulated them on such a lovely babe. When the thegn and his family had gone on their way, Eadgyth beamed at her husband. "See how the people love you? I am so proud of you, my lord husband."

They walked along the hedgerows to where the church was being built. Harold had commissioned the new structure to replace the old ramshackle chapel in thanks for overcoming a serious illness when he was a much younger man.

The dean, Wulfwin, and the chief stonemason, showed them around the foundations of the church. Father Wulfwin explained in a lively captivating manner, the machinations of the works.

But Eadgyth, lost in a world of her own, kept a quiet countenance throughout. As the party paused to admire the transept section, the laughter of the children echoed as they skipped around the half-built walls. Harold stopped and leaned closely to her, then repeated what he'd said to her earlier. "*Min Deore,* you're lost in a world beyond here, what troubles you this morning?"

"'Tis nothing, Harold..." She hesitated as if there was more.

"Nothing is never nothing when it is nothing," Harold said.

She glanced up and saw he was smiling. "There *is* something I wish to say to you, but I know not where to begin," she whispered.

"Then say it, sweeting. What is it?"

"Nay, I cannot here. Not with company around us."

"Then let us walk." He looked around to one of his captains, "Take the children for me, Skalpi, whilst I walk with my wife." The old veteran nodded, a slight smile on his scarred features.

Eadgyth diverted her husband to the millpond, partly surrounded by a hedgerow, a peaceful place where the huge wheel could be seen through the foliage, water gushing as it turned.

They sat on the wooden seating Harold himself had made so she could go there with the children and watch the waterfowl as it skipped on the ripples of the pond.

"I want you to marry," she said after a few moments.

He looked at her, bemused, and gave a little laugh. "After this morning? What on earth has got into you? Have you tired of me?"

She shook her head and put her hand in his. "Never, never, never would I tire of you, my lord. It is not for me I ask this, for I could never imagine being without you. It is for Wulfnoth and Hakon. It is the only way to set them free. If you were to wed one of the duke's relations –"

"Eadgyth, *lufestre,* there is no point in asking this of me for I will not marry elsewhere; not while I have you."

"Not even if it would get Hakon and Wulfnoth back?"

"How would my marrying help?" he asked.

"If you were to make an alliance with one of those women your sister is always urging you to, someone whose family could avail you of the influence you need at the court of the duke – perhaps even the duke's niece, Judith. Or – or perhaps one of the duke's daughters... Then... the boys would be bound to come home."

An amused smile hovered over his lips. Taking her hand, he said, "Judith, I believe, is a child, and the duke's daughters are babes."

"He must have other suitable relatives, or even the daughter of one of his closest advisors. We could ask Edith to send letters of enquiry."

"You *really* want me to do this?"

"One day I will lose you, we have always known that. If I must lose you to another woman, then I would rather it was for the sake of the boys." She looked away and wiped the corner of her eye. "It would make it easier..."

He sighed.

"You say this to me now, after all we've meant to each other? I thought you knew me, Eadgyth. I thought you knew me better than myself, but I must have been mistaken, for if it were true, then you know I would never leave you for anyone else, no matter the cause." He stood and took a few steps away from her.

She sensed his anger. It was rare that they exchanged heated words. When they'd first met, she'd thought him conceited and brash, mistaking his self-confidence for arrogance. The next time she saw Harold, he lay close to death, grateful for her care. She'd had to bathe him, change his soiled sheets, and spoon feed him like a child. She'd grown to love him in the following months and although she fought against it, he'd won her heart. She was later to tell him that she'd come to know of her love from the moment he'd brazenly kissed her hand, the mocking blue eyes gazing at her like some charming, lecherous rogue. Since the day they had become handfasted, rarely had either one hurt the other.

She went behind him, arms going around him. He tautened but did not pull away.

"If I've hurt you, my Harold, then please forgive me. It was not my intention." A lone tear rolled down her cheek. "I was trying to make it easier for us."

"Easier?" He swung around and faced her, grasping her arms. "Do you think that when I said to you, I would never marry anyone as long as I have you, that I did not mean it? There would never be a reason good enough for me to leave you, Eadgyth, not even if my life depended on it."

"Harold, please – don't be angry with me. When you asked me to be handfasted to you, you told me, as the son of an earl, you may one day need to make another alliance for the sake of the kingdom. I have known all these years that our time together is not infinite…"

"That was then, before I knew what my heart truly wanted. I couldn't have known then that I would not want to put you aside."

"But it will happen one day, Harold –"

"Have I not resisted any attempts the king or my sister has made to wed me to some foreign lady?" She went to protest again, but he caught her shoulders once more. "I wish I could shake some sense into you, my beautiful, selfless Swannehæls!"

She flung herself at him forcing his arms around her. "I only thought of it because I saw how unhappy you were for Wulfnoth and Hakon."

He stroked her hair. "My lady need never worry, for she will never lose her lord, no matter what happens. You, and the children, are all I ever need, Eadgyth. You are the one, most constant thing in my life, and will always be. You're my heart. I live only for you."

As they stood in the growing wind, locked in each other's arms, she said, "Your words comfort me, my love."

"Good. Now, there shall be no more talk of me marrying anyone else."

She nodded. "And Wulfnoth and Hakon? What of them?"

"For now, I shall take the advice of Wulfstan, and leave it to God. What will be, will be." He kissed her and nuzzled her neck, and Eadgyth felt a sense of relief, that for now, she had him. He was still hers.

Chapter Eight

King of the Britons

12th June 1056, Hereford

Bishop Æthelstan gave up his life on the 10th of February in the year of Christ our Lord, 1056. The last moments of his passing were peaceful, unlike those he'd endured some eight months ago when the town of Hereford had been aflame. Then, the streets ran thick with blood and the acrid stench of burning flesh and timber had permeated the air. The destruction of the church had devastated Æthelstan, hastening his departure from this world to the next.

His successor was Earl Harold's loyal priest, Leofgar. It was two months since his appointment, and in that time, the new bishop had listened, enraged, to the first-hand accounts of that terrible day. Gruffudd, self-styled King of the Britons and his vicious band of raiders, had shattered the great doors of the church and murdered the brave canons defending it with their lives. Appalled at the heinous deeds of the Wéalas, Leofgar heard how the walkways of Hereford were littered with the dead, how women were raped in front of their men and carried off into slavery, their children clinging to their skirts. Every day, he heard a new tale of misery, and it angered him that his flock had suffered such terror and torment at the hands of the Wéalas and that evil spawn of Satan, Gruffudd.

Leofgar was inspecting the work on the damage done by Gruffudd and his men to the ruined church when he was advised of a visitor, the newly appointed scīrgerefa, Ælfnoth.

"Bishop Leofgar, I come to warn you. There have been reports of the Wéalas raiding Englisc settlements along the Wye, destroying homes and carrying off livestock. It is reprisal for not adhering to the terms of the treaty."

"What terms?" the bishop asked, gritting his teeth.

"For not relinquishing the ecclesiastical rights of Ircingafeld to the diocese of Glamorgan. The agreement was endorsed by the king as we know, Lord Bishop."

"By all that is Holy!" Leofgar's face burned with fury as he paced. "The agreement also endorsed the return of our sacred properties. Of those precious holy relics – all our stolen raiment – we have seen nothing! Nothing I tell you! That Wéalas upstart, Gruffudd, cannot be trusted!"

Leofgar stormed across what was once the ruined church's precinct. "Are not the lands of Ircingafeld enough that he must as well have the diocese?"

Ælfnoth, running to keep up with his long strides, replied, "It seems he will continue to raid until it is confirmed, lord. He is goading you."

"So, it is a fight he wants. Then he shall have it."

"Lord Bishop?"

"I have listened to enough tales of blood and murder, theft of our goods, our livestock, our women and children, to last a bloody lifetime. The diocese belongs to Hereford and on this I will not budge."

"Then he will just keep raiding, Bishop," Ælfnoth said, "unless…"

Some days later, Ælfnoth called his men to arms at the bishop's request. They needed to show the Wéalas that the men of Herefordscīr would not stand for their impudence any longer and put an end to their raids. They would ride out to meet Gruffudd and make their demands. Their goods and those who had been enslaved should be turned over to them and if the Wéalas king did not agree, they would take them back by force.

Leofgar made ready to ride out with the local militia, casting off his bishop's clothing. The collegiate's dean, Æthelhelm, questioned his intentions. "Lord Bishop, you cannot mean you are going to fight the Wéalas? This is too much; a clergyman does not take up arms, it is against church law for a priest – or – or a bishop to spill blood."

Leofgar had found his sword and whetstone and was fondly sharpening the blade. "I am not going to spill blood, I am going to crush bones, I am going to cave in skulls. Not one ounce of blood will be spilled, Father Æthelhelm, you can be assured of that."

The little man looked aghast. "But they *will* bleed, my lord, if you use your sword."

"You see this?" Leofgar held his sword before the quivering dean's eyes. "It is a slashing weapon, you strike your opponent in his ribs, arm, leg, or head and they break. Therefore, I shall *not* be spilling blood."

Æthelhelm shook his head. "Lord, you are a bishop, you cannot do this. It would be a sin, lord. A sin!"

"Æthelhelm, did you not defend the church as did your fellow priests when the Wéalas burned it down?"

"Nay, my lord, I was hiding in the crypt – but I tried to put out the fire – unsuccessfully, I'm afraid."

Leofgar raised his eyes to the ceiling and then turned them back on the dean. "But your fellow priests, they did try to defend the church and even killed some of the marauders, did they not?"

"They were defending God's house, lord."

"And that is exactly what we are going to do, Æthelhelm. We will defend God's house, for if we do not put an end to these raids – to these Wéalas heretics – then they will come and destroy it once more."

"But it is already in rubble, lord. A ruin."

Leofgar signalled a young servant boy to help him with his mail. "Yes, it *is* a ruin, but the church's spirit lives on in our hearts. It is in our hearts." He thumped his chest as if to drive home the point and bent forward so the boy, staggering under the armour's weight, could shove the mail over Leofgar's hefty shoulders.

Leofgar put on his belt and strapped his sword to his baldric. Then, the boy threw the cloak across Leofgar's broad, warrior's back, and stood on a stool to reach the clasp at Leofgar's neck. Shield slung across his back, his spear in hand, Leofgar was ready for war. Gone was the bishop's mantle, his cross and mitre, and thus, he rode out at the head of an army with those of his priests who would willingly accompany him.

Leading his vengeful army over the border of Herefordscīr, they crossed Offa's Dike and moved along the River Wæg. Eight days before midsummer at a place the Wéalas call Y-Clas-ar-Wy and the Englisc called Glæsbyrig, Leofgar drew up his forces to face Gruffudd's army and were resoundingly beaten by overwhelming odds

Leofgar was mercilessly slain on the battlefield along with all his priests, his army, and the scīrgerefa, Ælfnoth.

Those that survived made attempts on horseback to escape but were hunted down. Their horses were confiscated or killed, and the prisoners abused and tortured. Word of Leofgar's foolhardy expedition finally reached the court of the king in Gleawecestre some days later.

*

July 1056

"That I should have to suffer the indignity of treating with my brother's killer, the same man who lured my son into treason – is too much to ask at my age and in my state of health. How *dare* the Wéalas 'nobody' expect *us* to make the crossing. These waters are making my stomach swirl. Why are we allowing this impudent fox to bait us like hunted animals? For all we know, we may be murdered when we get across the other side!"

Harold sighed and raised his eyes in frustration as he listened to Earl Leofric's bitter complaint. Was it *his* fault that Gruffudd refused to cross to meet with them? What was he supposed to do, row across there and forcibly carry the man back over the river himself?

So far Harold had managed to ignore Leofric's grumblings during the journey. After all, the old man *was* ailing, and he *was* great in age. The last thing he wanted was to get into a quarrel just as they were going to meet with the Wéalas king. He remembered how his own father died after falling into a rage of anger; he did not want the earl's death on his hands. Ealdred, however, newly appointed as Bishop of Hereford in Leofgar's place, was trying to placate the hoary old Mercian.

"Someone had to bend, unfortunately," Ealdred said. "Otherwise we might have been here for a very long time."

Leofric, though, was not for placating. "And why are we not taking the fyrd against him? After what he and his scorching army of devils did in Hereford – and now this, their latest provocation."

Harold, facing the prow, turned to look at Leofric, seeing the man's sagging features drawn into a scowl. He wanted to remind the old fool that it was *his* son who had brought the 'scorching army of devils' to burn Hereford, but Leofric would know it already, and Harold did not want to pour salt on the wound.

Instead he replied, "Remember, Lord Leofric, it was Leofgar who brought us to this point. He took his men to their deaths, without counsel. As for doing battle with them, it will do us no good to lose men in attacking the Wéalas – far better we should keep our men

80

alive for the defence of the realm. The Wéalas are like an ravenous fire; you put one conflagration to ground and another takes flame."

"The man's been sending raiding parties into Herefordscīr with impunity for years, he has no intention of keeping to his side of the bargain, so the provocation is indeed Gruffudd's doing," argued Leofric.

Harold gave the petulant earl one last look of impatience and the earl quietened. But in a few moments, he was cursing and muttering under his breath again. By the time they reached the bank, Leofric's moaning had become a frosty silence, even as Harold helped him ashore, grabbing his hand as he narrowly avoided falling in.

"It is good of you to come in person this time, Lord Gruffudd," Harold said, as Gruffudd alighted from a stocky, black-coated steed, and approached them with a confident stride. He was dressed in rich apparel. Intricately woven braid decorated his clothes, startling in beautiful shades of scarlet and blue. Harold admired the magnificent silk-lined cloak that billowed in the wind. It was purple, glorious in its rarity and cost, produced no doubt, from the dye of oysters.

The Wéalas king responded to Harold's greeting with a curt nod and offered him some mead in a silver cup from which Gruffudd drank first, to show that it was not poisoned. Harold accepted the vessel and took a mouthful, catching the Wéalas king's gaze as he looked over the rim. He saw then why Gruffudd's people followed him. The man's smile was enigmatic, his eyes spellbinding. Harold's own were inexplicably drawn to him.

The cup was returned and whilst Gruffudd passed it back to his half-brothers, men on both sides gathered around the negotiation party.

The place was a flat piece of shaded ground near the river, not far from the spot where Leofgar lost his life. Sheep, dotted around the meadows, bleated in the background. The sun broke through the clouds with the promise of a warm day as crows cawed and rustled in the trees, flying in and out to feed their young. It was good weather for an open-air meeting.

"I am honoured we can at last meet, Lord Gruffudd. Other opportunities have passed us by," Harold said, looking round for an interpreter.

Gruffudd responded, speaking in impeccable, accented English.

"We have a saying in the Cymru, *Cynt y cyferfydd dau ddyn na dau fynydd*: some things are not possible, like a mountain coming to meet a mountain, but there always exists the possibility men will meet some day." Gruffudd smiled as he paused. "I too am honoured, Lord Harold, although it is a pity that your king does not come himself to greet a fellow sovereign." Gruffudd folded his arms. "I command that you and your lords kneel, for *I* am king here and you are merely earls." His voice was warm, yet he carried an air of ice about him.

Leofric gasped and then the old earl spoke in a rasping voice, "I will kneel when you have been acknowledged as such by King Edward," Leofric retorted.

"And only when Lord Gruffudd has sworn fealty to *him*," added Harold, calmly.

Gruffudd's demeanour was hostile and Harold crossed his arms defiantly as their eyes locked in a battle of wills. Eventually Gruffudd laughed - a mirthless chuckle, intended perhaps to make light of their refusal to kneel. "I would be honoured to meet with the king of the Saes at his bequest, Lord Harold, for then we could discuss face to face, king to king, the subject of broken oaths, the invasions and repossession of our lost lands."

Harold was surprised at how sweet the Seaxan language sounded on the Wéalas king's tongue, yet the chill in Gruffudd's eyes seem to leave his words frozen.

"*Lost lands*? You were given possession of such territories that Lord Alfgar agreed on your behalf," Harold said.

"I was not there when Lord Alfgar negotiated on my behalf... as you should recall."

"You and he had an alliance."

"We did."

"And you sent him to plead for you."

"The king of the Wéalas does not plead, least of all to the king of Saes. Nor does he plead to any of his lackeys."

Harold coolly stroked his newly shaved chin.

"You make a habit of joining forces with those amongst our people who are traitors to their king," Harold said. "How can we trust you when you keep such bad company?"

Gruffudd looked pensive. "Alfgar, I know of. Perhaps you are also referring to another rebel, your brother, Swegn. Here in the *Cymru*, we say bad apples contaminate the rest of the apples in the basket.

82

How do I know that *I* can trust the rest of the fruit?"

"And in Englalond one bad apple spoils not the whole basket," replied Harold.

"That might be so… indeed, you are not much like your brother, Lord Harold. The difference in you is startling; mayhap that is why Swegn was apt to say you had different fathers."

Harold lifted an eyebrow at the veiled insult. Behind him, Leofwin drew breath. Harold threw his brother a look of warning over his shoulder. He was loath to turn the meeting into an aggressive confrontation, preferring to fight Gruffudd's insolence with cool equanimity.

"Are we here to discuss my brother Swegn, Lord Gruffudd?" Harold smiled.

"We are not, Lord Harold."

"Then tell me, *King* Gruffudd, what exactly is it that you want?"

"I would ask that Edward does not send armies into my lands after he has agreed the boundaries," Gruffudd glanced at Bishop Ealdred, "including the ecclesiastical control of those lands ceded to me, which your predecessor refused to acknowledge. You talk about trust, but I cannot with confidence expect *your* king, and those who serve him, will keep their promises."

"That was not Edward's doing," Harold replied evenly. "Leofgar took it upon himself to deny Ircingafeld to Glamorgan and then raided your lands. It was not endorsed by the king – nor was it by me."

"So not even the king of the Sæs can keep his own subjects under control? Why then should we trust you Englisc to keep your promises?"

"Because Lord Ealdred has been appointed the Bishopric of Hereford and he is a man of his word."

"And I will deal fairly with your bishop in Glamorgan, providing your end of the bargain is adhered to, Lord Gruffudd. That is… to return the property of the church along with those free citizens of Hereford who were carted off to be enslaved," said Bishop Ealdred.

"I shall see what I can provide, but I cannot guarantee all that was taken can be accounted for."

Again there was silence between the men; the only sounds were the bird songs and the distant bleating of sheep. Harold wanted the meeting over and for them to be gone from this place which, though beauteous in its rugged wilderness, held an atmosphere of malice.

Harold said when some moments had passed, "Lord Gruffudd," he gave a brief bow, I will convey your good wishes to Edward, our king, and your acceptance of his desire that you will come before him at the feasting of St Michælmas in Gleawecestre and swear your oath to him, that you will be a good and loyal sub-king, upholding the ancient laws that were agreed by our forefathers."

"And what do I get in return?"

"Peace."

"What if I want more?"

Once again Harold stroked the smoothness of his chin. "What more do you ask?"

"I ask for the lands beyond the *Afon Dyfrdwy*, the river that to you is known as the Dee," Gruffudd said, taking a roll of parchment from one of his brothers, unfurling it and showing it to Harold, "All these I want back in the control of my countrymen, as they were more than two hundred years ago."

Harold studied the map. "These lands you speak of have been inhabited by both our peoples for centuries, but if you Wéalas cannot live in peace with our countrymen, then –"

Gruffudd's cool melted. He raised his voice. "I am proclaimed protector of the Britons, what right do you Saes have to the lands that you hold from them in subjugation?"

Harold said nothing. Leofgar had been foolish, but he had also been his friend for many years. He'd heard how Gruffudd drove his sword into Leofgar's heart on the battlefield, and now he wondered how it would feel to disembowel Gruffudd, see him sink to his knees in a pool of his entrails, never to rise again.

Earl Leofric took advantage of Harold's silence to interject. "It is ours by the right of conquest. Lord God has deemed it so, and much Mercian blood has been spilled for those lands."

"You are Lord Leofric," Gruffudd said, eyeing the old earl with interest. "I see the resemblance between you and Alfgar. I remember your brother, Edwin. It was a shame that he died in my last encounter with him."

Leofric's fists clenched. Harold put a calming hand on his shoulder. "My Lord Leofric, let us not speak of old wounds, for they serve us not," Harold said.

"Our people have been singing about the dark days of the Saes invaders for five centuries. My ancestors were slaughtered by yours and driven into the mountains and into the sea and you dare to call *us* Wéalas, 'foreigners' in our own land. Yes, indeed, my lords, old wounds run deep. That injury is our life's blood, part of our very being, and what it means to be Wéalas."

Harold, incensed by Gruffudd's words, said, "What it means to be Wéalas? From what I see, if the Wéalas are not fighting or murdering each other, then they are harassing our borders, burning our villages, raping, carrying off our children, stealing our cattle and treasures from our churches – *that*, my Lord Gruffudd, is what it means to be Wéalas." Harold had not intended to lose his temper but now that he had, there was no stopping him. "You, yourself, slew your way to the throne, but then... perhaps we should be grateful. Perhaps we should be giving you thanks for having rid us of many other thorns in our side – Gruffudd ap Rhydderch, for one. We Englisc live in hope that if we leave you Wéalas long enough to your own devices, you will eventually rid us entirely of yourselves."

Gruffudd, sneering through most of Harold's tirade, said, "If I come before King Edward at Michælmas, the bargain shall be this: I shall be granted the lands beyond the Dee, the diocese of Ergyng will be returned to Glamorgan and Edward will acknowledge me as ruler of all of the Wéalas as well as the aforementioned lands."

Harold nodded. "Providing that my king will agree, and you return what we have asked for, if not, then at least in compensation which will go towards the building of the new church to replace the one that you burned to the ground."

Gruffudd turned to his brothers and spoke in their tongue. Then with a nod and a last glare at Harold, Gruffudd leapt upon his sturdy horse and left with his *teulu* as abruptly as he had come, galloping off into the distance.

*

Gloucester

"Why must your brother Harold always negotiate? Is it beyond his capabilities to just obliterate the damn Wéalisc?" Edward complained to Edith. He'd taken the opportunity to speak frankly during dinner that evening, whilst Harold visited the latrine.

Edward stared across the hearth to where Gruffudd sat celebrating his new victory. "Instead, I have to endure the sight of this upstart gurning at me with that stupid grin and look of triumph on his devilish feature. Was it not enough that I was forced to bestow him the kiss of peace on his side of the river, that I am now obliged to sit here and have dinner with him too?"

He wafted a graceful hand at Tostig who sat beside him enjoying the roasted venison that he and Edward had hunted the day before. "If I'd sent Tostig, *this* would not be happening. Tostig would *not* allow the Wéalisc peasant and his blood-crazed murdering swine to dictate terms to *us*. And Tostig would not have permitted Leofric's whelp, that godless Alfgar, to return to his lands after his brutal behaviour at Hereford last year, at least not without compensating those he'd harmed.

"What is more, had *Tostig* dealt with things, he would not presume to settle anything with those two foul ignominious creatures without my say so first! Your *other* brother, madam, is doing a fine job with those unruly men in the north, sorting out their taxes and enforcing the law! I should have sent *him* to deal with Gruffudd. Then perhaps instead of having to kiss the blasted thing I would have his infernal wolf's head on a platter. I swear, one day, I *shall* have that monster's head."

"Compose yourself, dear," Edith cajoled, patting his arm. "You know what your physician Baldwin says about keeping temperate and not getting yourself over-excited. I'm sure Harold did –"

"Harold did what?"

Edward, startled, looked around at his brother-in-law. He smiled as genuinely as his alarmed features would allow.

"Brother," Edith said, looking up at Harold, "we were just discussing the new peace between our kingdom and that of the Wéalas."

Harold knew by Edith's flushed cheeks, Edward's superficial grin and Tostig self-satisfied smugness, that Edward had been castigating him in his absence. All the court in Gloucester had witnessed Edward seething at having to make peace with Gruffudd. But no matter, for Harold was used to it. He was not going to risk a war that would only incite the Wéalas for years after and lose men to a cause that was better decided by diplomacy.

For the rest of the evening, his brother and the king were like star-struck lovers. Tostig hung on every word that passed Edward's lips, whilst admiration shone brightly in the king's eyes whenever he looked Tostig's way. But when Harold's gaze met with his brother's there was nothing but jealous hatred.

Chapter Nine

Secrets and Lies

Horstede, Autumn 1056

Father armed the sweat from his brow, leaving his forehead and hair streaked in scarlet. Outside the stall, Tovi waited anxiously, worried that Father laboured as much as the pregnant mare. All night Father and the others had struggled to calm the beast as she fought from the small hours to give birth to the foal. Tovi itched to get involved but he was not needed, so he had been told.

Rejection had been customary of late, since Tovi, who had never felt the sharp slap of Father's buckle across his backside before, had been punished for his assault on Mother. She had protested on his behalf, but had seemed a reluctant ally, and Tovi was certain she did so only to protect her secret.

She need not have worried, though, for Tovi had kept his mouth closed on that account, despite Father's attempts to beat the truth out of him.

The chestnut mare tossed her head, snorting and groaning, communicating the only way she knew to show her distress. Prayers formed on Tovi's lips in whispers. Father stroked the mare's strained neck and murmured words of comfort. Now in the autumn of her tenth year, Seaxa was Father's favourite broodmare. She and his stallion, Hwitegast, had never once produced a foal that was sickly or weak. All her labours had gone smoothly and without the trouble she was having now. Father's reputation as a high-quality breeder of horses meant that he was able to command high prices for her progeny. He'd been lucky enough to have bought both her and Hwitegast from a rich Iberian horse merchant at the yearly market in nearby Lewes some years ago.

Seaxa and Hwitegast had come as a pair and their blood, he'd been told, was of the popular Arab strain. Father often remarked that he'd never been too sure, for horse traders were notorious liars, but the pair had proven to be a good source of income for him, whatever the strain.

"Ælfstan, take over from me," Father said, and they swapped places.

As Ælfstan stroked, cajoled, and willed the mare to keep going, Father felt along her belly.

"There is no advancement from the foal," he muttered flatly. "It must have gotten stuck, damn it. How did we miss it? It's probably dead. If we don't get it out, she'll die too."

Seaxa began to sway and whinny in a high-pitched tone, tossing her head to proclaim her anxiety and pain. The three men held fast against the mare as she fought to collapse, quivering and covered in sweat.

"Hold her!" Father ripped the blood-soaked sleeve of his tunic, rolled it back and reached inside her up to his elbow. Seaxa gave a loud snort, stamped the ground, and panted her distress.

"Easy girl," Ælfstan said softly, as the mare ground her teeth, her throat thrumming. The smith's voice seemed to calm her.

"Can you feel the foal, lord?" Yrmenlaf asked Father. "Is it alive?"

Father shook his head. The mare's front legs gave way and she began to buckle, despite their efforts. Father pulled his blood-saturated arm from her as she went down. There was nothing any of them could do. The dead foal was stuck.

Father knelt, stroked her forelock, and whispered endearments. Tears pooled in Father's eyes and Tovi's stomach burst with butterflies. This could not be the end of this magnificent horse.

"What now, lord?" asked Yrmenlaf.

"It needs to come out. She cannot do this herself; she is spent and needs our help."

"We, too, will need help if we are going to do this," Ælfstan said.

"And rope to harness the foal. Yrmenlaf, go and–"

"I will go, Father!"

Father looked up, his matted hair, stuck to his head with perspiration made him look like a wild man of the forest. "Go then, Tovi, but be quick. She is losing blood – fast. Get the twins, and Herewulf, and anyone else who can make themselves useful.... And rope! Don't forget the rope!"

Tovi went swiftly out of the stables. He looked around the yard for any sign of activity. There was none. He ran into the longhall to find it occupied by the women.

Herewulf, he was informed, was in the kitchen with Sigfrith, preparing the slaughtered animals for the coming winter. 'Only God knew' where his brothers were, he was told, so he ran to the kitchen. There was no sign of Herewulf and Sigfrith was alone. Her father, she said, had gone to the village to fetch the butcher and that he should run there if he wanted him.

Out in the courtyard, the morning sunshine was fading. In the sky, dark, storm-filled clouds gathered overhead, moving rapidly like a blanket of shadows across the greying sky. A great gust of wind like the hand of an unseen giant held him back. He wrapped his arms around himself and charged against the forbidding storm as ice-cold showers slashed down to soak him. He thought to run back for his cloak, but Father's earnest instructions echoed inside his head, and he thought better of it.

The wind whipped the long strands of his hair into his eyes, and he struggled to reach the gates. Finally, he made it and opened the gate against the squalling wind, then, as abruptly as the storm had started, it stopped. The atmosphere brightened and he saw, waiting like a wælcyrie, a woman astride a dark horse. He knew her immediately. Shadows passed over the sun again, darkening the sky, but the wind and rain held off. *She* was there, like a spectre.

In the peripheral of his vision, he saw the shapes of men, but his eyes locked on her.

Though darkened by the hood, he felt the fierce glare of powerful eyes. She was both beautiful and harsh. Intimidating. The woman in whose bed he'd caught his father. The woman whose name Mother had always uttered with blistering contempt. Ælfgyva.

"Boy!" she called to him, a rich, throaty sound. "Tell your father that I would speak with him."

"He-he is tending the birth of a foal. It is not g-going w-well," Tovi stammered, heart pounding with unaccountable fear.

Her eyes narrowed, as though she were taking the measure of him. "Get him. It will not take long to say what I must. I shall not go until he comes."

Tovi stared at her, unable to move. There were men with her, blocking the pathway to the village.

"Well?" she glared.

"H-he c-c… can-not come. I was g-going to get help – f-for him…"

"Then fetch your mother."

"M-my m-mother? N-nay!"

She moved her horse closer. He wanted to run, but his legs were heavy. The rain started again.

"Go and fetch her. If you don't it will be *you* who must face the consequences."

Tovi felt sick. Was it rain or sweat that clung to his skin?

"W-what do you w-want with my m-m-mother?"

"Tell her I want my child back," the woman hissed. "Do you want me to come in there and rip the child from her arms, boy?"

The corners of her mouth lifted as if to smile; except it wasn't a smile.

So, she comes for the little foundling! Godfrida – the bearn was hers. Then that must mean… the child is my father's.

Tovi held his hands up to her. "Stay, lady, I will get your child."

Tovi rushed into the hall and was relieved to find Godfrida lying unattended in the wicker basket, peacefully asleep. He picked up the babe tightly wrapped in the blanket. Tovi heard Mother call as he ran across the courtyard. He hurried to the gate and was just feet away when she caught up with him and tore the screaming child from his arms. She slapped him so hard that he slipped over, his back soaked as he lay in a puddle.

Tovi, momentarily unable to get to his feet, watched as the witch rode in through the gates. As he picked himself up, Mother almost threw the squealing baby at Sigfrith who had come running from the hall. "Take her. Get her inside!" Ealdgytha shouted to the maid.

On his feet, Tovi grabbed Mother's wrist. "Get away, you stupid boy!" she cried, escaping his grasp. Her cold, angry face stared at him, then she looked back at the witch.

Squinting through sudden sharp rods of rain, Tovi saw that Ælfgyva was srating at the hurrying figure of Sigfrith. His mother's gaze followed the other woman's and they watched Sigfrith disappear into the hall.

The wind howled, and the women turned to each other like cats, readying themselves for a fight.

"At last we meet again, Ælfgyva," Mother said, as though she had known her adversary for years.

"I've come for my daughter."

"She belongs here now. You abandoned her, and now you want her back?"

"I was ill unto death and no one believed I would live, let alone myself. I wanted her to be with her father and the rest of her family, but now I am well again, she should be with me. I thank you for your care of her, Ealdgytha. I am truly grateful."

"I should have known..." Mother turned away from her. She was biting her lip.

"So, he didn't tell you?" Ælfgyva tilted her head.

Mother returned her gaze sharply. "Do not mock me," she said. "I know well how he has deceived me, you may rest assured, mistress. *You*, on the other hand, are the biggest deceiver here."

"It is not *I* who deceived you, Ealdgytha. It was not *me* who lied to you about the child."

"You pretended to be my friend when all the time you wanted my husband for yourself!"

"Can you never forget that? I did not wish for it to happen, but it did. I cannot change the past."

"And what of now? You snap your fingers again, and he comes running..."

Tovi whirled at the sound of another voice.

"What are you doing? You were supposed to get help!" Father grabbed his arm.

"S-sorry! I-I am g-going!" Tovi tried to make a run for it, but Father held him, the bloody handprint on his arm reminding Tovi what he'd failed to do.

"No need now, you are too late," Father said, bitterly. "She is dead."

Chapter Ten

A Dark Wyrd

Wulfhere stood by his wife but made no acknowledgement of her. Instead, he gazed at Ælfgyva and said, "What sort of *wiccecræft* is this? You were on your death bed when I last saw you."

Ælfgyva smiled. "It comforts me you are happy to see I still live." Her sarcasm was light, though unmistakable.

Wulfhere shivered, but the cold weather was nothing compared with the ice that came from Ælfgyva. He took some steps forward. Ælfgyva's men edged nearer to her but she stayed them with a hand. Her face like stone, she studied his hands, stained with the blood of the mare. The sensuous lips he had once kissed and often longed for were now set in a forbidding line.

There is no love there, not now.

Beside him, Ealdgytha grabbed his arm. "I won't let her take Godfrida!" Wulfhere's head jerked to face her. He wanted to speak comforting words to her; he wanted to feel ashamed, but he felt nothing.

He turned once more to look at Ælfgyva. "Who do you bring?" he asked, nodding to her escort. Two of the young men wore mail and a sword, and they grasped the hilts in anticipation.

"They," she said in frosty tones of hate, "are Guthlac and Thurstan, sons of my neighbours, and he," she indicated to a less equipped youth, though strong in appearance, "is Morcar, my tenant." Wulfhere recognised him. He saw too, that the woodcutter, Welan hovered in the background.

"Tell your young pups there is no need to reach for their weapons," Wulfhere said curtly, and then turned to the men directly. "You dare to come to the house of a king's thegn with your hands ready to draw swords upon him?"

Ælfgyva bent her head toward them and the young men relaxed.

"They are my escort, Wulfhere, and mean no harm as long as I am safe. I want my daughter, and *she*," Ælfgyva said, tossing her head at Ealdgytha, "will not return her."

"*She*," Wulfhere said, has cherished and cared for the child nigh on four months. Now you come here, risen from the dead like some she-demon, expecting the woman who has nurtured her all this time to hand her over without question. What game of witchery is it, that you are dying one minute, and then not? You begged me to take her, now you come for her – she is not a plaything to be passed around –"

"When you left me, Wulfhere, I *was* close to death," Ælfgyva interrupted, her face taut with anger. "You saw how ill I was with your own eyes. How would I have known that I would recover? Fritha, and Welan, cared for me and kept me alive. I owe my life to them. For a long time, I clung to this world by a thread, but now I am hæl again and the child… she should be with her mother."

Wulfhere's arm stung as Ealdgytha's nails dug into him. "You went to her? You promised me you would never see her again! Now I find that not only have you been seeing her, you have also given her another child!"

"I went to her because she was dying - *or so I thought…*"

Ealdgytha laughed without humour. "I really believed she had been left in the stables; God in Heaven, how you two have connived against me all these years!"

"Ealdgytha, go inside!"

"Why? So, you can plan your next tryst? Your next betrayal against me?"

"I want no more of your husband, madam. I just want my child." Ælfgyva retorted, raising her voice above the wind.

"You cannot have her. She is mine. You can have *him* instead, is that not a fair exchange?" Ealdgytha hissed.

Wulfhere pulled her back. "Don't, Ealdgytha. You have to give her back."

"I will *not!*" She gathered her skirts and lurched from him, hurrying back to the hall.

Wulfhere turned to his son. The boy was soaked to the skin, a bewildered look on his pinched face. "Tovi, go and look after your mother. You can do *that*, can't you?"

"Father, I am sorry – about Seaxa."

"I know you are," Wulfhere said. He felt the boy's anguish, but now was not the time for recriminations or forgiveness. "Now, go inside with your mother."

Wulfhere turned back to Ælfgyva. "You could have sent your woman to fetch her," he said. "You did not have to come yourself to torment my wife. Nor me."

Ælfgyva threw back her head and laughed for some time before she stopped and said, "You think I came to torment you both? God, Wulfhere, do you think so little of me and so highly of yourself? Am I the only one to blame for all this trouble? Have I not suffered enough? I nearly died that day and many days after that, if not..." She looked momentarily at Welan and then back at Wulfhere. "How am I expected to live now without my Wulfhild?"

Wulfhild. He had forgotten that was the name she had given her. She had named her for him. "Ealdgytha needs time. You cannot just wrench the child away from her arms. Besides, if you take her now... in this rain..."

"I want her, Wulfhere. Today. Damn the rain. I have come far to fetch her. Ealdgytha can say her goodbyes, we will wait. If not, then I will go to the scīr-reeve, but I *will* have her, even if I have to go to the king himself to get her back."

There was a grey pallor to her skin and translucent circles of purple rimmed her eyes. But she was still beautiful. How could he feel angry with her when all she had ever given him was love – and he'd returned it with broken promises and lies? She was alive, and he'd thought her dead, her 'demise' a constant ache in his heart ever since he'd ridden to her deathbed. Now she was here, like a dream, yet still he felt the despair that he could never have her. Never.

"Perhaps it would have been better if I had died after all," she said.

"I would not wish for that." He moved closer to her.

"Poor Wulfhere, is it too hard for you to accept that I am alive after all?" She put a hand to his face. "I'm sorry to come at such a bad time for you. Your son said you were tending a mare's birthing. The mare, she is..."

He stood motionless. She let her hand fall. The matter of a lost foal and mare seemed to fade compared to the loss of her.

"Dear God, Ælfgyva, I am sorry. If I'd known that you were still alive..."

"What would you have done? It wouldn't have changed a thing.

95

But I do want you to know I did not come here for anything else but my daughter."

Wulfhere nodded. "Give me a little while. You can wait in the woodshed out of the wind and rain. I will bring her to you."

As he turned to walk away, she called to him, "Wulfhere, I have been a slave in one way or another all my life. Today I am free from the yoke of men. Tell Ealdgytha I am truly repentant of the hurt I have caused her and that I promise I would cut off my hands before I ever see her husband again."

There was a pause, and their eyes locked.

Breaking the silence, Wulfhere asked, "Will I see Wulfhild again?" He gulped back a lump in his throat.

"Mayhap you will. You are her father, after all. Someday there will come a time in her life when she may have need of you."

He nodded, "I will be here for her," and with his heart heavy, he walked back to the hall to fetch their child.

*

Tovi stepped out from inside the woodshed where he had hidden, listening to them speak their evil. He had never really understood what had made his mother turn so against his father. Now he knew. He knew it all, and his world was torn asunder.

*

That evening Ealdgytha sat mesmerised as the little wicker crib burned on the hearth. All afternoon, she had been separating the threads of truth from the false – remembering a word here, recalling a look there. Realisation had come like an awakening, and the beautiful world she had created for herself was gone. She had known all along it wasn't real, she admitted, but her fragile mind had refused to accept it.

Wulfhere sat down beside her as the flames hungrily devoured the basket. The household was sleeping. It was just the two of them.

"See how it blazes as easily as my heart was deceived. You must think me such a fool," she croaked, poking the iron rod at the fire as though it were his eyes. Her throat was raw from sobbing, her eyes swollen and spent of tears. Now, watching the little cot disappearing to ashes, she felt the emptiness in her soul return.

Like the coward he was, Wulfhere said nothing, his head bowed. She'd waited all day for her wrath to find its way to him but was so tired of it all - his lies, his deceit... her own inability to influence him.

96

Now he was here, the burgeoning anger within her dissipated with the burning of the bearn's cot and all that was left to her was despair.

"Do you not have anything to say to me? Do I not deserve *something* for what I have had to endure?"

"What can I say, Ealdgytha, apart from I am sorry."

He sounded repentant, but it did not make her feel better.

"I knew there was no point in saying anything. You are always sorry. You are a thousand times over and over *sorry*. But what good is sorry when you can never keep your promises? You cannot justify your actions, Wulfhere – not this time…. Letting me believe the child was a gift from God! A child to replace the one I had lost, when all the time you knew it was *hers*. Do you know what that feels like? To be so duped by my own husband – and not for the first time!"

His sad eyes reflected the glow from the fire, and his words bitter to her ears as he muttered, "You look at me with such burning hatred that I am sure I will melt before long."

She had fallen into Wulfhere's deception through her blinkered desire to be loved and needed. Thierry had filled that need for a short while, but Godfrida's presence had offered much more. And he had even robbed her even of her beautiful memories, for they were tainted now.

She turned away from him, looking into the fire again, feeling the heat burn her cheeks. "What did I do to deserve such heartache and humiliation, time and time again? Everyone will be talking about how the thegn's wife had been deceived into looking after the child of her husband's lover… if they aren't already. And you just sit there!" she hissed. "Can you not say anything at all?"

"I have said that I am sorry, what more do you want me to say?"

For a moment she wanted to throw herself onto the fire, anything to be rid of the hurt within her. Instead, she said, "I want to know why you let me believe she was a foundling. I want to know why you didn't tell me who she really was when all the time you knew. I want to understand why you had to hurt me, when it is *I* who have loved you faithfully, borne you seven children, kept your home, woven your clothes, and put up with your wrongdoings for sixteen years. Oh, it was bad enough that you slept with this woman and gave her not one, but two children – but to do *that* to me too! It was a betrayal with a double edge, Wulfhere, just like your sword! You have slain me with your lies as much as if you'd killed me on a battlefield!" There! She had found her anger.

Wulfhere raised his voice. "I didn't say anything because I thought if I told you the truth it would hurt you even more than you have already been. I did not mean for it to happen that way, but it did. When they came to me with her – *my child*, I could not turn her away. Would you have me cast her out when I was all she had? They told me Ælfgyva was dying, for heaven's sake."

"And you went to her even though you promised me you would never see her again."

"She was dying! I could not let her die without at least telling her I would look after her child. And yes, I wanted to see her one last time. I couldn't let her die without that – that would have been too cruel."

She rose. "You did not think that what you were doing to me was cruel? And she did not even have the good grace to die after all!"

The bench he'd been sitting on crashed to the floor as he stood to meet her stance. His face flushed with anger, he said, "Christ on the cross, Ealdgytha, you are such a bitter woman. I think you would have been truly happy if she had died." He turned and almost tripped over the fallen bench as he paced towards the doors.

"Where are you going?" she demanded.

He turned. "Anywhere where you are not! I've had enough of your tongue lashing, Ealdgytha. I expected you to be angry and I am sorry for your hurt, but we have trodden this path before and there is only so much a man can take."

Seeing his face, a mixture of hatred and sadness, the tears ran down her face. She slipped to her knees, sobbing, her arms wrapped around her. Inside her, the pain was too much. Wulfhere went to her, an awkward child, holding out a hand to her. She stared at it. Did not take it.

"I loved her like she was my own," she said.

She allowed him to take her hands in his and bring her to her feet. "You have other children, Ealdgytha. And they have much need of you."

"A baby…Wulfhere, I wanted a baby," she sobbed.

"I can give you another babe, Ealdgytha, if you will let me."

She shook her head, tears running freely, soaking her cheeks. He held her to him.

After a moment, she pushed away. "No, Wulfhere. I am damned. We are both damned."

"It is not too late for us to start again. I will not see her ever again and I will do penance, I promise. I will request relief in my duties and go on a pilgrimage. Edward will allow it. He believes in such things. We can start again."

"You don't understand. Our marriage – it is damned. It wouldn't matter if you went on a thousand pilgrimages, we will never be absolved... never...."

That night, Ealdgytha slept alone in her bower upstairs. She dreamt of Thierry. Images of his dark, seductive eyes tempted her as they sat playing dice. He won the game, and she was the forfeit – her body and her soul.

Since that night, she'd pushed the sin of Thierry to a corner of her mind where she'd locked it away. Something had stirred the memory earlier in the hall with Wulfhere. As she sat up in bed, sweating, she realised the enormity of what had gone between her and her handsome young Franc. She'd committed adultery, one of the greatest of sins. The cloud of dream-like happiness she'd been floating on had dispersed and in its place was doom.

She'd fallen into a web of enchantment: Godfrida, Thierry... they'd been part of it. The norns had spun a dark *wyrd* for her – a deadly magic – and she'd allowed herself to become enmeshed, like fish caught in a trap. She'd failed the test.... And would be forever cursed.

Part Two

An Ill Wind Blowing

1057 – 1058

Chapter Eleven

Death of a Prince

Súþrigaweorc April 1057

The man known as 'The Exile' watched with his wife Agota, as his children romped in the courtyard of Lord Harold's manor at Súþrigaweorc. The air rang with laughter as they enjoyed a game with the Godwinson's offspring. Edvárd was pleased to see them happy after such a long and arduous journey. He laughed as the two younger ones, Kristzina and Edgar, scooted here and there to avoid being caught by the 'it', squealing with delight as they narrowly missed capture. Eldest daughter, Margita, joined with less enthusiasm, for now that she was somewhere between girl and womanhood, her inclinations to participate in childish pursuits were gradually diminishing.

Beside him sat Agota. A cool late afternoon breeze caressed the silky folds of her wimple. His Germano-Hungarian princess, espoused to him since she was little older than their eldest daughter, had been a true companion for nigh on two decades, bearing his anger, frustration, and episodes of melancholia with stoic resilience.

In exile, Edvárd had not been treated unkindly by his adopted royal family, and yet his resentments were deep-rooted. He'd been a young boy approaching adolescence when he and brother Edmund had discovered the truth about who they were and from whence they'd come and why. Since then Edvárd nurtured within him the damage of many indignities, the first of which happened when he was just a bearn in arms. Over the years he had learned to disregard them, making a name and life for himself in his fostered land. But with this new chapter in his life, old hurts had resurfaced.

Instead of fighting for Edvárd's birthright, the Englisc thegns and nobles had capitulated to Cnut. They should have protected the babes of their deceased king, but they did not, and Cnut had, Edvárd, brother Edmund, and their mother, secreted away to be disposed of. Overnight, the brothers' claim to the English throne had dissolved like white snowdrops in winter sunshine.

Edvárd looked lovingly at their three children. At first, five-year-old Edgar had cried all the way from Mecseknádasd, knowing that he would never see home and his childhood playmates again. With time the little boy's fears gave way to inquisitiveness and he adapted to this itinerant life and each new surrounding. The two girls, Margita and Kristzina, had embarked on their journey with a mixture of puzzlement and excitement. They were going on an adventure, Edvárd had told them, and they were to live at the grand court of their great uncle, the King of Englalond. There, they would find handsome husbands amongst the great nobles of that country and live a life of splendour and comfort in their father's old land.

Agota squeezed her husband's hand. "No regrets, Edvárd?"

"I hope not," he replied, trying not to sound too doubtful. He knew what she had given up by uprooting their family from all they had ever known.

The decision had not been made lightly. They'd given it much thought, mulling it over with their closest companions and advisers, day after day. Almost a year ago, Edvárd had heard that an Englisc bishop was making enquiries about his whereabouts, but it had not been the first time, and he'd thought nothing would come of it, and nothing did, until a year later, when he received a letter brought to him by a messenger sent from the court of the Holy Roman Emperor. It was from an Englisc noble, a man called the Earl of Wessex. Written on behalf of the King of Englalond, it requested Edvárd meet with the Englisc embassy, waiting at Henry's court in Cologne. That one day he would return to the country of his birth and take his rightful place on the Englisc throne, had been his lifelong wish and now the day was here. However, when he read the words that the Englisc earl had dictated, his anxieties rose. Were there still men in Englalond who would see him dead?

The Lord Harold, Earl of Wessex, requests your gracious presence so that he may enlighten you with the intentions of your royal uncle, Edward, Rex Anglorum.

He should have been ecstatic, yet feelings of longing had been replaced by fear. Would it be safe for them in the place he'd been forced to flee as a child? Would the journey be worth what they were giving up at home?

It was Agota who'd finally persuaded her husband that a move would be beneficial to them all. Hungary was not a safe place to be right now and the prospect of better things seemed more likely in Englalond. As the king of Englalond's heir, their lives would be a lot more secure than if they stayed in Hungary.

"You are hesitant, my love." Agota said, breaking into his silence.

Edvárd coughed and took out a strip of linen to wipe his nose. He coughed again and felt pain in his chest, neck, and throat. "We have no guarantee I will be king after my uncle dies."

He'd pressed Harold that the Englisc nobility would swear oaths that he would become king on his Uncle Edward's death. But Harold emphatically stated that such an oath was not his alone to give and could only be given with the agreement of the witan. Edvárd was bemused. Did they think him a man of no standing where he'd come from? He and his family were not in need of charity, for they had brought with them much treasure and gold to support them very comfortably.

"But surely, Edvárd, these Englisc…they would not have gone to so much trouble to find you and bring you back, if not for the kingship?" Agota said.

Edvárd shrugged. He was forty-one now, well past his prime, and looking much older recently, with a head of lightly greying hair balding on top, his hands showing the first signs of age. Agota, in contrast, had aged well, her looks hardly marred by advancing years.

Edvárd sniffed and wiped the mucus from his top lip. "You know nothing of the customs of these people, Agota. A king may nominate his successor, but the choice made must be sanctioned by the witan. And the king has yet to see me. What if I do not meet with his approval?"

"Of course you will, my love." She placed a hand on his wrist. "You are a good, honourable man, a warrior, with the blood of kings running through your veins. Furthermore, it is your birthright. You
have waited for this moment all your life." She paused, seeming earnest, like one who saw her dream, wavering, just within reach.

"We have waited much of our lives for this moment. You must trust

104

in God, Edvárd; He would not have brought us this far to have our hopes dashed like waves against rocks. And Earl Harold will speak for us. He is an honest and righteous man, of that I'm certain."

Turning away from the burning in her eyes, Edvárd shook his head. "We hardly know him, Agota. And you forget he is a Godwin."

"And so? What has that got to do with anything?"

"After my father died fighting for his kingdom, Godwin betrayed him by pledging allegiance to the usurper Cnut. We were banished from this country, my mother encumbered with child - myself a babe in her arms - to be murdered on Cnut's orders - and we would have been if not for King Olof's kindness. What makes you think we can trust a man whose father sided with such a person?"

"That was the father, not the son. It was long ago and Harold himself could not have even been born when your father, God rest his soul, died. You cannot blame the son for the actions of a dead father. Edvárd, you grew up at the Hungarian court, I am sure that it would be the same anywhere. The loyalties of men ebb and flow with the tides of politics and war. Godwin most likely made the most expedient choice at the time when he chose to accept Cnut as his king."

"He should have remained loyal to my father. He was supposed to have been his friend."

"One thing I have learned on this journey, the will to survive is the greatest driving force of any man. Do not let the past embitter you, for if you do, it will forever mar our future. Do you want that for your son? For your girls?"

Edvárd gazed at her entreating eyes. "You speak wisely, wife, as always," he said, "but I fear it would be naïve to trust them implicitly. I would wager there are many men who would not be content to see the son of Ironside return. Most of all, the good earl – for he himself may have designs on the crown of Englalond."

"Sometimes, husband, I feel as if I alone carry the burden of hope for this family… and I am afraid it is too heavy at times."

He felt guilty. "I am sorry, Agota."

She took his hand and placed it in between hers. "I came here to follow your dream. Now it seems that the dream is no longer yours, but mine. Yet we must believe in it, if we don't, then what has this all been for?"

Edvárd shivered.

"Your hand is as cold as ice," his wife said.

He felt unwell, drifting in and out of himself. The children's voices, which only moments ago had sounded loud and vibrant, now seemed distant, as though they were no longer nearby but somewhere further away. Agota's hands warmed his, and the sadness that consumed her brought him back, realising that he had been crushing the life out of her with his own fears.

"Dear Agota," he said in a low voice. Now it was his turn to take her hands. "I am here with you. We will face this together whatever God has in store for us."

At once she smiled and said, "No, Edvárd, it is I who am here with you."

*

A warm smile spread across Eadgyth's face as she pictured the gifts Harold had brought home from the continent, strategically placed around her home in Waltham to their greatest affect. Harold had been abroad since last October and had sent word that she should come to Súþrigaweorc to greet him when he arrived with the Exile's family.

"Harold, you have bought all manner of things back with you: perfumes, oils, lotions, silk, earthenware, leather belts, and pouches – just look at these precious gems. Not to mention all the holy relics in their bejewelled caskets," Eadgyth gushed. "These relics, I take it they are for our church at Waltham. Ah, Harold, the church will be the finest ever with these things. Edward will be oozing with envy. All this must have cost you a pretty penny!"

"Not really, sweeting. My unique charm could not fail to affect the staidest of characters. My hosts were falling over themselves to endow me with gifts."

"And who are you to deny them that pleasure, dear husband? Of course, to say no would offend them dreadfully," Eadgyth said with a teasing smile.

"Would you insinuate, *lufestre*," he said, his hands going to her waist as he turned her toward him, "that I used my charisma and wit to procure these things falsely?"

"I swear, my lord, you could lure the devil out of his lair in Hell." Eadgyth laughed warmly, her hands resting in his shoulders.

"That, my dear Lady Eadgyth, is a terrible thing for a noble lady to say to her loving husband. I wouldn't let Father Wulfstan hear you say such a thing." Harold looked so serious that for a moment Eadgyth thought he truly disapproved of the jest. Then he smiled, drew closer and kissed her mouth. "But worry not, for it will be I later, demanding penance from *you*."

"Will it now? Then I shall be happy to perform whatever penance you should prescribe for me, my lord." Eadgyth giggled as Harold playfully nipped at her neck and rocked her gently in his arms.

"Eh-hem!"

Eadgyth turned to look at the intruder.

The woman spoke in halting, accented Englisc. "Excuse me – I interrupt, Lord Harold."

Harold drew away from Eadgyth. He smiled at the woman they both knew to be a servant in the household of the Lady Agota.

"Of course, madam, what can I do for you?" Harold asked.

"My lady – she asks go to her chamber. Prince Edvárd, he is need to... He tired after journey – he is needs to –" The pleasant, middle-aged woman bent her head to one side, her hands clasped together against her cheek.

"Tell your lady 'yes', I will see that her quarters are made ready." Just as Eadgyth was replying, Lady Agota appeared in the doorway of the hall, somewhat distressed. Leant heavily against her, a fist clasped to his chest, was her husband, pale and clammy with sweat.

"S'il-vous plait! Aide moi!" Agota cried, using Francisc, the common language that they all understood. "Mon mari! Il est malade! Please, you help, yes?"

The evening shadows were lit by the brazier as Agota sat beside her husband who lay weak and pale.

"Here, my lady, take this water and sponge, it will cool him."

"Thank you, for your kindness, Lady Eadgyth," Agota said.

"You are very welcome, Lady Agathe." Eadgyth placed the bowl and its contents beside her.

Agota was used to having people defer to her, but here in Englalond, she was no more than the wife of an exiled man whose status was yet confirmed.

Now her husband was inexplicably gravely ill, a very uncertain future was on the horizon. What if he died? What then? Would these Englisc, who had gone to so much trouble to find them still desire her and the children's presence? Edgar was but an infant. Would they consider him too young to be proclaimed the king's heir?

As Agota gave an involuntary shiver, a guttural sob emitted from her throat. Eadgyth edged nearer and put an arm about her shoulders.

On the bed, Edvárd's eyes flickered and beads of sweat layered his brow. He must be in deep anguish to be thrashing about like he was, babbling incoherently. Agota dabbed at his forehead with the dampened sponge. *Come back to me, dearest Edvárd.*

She spoke soothingly in Hungarian to him, words of endearment. He called out, staring blindly, and Agota tearfully told Eadgyth that Edvárd cried for his mother.

"He is fighting the fever so hard." She sat back in despair. "I do not know why this has happened. He had nothing more than a cold for a few days. Now it has become a fever and he labours for breath."

"Perhaps the journey had been too much for him. He may just need to rest."

"You do not need to stay, Lady Eadgyth." Agota saw that Eadgyth had brought a chair to sit beside her.

"I will not stay if you do not wish it, Madame, but if it would give you some comfort, I would be happy to stay awhile with you."

Agota smiled her thanks. "I would be greatly comforted if you should stay. I feel so alone here in this strange land. I welcome your friendship, my lady."

"Then it is yours, Madame."

*

Harold sat in his private apartment, sharing the fine red wine he'd brought back from St Omer, and playing *hnaftafl* with his brother, Leofwin. Earlier that eve, a maidservant had come to tell him that Eadgyth was in attendance with the Exile's lady and would come to bed later. Harold was disappointed. He'd waited months to bed with her again. During his sojourn on the continent, he'd met with many chances to bed both noble and lowborn ladies. Once, Harold would have taken advantage of the opportunities, but not anymore. He reasoned that he was too old and, besides, for a long time now, he'd come to believe that lovely Eadgyth was all he ever needed.

But that did not mean Harold was averse to a flirtation. He'd indulged many a rich noble lady who'd hoped to secure a match with him. Harold, however, using his inexorable wit, managed to sidestep any attempts to marry him off without causing too much undue offence.

"A penny for your thoughts, Hal," Leofwin said.

Harold stared blankly at his brother.

"'Tis your go," Leofwin prompted.

Harold grunted and rubbed his eyes. "Sorry, I don't think I can continue with the game. I am sorely tired from journeying. Damned muddy roads. I was rather hoping for an early night with Eadgyth, but the Exile has gone and got himself a fever, which means that she is there having to see to their comfort, and me, well, I haven't held her for nigh on six months and I'll just have to… well, you know."

"I will leave you to rest then, if you prefer. I was hoping to have met the man myself this eve. But it looks like we will have to wait until tomorrow. Has he seen a physician? After all, it wouldn't do for him to leave his worldly body just now 'ere he gets a chance to go before the witan and meet with the king." Leofwin laughed at the irony.

But Harold was not laughing. He stood up to throw another piece of kindling on the hearth which had almost gone out.

"Hal, what is it?" Leofwin asked, turning serious. "You look like a man with a heavy burden. Did something happen whilst you were abroad?"

Harold shook his head. "I'm just weary, brother. And missing my woman," Harold replied.

"No, Hal, there is more wrong with you than you are telling."

Leofwin poured two glass goblets of Flemish wine that Harold had brought back with him from St. Omer. "Here drink this, it will loosen your tongue. You haven't been yourself since I got here. Let's talk. Tell me what is on your mind. Father always said never to sleep on a problem and to find a solution by sharing it with another."

Harold had joined Leofwin in echoing his father's old maxim. He sat down and took the wine, gulped a few mouthfuls, and leant back. The wine had an instant effect and he licked his lips as the last mouthful went down. He felt a slight dizziness and his eyelids started to droop.

"All right then, little brother, perhaps Father was right. But I doubt if there is an immediate solution to this predicament."

For a few moments, Harold stared into the fire without saying another word.

"What predicament?" Leofwin urged. He sat forward in his chair and looked at Harold intensely.

"Our brother and our nephew."

"Ah, Wulfnoth and Hakon. Do you have word of them?"

Harold shook his head. "Not exactly. The Count of Flanders, is not

109

only the brother-in-law of our brother, Tostig, but also the father-in-law of Duke William, our boys' host in Normandy. Do you know that William is known as the 'bastard' over there?" Harold paused, "And not just because his mother was a tanner's daughter."

Leofwin smirked and Harold continued, "I was once told a story by a fellow called Brihtric, who claimed that when he was an ambassador at Baldwin's court, the count's daughter Matilda had refused to marry William. She considered the duke too lowborn a bastard for one with such a pedigree as hers. After all, she is descended from King Alfred."

"Ah, I think I know this man, Brihtric." Leofwin looked pensive. "That's it, I remember hearing a story that Matilda took a fancy to Brihtric, but he claims he had to reject her advances on the grounds that her father would have gelded him."

"Strange, for I heard that Ambassador Brihtric found her unnaturally short and he, being of tall stature, felt repelled by her." Harold laughed. "Whatever, she went on to marry that lowborn bastard William, just the same."

"I wonder what persuaded her."

"Apparently when Matilda refused his offer of marriage, he beat her. It is said that she enjoyed it so much and happily agreed, to be his wife."

"I would happily agree to marry such a woman," laughed Leofwin. "But we digress, brother. Continue with your account."

"The Count of Flanders, as you know, has always been a friend to our family, giving our father and mother refuge during our exile of '51. He himself has not much liking for his son-in-law. William's reputation for ruthlessness and greed far exceeds the normal limits, even for a descendant of Norse savages. The count warned me that the duke has definite designs upon making the throne of Englalond his. Furthermore, he advises that William claims our boys were sent with that cunning bishop, Champart, as surety for Edward's intention to name him his heir, which is what our cousin Ranulf confirmed."

"What will William do if Edward names the Exile as his heir?" Leofwin asked and drew his eyebrows together in a concerned furrow.

"It is not for the duke to make such claims upon the throne."

"But if Edward has offered it to him?"

"Aye, and there is the rub, for William does not understand the way things are done here and will be greatly angered."

"Then, perhaps our boys might be in danger," Leofwin concluded.

Harold poured more wine; he felt like getting drunk. "The man is ruthless, from what I hear. He would kill his own grandmother to get what he wanted."

Leofwin looked horrified. "Why didn't you go to Normandy to speak with him yourself?"

Harold gave his brother a reproachful look.

Leofwin was wide eyed. "You were there in the vicinity. You could have gone to the duke and demanded that he send the boys back with you. That's what I would've done."

Harold was in the middle of another gulp of wine and almost spat the contents. "Christ, Leofwin, don't you think I feel guilty that I did not? My conscience plagues me daily about it. Normandy was still unsettled, with the conflict between the duke and the Franc king still not fully resolved. I might as well have just thrown myself to the bandits if I'd chosen to travel through that lawless country without an armed escort. The likelihood of getting in or out of Normandy without being set upon was pretty much non-existent... and there was no guarantee the duke would have granted me an audience, even if he was not occupied with more pressing matters."

Harold sighed and continued, "What would I hope to gain by going there? Can you imagine it? My dear Duke of Normandy, please may I have my brother and nephew back? Oh, yes, my lord, of course you may have the crown in exchange for them. What's that, they must stay until such a time you are king? And then what must I tell the witan: I have just confirmed our new successor to be that Norman bastard! They would have my guts for leg-bindings. No one wants William of Normandy to sit on the throne except the Normans."

Leofwin shrugged sheepishly. "So, it seems unlikely William will ever hand the boys over until he has the Englisc crown upon his greedy head." He eyed Harold with a sour look. "What of our boys, then?"

Harold shrugged and leaned forward. "That is the dilemma, dear brother. The fate of our boys is inescapably woven into this plot. I can see no way out of it."

*

Eadgyth finally left the Lady Agota's side long after midnight to return to her bed. Harold stretched out an arm as she settled down beside him in their bed. The urge to make love to her had dissolved into a desire for sleep and he was content to lie close to her with the comforting warmth of her soft skin. The wine had dulled his senses,

111

speeding him into a deep sleep, something that had not happened for some time.

When morning came, light filtered into the bedchamber through the open slats of the shutters. Harold turned over and reached out an arm for her, only to find the space empty. He moaned, annoyed that she was not there to help rid himself of his erection and thinking how inconsiderate it was to leave him to deal with it alone. But before he could do anything about his swelling manhood, Eadgyth burst into the room.

"Harold! Dear God in Heaven! There is terrible news!"

Harold sprang upright. "By the Saints, woman! What ails you?" He reached down to the floor for his braies and hose, and heard a woman scream somewhere out in the hall.

"The-the Exile, Lord Edward," Eadgyth stammered. "Harold... h-he is... Oh God, he is dead!"

Wulfhere and Leofnoth left the Exile's vigil in Harold's chapel to convey the sad news to the king at Westmynstre. No doubt the body would soon be made ready to be brought across the Thames for burial in Lundenburgh. Wulfhere could hardly believe that only that morning he had been assigned to escort the long-lost prince to the king, and now, instead, they were bringing back the Exile's corpse. The man had set foot in Englalond for just two days. Now he was mysteriously dead and had drawn his last ever breath before he'd had a chance to look upon the face of his uncle, the king.

"You know what they will be saying now, don't you?" Leofnoth asked as he and Wulfhere were being rowed to the other side of the Thames.

"Aye, they will be saying that there are sinister powers at play here, working to rid the country of an heir to the throne." Wulfhere pulled his cloak closer to him against the chill. The dark clouds had not dispersed, making the atmosphere, like the sad demise of Englalond's hope, a pall of misery. The two men became silent, and the only sounds were the oars in the water against the plaintive cries of gulls flying overhead.

After a while, Leofnoth resumed the conversation, keeping his voice low. "There may not be many who are saddened by the sudden death of the Exile."

"I can almost hear the sighs of relief floating from Normandy across the narrow sea, even at this distance," said Wulfhere.

Leofnoth smiled in reply and nodded. *"Wyrd bið ful aræd.* Man cannot escape his fate, whatever that might be."

Harold and Eadgyth watched as the swathed body of Edward the Exile was borne down to the water's edge. It was transferred to the barge that was to carry him to be buried with great honour in St Paul's Mynstre with his grandfather, Ethelred. Harold assisted a dazed Princess Agota and her weeping children into the boat. Another vessel would follow them to take their belongings. Before he climbed aboard, he went to take leave of Eadgyth and his children, who stood, downcast upon the quayside to wave them off.

"What will become of them now?" Eadgyth asked with a pitying glance at the woman and her fatherless children as they sat grief-stricken with Ætheling Edward's body. "The poor woman doesn't seem to have been able to take it all in yet. Oh, Harold! It seems like such a waste. All those months you were gone… and the effort put in to find him."

"Nay, my love. Not a waste. At least we have the boy, Edgar. He is our one hope now. That is, if the king lives until the boy comes to manhood."

"Let us hope that he does," murmured Eadgyth.

And as Harold made his way to the boat that was to carry the family of the Exile to London, he could not help but sigh inwardly, almost relieved, at the turn of events and that for now, the boys in Normandy were safe.

Chapter Twelve

The Runaways

Late May, 1057

May was coming to an end. The light chill winds of early summer had receded and made way for longer, warmer days. This was the season when the forest of Andredeswald was covered for miles in an exquisite blanket of emerald foliage. Tovi knew which paths were safe to follow, but somewhere off the beaten tracks so familiar to him, he now wandered, a runaway from home.

Riding his young gelding among the ancient trees, Tovi took in the warm sunrays. Ash and beech stood like great leaf-laden sentinels along the pathway, and he imagined they protected him from what lay beyond. It was daylight still, but before long, would come nightfall and fear.

It was said that murderous outlaws hid in the forest, waiting to accost the innocent traveller. Vicious animals, too, lurked amongst the woodland: boars, wolves, and possibly, though rarer, a bear. However, worse than these, were the *nihtgengan*, ghostly walkers that dwelt in the shadows of night. He clutched the charm around his neck and said a quiet prayer to the wolf spirit it was for. But even this did not fully allay the fear about the uncertainties ahead.

Nonetheless, he would rather face the night terrors of the dark woods than what his parents had in store for him. Since he had been a little child, his head had been filled with the idea he would someday join his father and brothers in the shieldwall. Now Mother and Father had other plans for him and wished him to finish his education far away from home in a place called Waltham. The twins had been sent to acquire the skills of a warrior. Why not him too?

Tovi had not wanted to run away, but there was no other option. He did not want to end up like Father Paul, listening day in day out to the

114

moans and groans and needs of his parish flock. He wanted to be a warrior, like his father.

Mindful that he would soon be missed and to avoid being found, Tovi stayed away from the main pathways. He came to where the underbrush and foliage were less penetrable. Dismounting, he took hold of Grendl's reins, and waded through the brushwood and entwined branches.

Having battled his way for some distance, Tovi was relieved to feel that cool air brushed against him as the woodland shifted into something more permeable. He kept his eyes downwards, checking for any roots or stumps that might trip him or lame Grendl. The ground began to level out and eventually an obvious well-used pathway joined it. Looking straight ahead at a vast curtain of tall beech, ash, and oak trees, he sighed with relief. He had no idea where he was going, but this would be his route.

Tovi crossed the pathway and led Grendl to the edge of the dark, deep woods before him. The horse snorted and hoofed the ground, refusing to go any further. Something was spooking him. Tovi pulled on his halter, but the creature remained stubborn and repeatedly turned his head as if to warn of some terrifying omen.

"Come on with you, you stupid horse." Tovi pulled him harder and smacked the horse's withers, but it was no use. Grendl would not move, not even for the carrot that Tovi offered him. "Look it's a tasty carrot. You like carrots."

The sudden tang of rotting flesh assaulted his nostrils and he paused to listen carefully. The sound of buzzing reached his ears and a movement amongst the mesh of thickets caused him to cry out. A couple of woodland birds were startled into flight and he sighed.

"Come on, Grendl, 'tis just the birds, no more. Nothing to worry your big head about."

Frustrated, Tovi let go of the reins and walked forward, hoping Grendl would follow. The creature stayed put, so Tovi backtracked and grabbed the reins again.

"Walk on!" Tovi tightened the reins around his hands and pulled hard. This time the horse moved reluctantly, whinnying to show his displeasure.

They walked on through the web of trees, the air becoming increasingly cooler. The light began to fade, and an eeriness filled the unknown woodland fortress. He shivered, his skin prickled, and he stopped – *was that footsteps?* After a few moments he carried on, chiding himself for his cowardice. Every now and then Tovi paused to remove barbs caught in his clothes and Grendl's flanks. The constant movements in the shrubbery unnerved him. He told himself not to be afraid and that it was only one of the many woodland creatures, a mouse, a hare, or a badger – not the little spirits that had been known to shoot men with their poisoned arrow tips. Not a wolf or a *nihtgenga*. Occasionally he stopped and looked over his shoulder, expecting to see something alien following, only to see Grendl's long nose and large staring eyes.

Moving deeper into the greenery, gnarled and knotted tree trunks seemed to grin as he passed by. They were reminders of the times he used to run to the forest to carry messages to Edgar from Freyda. Those were happier times, in the days when Edgar had once meant something to his sister. The sound of a rippling stream brought memories of his fondness for his sister's lover. Tovi recalled waiting, sprawled nonchalantly on the enormous boulder at the edge of the rock pool. A huge grin on his face, Edgar would greet him with: '*Wæs hæl*, Tovi, what news?'

And Tovi would speak with a grin of his own, excited to be part of their secret assignations. "My sister sends greetings, and that the 'great oak gives good shelter in the moonlight'," which was obviously something that only his sister and her lover were supposed to understand. Hearing this, a smile would creep over Edgar's face, and his eyes danced as he laughed. They would talk, hunt, or whittle, and Tovi had learned how to fashion his first wooden figure out of wood: a stag with horns. After all this, Tovi would run home before dark, to tell Freyda that the 'great bear was alive and well'.

Thoughts of all this made him think of home, and he had to remind himself why he had run away. Oh, yes. Waltham. Replaying the scene in his head, he heard Mother's voice as if she were there with him now.

"You are well past boyhood now, Tovi. 'Tis more than time you left home and continued your education." She'd paused as if expecting a reaction, but he'd stayed silent and expressionless. "You will be leaving here soon to take your place in the world. The Earl of Wessex has a successful collegiate at his manor of Waltham, so I hear. You will be assigned to the care of the canons there. You will learn to read and write your letters properly. And if you learn your craft well, who

116

knows what you might be able to do. You may even get a bishopric one day."

His jaw dropped. He'd stared at them speechless in their places on the dais in the hall that raised them above all others to dispense their justice to those beneath them, just as they were dispensing their justice to him, their own son.

She had spoken with such resolve. And Father had said nothing, avoiding his eyes.

"The good dean has agreed to accept you," Mother continued, "despite you being well beyond the usual age for new pupils, but we have assured him that you have had some education already, so you won't have much catching up to do. It is a great honour, Tovi, that the earl himself arranged it. Fortunately for you, he has not forgotten what you did for his daughter the day you saved her from drowning."

Father Paul had spoken about the kind of life that monks led, languishing in a cold, sparse, draft-ridden scriptorium, the writer's cramp searing through their frozen, ink-stained palms. It sounded like torture. Tovi had looked to his father, willing him to turn his eyes on him. But nothing.

"Well Tovi, what do you say?" Mother asked.

"I do not wish to go."

"You have no choice," she'd replied.

"Then why ask me?"

Mother's head jerked toward Wulfhere. "Tell him, Wulfhere. Tell your son, it is for his own good. He *must* go!"

"Your brothers went away, Tovi, now it is your turn," Wulfhere muttered, looking at him for only a moment before turning away again.

"But I am not going to Leofnoth's. I am going to Waltham – to be a m-monk!" Tovi protested. "They went to be warriors. F-Father, don't send me away."

"You are not going to be a monk, Tovi, silly boy," Mother interjected, laughing. "A collegiate is not a monastery. It is a place of learning, and a church. If you're lucky you can make your profession as a priest, like Father Paul."

"I don't want to go!" Tovi threw himself onto the steps of the dais and in front of all the household, begged them. He reminded Father of all the years they'd spent together, learning to fight with shield and spear so one day he could stand by him in the shieldwall.

117

But all Father had said was, "You will go - as your mother wishes."

*

As late evening approached, Tovi looked for a suitable place to make camp. The undergrowth grew denser again and to carry on into the night would be foolhardy. The quiet rustling of bushes and the distant howling of wolves followed him. Clutching his wolf amulet, he chanted the prayer he hoped would keep him safe. "Oh, Lord of beasts, harbinger of death, feaster of carrion, guard me, for I am of your blood and need your protection."

Eventually a small clearing came into view near the edge of a steep gully. Broad branches would provide ample shelter from the cold and there was enough space between the tree's giant roots to nestle for the night. It would not be as comfortable as the goose feather mattress at home, but at least he would be able to endure it. He tethered Grendl to a tree branch and set about collecting twigs and kindling to start a fire. He climbed carefully down the steep ravine, collected some small rocks from the stream, and flung them up the incline one by one as he struggled his way back to the top.

Placing the rocks in a circle, Tovi made a little hearth and sat shaking the dust from his shoes and warmed his hands over the flames. Daylight was gone. The long days of summer were warm, but it would be a chilly night and he would need to keep the fire going until he settled down to sleep. He munched on some bread and cheese taken from the pantry and gave a satisfied sigh – the plan had gone well so far. He smiled and listened to bullfrogs croaking, the stream babbling, and the night owl's soft gentle hoot.

But his contentment soon turned sour and eventually he began to think about his recent resentments: mother and her Norman *cniht* and the beating he'd taken because of it. Catching his father in bed with that black-haired witch, Ælfgyva. Godfrida, the child Father had deceived them all into caring for. And the final insult: his banishment to a life of clerical drudgery, as if *he* should be punished for all their wrong doings.

Tovi tried to banish the thoughts, but the voice that bounced off the trees around him, would not go away. *They hate you. They think you're useless. Useless - worthless, Tovi.* The words echoed until it sounded like a multitude of voices instead of just one. He leapt to his feet, clutched at his amulet as fear tingled through him.

"Who-who are you? W-what do you want?" The voice had sounded

118

familiar – his brothers, perhaps? He dismissed the thought as quickly as it had come, for how could that be possible?

Tovi stared into the darkness. In the distance came the sound of branches swishing and wings flapping. Then the voice manifested again, this time inside his head, malevolent and somehow familiar – yet – also unknown.

They hate you, Tovi þorléas; Tovi the Useless. Not like your namesake, your great grandsire, that grand lord, Tovi the Proud. You think Father will be worried about you? Think again. He cares nothing for you. He is glad to be rid of you! They have bewitched him, your whoring mother, and that black-haired daughter of the devil!

The disembodied voice began to multiply, and he clasped his ears to quell the noise. But it was no use. It was inside him.

The voices increased to a crescendo, rebounding in and out of his head. The trees swayed eerily. He wanted to run, but fear rooted him to the spot and his heart beat like a hammer and anvil inside his chest. Crouched down into a ball, he covered himself with his cloak. Unseen hands grasped at him with their bony fingers. The sound grew louder, like a bell ringing, it permeated his brain until he thought his head would burst. *I'm going to die!*

He'd no idea how long he'd stayed like that but after some time, he opened his eyes to a dog barking. Someone familiar called his name and he realised he had been asleep; it had been no more than a nightmare.

"Tovi! Thank goodness! I thought I'd never find you in this darkness and gloom!"

Relief overwhelmed him. "Winflæd!" he cried, laughing nervously, pleased to see her. "What are you doing here?"

"Where are you going?" Winflæd stood before him, a grin on her face.

Her hound, Elf, tail madly wagging, bounced up at him, paws padding Tovi's chest in greeting.

"Hey, stupid dog, stop that." Tovi ruffled the hound's ears.

"It was hard to keep up with you, but then I lost track somehow, and oh – I am so pleased to have found you again!"

Tovi gave another nervous laugh. "You scared me half to death. I thought I was being hunted by woodland spirits. Nice try though, Froggy. You had me really believing it for a while!"

Winflæd frowned at him, then said, "If you are going to run away, you could at least take me too, instead me having to follow you secretly."

Morning came at last. In between the roots of the old oak, Tovi and Winflæd were snuggled together wrapped in his cloak. Elf, lying across their toes, had kept them warm as they slept. Tovi sniffed, head heavy from the previous night's mead that Winflæd had brought with her. As rays of light pooled through the trees, he squinted in the brightness.

Shifting, he realised how much he missed his goose-feather mattress already. Carefully he extricated his aching body from the space in which they were lodged, so as not to wake his sister or the dog. Winflæd did not flinch, even when her head lolled and slipped onto a root with a thud. Elf, easily disturbed, bounded after him barking, and the noise was enough to wake her.

She sat up and rubbed her eyes.

"Morning, Frog Spawn," Tovi replied without much enthusiasm as he gave water to Grendl. Winflæd pushed the excitable Elf aside and got to her feet.

"I'll go and refill it," she said, pointing to the empty water flask.

"Nay, little sister, you can't go down there, 'tis too dangerous. Too steep."

"I can do it!"

"I said, nay!" Tovi snapped at her. "I'm sorry, Frog Spawn, but you are going to have to go back home. You can't stay here."

"But last night you were glad to see me." Winflæd's eyes were wide and watery. "I know you think that I am a useless girl, but I am not. You know I can hunt and fish. See, I have brought my bow. And I can make a fire… I won't be in the way, I promise."

Tovi shook his head. "I was glad to see you, but now you need to go home."

"But why?"

"You cannot stay. You must go back. This is no place for a girl."

Winflæd's face began to crumple as if she were about to wail. "I can't go back without you, Tovi," she entreated. She wiped away a tear.

Tovi observed her awkwardly. "Don't cry, Froggy. I hate it when you cry."

"I am not crying, there's something in my eye."

120

She turned away, and Tovi saw she was rubbing her eyes.

"You *are* crying, don't deny it. This is no place for a wailing little girl!"

"Don't make me go back, Tovi, please!"

"*I go* because Mother and Father hate me. It is not the same for you. You have always been their favourite."

"That is not true, Freyda was always the favourite."

"Well you are the favourite now. It is me they want rid of. And I cannot and will not go to Waltham."

"Then, what will you do?"

"I don't know yet. Maybe I will just live in the forest, here. I can hunt for myself, build a shelter. It will be all right."

"I can hunt too; you know I can. And I can build shelters. You know that too!"

Tovi sighed. "Why do you want to come with me?"

"I don't want to be at home if you're not there."

Tovi sighed. He shook his head at the state she was in. Her dress was smeared with dirt and full of loose threads. As for her hair... How could he look after her? If Mother could see her now, she would faint with disgust.

"I cannot be responsible for you, Win. You must go home."

"But you will be alone. I couldn't bear for you to be alone."

Tovi shrugged. "Alone is good for me."

"Nay, alone is not good, and I don't want to go back to Horstede without you there! I hate it there too! Mother ignores me, Father never plays anymore... and Aunt Gunnhild hits me with her broom."

"Nay that isn't true. You're making it all up." He gripped her elbow. "You are going back and that's final! So you may as well stop your whining."

Winflæd shook him off. "You want to leave me to find my own way?"

"I didn't ask you to come after me. You found your way here; you can find your way back."

"How can you do this to me? You promised me once that you would never leave me. You lied. You always lie."

Her words stung him, but he could not give in. She had to go. Turning his back, Tovi started to gather his things together.

"I didn't say that I would never leave you, Froggy."

He bent to pick up his cloak from beneath the old oak. A sharp blow to the head felled him. Blood trickled through his fingers as he touched the wound above his temple. A few feet away lay the stone, blotched with red. Elf barked at him as though to say, 'There, you deserved that!"

Tovi got awkwardly to his feet. "You little bitch!"

She stood by the ravine, laughing.

He looked for a stone to retaliate with, found one bigger, almost a small rock. Elf growled. Tovi lunged, swung his arm – and gasped, "Winflæd, look out!"

Too late. She was gone. He let out a cry, ran to the ridge, and looked over. Bouncing this way and that, he saw that she had fallen. Her limbs flailed as she tumbled head over feet. A yelping, twisting bundle of tawny fur shot past him down the slope after her. "Elf!"

Tovi launched after them and came to rest a few feet from the stream. He leapt up, and Elf, his fir scuffed by the fall, whined and nudged at Winflæd's lifeless body in the shade of an old yew.

He pushed Elf out of the way and knelt to examine her. Deep scratches etched her forehead, the bridge of her nose, and over her brow. Wisps of hair torn loose from her braid were entwined with twigs and the little cap was off, caught somewhere up the ravine, he supposed. A glance upwards confirmed he was right.

"Oh, Winflæd, I-I-I am s-so sorry!" he sobbed.

Elf yelped pathetically, but Winflæd made no sound, though her little girl's flat chest rose and fell. He thanked God she still breathed. A large swelling developing on her forehead explained her unconsciousness. He gathered her to him and cradled her head in his lap. "Dear God, I didn't mean to hurt her." Looking up at the ridge he saw it would not be easy to climb with an unconscious body in tow, even one so light as she.

He thought of a stretcher but could not find any vines or hazel to make one. If only there was some rope....

He would have to carry her, get her up to the top; lay her over Grendl and take her home. Bracing himself, Tovi bent down under Elf's mournful gaze, and pulled her into his arms. He was about to stand and startled when she let out a scream, he let her drop.

"What?" he cried out, his heart racing. "Did I hurt you?"

"Wh-what happened?" she asked, looking up at him with a frightened expression. "It hurts...." she wailed. "I'm all broken!"

He wanted to vomit at the sight: the blood, the ripped sleeve with the broken bone protruding through the hideously torn skin. Carefully, he propped her up against the yew and inspected her other arm, which was now the shape of a wolf's back leg, obviously broken too. She fought against him as he struggled to reset it, with splints hastily made from branches, using torn strips of her under tunic to secure it.

Done with that arm, he contemplated nervously on how to mend the bone in the other. As Winflæd whimpered beside him, it came. Once he and his mother helped a man with who had fallen from a cart on a boggy path, his leg caught under the heavy wheel. He remembered the man's broken limb like it was yesterday: the skin all torn and bloody, the bone below the knee protruding. He remembered how Mother had realigned the bone, her hands covered in blood, then splinted the leg to hold it in place. He'd spewed afterwards when it was over.

Trembling at the memory, he knew he must try.

Winflæd howled as Tovi tried to push the jutting bone back into the gash in the muscle so he could reset it. "Don't touch me!" she cried.

He crawled in close and turned his back to her so that he could manage the arm easier. Damn, she would not stop struggling, and he had to press against her to hold her still. It made fixing the bone all the more difficult. "Froggy! I cannot help you if you do not stop your thrashing!"

"It hurts!" she screamed. "It hurts!"

He let go of her arm, turned to her, and shouted in her face, "I know it does, but unless you let me do this, the elves will get into the wound and it will become poisoned! Do you want to lose your arm?"

It shocked her into stillness.

"Now are you going to let me do it?"

She nodded.

He gave her a stick to bite on. Whimpering, she put it in her mouth. "Froggy, keep still and bite hard."

She yelled and bit down on the stick as he manipulated the bone to realign with the other. The sound was terrible, but he did not falter in his mission. When it was over, Winflæd lay panting, the piece of wood still in her mouth.

"Winflæd, I am going to have to get you up the slope, now, can you walk?" he said after they had both rested.

"My leg hurts." Her face crumpled.

To further dismay, he saw that her right ankle was swollen twice its size and a pool of blood was forming on her skirt. Cautiously, he lifted her tunic to expose a large open gash in her right thigh and groaned.

"What have you done to me?" she sobbed, staring at the wound in her leg with wide fearful eyes.

"I am so sorry," he replied. "I didn't mean for this to happen, Win."

"My head hurts. I want my papa!" She let out a stream of wails.

Cradling her head in his lap, he stroked her hair, and after some moments a glazed look settled over her. She looked feverish; her eyelids closed.

"Winflæd?" Tovi tried to rouse her. Her pupils moved under their lids but there was no response. "I am so sorry," he whispered.

*

Leading Grendl, Tovi waded through the thorn bushes, disappointed that he'd failed to think of a way to get Winflæd safely out of the gorge. So now, after making her as comfortable as possible, he was heading to Horstede to get help. Winflæd's life was in danger, of that he was certain. He'd seen enough people die of the elfshot and wound fever to know he *had* to get her home soon, but he could not do that himself.

He would be blamed for her plight, no doubt, but to save his sister, he must brave whatever punishment befell him. Father was going to be so angry. He would go white first, then start cursing and growling – then he would break something. Perhaps even beat him.

But now he was lost, certain he'd made a wrong turn. His stomach reminded him he had not eaten since the night before and he was weary and scared. As he tried to get his bearings, the notion to run away no longer seemed such a good one after all.

Chapter Thirteen

The Search

"Tovi, Winflæd, why are they not here?" Munching on a piece of stewed meat, Wulfhere looked at the empty spaces at the table, then at the twins. "What have you two Sons of Loki done? Where are they?"

The boys glanced at each other, shrugged and shook their heads.

Ealdgytha sat beside him, pale and thin, poking impassively at her food. She said in a dull voice, "I suspect they're running wild in the woods with those little urchins from the village."

It was as if the absence of her children hardly concerned her.

"Why do you allow our daughter to run around the woods like a forest creature when she should be here, waiting at table like a dutiful Christian maid? Do you wish to see the same thing that happened to Freyda happen to Winflæd? Good God, woman, have we learned nothing at all? And why is Tovi is not here pouring my mead and sharing table with his father this eve? Tomorrow, the boys and I will be off to muster. This will be the last time I shall see him before he goes to Waltham...." He paused, buried a hand in his hair and massaged his head, peeved that his son should have been going with him and was not. He sighed. "The boy should be *here*!"

Ealdgytha turned to him with hostile eyes. "Am I the only one responsible for the behaviour of our children?" She spooned the stew delicately through her lips. Wulfhere bristled, annoyed that she rarely took any sustenance these days and wore her misery openly.

"I will go find them, Lord Wulfhere," said Sigfrith, as she stood from her place at the table. "Mayhap they be somewhere in the village, playing with the children."

"Stay and eat your supper, Sigfrith," Ealdgytha ordered. "They are often late. 'Tis nothing unusual. They will come home before dark, their stomachs rumbling and their eyes bulging, no doubt."

Wulfhere was not pleased. "Thank you, Sigfrith. You may go and seek them out and when you find them, you can come back and finish your meal. 'Tis way past the time they should be out."

Sigfrith nodded and made to leave.

"Stay, Sigfrith," Ealdgytha demanded. Sigfrith stopped in her tracks.

"I said, you may go, Sigfrith!" Wulfhere banged a fist on the board and glared at his wife.

Ealdgytha did not even flinch, but she said no more. Wiping the corners of her mouth delicately with a napkin, she pushed her plate away and left the table. Once she was gone, the twins both let out a long breath and shared a look between them.

Wulfhere sighed. He let go of his spoon dropping it into his bowl, slopping the contents all over the place. "God's teeth," he muttered and sat back with crossed arms.

Wulfric and Wulfwin stared at him with wide eyes.

Wulfhere turned an angry gaze on them. "What?!"

*

Ealdgytha stood on the porch, shielding her eyes from the evening sun. She let out a long breath when she heard the horn. Ælfstan's new cherubic-faced apprentice, Thurkill, ran down the steps to open the gate. The search party was back. They'd been out since the previous dusk searching. Ealdgytha ran down to the path, past the chapel, past the wood store, past the stables and the forge to the gatehouse where the men were dismounting. But there was no sign of the children. She ran sobbing into her husband's arms.

"We will search again, Ealdgytha." Holding her to him, he added, "And we will find them."

Ealdgytha whispered, "Dear God, return them to us."

*

Tovi had not been sure how long he'd been wandering in the forest, alone and scared. Dazed and weary, with Grendl trailing behind him, he collapsed with relief when he spotted Ælfstan and Herewulf.

The sun had been up for just a few hours and blood from numerous scratches smeared his face, hands, and clothes. Grendl had not escaped the thorns either; a mass of cuts criss-crossed the horse's flanks.

Weak from hunger and thirst, Tovi was borne on the shoulders of

Ælfstan, to where Father was, wading through the foliage as he hunted for him, calling his name. Wulfhere's anguished face changed to a smile. He cried out as he hurried toward them and Tovi slipped from Ælfstan's shoulders to feel himself engulfed by his father's muscular arms.

"Where's your sister?" Father asked, releasing him from the bear hug.

"Are you going to belt me again, Father?"

Wulfhere cupped his face, turned it to one side and rubbed a finger over the dried, crusted blood at Tovi's temple. He sighed deeply and stood back, fists on hips. "What mischief has befallen you now, boy?"

Tovi looked at his feet and made no attempt to answer.

Father said, "Tell me the sorry tale, then, where is she? In truth, I always thought it was those other two sons of Loki that needed a good thrashing, but now I know your mother has been right all along. We should have sent you away a long time ago."

Father's words ripped into Tovi's heart.

"Well? Where is the little minx? How is she not with you?" Wulfhere demanded. "I am not going to thrash you, boy, just tell me where she is."

"I didn't want her to come. She followed me. I told her to go back home, but she wouldn't listen!"

"Go... with you? Where?"

"I was running away."

"Running... Why for God's sake?"

"I don't want to go to Waltham!"

"God's teeth!" Wulfhere cried, hands going to his head. "Where is she? Why have you not brought her back?"

In a torrent of sobs Tovi said, "She's in the w-woods, Father, she.... I made her f-fall!"

Father caught him by the arm. "What? And you left her there? How badly is she hurt?"

Tovi winced as Father's grasp hurt him. "Badly. She fell, and she f-fell over and over again... and it was my f-f-fault!"

"Where?"

"Down a wooded slope into a ravine." He wiped the snot from his nose with his sleeve.

"God's teeth!" Wulfhere bellowed again. "You left her there – in the woods?"

"I had to, I had to get help – I could do nothing myself. Then I got lost."

"You had better take me to her, then! Can you remember which way you went? Better pray we are not too late! If anything has happened to her, I will skin the hide from you!"

It was easier to find the way back to the ravine than it had been for Tovi to find the way home. He, Father, Ælfstan and Herewulf rode through the woods until Tovi cried out, "Here! Here is where we were!" He slipped off the saddle and ran ahead through the trees and into the clearing.

"Are you certain, Tovi?" Wulfhere called after him.

"Aye, see? Here… here is where we camped." Tovi indicated to the little circle of stones and then pointed. "She fell at the edge there."

Wulfhere followed Tovi to the ridge and looked over. Tovi cried, "No! This cannot be!"

She was not there.

*

Winflæd tossed and turned upon a bed of animal skins. Suspended above were the blurred images of faces. Voices whispered as, with a vicelike grip, something grasped her. Excruciating pain and alternating waves of heat wracked her sweat-drenched body.

In the delirium, she was taken to Horstede, to the longhall. Shadows hovered around the hearth, cried, and called out her name. Back at the ravine again, she floated, then spiralled downwards until she lay sprawled, staring up at never-ending treetops. A face laughed down at her, a demon with narrow, slanting, devilish eyes. There were pointed ears and serpent's teeth, but as the face transformed into the more human-like features of Tovi, it gave a malignant smile. *There, we are rid of you now,* the demonic Tovi said, and the evil faces of the twins wafted into view alongside him. So Tovi had joined forces with them. The fiendish brothers were laughing, mocking her. She closed her lids to shut them out and prayed for sleep. At last, Winflæd's eyes felt heavy and mercifully, she slipped into unconsciousness.

*

Ealdgytha sat on the cot where Winflæd usually slept. Clutching a little woollen shawl, she wept. Her daughter had been missing for a week now and each day Wulfhere would round up the searchers. At first, Ealdgytha had been hysterical, Sigfrith inconsolable, and Tovi,

Ealdgytha was certain, had taken Winflæd on purpose to punish her because of what she had done.

"Mother?"

Ealdgytha turned. In the doorway, framed by the evening light, stood her youngest son. As always, the floppy fringe all but concealed his eyes.

"What do you want?"

"Can you ever forgive me?"

From under the fringe a tear rolled down his cheek, but she refused to feel anything for him. "Not now, Tovi, please. Leave me be."

She averted her eyes, swollen from incessant crying, and stroked her cheek with Winflæd's shawl. She could have sworn him gone, but as Ealdgytha turned her head again toward the doorway, she saw her son was still there, poised as if about to leave. He waited, perhaps hoping she might change her mind and she caught a glimpse of sad eyes through wisps of the fringe.

Ealdgytha knew that Tovi's banishment to Waltham was a penalty for knowing too much, and his suffering lay heavily in her heart, but every time their eyes met, it was like a banner that fluttered in the wind for all to see…. Her secret.

"I forgave *you*," he murmured softly, his pale face empathic, sharing her pain.

She turned away again. There were no words to heal her own wounds let alone his. Only tears; sobs that wracked her body. Ealdgytha clung to the blanket, as if somewhere wrapped inside was her lost daughter.

"Please don't… don't send me away, n-not n-now, Mother."

"*I* am being punished, Tovi, not you. Winflæd is lost to me. That is *my* punishment, not yours."

"Nay," he sobbed, "She isn't gone. She – she m-must have crawled away... Let me stay, at least until I f-find her! I will go out every d-day and I will f-find her, Mother! I *will* – f-find her!"

"*Please*, leave me…" she said. "I cannot bear to see you right now."

"I've n-never told. I keep your s-secret – do you know how hard that is? And th-this – is wh-what you do to me…"

"Leave me! Just leave me, Tovi!" Ealdgytha shut her eyes tightly.

When she opened them, he had gone.

She lay on the cot, tears overwhelming her. If Winflæd's loss was her punishment, then losing his mother was Tovi's. Though she would never admit it, someone had to suffer for her pain, and it had to be him.

*

Unlike his wife, Wulfhere had not resigned himself to Winflæd's death and was certain she was still alive. He felt it, but the rest of the household were not as certain, and although they did not say it outright, Wulfhere could tell what they were all thinking - that she was gone forever.

Three more days of searching passed. Wulfhere called a meeting to work out a new strategy. As they stood in the courtyard, Ælfstan pleaded with him not to send them out to look for her again.

"Lord, we have our work to do. Ten days have gone by and there has been no sign of the poor little mite. You cannot expect the men to keep going. They are bone weary, so are you. We are never going to find her now."

Wulfhere was furious. "She is alive, Ælfstan, I know it," he closed a hand over his heart, "in here. She is out there, waiting for me. I cannot give up now and you should not ask it of me."

"Lord, anyone could have taken her." Ælfstan's eyes were moist.

"But we found no trace of anyone else being there," Wulfhere protested. "If she wasn't there in the place where Tovi says she be, then she must have wandered off.... And where is the hound? That dog never leaves her side. If she *was* dead, we would have at least found *him*, or - or he would have come back. *She has to be alive!"*

"Lord, even the hounds cannot get her scent. I am afraid we must fear the worst."

Wulfhere, though not yet ready to give up the search, knew what Ælfstan meant. The familiar glades of the forest were not so unwelcoming a place, but in the darker, more camouflaged trails, outlaws, wolves, demons, and spirits roamed, and it was more than enough for a mere mortal man to withstand let alone a small girl.

An image came painfully to him: his little bird, lost, hurt, and frightened. She would be desperate for him to help her. He shuddered involuntarily and fought back the desire to break down and weep. He stared at the men accusingly, their feelings of guilt plain on their faces. Then Herewulf, as if compelled by Wulfhere's anguish, and possibly to ease the gloom that floated around them like mist, said, "Perhaps we should go back to the place and see if we can find any other tracks. The little mistress might have been found after all and mayhap be in

130

the care of some forest dweller as we speak."

Wulfhere swung his arms agitatedly. "We have been to every charcoal burner and woodcutter's hut for miles and found nothing –" he broke off as an explosive thought came to him. "Unless… Helghi! God dammit! I'd wager my teeth he has my daughter. He said he would come for her one day!"

"Lord? Could this be so? Edgar has been banished, after all. Surely that would make the agreement null and void," Herewulf said.

"I know neither of you relish another visit to Helghi's, but –" Wulfhere's words were cut off in mid flow, this time by a horn sounding. There was a commotion at the gates and one of the cottars came rushing toward them, shouting that Wulfhere should come out to the green.

Once there, he joined the gathering crowd watching a cart trundling across the meadow, being hauled by an old ox. Elf, bounding in front of it, saw Wulfhere and quickened his pace, barking loudly. In the cart was a woman and walking beside her, a hooded figure drove the ox. The villagers gathered around them as the woman alighted, helped by the hooded man. She was youthful, wearing a full wimple that covered her chest and shoulders. A drab grey linen tunic hung loosely on her and a dark braid could be seen beneath the folds of her veil. Wulfhere recognised her fawn-coloured eyes. Once they had gazed at him in gratitude when he'd saved her child from a burning hut. She was much changed, had become wraithlike, drawn and pale, but her eyes still had the same ethereal look.

He knelt to rub Elf's ears. "Where is your little mistress, hound?"

The hooded man stood in the background as Mildrith approached.

"Lord Wulfhere," she called to him, "we bring your daughter to you safe and alive." Her companion lifted a bundle wrapped in a woollen blanket from the cart. He saw the fair hair and immediately lunged forward to gather her in his arms.

Mildrith put a hand up. "Careful, lord. She has been wounded badly."

His daughter was pale, exhausted, and as light as Gerda. He kissed her again and again, dripping tears of joy over her scarred face.

"Papa," she murmured in a weak voice.

He stopped to gaze down at her, needing to believe it was really her. "I've not been well. Tovi… I'm sorry… I don't know what happened to him. Is he home?

Wulfhere could not speak, so overwhelmed was he. When able to, he turned to everyone and declared with a beaming smile, "Look, my little girl has returned. Give thanks to God."

There were cheers and gasps of relief from the villagers. Some of the youngsters clapped and leapt with joy, and Father Paul said a prayer of thanks.

His little girl, his little bird had flown back to him. He gazed at Mildrith gratefully.

Mildrith said, "Have a care, Lord Wulfhere, for she is not fully mended yet. She has two broken arms, and her ankle was sorely swollen, though we could not feel any serious damage there. The bones are fixing well, but one broke through the skin... and some elf poison got into her blood through a nasty gash in her right leg. She has lain in a fever for days, burning hot to the touch. I can hardly say what it must have been that kept her with us. Only God's will perhaps and..."

"I am indebted to you, lady," Wulfhere said.

"Once I was indebted to you, my lord. Now we have a daughter each to be thankful for, though truly, she would be dead if not for..." Her voice trailed off and Wulfhere followed her gaze to her mysterious companion.

"Papa," Winflæd whispered. He looked down at her. She gave a faint smile and then said in a strange low voice, "The wolves saved me, Papa... and brought me to *him*." She pointed at the figure standing quietly by the cart.

Wulfhere called to Ælfstan. "Take her home to her mother. Lady Ealdgytha will be anxious to see that she is safe." Wulfhere handed his daughter to the burly blacksmith and went to the hooded man who stood, passive like one of the standing stones left by the old folk. Pulling back the cowl, he cried, "Edgar?"

Edgar recoiled and Wulfhere was shocked by the change in him. He looked like one of the wild men of the forest, a *wulfeshéafod*, forced to live as an animal.

Mildrith caught his arm. "Please, lord, she would not be alive were it not for Edgar. It was he who found her and cared for her, kept her from being molested by the elven spirits and wolves. She would have died if not for him."

Wulfhere glanced at Ælfstan carrying his daughter toward the hall. *She would have died...* A moment ago, he had wanted to take the chains

132

that hung on his belt and clap them on Edgar's hands. Now, as he looked at the pathetic creature, the impulse for revenge fought against the desire to forgive. How could he hurt this man when he'd given him back his precious daughter? Had saved her life. Perhaps Edgar had earned his own redemption now. For a moment, as he gazed at Mildrith, her eyes burning with hope, he recalled how he had returned home from war with so much guilt in his heart – the things war had made him do. He'd earned his own salvation the night when Helghi's hall had burned and he had saved Mildrith's child from the fire. Perhaps this was Edgar's chance to absolve himself and who was he to deny him? He recalled the words in the *Pater Noster* that Father Paul had taught him: *Forgive us our trespasses as we forgive those who trespass against us....*

"He has a shelter in the forest," Mildrith explained. "He took her there. I sometimes go to him to see how he thrives. I know I should not, but Edgar was never truly wicked, not like..." Her eyes looked downward momentarily as if on the ground she would find the words. Then, tilting her face to him once more, she said, "He was not himself when..."

Wulfhere stayed silent, letting her speak her truth, studying her with a mixture of interest and pity. Her eyes were lit by sunlight, the gold flecks in her irises shimmered like sunrays dancing on water. Beautiful eyes, untouched by the harshness of her life.

She struggled to find the words, but Wulfhere understood her completely. *Edgar is not like his father.*

"He suffers, my lord, tormented. Nary a word has he spoken since that day when..." Her gaze wavered between him and the ground.

"Why would he do such a thing... for me... for Winflæd, when it is our family that has caused him so much hurt?"

She shrugged. "Perhaps because you saved his little sister from the fire." She went to the cart and lifted out a small dark-haired child. "Remember her? You risked your life to save her. Now he risks his life to come here and give you *your* child. Not only for the debt we owe you, but also because he is a good man."

Mildrith's daughter was now an infant of at least four, with Helghi's dark curls and eyes, but she had the same haunted look of her mother.

Wulfhere nodded. A memory of that night came flooding back in a torrent of images. He gazed at the woman holding her child, and in his mind's eye he saw the scene as though it were happening again. He

133

saw the flames, just as they were, heard the cries of people darting here and there, getting water. The smell of burning and the look on Mildrith's tearful face as she walked away, mouthing her gratitude, the baby held close to her.

The same sense of peace that had breezed through him that night, touched him again. He remembered how it felt when he saw her clutching her child, safe from harm, knowing it was because of him the little mite lived.

Hearing voices, he looked toward the towers that defended his gates and saw Ealdgytha running across the ford and down the path, Sigfrith in tow.

Sigfrith cried. "Little mistress!"

"My daughter!" Ealdgytha made straight for Ælfstan without a glance at anyone else. "You are safe! Winflæd! God is gracious indeed!"

Wulfhere smiled as the women went with Ælfstan up the path back to the hall's enclosure. He could hear Ealdgytha weeping tears of joy and Sigfrith's heralding Winflæd's return. Somewhere within the din, Gunnhild's booming voice could be heard remarking something about what happens when children run wild.

Mildrith put her child in the cart and Edgar led the ox by the reins ready to wheel it around.

"Wait!" Wulfhere called to her. Both she and Edgar halted. He approached them. "I wanted to tell you, and the lad, that he need not fear anymore from me. It is not because I have forgiven, but because a debt has been paid and a wrong has been righted."

Mildrith's eyes narrowed. "Edgar was more wronged than your daughter. You think she was so innocent, lord?"

He had not expected that. Her words stung him. His legs parted and his hands went to his hips. He wanted to remind her that Edgar had killed a man beloved to him. Then he thought, *Nay, Freyda was not always the innocent. If not for her, Esegar would still be alive.* He said, nodding, "I know my daughter. I know what she did."

Mildrith's face softened. "Do not be troubled, lord, for it is done now. It is the past. I thank you on my stepson's behalf for your clemency and I would not wish to speak out of turn, but he deserves much more than just your good will."

Wulfhere looked at Edgar. "Will he go back to Gorde with you, now?"

A bitter smile appeared on her face. "Edgar is no longer – Helghi has disinherited him and replaced him with his other son as his first. An outlawed man cannot inherit his father's land; you should know that, my lord."

"Then as the man who petitioned to have him outlawed, I set him free."

"And what use will that be for Edgar? His father will not want him back. He is bad seed, according to Helghi, useless to him. He lost him the day he was crippled by that horse you sold him." She paused, "I bid you good day, Lord Wulfhere."

So everything was his fault, Wulfhere thought. He wanted to deny that he was to blame but instead he said, weakly, "Thank you… both... for your trouble," Wulfhere said.

Mildrith smiled wanly and went to leave, then turned back, as though she had thought of something important to say, "Heed this warning, lord. Helghi still believes Winflæd will marry his son – not Edgar now, but the other one, Eadnoth. He will come for her soon, so keep her safe. They want her."

"Why is Helghi so intent on having her?" Wulfhere asked, clenching and unclenching his fists.

She smiled. "You still don't know? You have not worked it out? Then, you are not as clever as my husband." She hesitated, her thin shapely eyebrows drawn together, as though frowning at an idiot. "It is through her they will get your land."

"*They*? Who is this 'they'?"

"Helghi's kinsmen."

"I know them." Wulfhere nodded, remembering the men that fought alongside Helghi at Freyda's rescue. Whenever there was trouble with Helghi, those men always appeared.

Mildrith became suddenly animated. "One of them, Hengest, once owned property in the burgh of Lewes and a homestead on the other side of the river. He lost one in a dice game – it was said that the new owner died mysteriously. The other property he forfeited for neglecting to pay his dues. He and his brothers are lazy, idle creatures. They are useless and have taken over my husband's hall. They ply Helghi with strong mead and fill his mind with ideas - evil ideas. They abuse our tenants' daughters, steal their food and property, and lately they have been making raids into neighbouring outliers. They are nothing but thieves and brigands but Helghi allows them to do terrible things within our home. He cares not as long as he can have more mead and wine."

"But the bargain was for Winflæd to marry Edgar not Eadnoth. It cannot be transferred to another," Wulfhere said.

"Not in Helghi's eyes. He will argue differently, and he reasons that the Earl of Wessex will agree to support his claim because he wants peace in our hundred."

Wulfhere shook his head in disbelief. "My daughter has not yet reached the marriageable age."

"Fathers always forget their daughters grow up quickly. How long before she reaches her twelfth year?"

Dread rose within him. He still thought of Winflæd as a little girl. But Mildrith was right. Soon after next winter, she would pass into womanhood, the signs were already there.

"Yes, you see now what may come. Helghi wants your lands to pass to him through your daughter."

"Then he is a fool. I have three sons."

Again, she eyed him as though he were a dim-witted fool, lightly shaking her head.

"What?" he asked and shivered. It felt as though someone had walked over his grave.

"Forgive me if I speak out of turn, but I was wondering if the thegn of Horstede was as foolish as he is blind."

The meaning of her words filtered through his mind. "Would Helghi really stoop to murder?" She said nothing. He whispered, "Of course he would...." He clutched at his forehead. "God, he would never get away with it! Would he?"

"Accidents happen, my lord. It is not uncommon for young men to die in a drunken brawl, or some game of sport, or at hunting. You all think I am just a stupid woman, no wits to see or hear or speak sense. But I know... *I know.*"

"God's teeth, you *are* serious, aren't you?"

She nodded slowly. She glanced back to where Edgar was waiting with the cart and her child. "After Eadnoth weds your daughter, all your lives will be in danger. Helghi has wanted revenge for many years."

"This I know. But kill my sons? For what? Five hides of land?"

She looked around, the calm exterior gone. "He would kill me if he knew I had been here today."

"Then do not go back there," Wulfhere said.

"Where would I go? The only place is the forest. Believe me, I have thought about running away, but my parents will be at risk, for Helghi threatens me constantly with their harm. My father is unwell and my mother... I am their only living child. My father thought he would gain by marrying me to Helghi." She laughed, a bitter despairing sound. "Instead, we are all his hostages."

"These men are animals. They should be brought to justice."

She shook her head. "There is no justice for the likes of me.... Now I must go."

He caught her wrist as she turned to leave. She looked into his eyes and he felt an unexpected spark kindle between them. He fought back the instinct to cloak her in his arms, but instead he kept his distance, knowing that a deadly pattern would be repeated if he did not.

Mildrith stared at his hand on her wrist and then at his face. Wulfhere was sure she felt something too.

"My lord?"

Wulfhere clung to her wrist wordlessly and stared at her.

"Lord Wulfhere..."

He woke from his silence and said, "If ever you have need of help, lady, then come to me. I will be here for you."

She paused and with a half-smile, gently freed her hand from his. He watched her walk to the cart. The exhilaration as he'd touched her disconcerted him, but also left him longing for more. As he gazed after her diminishing figure, he knew from that moment, Helghi and his murderous intentions would never be far from his mind. And nor would she.

Chapter Fourteen

Wolf's Head

One week later

Tovi was lazing on the porch, leaning back on his elbows, legs outstretched, gingerly, because he was still sore from the thrashing he'd been given. Not quite the tanning he'd been threatened with, but enough to leave his arse battered and bruised from Father's leather belt. He gazed up at the heavens, remembering that many a time during the bright evenings of summers past, he and Father had sat there in the very same spot, waiting for nightfall. Tovi would hug his knees whilst Father told the stories of their saga and of the wolf spirit that guided the warrior. When darkness came, they would try to catch a glimpse of Tovi's wolf in the sky until one day Tovi shouted, "There it is! Right there where I am pointing. There's my wolf's head."

"I can see it."

"So, I *will* be a warrior then, Father? A ferocious warrior? With the heart of a wolf?"

"Aye, son. Once your wolf appears amongst the stars, your *wyrd* begins. 'Tis the way of the old ones, our forebears who came here from across the sea. The wolf was their *tácen*, and when they wore the wolf's pelt, they believed the animal's soul was within them."

From thereafter, whenever he saw it again, he believed his *wyrd* was being forged day by day in the heavens. But now, the wolf's head was gone. No matter how hard he looked, it was nowhere to be found. Could it be that the spinners were spinning a new thread for him?

Something dropped into his lap. Looking down, Tovi saw the beautifully crafted scabbard of his *seax*.

It had been a gift from the Earl of Wessex as reward for saving the earl's daughter from drowning. Father had confiscated it as further punishment for running away and for what had happened to Winflæd.

Tovi turned his head. Father was standing behind him. "You might want to take this with you, when you go."

"I thought that... You – you said I was not worthy of it."

"It is yours, lad. I have no right to withhold that which was given to you by Lord Harold."

"Thank you...." It seemed more precious than ever now. He glanced up at the sky.

"What were you looking at up there?" Father asked, sitting down beside him.

How could he have forgotten? "I'm searching for my wolf's head. I know when I was a *lytling* I believed anything you said, I'd no reason not to. But now, it makes more sense that my father had pretended all along."

"Things change, it is the way of *wyrd*."

"But why? Why spin a thread one way, then spin it another?" Tovi was confused.

"I - I do not know, son."

"I do not want to go to Waltham, Father."

"I know, but perhaps there will come a day when your *wyrd* will change again."

But Tovi did not want to wait for something that might never happen. He wanted it to change now! "Surely we can change it. If you would just speak to Mother – tell her I should not go – then my *wyrd* need not change at all!"

For the first time in a while, Father looked him straight in the eyes. "I cannot, Tovi. I wish I could, but I cannot."

"But why...?"

"I –"

"I know why. M-Mother."

Father looked down at his hands and rubbed them. "Then you will know it is difficult for me, Tovi."

"But it is *you* who is changing my *wyrd*, by sending me to become a priest!"

"I know, but for now, it is as it must be."

They sat in silence. Tovi flicked pieces of straw as Father fingered the braid on his collar.

Eventually Father said, "Put on your *seax*."

Tovi stood up slowly, undid his buckle and threaded the scabbard's loops through his belt.

"Look carefully after that *seax*, it is worth more than you might realise, especially since it was a gift from the earl," Father said.

"I will." Tovi looked down at it from where it hung from his waist. It felt good to wear it, made him feel manly. "How do I look?" Tovi asked, descending the steps to stand before his father.

"Like a man grown." Father gave him a half-hearted smile.

"*You* look defeated," Tovi said, "and I don't like it."

"Tovi, I have told you – I have no choice."

"Father, this is not you. This is *her*."

"I'm sorry, Tovi. If not for me, you would not be in this position. 'Tis my fault. All my fault. I'm sorry... I wish I could change it, but..."

Tovi saw a moment of hope. "You *can* change it, Father. All you have to do is tell her I'm not going. *Please!*"

Father got to his feet, shaking his head. "I cannot." He turned to leave.

"You admit you are at fault, and then you walk away? If you turn your back on me, I don't know who you are – but this I know –my real father would never do that!"

Wulfhere hesitated, his foot on the next step.

Tovi fought back the tears. "You once promised me that I would fight in the shieldwall with you, side by side. You, me, and my wolf brothers – just as our ancestors had done. And n-now… you-you snatch it away from me because you are too w-weak to stand up to M-Mother. You would rather see me with a qu-quill in my hand than a sword. And all because you m-must m-make amends by giving into every little thing M-m – what she says. I don't know who is w-worse – you – or-or *her*!"

During Tovi's tirade, Father had turned back to face him. Pointing a shaky finger he said, "One day you will learn. Being a man is not just about fighting wars and battles. It takes courage to right the wrongs one has made. Do you think I like the way I am? I wish I had not done the things I have. That I did not have to see you suffer. But here I am, with this cross I must bear. And I *will* bear it, God damn you – because I have to."

He paused to draw breath. "Tovi, I know this was not what you wanted, but you will get used to it. Fate has spun us a different course, and we must accept our destiny and make of our lives what we can."

"*Our fate?* It is not yours – n-nor that of my brothers, nor anybody else's but mine that you have changed."

"You cannot see how lucky you are, can you? At least you will be out of the reach of the *Déapscufa*, unlike myself ... and your brothers."

Father's words were like a blow and Tovi's head jerked upwards. "I would look *Déapscufa* in the eye any day than some shaven cockhead, preaching scriptures all day! Nay, Father, I will never get used to it!" Tovi ran past Wulfhere up the porch steps, pausing at the door to the hall. "God curse you, Father. God curse you - and Mother - for punishing me for your sins. Yours, not mine!"

The next day, to make a good impression upon the dean, Mother saw that Tovi's cart was laden with cheeses, jars of honey, salted meats, and flasks of ale, mead and even a basket of freshly spun wool, all gifts for the canons at Waltham. She'd made sure Tovi had a spare set of clothes and that he had been scrubbed as clean as dirty linen on wash day for the trip.

Father Paul was to escort him. The good-natured priest was excited having spent some of his education as a young, newly qualified monk there, before making the transition to secular priesthood. He sparkled with enthusiasm and looked forward to see what Earl Harold was doing with the new church. It would be a long, perilous journey through thickly laden woods, a haven for robbers and it was lucky that Tovi's escort included a couple of robust youths from the village who were handy with a knife and bow if necessary.

Tovi said his goodbyes, stiffly shying away from Mother's obligatory kiss. He'd side-stepped Father's attempts at farewell, content to see the hurt in Father's eyes. *Served him right,* Tovi thought.

Despite his earlier efforts to avoid them, his brothers managed to find him, their goodbyes given with their own peculiar brand of humour.

"You're too skinny for a warrior, Tovi. Is he not, Wulfric?"

"You're right, Wulfwin, best used as a fire poker for the priests!"

"I don't know why we never thought of it before!"

They fell into a bout of laughter that was uproarious and as they went off, arms around each other, their guffaws could still be heard moments later. Of all people, he would not miss them.

Tovi waited, hoping that his sister would come, but there was no sign of her. Sadly, he accepted she was not ready to forgive him and mounted Grendl as the party began to draw off. Then when they had passed through the gates, Tovi heard a familiar voice call out to him. He leapt from the saddle, unable to quell a tear, and hurried across the ford as she came, limping, supported by Sigfrith.

"I could not let you go without saying goodbye, Tovi." Winflæd burst into tears.

Tovi threw his arms around her and held her tightly to him, forgetting her injuries. She winced, and Tovi withdrew.

"I didn't want that to happen to you, Winflæd." He held her close again, this time carefully.

"I know," she replied softly, choking back her tears.

He studied the unsightly scabs on her face and guilt struck him in the stomach.

"I am sorry. I was unkind." Tovi gulped back a lump in his throat and palmed away tears from his cheeks. "Please forgive me."

"The fault was all mine. I should not have made you angry –"

"Nay." He shook his head. "It was my fault. I am to blame. I threw the rock."

"I threw the first. Besides, your aim is terrible. It did not even hit me. At least I got a good shot at you."

"But I thought you fell because I hit you – I threw that rock at you."

"It was hardly a rock; besides it didn't hit me. I fell because I lost my footing and I slipped. So, you can stop blaming yourself, silly, stupid boy."

"I will miss you, Frog Spawn," he said, cuffing a tear in his eye.

"And I you, Tovi the Terrible. Who is going to torture me now?"

"I wouldn't worry; our brothers will keep you busy. They were always better at it than I was."

Their precious shared moment lifted his mood briefly. Then it clouded over at the thought of her being tormented by the twins and not being there to protect her.

"Mayhap some day you will come back to Horstede and rescue me from their clutches," she said.

She gave him a half-smile and looked across at Father and Mother. "Please forgive him, it is because of Mother that he is sending you away."

Father's face was white; his sad eyes stared blankly. Mother, however, seemed unrepentant. Her arms were crossed; her face set like stone. "I cannot," Tovi whispered. "Neither of them."

Winflæd looked unhappy for a moment, then shrugged sadly. Tovi kissed her, "Take care Frog Spawn," he said and re-mounted. He signalled to Father Paul that he was ready to leave.

Wulfhere hoped his son would glance back, hand ready to wave one last goodbye. Tovi did not turn. He was gone. Wulfhere was filled with silent grief at the loss of his youngest boy. It should not have been that way.

Chapter Fifteen

Death of an Earl

Bromley, Staffordscire, August 31ˢᵗ, 1057

Despite it being summer, Lady Godgifu closed the shutters to keep an unseasonal chill from the chamber. Her husband, the Earl of Mercia, lay gravely ill, needing warmth and comfort. Godgifu sat down beside him, her hand on the elaborately carved bedpost. Past the springtime of her own life, Godgifu felt the strain as her beloved Leofric courageously endured his illness. She'd always taken pride that even at a great age her husband was able to manage his affairs, but this year he'd gradually lost strength until he woke one morning unable to rise with his usual zest.

Godgifu dabbed at her tears and helplessly waited for the inevitable. She'd kept to his side these last few weeks, feeding him what little sustenance he could manage, cleansed him when he needed it, and changed his bed sheets when he'd soiled them.

Through the gap in the curtains, she briefly glimpsed the attendants who morosely lined the plastered walls, draped with expensive carpets depicting scenes from the bible. They had not always been able to afford such luxury, but it was a reminder that she and her husband had done much together throughout their marriage in a shared love of God and religion.

Her life with Leofric had not always been as harmonious as it had been in their autumnal years. Once, Godgifu remembered, she had threatened to ride naked through the streets of Tameworth if Leofric did not lower his taxes. He eventually relented and agreed to reduce them. She had been a young girl then, but even Godgifu herself would never know if she would have carried out the threat. Leofric, at least, thought he knew her well enough to believe she would.

Just then her grandson, Burghred, entered the chamber, bringing her out of her reverie. He placed a hand on her shoulder, and she lay her own over it. Leofric's flickering eyes caught her gaze before he looked to his grandson and stretched an arm out to him. Burghred moved closer to kneel at his grandfather's side, taking the old man's bloodless hand. The wind whistled through the shutters and the candle flames danced. Godgifu felt the chamber chill and got up to stoke the brazier.

"My son..." she heard the old earl say, in a low, faltering voice. "So glad... you have come."

"Nay, Grandfather, 'tis not Alfgar, but Burghred, your grandson. Father has been sent for –"

"And he is here, at last." The curtains were roughly pulled aside and Alfgar threw off his cloak and stepped closer to the bed. Godgifu bent to pick the garment up and hung it on a hook.

"Alfgar, thank God you came." Godgifu went to embrace him but Alfgar avoided her.

"Father," muttered Burghred. He extracted his hand from Leofric's grasp and dutifully found a stool for his father.

"Leave me alone with him," Alfgar demanded as he drew close to Leofric's bed.

"I would rather stay," Burghred said, looking at Godgifu.

"What do you think I'm going to do? Suffocate him with a pillow? He is dying anyway. There is no need to hasten his death."

"Alfgar, your father might be ill, but he is not deaf. Burghred just wants to be by his grandfather's side. Must you be so accusing?"

"It was not I who spoke accusingly. Do I not have the right to be with my dying father in privacy? I have a chance to settle things with him and I would do it alone."

Godgifu glanced at her husband, seeing the pain their conflict caused him. Leofric nodded and her son's expression turned self-righteous. She ushered a reluctant Burghred out of the chamber, leaving Alfgar and her husband to make their peace.

Alfgar sat down. He swept his hands through his long, wild hair to tame it and sought his father's eyes.

"Father, I would beseech your forgiveness. I know I have not been the best of sons, that I have been a disappointment to you... that sometimes I let my hot-headedness get in the way of dignity, and I have brought much shame, but..."

"What is done is done, my son."

Alfgar reached for his father's hand and Leofric summoned the strength to pull him close to give him the kiss of peace and forgiveness. Alfgar wiped away a tear and nodded.

With great difficulty Leofric spoke slowly. "Forgive the lad. Unite with him," he wheezed, "for only together will you survive... The Godwins – they are on the rise... Harold... he is not like his father... but he wants... power ..." He broke into a cough and took a moment to regain his breath.

Alfgar poured some wine and caught the scent of pain-relieving herbs. He held the cup to his father's pallid lips. Leofric sipped a little, then pushed it away before continuing. "The Godwins... do not let them... the kingdom... Tostig will... destroy the north with his heavy-handedness, and... if Gyrth gets East Anglia, what will be left for your sons? You will have Mercia... Burghred must... must have East Anglia. Gather support... the other nobles... When the time comes, Burghred must be... nominated... for East Anglia."

Alfgar nodded and wiped his nose on a strip of linen. He was heartbroken. He was losing Leofric before they'd a chance to benefit from their peace. A surge of frustration rose within him that the Godwins should cloud every moment of his life, even these last he shared with his father.

Leofric lay back against the bolster, his hand slipping from Alfgar's. The effort of speech seemed to drain him. Alfgar leant closer to him as he beckoned and whispered his last rasping words in Alfgar's ear. "Not Gruff... not Gruffudd..."

Alfgar closed his father's eyes and left Leofric's side. He pulled back the curtains.

"Is he...?" Godgifu asked.

Alfgar nodded solemnly. His mother pushed past him through the curtains and a sorrowful wail was heard.

Alfgar grabbed Burghred's arm as he went to console her. "Tonight, we ride for Wales," he said. "Make sure you are ready."

"Ready for what? We have not even buried him."

"A wedding."

"Nay, you don't mean...?"

"You heard what the old man said?"

"I heard nothing about Aldith and Gruffudd."

Alfgar continued, "You know that the Godwins will never allow you to have East Anglia. They will give it to Gyrth. They want Edward

146

to be their puppet king so that between them they can carve up the kingdom with the balance of power tipped firmly on their side."

"So, you want to go to war again, do you?"

Alfgar answered him with a glare.

"My God, you do!"

"I make no such claim yet. An alliance between Gruffudd and our house is necessary and will boost our support in the west. The Godwins stand in our way of East Anglia. As my son, you should be the natural candidate, but they will say you are inexperienced. With the east and the south-west at their command, there is nothing we can do to defend ourselves without the Wéalas."

Burghred tried to distance himself from him, shaking his head. "Gruffudd has always been our enemy. Leofric would never have agreed to this. And how can we leave him when he is not even in his grave yet?"

Alfgar grabbed Burghred's face and forced his son to look at him. "We cannot allow the Godwins to take everything! Your grandfather's dying wish is that we fight."

Alfgar's fingers dug into Burghred's cheeks, and he pushed the lad's head so it hit the wall with a thud.

If Burghred was hurt by the impact he did not show it. "Nay, Grandfather would not wish Mercia to be allied with the man who killed his own brother. Did you tell him that his granddaughter is to be married to his brother's murderer? I was with Leofric all the time he was ill. He spoke of many things but an alliance with Gruffudd was not one of them. It is true that he desired East Anglia for me and you Mercia, but he did not want us to take up with Gruffudd again. Nor did he want that we should risk losing Mercia by going to war with the king and the Godwinsons. If you truly want to fight them, do not put Mercia at risk!"

"I should not waste my breath on you. Call yourself my son? I should have dashed out your brains after what you did at Rhuddlan two years ago. You know nothing of honour or loyalty! You're no son of mine! *You are níðing!*"

"What right do you have to call me a *níðing* when it is because of you we were exiled? It was you who brought shame on the House of Leofric, not I."

Alfgar grabbed Burghred by the throat, his fist drawn, ready to smash it into his son's face when Leofric's mass priest emerged from

147

behind the bed chamber curtain, with Godgifu behind him. The lines of her aged face were furrowed, with obvious dismay.

The priest spoke. "Contain yourselves, my lords. This disrespect at such a time will not go unnoticed by God! Your good lady mother has great need of comfort and support – and you choose to dishonour her and the earl's memory by squabbling!"

"Let him go, Alfgar!" demanded Godgifu. "Father Wiglaf is right! Would you sully Leofric's memory with conflict at his deathbed?"

Alfgar released Burghred roughly.

"Grandmother," Burghred said, "Alfgar wants us to go to Wales – tonight. He wants to wed Aldith to Gruffudd – I will not go!" Burghred shouted. "I do not wish to be part of it!"

"You would do such a thing, Alfgar?" His mother stared at him with wide eyes.

"I am the Earl of Mercia and I will do what is best for my people. Are *you* with me?" Alfgar called to Leofric's men and upon replies of assent, he said, "Then we go!"

"But your father – will you not stay to see him buried?" Godgifu asked, looking dismayed.

"Look to your grandson, woman. If he would rather not attend a wedding, then he may as well attend a funeral!"

Aldith was wed to Gruffudd on a cold autumnal day about the time that Leofric was being buried in his beloved church at Cofantreo. Alfgar was noticeably absent from his father's funeral and when King Edward heard the reason was due to this wedding, he was scarlet with rage. Alfgar had gone too far this time.

Upon Alfgar's return from Wales, he and Burghred were united, at least in their anger, when, as Alfgar predicted, Gyrth was invested with not only East Anglia, but also Oxfordshire that had once been a part of the old kingdom of Mercia. Furthermore, Alfgar was to release the East Anglian men from his control and they were to go home to their lands and their new lord.

"This was always going to happen – I told you so," Alfgar said when Burghred told him the news. "The Godwins' scheming for dominance is proving to be very fruitful for them."

Godgifu joined in with her womanly sarcasm. "Edward is surrounded by Godwins – the queen is one; her darling brother, Tostig is also a much-loved favourite of the king's. I have heard some speak that Tostig is closer to Edward's bedchamber than she is."

Alfgar laughingly agreed. "Aye, when he should be in the north seeing to his affairs. Instead he is scheming at court with his brothers. I tell you, Leofwin will be the next to rise to power. Thank Christ on the Cross that the youngest brother is a hostage in Normandy, or they would be looking for an earldom for him too."

"Give them time and I'm sure that will be arranged," Burghred said, with a crooked smile.

"And there is the rub, the more positions and land they hold, the more wealth. And the more wealth, the more power. What chances are there for my sons – even you, Burghred?"

Burghred eyed him resentfully. "Why must you always make little of me?"

Alfgar shrugged, turned away and poured himself some mead. "Alfgar," his mother said as she went to him and put a hand on his shoulder, "there may be another reason for this snub. Aldith and Gruffudd."

Alfgar shook his head angrily. "She is *my* daughter – it is my right to wed her to whomever I see fit! I do not need to seek anyone's permission – not even from the King of Englalond!" He swallowed hastily and poured another mug. "Our family is a lone island in a sea of Godwinsons, drowning in their greed."

Gleawecestre
Crístesmæsse, 1057

It was an angry and resentful Alfgar, who was summoned to attend court that *Crístesmæsse* and forced to stand outside the king's great hall in the pouring rain and cold wind. The king, himself, sat in the warm glow of a burning hearth with his wife, surrounded by his earls and their ladies. Alfgar's simmering temper began to boil at the slight and by the time Edward deigned to grant him an audience, Alfgar was seething, cold and wet through. Conversation faltered and heads turned to watch him force his way up to the dais, his barely contained anger clear on his face.

The whole court strained to hear the muttered curses under the huffing and grimacing as Edward took him to task over his daughter's marriage to Gruffudd. And when it was announced he was to lose his office and his Mercian lands, there was no withholding his rage.

Harold watched, amused, as in almost an exact replication of his

149

disgrace at Westmynstre more than two years ago, Alfgar unleashed his vehemence against the king, making for the doors.

"May all of you that serve this incompetent Godwin puppet rot in hell!"

"Seize him, Tostig, seize him!" A maddened Edward shot off his throne. "Detain that man!" he screamed. "Am I to be harried in my own household; *I,* who am king, anointed by the Grace of God?" He pointed at Alfgar. "You will burn in hell for this heinous crime against me!"

Edith had taken to her feet to stand with her husband, her mouth moving beneath her trailing wimple. Amused, Harold could only imagine what expletives were coming out from underneath it.

Alfgar's men formed a protective ring around their lord. Several of the king's men rushed toward them as Edward yelled for Alfgar's blood, but before anyone could break through, Alfgar had taken the steps up to the doors two at a time. In his grasp was the king's chamberlain, Hugolin whose frightened squeals were like that of a hunted pig. Alfgar had the frightened Franc by his neck holding a blade to the quivering chamberlain's throat.

"Harold! We must go after him!" Tostig cried, a hand on Harold's shoulder, pulling him toward the chaos at the doors.

Harold held back and shook his head. "And risk incurring the death of Edward's favourite chamberlain? You heard the man. He will kill Hugolin if we do. And we know Alfgar is capable of such an act, do we not? I don't particularly relish a lambasting from Edward, do you?"

"So, we just let him go, after threatening murder and insulting us and our king? You know he will be riding to Gruffudd again, don't you?"

Harold glanced up at the dais to see his sister fanning a stricken Edward with her wimple whilst Baldwin his physician, tried to soothe him with a goblet of wine. Turning back to his brother, unable to contain the smirk forming on his lips, Harold said, "Aye, to Gruffudd he will go, and this time we shall be ready for him."

"But the Wéalas are like wolves, you never know where they will attack," Tostig said. "We need to know what they mean to do."

Harold looked over at Burghred, surprised that the young man had not gone with his father. "I have an idea that may help us kill two birds with one stone," he said, "Come with me, Brother, let the king's men

150

do their duty and go after Alfgar. I have another idea."

Harold approached the Mercian and followed him through to the antechamber. "You do not go with Alfgar, Burghred?"

The young Mercian was collecting his gear from the door thegn. He turned to Harold with a red face. Averting his eyes, he looked ashamed. "I cannot follow a man, father or no, who speaks treason against his king."

"You do not share your father's views?" Harold asked. "You *were* overlooked, after all."

"If you are asking me if I feel resentful towards Gyrth because he has what I should, then yes, I share my father's views. But I would not cause unrest because of it and I do not harbour any ill will toward the king – nor any of his loyal officers."

Having stuffed his gear into a sack, Burghred threaded his scabbard onto his belt, buckled it, and sat down to re-tie his bootlaces. Men were storming past them out the door to rallying cries, on their way to catch Alfgar.

"Where will you go?" Harold asked.

"Well, that might be a bit difficult, since I can no longer serve my father. And now that I have no earldom of my own and not much in the way of lands to sustain me as a lord, I truly don't know. It seems I am a man without honour."

"Without honour?" Harold asked.

"My father is a traitor; his lands are confiscated, where does that leave me?"

"There is still Mercia."

Taking the offered hand, Burghred allowed Harold to pull him to his feet.

"Alfgar will fight for Mercia. He will go to Gruffudd, again." Burghred said.

Harold shrugged. "I suspect that to be so, Alfgar is the Wéalas king's father-in-law now. It is inevitable. Besides, Gruffudd seems to be the man for the outlawed Englisc to flock to."

Burghred was fastening the brooch on his cloak. "What do you want from me, Lord Harold?"

"You may be able to serve your king, yet."

"You want me to help you destroy my father for good, so you can give Mercia to another one of your brothers? Which one will it be this time, Leofwin?"

"'Tis not your father I want to destroy. I want to send Gruffudd back to his mountains for good – and there lies the way for you. Go to Gruffudd's stronghold and find out their plans. It will be imperative to be sure of their movements this time if Hereford is never to happen again. You may after all, find favour with the king... and Mercia could still be yours one day."

Burghred, one hand on the door, stopped in his tracks, staring at the wrought-iron handle.

"What would happen to Alfgar?" he asked, turning to look at Harold.

Harold shrugged. "It depends on you... and the threads the spinners weave."

"I have betrayed my father before. I cannot do it again."

"Not even for Mercia?"

"Not even for Mercia." Burghred's eyes met Harold's. They locked gazes and after a moment, Harold nodded.

"Then God speed you, Burghred."

As Burghred left through the heavy door, Tostig, his words laced in sarcasm, said, "So, you thought you could win him over?"

"Doesn't look like it at the moment, but my gut feeling tells me he will come back."

"And what do you mean Alfgar is not the one you want? We *should* have gone after him!"

"He'll be long gone by now. They'll not catch him. We do not know how much support he has in Mercia. He is an ill-wind, for sure.... But Gruffudd? He is an even iller wind. Get rid of him, and hopefully Alfgar will have no choice but to rot in exile."

*

Burghred rode out of Gleawecestre along the open road to his grandmother's manor of Evesham. He'd planned to see her one more time before he took a ship to Normandy. Harold's words whistled through his ears as he rode and though he tried hard to forget them, they would give him no peace. *The promise of Mercia....* But could he trust Harold?

He liked Harold, had always found him to be fair and decent, a world apart from Alfgar. Though to betray his father again would be betraying not only his grandfather, but also himself. *Blood was worth more than gold, was it not?* Though Mercia was a great prize for a second betrayal; at least then Mercia would stay with their bloodline. Or would he simply be a game piece for Edward and Harold to use as

152

they wished?

What had he to lose? He had no lord, no father, few lands to call his own. This might be his only chance to win an earldom for himself. *Mercia. He had to take it.*

Burghred reined his horse to a stop, turned his mount's head in one swift movement and rode back towards Gleawecestre.

Chapter Sixteen

Web of Deceit

Rhuddlan, March 1058

Burghred dismounted and tethered his horse to the nearest branch. He waited for Aldith to do the same, then took her arm in his. Together they walked through the grove of blossoming fruit trees filling the orchard. She had brought him there, she said, to show him the early spring beauty of the hilltop and perhaps to snatch a little time to themselves.

"You and Father seem to be getting on much better now," Aldith remarked.

Burghred grinned wryly. "Just like a house on fire, eh? Nothing has changed, then."

She laughed and said, "You two could ignite a tinder box with one look."

Burghred paused to take in his sister's newfound beauty. She was no longer the half-grown dimpled girl he remembered. Her eyes shimmered like gold in the sunshine, and a light smattering of freckles dusted her well-formed cheek bones and the bridge of her nose. When she smiled, the deep-set dimples of her childhood he thought had gone, reappeared and he realised how much time had passed between them. Their father had left her in the care of Gruffudd's sister when she was no more than twelve summers. Now, approaching fifteen, she had matured into a refined young lady.

"I know that you dislike Gruffudd and you are angry at Father for making me marry him, but..." She hesitated.

Sensing her discomfort, he interjected, "I only want what is best for my sister. If you are happy, then what more can I ask for?"

As if to reward him, Aldith gave him a griddled honey cake from her pouch and took a bite of her own. He examined the cake absent-

154

mindedly.

"'Tis not poison, Brother, or filled with dark magic. Do you think it will corrupt you and turn your heart *for* Gruffudd instead of against him?" She laughed in a soft, husky voice. "Am I such a witch?"

Her mocking tone irritated, but her smile and the dimples melted his heart, and Burghred could not stay annoyed for long. He took a hungry bite from the cake, nodded in appreciation, then crammed the rest of it into his mouth. She giggled as he struggled to make it fit, crumbs flying from his mouth.

"Are you glad you married him?" he asked, still munching on remnants of cake.

"I am a queen; would that not gladden any girl's soul?" she replied as a chill breeze rustled her veil and threatened to reveal her hair. She felt for the pins that secured it and ensured it was still in place before skipping girlishly along the tree-lined avenue. "I have all this!" She laughed gaily, throwing her arms out as if to encompass the whole of the hills and valleys below. "Here I am free! I am a *queen*, dear brother, and my people love me because they love my Gruffudd. They think of me as one of them now, so it matters not to them that my blood is not Wéalisc, for they know that my spirit is."

He noticed for the first time the soft lilt and within her, he sensed the spirit of the Wéalas. "Do you love this man?" he asked.

"Of course, and he loves me!" She spun herself around, laughing like a child. "You do not believe he does?"

Burghred gave her a sceptical look. She picked up a mountain flower and began to pull at its petals.

"On our wedding night," she said, "he promised me I would never want for anything... neither love, nor respect, nor comfort. So far, he has kept that promise and I believe he means to do so for as long as he lives. He is a good man, Burghred... and I would like you to be happy for me." There was a ferocity in her loyal defence of her husband.

It was hard to believe that a man who had treated her like a prized cow three years ago when she was no more than a girl, could ever be that tender. But Aldith had never spoken falsely, as he remembered.

Still, this did nothing to allay his misgivings, even though he hugged and gave her his blessing.

Gruffudd's reputation was brutal. He'd killed their uncle in an ambush and coerced their father into destroying Hereford. It would be

155

difficult to forget who Gruffudd was and what he had done.

They walked on in silence to the edge of the grove, found a dry patch of grass on top of the ridge and he lay his cloak for her to sit. He sat down beside her. Looking out over the valley at its vista of clustered woods laced with snowdrops and anemones, Burghred understood why his sister was so taken with this place.

"This is a beautiful land, Aldith."

She turned to him and said in her lilting accent, "I am with child, dear Brother." The joy in her smile touched him. He glanced down at her belly. "I hardly show yet, but I am four months without my flux."

He wanted to say something positive to her, instead he said, "Gruffudd already has sons."

"Oh, this child is not a boy."

"How do you know?"

"The soothsayer says that I am carrying a girl and I am going to call her Nest."

"Do you really believe that pagan nonsense?"

She burst into laughter and pushed him playfully. "I *have* to believe her. My ladies say she has never been wrong. Burghred, you are so amusing at times. You take everything so seriously. If you could see the look on your face." She took his hands. "Come, help me up. We should celebrate."

Burghred allowed her to pull him into a dance, singing a lively Wéalisc song, spinning him round until they collapsed in a heap of laughter.

"I can scarcely believe that my little sister has now become this old married woman – a queen, no less. And I cannot believe she is to have a child when it seems like only yesterday, she was a child herself."

They lay side by side looking up at the sky, and she took his hand. Above them, the sun fought valiantly against the clouds. Burghred, concerned that the weather would suddenly change, thought about going back. There was a faint growl of thunder as he pulled her gently to her feet. They both laughed and embraced. "See, even the storm clouds declare it to be true, you are to be an uncle."

"Aye, Uncle Burghred, I like the sound of it."

The darkened sky rumbled again, only this time louder. The air had chilled and there was the damp smell of rain.

Aldith shivered and just as she pulled her hood up, large drops fell.

"We'd better go," Burghred said. "There is a storm coming."

"Looks as though it's already here." Aldith looked up, covering her head with her cloak.

Burghred helped his sister to mount her horse. She gazed down at him, not caring that she was getting thoroughly soaked. "Please say you are happy for me?"

Burghred's heart quickened and his stomach rolled. It sickened him to think of the betrayal that was to come. But he must keep his own counsel as he had done since his arrival in Rhuddlan and smiled brightly through the downpour. "If you are happy, dear Sister, then I am happy also."

"Burghred, come. Dice with me! There's nothing else to do in this Godforsaken place with weather like this," Alfgar spluttered, as Burghred and Aldith arrived back at Rhuddlan, scurrying into the building like drowned rats.

Alfgar's face was flushed with mead as he sat with a group of men, dice in hand ready to throw. Burghred was cold after riding in the storm and made his way to the firepit to warm himself, ignoring his father's request. The hall was full of activity with everyone piled inside to benefit from the shelter and fire pit. He warmed his hands over the flames, nodding to a Wéalas next to him who was doing the same. His father called to him again and Burghred thought he'd better oblige him.

Approaching Alfgar, he saw that among his father's hearthmen were many new faces, and he felt a sense of unease. The frizzy, sun-bleached hair, their seafarers' boots and salt-stained clothing gave away their identity. These were Wícingas, pirates who roamed the seas and coastal lands, looking for plunder, slaves, and whatever else they could get their hands on. Norþmenn. Burghred's heart sank, for he had hoped that it would not come to this – not again. Not another Hereford. Since he'd been in Rhuddlan, he and Alfgar had started to form amiable relations again. Burghred began to hope that he would be able to talk Alfgar into seeking justice using passive means. But now, with the presence of so many of these raiders and plunderers, his hope faded.

That evening as they sat at supper, Burghred watched as Aldith interacted with her husband at the high table. She was blissfully happy with this man and she hung on his every word. Gruffudd was gracious towards her, but it was easy to see that her regard for him was far greater than his for her. The way Gruffudd followed other women at court with his stare was not lost on Burghred, though it seemed lost on Aldith.

"You don't approve, do you?" Ælred said. Burghred's old childhood friend looked at him curiously. He was the son of Alfgar's captain, Ragnald. Once Ælred and Burghred had been close. Nowadays their friendship was less convivial, mainly due to Burghred's dislike of Ragnald's influence over Alfgar.

"Approve? Of what?" replied Burghred. Ælred was the image of Ragnald, with his father's strong features, well-groomed long hair, and deep-set, watchful eyes. But he was only a shadow of the appalling man his father was.

"The whole alliance: Alfgar and the Wéalas... your sister and Gruffudd," Ælred answered. "I've seen how you look at Aldith, as if you cannot stand to see her with Gruffudd."

Burghred had ceased long ago to share his innermost thoughts with anyone, but strong mead always loosened his tongue. "Ach," he began with a shake of his head, staring at a piece of roast meat impaled on his knife, "can I help it if it sours my mood to know my sister is sharing the bed of a murderer?"

"Keep your voice down," Ælred hissed, looking around. "You would burn alive if it got back to Gruffudd. They still don't trust you – not after your betrayal of Hereford. Any little thing they hear against their beloved king and you would be fodder for the pigs in no time. You'd do better to keep your mouth shut."

Burghred lowered his voice but did not feel much like shutting his mouth. "Remember how Gruffudd ambushed and murdered my Uncle Edwin? He also murdered Hywel of Powys and took Hywel's wife, who was Edwin's daughter, for his own." Burghred lowered his head and quietened his voice further. "I cannot understand how my father can just put that aside and forget." He picked at the meat on his knife.

"Some may see it this way," Ælred began and gulped down a mouthful of bread, "the fact that Gruffudd's current wife is Mercian negates the past and strengthens the alliance." Ælred took another bite of his supper and smiled as he masticated his food, reminding Burghred of a dog.

"Edwin's daughter was a Mercian. Did it make a difference then? And Gruffudd already has sons from his first wife, the wife that was *not* a Mercian." Burghred looked over at the Wéalas king's adolescent sons, Maredudd and Idwal, laughing with their friends.

"And a flock of bastards too, so I'm told." Ælred smiled. "I hear that you are to be handfasted to one of them, that pretty thing over there." Ælred nodded to a dark-haired serving girl.

Burghred gave him a sceptical look. It was the first he had heard of it. "*She* is one of his bastards?"

"So I am told, but her mother is no lowborn wench, and Gruffudd cares for this daughter dearly."

"I care not that her mother is a highborn whore," Burghred remarked. "I will not be settling down with any bastard of Gruffudd's."

"Well, perhaps I should make a bid. I would not say no." Ælred's eyes were lustful.

Lord, he looked like his father.

Burghred was absurdly irritated by Ælred's interest in the girl. He had seen her about the palace and knew she was called Heulyn, meaning 'sunshine' in the language of the Cymry. Though Burghred had no desire to become handfasted to a bastard daughter of Gruffudd's, he found himself suddenly unable to take his eyes off the wench. He licked his lips as he gazed at her ample backside, bent over the ale boards. It was a long time since he'd loved a woman, and Heulyn was not unattractive, in fact quite the opposite.

Burghred's eyes followed her, oblivious to Ælred's musings. At one point her gaze caught his and she smiled knowingly. The musicians played in the background, a wild whirling music whilst Gruffudd's people and his foreign visitors made noise of their own. The serving girls were used to fighting off their master's guests, but the Norþmenn were unruly and without propriety, taking liberties that stepped way beyond what was grossly unacceptable. One such boisterous handsome young Wícinga grabbed Heulyn's arm as she attempted to fill his drinking horn. Burghred felt his hackles rise and he tensed, clenching his fists.

Ælred chuckled. "She doesn't take your fancy?"

"I didn't say she didn't take my fancy, just that I wouldn't be wedding her. I said nothing about bedding." Burghred stared at the youth who playfully slapped the girl's arse.

"Don't cause trouble with that one," Ælred warned.

"I do not intend to."

He tried to focus elsewhere, but out of the corner of his eye he saw

Heulyn deftly extricate herself from the grinning man's grasp.

"So, Ælred these Wícingas? They are not just here for the hospitality, are they?" Burghred asked, distracting himself from the ridiculous jealousy emerging within him.

Ælred leaned forward to hear him above the musicians and the noise of the dancers as they clapped and stamped their feet in time to the rhythmic music.

"Apparently, they are men led by the young Magnus, son of Harald of Norwæg. I thought you would know why they are here. The fellow you were staring at with murder in your eyes, his father is one of the Magnus' men. A jarl. He is their leader and is here to negotiate an alliance with us. 'Tis why I warned you."

"Magnus... son of Harald of Norwæg?"

Ælred nodded.

Burghred's heart sank. It *was* happening again.

Later, Burghred caught Alfgar going to the latrine. He pulled his father to one side and said in a hoarse whisper, "So, you are going to war again." Alfgar stared at him, baffled. "The Norþmenn. You want to go to war again, don't you?"

"Do you think I would be here in this murderous Godforsaken hole otherwise?" Alfgar slurred. His face was flushed, and the strong, sweet tang of mead flavoured his breath.

"Is this truly the way for us, Father? Maybe we could go back to Edward and –"

"Foolish idiot! Do you think I can go back now? 'Oh yes, Alfgar. You've been a bad boy again... but you can have Mercia back if you play nicely!' Yes, I can see *that* happening! No, force is the only way. It's what they know."

"But to fight your fellow countrymen – *again*?"

"Countrymen? Mercia is all I care about! They will come to me, wait and see. The thegns have sent messengers already to pledge their support." Alfgar eyed him charily.

"Are you here to convince me to go back to Edward with my tail between my legs, grovelling on my knees to him and to those lickspittle devil spawns of Godwin? You swore to me, Burghred, that you would be loyal to me this time. Are you going to betray me again?"

"Nay, Father, but you never seek my counsel on any matter. I would that you did."

"You want me to go back and beg for my lands… for my life? You know I am declared outlawed, to be killed on sight – just like that?" Alfgar snapped his fingers. "Edward is merely a puppet in the hands of Harold Godwinson. Everyone knows that nothing happens in the kingdom without the Earl of Wessex' approval."

"Father, I hate them just as much as you do, but how can you be sure the Mercians will stand with you? How do you know that they will not be swayed by the might of the West Seaxans and Tostig's men in the north?"

Alfgar looked at him with one eyebrow raised. "I know the men of Mercia. They have always been loyal to their earl, unlike some."

Burghred was defeated. It was not going to be easy way to change Alfgar's mind, but that did not mean he couldn't work on him. For now, he must play the loyal son. Looking at his father, he nodded and said, "I do not wish to gainsay you, Father, I only desire to advise you of the possible pitfalls we may face, but if you are certain, then I trust your wisdom. I would not ask you to do anything you were not able to. I came here to support you, and I will. If you want to do this, then I am with you!"

Alfgar smiled, clapping his son on his shoulder. "It gladdens my heart to hear you speak those words, my son. I thought at first that I would never see you again and that you would be with the Godwinsons. Last time..."

"Father, I am truly remorseful of what happened last time; it will not happen again. I despise the Godwinsons as much as you. I would be loyal to the king, but the Godwinsons are everywhere and their power must be wrested from them."

His father looked at him curiously as if trying to gauge whether to believe him or not. But after a moment, Alfgar laughed, and smiling, clapped Burghred on his shoulder again. "Good lad, now let me tell you our plans."

*

That night the girl came to him and Burghred, absorbed in Heulyn's caresses, allowed her well-trained hands to massage, rub, and stroke him. She was still there when he awoke in the morning, her breath gently fanning him as she slept. Her long, dark hair brushed over her high cheek bones, flushed with the excesses of the previous evening. He smiled and closed his eyes, recalling with pleasure their night of passion. He'd tried to resist, for he'd not wanted to embroil himself too deep into Alfgar's plans. If he plighted his troth with this girl, he would be well and truly enmeshed in Gruffudd's trap.

He'd come to Rhuddlan to spy for Harold and the king, not to join sides with his father, but last night his heart fought with his head. In a rare moment, Alfgar had shown him something akin to a father's love, something he'd longed for all his life. He thought of the assurances Alfgar gave him about Mercia and wondered if Alfgar was right after all. The Godwinsons *were* greedy and ambitious. Burghred *had* been overlooked for Gyrth. Last night his heart emerged as the victor, aided by the sweet honey tasting mead, and a pretty, young girl.

Not long after he had satisfied himself again with Heulyn, he fell into a dream that he was riding in Gruffudd's warband on his way to fight Harold's army. Heulyn was standing at the gates of Rhuddlan waving him off, her belly swollen with child. He awoke with a jolt of panic. He sat up, sweating. Heulyn stirred but did not wake, breathing lightly and contentedly beside him. Beyond the curtained partition, Burghred could hear his father snoring loudly and the soft burr of a woman lying with him.

What in God's name are you doing? he asked himself. *If I don't get out of Rhuddlan soon, I will be caught in this web of deceit forever!* In the cold light of day, his head had started fighting back.

The days that followed were like torture to Burghred. Heulyn continued to share his bed at night and there was talk of a celebration of their union sometime soon. Try hard as he might to find ways of avoiding it, he could no more resist her when she came to him than he could resist taking a piss when his bladder was full.

In his dreams he was a fly, trapped in a spider's web, desperately seeking a way out of the sticky fibres. The more he floundered, the more entangled he became. And as he struggled in the network of threads, the closer he was pulled in. The spider in the centre of the web threatened to devour him. And the spider was Gruffudd.

Two days later
Burghred sat in grim anticipation at his first council meeting in Rhuddlan since he arrived there. Rays of sun filtered through the chamber's high windows, illuminating the brightly painted battle scenes adorning the walls. Gruffudd's achievements were embedded with biblical references scrawled in Latin, implicating him as a current-day messiah of his people. In these scenes, the devastation of

Hereford was compared to the Fall of Jericho, with Gruffudd playing the part of Joshua in the overwhelming victory.

Burghred shivered. It was a sickening reminder of how he had tried to prevent the slaughter of his fellow countrymen but had been too late. And now he found himself sitting amongst the very same men he had tried to stop committing this terrible massacre – their evil victory compared to holy scriptures.

Aldith, sitting with Gruffudd at the head of the board, seemed uninterested in the proceedings as she yawned unashamedly. Burghred caught her eye and she smiled brightly at him. He winked at her, then looked away, finding himself face to face with the Norþmann who had been discourteous towards Heulyn a few nights before.

The jarl's son smiled and raised the peace cup to his lips. He was a handsome youth, a little older than Burghred, and heavily muscled. His hair was well-groomed like the finely trimmed beard. Brightly dyed clothing spoke of the man's status, but his hands looked rough like those of a well-seasoned sailor. There was something about the way this brash Norþmann eyed him, that made Burghred feel uncomfortable and he averted his gaze.

When everyone had their fill of the peace cup, the handsome son of a jarl stood. All eyes were on him as he addressed them all. "My lords, I am Ivar, son of Jarl Ótryggr. I come here to do terms on behalf of our prince, Magnus, son of Harald, King of Norwæg. King Harald has commissioned his son to make claim to the throne of Englalond on his behalf."

There were looks of astonishment. Roars of laughter came from the English faction who stood against the walls. "Magnus is but a child!" someone guffawed.

"A babe in arms!"

"Every man on earth wants to rule Englalond," Ragnald said with disdain. "What makes this one think he can do it better than the rest?"

Burghred turned to look at Alfgar to gauge his reaction. His father was silent, a finger resting on his nose. When the noise abated, Burghred spoke. "On what grounds does your little prince make his claim?"

Gruffudd raised his voice over the hub. "Quiet! Let him speak," he ordered, meaning the Norseman.

Ivar remained calm, waited as the room quietened in the face of

163

Gruffudd's disapproval. Burghred watched him thoughtfully. He was a cool character, this son of a Norwægian jarl. Then Ivar spoke, "Not my *little* prince, but his father, King Harald Sigurdsson." Ivar's voice was deep and resonating. His gaze swept the chamber. "When Harthacnut was King of Denmark, he made a pact with King Magnus the Good, that whosoever died first would succeed to the other's kingdoms. Later, as we all know, Harthacnut was to become king of Englalond."

"How is this relevant?" someone shouted from the stalls.

"Quiet! Let him speak and hold your tongues!" Gruffudd thumped the table.

Ivar continued. "Since my illustrious King Harald is now king in Norwæg, this legacy, by rights, is now his."

The Englisc contingent showed their disagreement by shouting and cursing. They jeered and stomped their feet.

"That's an illogical notion!" Ragnald shouted, his voice getting lost amongst the uproar.

Ragnald turned to Alfgar as though to appeal, but Burghred's father ignored his captain and said, "So where is this Magnus? Where be this King of Norwæg? And why is he not here himself to make his claim?"

Ivar's smile was charming. "My lord, the King of Norwæg is not here because he has gone to secure the other half of his inheritance, Denmark."

The chamber filled with laughter. Burghred glanced sidelong at his father. There was a faint, calculating smile upon Alfgar's lips. Burghred knew the scheming look very well. If Harald's mission was successful, his father would be the most powerful man in this new alliance with a Scandinavian king on the throne. It had been done once before. Could it be done again?

Burghred reflected: with Alfgar's daughter married to the Wéalas king and his new friend, Sigurdson, on the Englisc throne, Alfgar would no longer feel threatened by the Godwinsons. It made perfect sense to Burghred, that his father would take up Harald Sigurdson's cause. His stomach turned at the thought. That he should be involved in an invasion, was one thing, but it was another thing entirely to replace an anointed king with a foreigner.

A discussion began about the validity of Harthacnut's oath with the old Norse king and whether it would be right for the current king of

Norwæg to make a claim through an old legacy. Burghred ceased to listen. He thought only about how he could get his hands on Gruffudd's map, steal away unseen, and warn Edward's spies. Recently it had been harder to smuggle information out of Rhuddlan, for he was sure he was being watched.

The midday meal had come and gone, and Burghred struggled through the discussions as they went on into the afternoon. If anyone looked his way, anxiety and paranoia pricked at him. His heart raced and he could not wait for the proceedings to end, certain that everyone in that council chamber knew that he was a Godwin spy. He felt trapped. On one hand he was betraying his father and sister – on the other, his king and countrymen.

Who to choose?

Either way, he was the loser in a game he could never win.

At last Burghred felt he could breathe as the meeting came to an end, and men were leaving. He remained seated. Thoughts about what he should do sprinted through his mind like the rapid movement of white waters.

Startled out of his rumination by a clap on his shoulder, he jerked his head around and saw it was Alfgar. "Son let us celebrate, for soon we shall be fighting beside one another. This time, we will show them together that the courage and steel of ancient Mercians still flow in the veins of the sons of the great Ealdorman Leofwine…"

Burghred was aware of sweat beads gathering on his brow.

"Hell's teeth lad, you look green-sick! Are you ill?" Alfgar showed rare concern. "Maybe the wine was too strong?"

Burghred rose to his feet unsteadily, a hand over his pounding chest. Alfgar caught his arm to stabilise him.

"I-I am sorry, Father, I believe I am ill. I should lie down – if you don't mind."

Pressure was building.

His head hammered in time with his heart and his ears rang with noise.

"Come now son, you will be expected in the feasting hall," Alfgar said. "It will pass."

Burghred gently shook him off. "No, Father. Go and be with the others. You have much to celebrate, as you say. It is most likely the wine has upset my stomach. It will pass, and I will join you after a rest."

Alfgar eyed him darkly. Burghred wilted and put a hand on the wall to prop himself up. After a moment, Alfgar nodded. "Get some rest then," Alfgar said. "You look terrible." With that he left him.

Burghred scarcely made it back to his chamber when he was violently sick in the piss bucket. He lay back on the pallet, body trembling as he tried to fathom a way out of the entanglement.

Chapter Seventeen

Swica

Burghred squeezed through the throng searching for familiar faces. The feasting hall was noisier and busier than usual. Ælred waved at him from a shadowy corner and Burghred made his way up the benches and sat down next to him, giving him a curt nod. Unconcerned that his friend still brooded over their previous conversation, Burghred sliced some meat then stared at it impaled on his knife, unable to bring himself to eat it. His stomach was still a pit of nausea and his chest was tight with worry.

Loud bagpipes played, and dancers spun to clapping, whooping, and stamping. Burghred gulped down the mead. It eased his shaking hands, and he relished the warmth that entered his veins. A laughing girl pulled him up without warning and propelled him into the jig. Whirling around the floor, the beating of tables thundered in his ears and he saw the blurred faces of his father and Aldith, as they sat with Gruffudd at the high table on the dais.

The wheel of tumultuous commotion continued all about the hall, but in Burghred's mind, time stood still. The noise was muffled as if he were underwater, and caught by the king's stare, unease pricked at him. The spider. *He knows; he sees right through me.*

In a flash, he was dancing again as though he'd never stopped. Gruffudd was laughing in Aldith's ear and it seemed as though he must have imagined the king looking at him after all. Burghred disengaged himself from the dance and looked for Heulyn. He saw her in a far corner of the hall, jug in hand as she hovered around a group of Norse.

She laughed, weaved her way through carousing men, and expertly dodged attempts to grab her backside or breasts.

Burghred called out her name, was buffeted by the dancers and lost sight of her. When she came into view again, a tall warrior hovered over her. The man reached out, caught her to him, and mead spilled as she tried to remove his hands from her.

Burghred's face reddened. It was Ivar.

The Norþmann's mouth closed over Heulyn's spurred on by cheers from his companions. Burghred's irritation was spiked with jealous rage and, as Ivar withdrew from her momentarily, their eyes met across the hall.

As Ivar resumed his amorous attack, Burghred snatched up a flask, emptied it into his gullet and tossed it away. He moved closer to them.

"Let – her – go!"

The big Norþmann looked up from where he had been gnawing at Heulyn's neck and grinned. "Oh, does the filly belong to you, *lyttel Englander?*"

"You dare to speak so of the king's daughter?"

Laughing mirthlessly, Ivar continued to grapple with his captive.

"I said, let her go!"

Ivar's smile as he glanced over Heulyn's shoulder was malicious.

The bastard! Burghred flew across the floor. A vicious kick sent Ivar and his hostage sprawling among the upset tables. Heulyn jumped to her feet, screaming, escaping from her captor. Ivar made to get up and Burghred knocked him flat, straddling his chest. He gripped Ivar's throat, drew back his head and butted him. Suddenly there was a burst of crimson.

Burghred was dragged arms and legs flailing from his victim. Ivar, helped by his friends, was covered with fragments of food, stuck to his clothes and hair.

Straightening himself, Ivar said in a voice filled with mockery, "You want to fight me, *lyttel Englander,* huh?"

"I am a Mercian," Burghred growled, struggling to escape. "Burghred of Mercia."

"Burghred of Mercia?" Ivar considered. His forehead was swelling and a cut on his forehead bled, but he showed no discomfort. "I heard that you are called *Burghred Swica.* You betrayed your own father, didn't you?" He thrust his face towards Burghred. *"Oathbreaker!"*

Burghred stiffened and clenched his fists, hot with shame at the taunting.

"The girl – she is mine, and she is no whore, but the daughter of

168

King Gruffudd. You may insult me, I care not, but do not insult *her*."

"This little mare?" Ivar slung an arm around her neck as she was thrust forward by one of his friends. "A king's daughter? She did not tell me that when I was riding her in my bed!" Ivar and his friends roared with laughter again as Ivar planted a loud smacking kiss on her cheek.

Heulyn's tortured eyes were piteous. Her lips moved in silent appeal, though he did not understand what she was trying to say. Burghred struggled, seeking a way out, then swung back a leg and kicked the man to his right who fell to the floor, clasping his knee. Burghred smashed his freed fist into the face of his other captor, bloodying the man's nose. Reaching for his *seax*, he unsheathed it, only to have his arms forced behind him once again and his weapon dropped out of reach.

"So, you want to kill me, *Swica*?"

Again Burghred grappled with them and a large muscular arm encircled his neck. Rock hard flesh choked him. He was in trouble, but death seemed preferable at that moment. He was dead anyway. He was an oath-breaker… *swica*. A disgrace to his father. No one would come to aid him. If he were to die, he'd do it fighting.

Burghred managed to free an arm and tried to lever the huge muscle from his neck. The grip was vice-like and all his arm could do was hang limp and useless.

"Fight me, coward," he muttered,

Ivar towered before him, smirking. With Heulyn still struggling in his grasp, he bent to pick up the blade and held the point to Burghred's face. "What will you say when I am gouging out your eyes on the end of your knife, *lyttel Englander*?"

"Why don't you try it and see?"

"Burghred! No!" Heulyn cried. "Don't fight, please, just let it go."

That she may have thought him no match for Ivar irked Burghred. He was no coward.

"Give me my *seax*, Ivar and we will fight."

Ivar grinned like a child allowed to join a game. He signalled to his men to release Burghred and handed him his knife, clutching his own in readiness.

Around him, Burghred was aware that the musicians continued to play, and the dancers danced on, as though nothing untoward were happening.

"My people call this the *hólmgangr*." Ivar smiled, showing strong white teeth as he readied himself.

"I call it *killing scum*." Burghred quivered with the energy that rushed through every fighting man's veins when survival was all that mattered.

"Burghred, stop! Do not fight this man," urged Heulyn once more.

He jerked his head in her direction, his guard dropping.

She screamed and he was jolted by a stinging sensation in his midriff. Taking advantage of his inattention, Ivar's blade caught him. Burghred staggered back, looking at his abdomen. A long, bloody laceration leaked crimson through a slash in his tunic.

Ivar came for him again, and Burghred quickly focussed himself. Their forearms collided, and Ivar's weapon-hand was knocked aside. Burghred thrust his blade forward, and his opponent sprang gracefully like a cat from its path. "Nice start, *Englander*, but you need to try harder."

Burghred edged cautiously toward him. Ivar skirted to the left, occasionally darting and feigning his weapon one way and then the other, teasing – trying to unnerve him. The Norþmann appeared confident, but Burghred had nothing to lose, and a man with nothing to lose was dangerous.

Ivar smiled, and in a movement designed to unnerve, he spun his *seax* and flicked it in the air, catching it neatly in his grasp as it descended. In a flash, the blade was poised again and Ivar lunged aiming at his neck. Burghred chopped at Ivar's wrist with the side of his palm and knocked the knife so it skidded across the floor. Jumping, he slammed his boot into the Norþmann's groin causing him to stumble until he regained his stance.

Burghred remembered his father's words… *Become complacent and you die. No man holds victory over another until the last breath is drawn.*

Ivar snatched up his fallen weapon and continued the offensive. Burghred kept his guard. He slid and dodged his rival's attempts to strike him.

"Still think you can beat me, Norþmann?"

Ivar's eyes narrowed. His lips stretched into a menacing grin, and he began to close in on him. "I'll beat you, *lyttel Englander*. I am going to rip you to shreds and feed you to the hounds. I'm going to cut out your tongue and give it to your woman for her to lick herself

170

with…"

Busy with his words, Ivar lowered his arm.

Lunging, Burghred felt soft warm flesh against the side of his hand, as he brought his blade down upon Ivar's chest. He slipped on the ale-drenched floor, steadied himself and waited for the expected return. Ivar made no such movement. Instead he stared down at the blood that blossomed over his torso. His eyes, wide with surprise, glared at Burghred. At first it seemed the injured man would pass out as he swayed, then he became enraged, and rushed, a roaring sound emanating from his open craw. They wrestled and slid; arms entwined as they went down like lovers in a frantic embrace.

Burghred gasped for breath, pinned under the large frame of the Norþmann. Tearing a hand free, he grappled for Ivar's wrist. Holding off the blade at his neck, he felt hot liquid trickle down his throat to pool in his collarbone. Blood squelched between their tunics and the stench of urine assaulted Burghred's nostrils. His enemy's bladder had let itself go.

Burghred, attempting to release himself, forced his knee up into his assailant's abdomen. He pushed, but Ivar battled against him, and Burghred was unable to shift the man's bulk whilst staving off the blade at his throat.

He did not want to die – not like this. Summoning all his force, Burghred rammed hard with his knee again and this time, Ivar's strength waning, struggled to maintain balance. Burghred gave one more push and heaved the Norþmann until he rolled onto the floor. Burghred leapt on him. He had to get the knife! The blade bit into his hands as he grabbed it and then lost it again. The two of them rolled and Burghred felt for his own weapon. Had he dropped it in the scuffle? The cuts in his hands streamed with blood and pain and Ivar was now on top of him again, his grunting, contorted face staring at him. Something cold and wet was beneath him. His *seax*!

Burghred fumbled for the weapon and grasping it precariously in his injured hands, plunged it into his enemy's neck.

Ivar cried out and scrambled unsteadily to his feet, holding a hand to the wound. Burghred flipped himself onto all fours, and as he slipped and slid in the glutinous mess a boot thudded into his face.

Burghred twisted, blinded with pain, struck out with his weapon, and felt his blade sink into linen and flesh. The floor thudded as beside him Ivar collapsed. Dragging himself closer to his enemy, Burghred thrust the *seax* once more into Ivar's body.

The music had gone and Burghred was aware of the hushed silence. Ivar's body twitched. Burghred stabbed again and again until the body went limp and twitched no more. He rolled on to his back breathing heavily, blood blurring his vision. Had he killed him?

Aldith shoved her way through the crowd and gasped in horror as a figure of a man slowly got to his feet. Was this monstrous image really her brother? As Burghred stood rigid and dazed, rivulets of blood dripped down his cheeks from above his eye. At his feet, a man lay bloodied and prone, a pool of dark liquid seeping from underneath him.

Heulyn pushed past Aldith, sobbing. The girl threw her arms around her brother. She was hysterical. A sound from the man on the floor made Aldith turn as he tried to sit. He was alive after all. Friends surrounded him, disbelief on their faces as they tried to lift him. But it was useless, death was too near. Dark glutinous blood was everywhere.

Someone had fetched a sword and handed it to a distressed youth who knelt beside the dying man and gently placed it in his hand. Then, choked with tears, the young Norse warrior said, "Here, my brother, die as a good warrior ought. Go to Valhalla knowing you are worthy of Odin." The lad's tears dripped onto the body as he closed the red-stained fingers around the hilt. Death ravaged the man's face as he turned to look at his companions briefly before the life went out of him.

Aldith's heart pounded as the slain man's brother, rising to his feet, glanced over at Burghred. "It was meant to be you! It was not meant to be Ivar!" he screamed. Knife drawn, the youth moved toward the shadowy figure of Burghred.

"No!" Heulyn stood protectively across him, her outstretched hand shaking as she too held a knife.

"Heulyn, put the blade down," Aldith demanded. She feared for Burghred and searched her mind for what to do.

"Don't any of you come closer, I am Gruffudd's daughter and you will have to kill me first!"

Ivar's brother halted. "Move, girl! You think your father cares?"

"*I* care," intervened Aldith.

One of the Norþmenn held the youth gently and spoke quietly to him in Norse.

"There has been enough violence already," Aldith said. Tears of anger and confusion stung her eyes. *What did he mean it was not meant to be Ivar?*

As the Norse knelt around their friend's corpse and swore oaths of vengeance, her mind worked to piece together what had just happened and trying to fathom the brother's words. Why was Burghred supposed to be killed and not Ivar?

She turned to look at the dais where her husband sat unmoving, his chamberlain speaking in his ear. He looked directly at her, and in the dim light of the hall, she could see his face was expressionless. Aldith looked to the bloody image of her brother, vomit churning in her belly. Heulyn's arms went around him as he swayed, his eyes glassy. Aldith suppressed the need to burst into hysterics. It was important to remain calm if they were going to save Burghred's life. She needed to get him away from Rhuddlan, but how? There would be guards on every gate. Her mind raced and her body shook. *Stay calm...* "You must go, Burghred!" she said to him.

"He can't, he is hurt," sobbed Heulyn. "Can you not see?"

Her father burst through the swelling mob. "What in God's name have you done, Burghred!"

Burghred opened his mouth. Nothing. His eyes rolled and his head flopped as he sank, legs collapsing.

*

Warm light fell across his eyes. He'd been happy in his slumber, dreaming of when he was a small boy, his mother telling him a bedtime story as he lay in her arms comforted by her smell and softness.

He looked up at the face that hovered over him, features blurred by the sunshine that burst through the open window.

Burghred whispered, "Mother," and smiled.

He tried to sit, and his thigh throbbed, reminding him of the fight and what had happened the night before.

"Aldith?"

Her eyes and cheeks were wet as she embraced him and gathering her close, Burghred's shoulders heaved, his tears staining her wimple.

Over Aldith's shoulder, in a shadowed corner, he saw her. Heulyn. It was then that he realised he was not in his usual chamber and the itchy straw pallet he was lying on was not his. The furnishings were feminine, and he guessed he was in his sister's apartments.

"How long have I lain here?"

"For two days and two nights now," Heulyn replied, coming forward. "You have been in a fever, but your leg heals. You must leave here. The Norse have gone to take the body of Ivar to his father. But they will want revenge. My father wanted you hung from the highest tree."

"Then why do I still live?"

"I reminded him that you are his brother-in-law and that his loyalty should be to you," Aldith interjected. "Of course, he denied any loyalty to you, but has agreed to allow you to live so I can nurse you until you are well."

"Well enough to die," he said cynically. "Then I shall stay and face my fate."

"If you stay, your fate will be to die," Heulyn said.

"Gruffudd caused this, didn't he?" Burghred's voice was bitter.

Heulyn nodded. "My father did not trust you. They say it was you who warned the Saes king about Hereford, and that you were going to do it again. It was *you* who was meant to be killed, not Ivar. Everyone thought he would be the stronger of you. They'd even put something in your drink."

"If they did, I felt nothing," he said, but… *Ælred? Could he have?*

"Gruffudd needn't have gone to this trouble. Why didn't he just have me hung and done with it? I wouldn't have struggled. I'd have gone to the gallows willingly."

"He didn't want a rift with Alfgar. He needs him. He didn't want anything to risk the Englisc alliance. The plan was for you to be provoked into a fight and your death to be the outcome. It was the best way to get rid of you."

"It worked well for him, then, that plan?" Burghred smirked. "Did he not realise my father hates me and would have been glad to have me dead?"

He lay silent for a moment, then continued, "And you, Heulyn? You were part of it, weren't you?"

"I am sorry." She hung her head. "I was supposed to bed you and find out your plans. I had no idea they wanted you dead until it was too late to warn you. I tried to warn you during the fight – I-I told you not to fight him. I should have told you what I knew, it's all my fault! I'm sorry – I was scared. My father would kill me if I betrayed him."

Burghred laughed without mirth. "And I am alive, and Ivar is dead."

"Burghred, 'tis not true what they say about you, is it?" Aldith knelt by his bed. "That you betrayed our father for Edward, and you have been passing information to Harold Godwinson's spies? Tell me it isn't true that you are faithless and a deceiver – that you are... *swica*?" Burghred did not answer. "They say you will betray us again. Once a traitor, always a traitor, so they say."

"*They* say? The Wéalas are always betraying each other, and they call *me* - *swica*. Did Alfgar know what they had planned to do to me?"

Heulyn shook her head. "I think not. Gruffudd didn't want to risk their alliance."

"Aldith?"

"He couldn't have, he wouldn't..."

He took Aldith's hand and pulled her to sit down beside him. It broke his heart to confess what he had been sent there to do. He left out the part about Harold Godwinson's offer of Mercia. He could not face her with that.

When he'd finished his story, tears flowed silently down his cheeks, and he wiped them, ashamed. Aldith held his hand and said, "You have been used, Burghred, my poor sweet brother, badly used... it was that self-serving Harold Godwinson who caused this, for his own ends no doubt. How dare he use my dear brother to betray his own family?"

Burghred tried to protest. "No, Harold has promised –"

"Promised? Promised what?" she asked.

"It doesn't matter –"

"He promised you Mercia, didn't he?" She looked at him with a mixture of incredulity and sadness. Burghred closed his eyes. "Oh, Burghred," she whispered.

A day later, Aldith and Heulyn came to him with a plan. Gruffudd had given them five days to nurse him back to health and then they were coming for him. Aldith told him, "The local weaver comes weekly to sell his woven cloth and a handsome bribe was all it took to persuade him to hide you in his cart – no questions asked."

"This is too dangerous for you girls, I cannot let you do this," Burghred said.

"You are my brother, Burghred, my blood, and though I do not like what you have done, I cannot see you die. Not for that leech, Harold Godwinson."

"I will not go without my horse," Burghred said, as Aldith and

Heulyn readied him for escape.

They dressed his wounds afresh and gave him clean clothes. He had been severely injured, the worst being the slash to his inner thigh. During the tussle when he and Ivar were wrestling on the floor, Ivar's knife had caught the big vein in the leg through which a man's lifeblood flowed. He had lost a lot of blood, but the girls had been quick to close the wound and stitched the gash with linen thread. Burghred had been strong in his delirium and they'd needed help from the guard at the door to hold him down. The wound was wide and deep having torn into his muscle.

He was still very weak, and his head where Ivar had kicked him throbbed painfully. His hands, cut to ribbons, had been bandaged, the slash in his chest also stitched, but it was not so deep that it worried him as much as his leg. Shallow knife cuts covered his neck, but they would soon mend. There was no time for him to stay and recover more. If he didn't go before the five days were up, his life would be forfeit. The Norþmenn wanted revenge. Gruffudd would let them have it. And his father would also be happy for them to have it, no doubt.

"You cannot ride out on your horse, Burghred," Heulyn said. "I will bring Aries to you, somewhere in the grove," she added.

He nodded and then turned to Aldith as she gave him a bag of provisions for the journey. He went to embrace her, but she baulked. "Don't," she said. "I just hope it is worth it."

"What is worth what?"

"What you are getting in return for your deceit."

Burghred tensed. "I am doing this *for* the good of Mercia, for us all," he said. "'Tis my birthright and I cannot stand by and see my father throw it to the Godwins."

"And if Harold does not keep to his side of the bargain?"

Burghred shrugged. "Then I will get what I deserve."

He took his leave from Heulyn and went without the embrace from his sister he sorely needed. His heart was heavy, but he knew there was no other choice. Alfgar would never forgive him, Gruffudd would not allow him to live, and Aldith would no longer love him. All he had left was Mercia. He limped painfully to the door where the guard lay unconscious, drugged by something Heulyn had mixed. Aldith called to him. He turned and saw her, proud and beautiful, his sister, the queen.

"God speed you, my brother."

*

Heulyn was true to her word. She came to him in the early hours of the morning. From the undergrowth hiding place, he heard horses' hooves thump the damp grass. The pain in his injured thigh made it uncomfortable to sleep in such conditions so he'd lain awake all evening with only his cloak and the brushwood to keep him warm. Peeking through the foliage, he watched a rider approach, leading another horse in tow. He crawled out of the scrub, pushed himself awkwardly up on two feet, and flagged her down.

He took his horse's reins and rubbed Aries' nose who snorted appreciatively. Heulyn dismounted and he embraced her.

"Thank you, he did not give you any trouble?" Burghred asked. "I could not leave without him."

She shook her head. "He was as good as gold," she said and opened a sack, pulled out some ale and more food. He took them gratefully. "Oh, and here is a salve to help heal your wounds, and medicine for sleeping." She put the latter back in the sack and gave him another.

"What's this?" Burghred pulled out a thick brown tunic and a hooded cowl.

"You will travel much better as a monk than a runaway Englisc lord."

"I won't ask you where you got them. What are those for?" he asked indicating the scissors and razor in her hand.

"I am going to give you a haircut, Brother Burghred. "All good monks must have a bald patch on their heads." She giggled.

Burghred smiled, doubtful that he needed to go to such extremes. "I have done this before, you know."

"Last time you had not killed the son of a Norwægian jarl."

They sniggered nervously, and standing on her tip toes, she lifted her arms over his neck. It brought home to him just how small she was and how much she risked.

She let go and put something in his hand. "Here is a purse with a few coins and this," Heulyn took from her neck a little cross made from silver and placed it around his own, "is to remember me by."

"Why do you help me?"

"Because I would have loved you if I had been allowed to. You alone are the only one I have ever wanted to spend my life with. I could not let them kill you. If I'd known that I would grow to love you..."

"Then come with me."

She put her hand to his cheek. "If only, *cariad*...."

"I will make you my wife, my true wife, blessed by God."

"In the lands of the Saes? I would be hated," she said, and shook her head.

"No... you would not."

"Burghred, this is my home. My heart is here."

"And I have no father. No lord, and no worth," he replied, downcast.

"What will you be, without a home, or kin?"

"I will be what I have always been, just a man. I have some lands, but they are not many. My father and I have never seen eye to eye. Some years ago, I learned that my mother was not my real mother, though she treated me as her own. My real mother had been the daughter of a traitor. I have a traitor's blood, it seems. I fought hard to make Alfgar love me, but in truth it was I who found it hard to love him."

She touched his face again tenderly, with a look of regret. "If only we had been born on the same side of the dyke... perhaps then we might have been allowed to love and not used for someone else's gain."

"What about you? They will know it was you who helped me."

"Do not fear for me, my love. I will be safe. My father will be angry, but I am hopeful he will not hurt me."

"Come with me, please..."

Heulyn paused and for a moment it seemed she would change her mind. Instead she shook her head once more and said, "Now, let me transform you into Brother Burghred, and then I must go, it will be a long ride back to Rhuddlan. But I will never forget you my Saes love."

"I would that the *norns* had spun a different web for us. Please tell my sister I am sorry that I could not be the brother she wanted."

When she had finished cutting his hair, he kissed her and then as she held Aries' halter, he mounted. Handing him the reins, Heulyn said, "Ride this track south and it will lead you to the River Conwy. Take the riverside path to where it joins the River Elwy. There you will find sanctuary in St Asaph. The canons there are kind and if you mention my name, they will look after you unconditionally, asking no questions."

As he rode up the woodland avenue a faint hint of a breeze touched his face. He sniffed the aroma of the mountain air, sighed heavily and turned to see her still there, a small, shadowy figure in the darkness.

He put an arm up to wave to her and felt heartened when she waved back. He would miss her. He would even miss Wales.

Chapter Eighteen

Escape

Dawn broke above the church tower as he reached the walls that surrounded the little commune. He heaved a sigh of relief and crumpled from the saddle, passing out before he hit the ground.

He awoke to the pleasant smile of a woman whose lined face would have once been pleasing to the eye. "*Iechyd da* to you, young brother," she said, which was ironic when he was in anything but good health.

He licked his lips and tried to reply, but his mouth was as dry as a drought-ridden stream. He lay on his back and discovered that beneath him was a comfortable feather mattress. Despite his sweat-soaked body, he shivered, and the lady covered him with blankets retrieved from the floor, babbling away in a calm voice that was definitely not Englisc. She offered him some water, gently supporting his head. When he'd taken only a few sips, Burghred rolled onto his side, curled himself into a ball and trembled uncontrollably.

Upon hearing a male voice speaking the Wéalisc language, he thought he was back in Rhuddlan and panicked. Then he recalled his night's painful journey, and the last thing he remembered was arriving at the walls and collapsing, then nothing after that. He wanted to speak, to ensure that he was safe, but was overcome with exhaustion and his fear dissipated as he floated into a restful slumber.

When Burghred finally emerged from his fever, still a little delirious and weak, he had no idea how long he had lain there. The lady was sitting nearby sewing, and she gave a startled cry as he sat up abruptly.

"Well, well, there's a surprise you gave me," the woman said brightly in well used Englisc. "My, you are a strange one." She put her stitching aside and fetched some water from a sideboard.

"Olwen? Is he awake?"

"Aye, Rodric, he is," the lady called out as she turned to Burghred with a cup. A man in his middle years, came through a curtain.

"Greetings, lad," Rodric said, also using Englisc. He gave Burghred a warm smile. "'Tis glad, we are, that you are recovering."

Burghred threw off the blanket and naked, leapt from the bed. He yelped as hot pain tore through his injured thigh and his knees buckled beneath him.

The man caught him in his arms. "Now just where do you think you're going, young brother?" The older man fought off Burghred's pathetic attempt to grapple with him. "Come, let me help you back into your bed."

"I need to get out of here," Burghred protested and tried his escape once more, crying out in pain.

"Don't fret," Olwen said, as Rodric laid him down. "You are safe here."

"No, I am not safe – not safe. I must go…" The effort had sapped what little strength Burghred had, and his eyes began to close again.

Later, Olwen brought some broth to him. At first, he was so feeble he had to be spoon-fed, sometimes by Olwen, or at others, their young daughter. Gradually, over time, he regained the ability to feed himself.

Ten days passed and he'd become stronger, venturing out on shaky legs into the grounds of the community. He'd been in such an awful state, Olwen and Rodric had told him, with his hands all cut up, a discoloured lump and deep wound over his right eye, and the weeping gash in his leg, not to mention the assortment of cuts and bruises all over his body. He learned that the priests had found him outside the gates on the ground, with Aries standing guard over him. They had carried him on a stretcher and settled him in Father Rodric's house where he had tossed and turned in a fever that had raged for days.

As he limped his way around the cluster of domestic buildings and workshops that surrounded the stone church, he would pass pleasantries with the inhabitants as they tended their gardens, their herbariums and other work.

Speaking in the little, but sufficient Wéalisc he knew, he told them he was Brother Dunstan from a monastery on the other side of the Englisc border and had been with a group of pilgrims to the shrine of St Werburga when robbers attacked them. His companions were killed and he, the lone survivor, left for dead. They neither questioned his story nor asked him again once already told.

One day, when Burghred was feeling more recovered, he was helping Father Rodric in his workshop, boiling up potions, and mixing salves. As they worked, Father Rodric was telling Burghred he was from Scrobbesbyrig, his father was Englisc, and his mother had been of Wéalas blood. Rodric had just begun relaying the story of how he had come to live in St Asaph when there was a commotion near the gates and horses' hooves could be heard as riders crossed the precinct. Burghred joined Father Rodric looking out of the doorway and saw men armoured and dressed in the garb of Gruffudd's officials. Burghred sucked in his breath. Rodric must have seen the panic in his face for he asked him in a fearful voice, "Do you know those men?" Burghred nodded. "Then chances are they will recognise you?" Burghred nodded again.

Father Rodric pushed Burghred under the work bench. Burghred did not protest as the priest covered him with what he could find to camouflage his presence until baskets, chests, and sacks of herbs completely hid him.

Burghred listened to Father Rodric speaking in a muffled voice to the men outside.

"We're just wasting our time here," one of them said. "He won't be here; we've already looked anyway. He can't have got far with those wounds. I heard he was near to death before he disappeared. Most likely he's lying somewhere dead and the beasts have got to him."

"You can come out now, they've gone," Father Rodric said eventually and Burghred crawled out of his hiding place.

Father Rodric helped him to his feet and stared at him. Kind, green eyes flickered in the sunlight from the open window. "If you were, as you said, from the other side of the border, how do you know the king's daughter, Lady Heulyn?"

"I-I don't know what you mean."

Rodric folded his arms across his ample waist. "The morning we found you outside our gates, we picked you up and you opened your eyes, looked right into my face, and said, 'Rhuddlan' and 'Lady Heulyn'. They were the only three words you spoke with any coherence, and then you lay unconscious for days. You tossed and turned for hours on end, calling out for her – and occasionally for a lady called Aldith."

"You know her?" he asked, "You know the Lady Heulyn?"

Father Rodric nodded. "St Asaph knows the Lady Heulyn well. She comes often to bake bread and work with us, help the sick, and to give alms. Sometimes, the queen also comes."

Burghred was surprised, for that was not the Heulyn he remembered. He gave a little smile at this softer side of her. It made him feel better about what she'd been forced to do. She had just been a playing piece, in the game. It had not been her fault.

"Did she come to see me when I was ill?" he asked, hoping she had.

Father Rodric shook his head. "Lady Heulyn? She hasn't come recently. Not since you arrived."

Burghred felt disappointed. He'd hoped that she would change her mind and come to be with him.

"So why are you helping me?"

"Because it is our obligation to serve God, and by giving sanctuary to any one of his creatures who needs our help, no matter the cause, we are fulfilling our duty. When they first came looking, you were almost unconscious with fever. We were worried that it was you they wanted. So, we hid you. Just now when that soldier said that the man they were looking for was injured, I thought that it must be you. Besides, you don't seem very much like a man who has lived in a monastery all his life."

Father Rodric smiled and returned to his work sorting out the herbs and plants.

"I am sorry, Father Rodric. I have deceived you, and your good lady wife, and the other members of the community. Can you ever forgive me?"

"It is not my business to ask people who are sick and in need what they have done or why they need my help. All I hope for is that whatever you do from now, you will help someone as we have helped you."

That night Burghred ate his last supper in St Asaph, for he knew he could not endanger the community's lives by lingering any longer. He was anxious to get back to the king and Harold. First, he wanted to go to Scrobbesbyrig to gather support. If he could rally the men of Mercia to his banner, then he could bring them to the field, and it would be beholden upon Edward to give him Mercia.

Burghred left in the early hours of the morning, before dawn, wearing his monk's guise but declining Olwen's offer of shaving his head again. He would keep his cowl up, he had told her, until it was safe to become himself again. He took into his service a young lad from the community called Beric, who had recently lost the only relative he had. Beric was a red-faced youth of fifteen with greasy black hair and eyes like a toad. He had a spear, a shield, a knife, and an old nag. Although it was hardly an army, Burghred accepted his offer of companionship and they went with the good blessings of the people of St Asaph.

Scrobbesbyrig
One week later
The hall, built on the summit where the town was situated, had its own stockade. The brightly painted gables and doors stood proud as Burghred and his servant approached, escorted by the townsmen. They were brought before Wulfgar, the scīr-reeve, a man whose face was lined beyond that of a man in his prime.

"So you are Burghred, son of Alfgar, outlawed Lord of Mercia," Wulfgar said slowly, pensively rubbing his bristled chin. "Your father is in exile, but *here* you are, his son, betraying him, seeking support of your own, rallying men to your banner against him. Could it be that you are about to betray him a second time?"

Here we go. Mentally, Burghred brushed off the accusation and said, "My father is the traitor, not I. Right now, he is plotting with the Wéalas to overthrow our rightful King Edward; plotting once more with the very same dogs that killed my father's brother, Edwin, as most of you will remember." Burghred looked around at the hoary, listening faces of the men within the hall and recognised many. "Alfgar is with Gruffudd, a man who has caused the deaths of hundreds of Mercians, your own kin amongst them."

"Your father has not always been a man of the greatest integrity, but he is the heir of old Leofric, who was well loved. It was Leofric's wish that Mercia does not fall to Godwin control, just as the old Mercian lands of Scrobbesbyrig and Gleawecestre have already been given to that greedy family to hold. If anyone is plotting it is them. Whenever Alfgar is in trouble, one or other of those brothers are always nearby. They already have the north, and the east, as well as Wessex in the south. Harold will manipulate the king as usual – just like his ill-begotten father used to – may he rot in hell - and Mercia will have one of his self-serving clan foisted upon us so that they will rule the whole kingdom."

"If you loved my grandfather as you say, then you know that he would not have wanted this alliance with the Wéalas."

"Aye, I loved the old earl, I was at his funeral, you recall."

"Then you shall know that my father wasn't. I was with my grandfather when he died, I know his wishes, and he would not have wanted war against the king, nor for Mercia to ally with that Wéalisc butcher, Gruffudd."

"Leofric would not have wanted a Godwinson to rule Mercia!"

Around the room, Burghred heard murmurings of assent. He had been travelling through difficult terrain for days, was dirty, weary, and hungry, and in need of rest on a soft goose feather pallet. He had cast off his monk's habit and was simply dressed in clothing borrowed from the canons. It occurred to him then that there was little difference between him and his servant Beric. How was he going to convince them of his worth looking like a peasant? His grandfather had always said that words were more important than a man's garb, so if all he had were his words then so be it.

"Listen to me, Wulfgar, Alfgar and Gruffudd have made an alliance with Magnus Haraldsson of Norwæg. They want to oust Edward and put Harald Sigurdsson on the throne in his stead. Alfgar and Gruffudd would have us live under the yoke of those northern barbarians. That is why Alfgar is *there*, and I am *here*. I do not have the stomach for that – do you?" Burghred moved closer to the dais. "Follow *me*, Lord Wulfgar. Let *me* be your *hláford*. My blood is just as Mercian as Alfgar's. Let us fight together against our enemies, the Wéalas, the Norse, and that traitor – Alfgar, that *níðing* – betrayer of kings, betrayer of fathers. Do you think that he won't betray you also? That he won't have your lands taken from you and given to his Norse scum? How else will Harald's army be paid but with your homes, your gold, your silver, your land? And they will not ask for it, they will take it." He paused, searching his mind for some caveat that would ram home the message. He took a deep breath and said, "What will happen to your women and children then?"

The lines on Wulfgar's mottled face were drawn as he contemplated what Burghred had said against the background of mutterings.

"You want us to join *you* to fight against your father?" he asked.

"Not just Alfgar, but Gruffudd also. And the Norse. I was little more than a child of four when my uncle and many good men from this burgh were killed by the Wéalas, but I know the enmity that it caused and I know that it is etched in the minds of our elders, Mercians like yourselves. Some of you are kin to Alfgeat and Thurkill. And yet you forgive so easily that cowardly ambush."

A thegn stepped forward and addressed Wulfgar. "He is right, my lord. Alfgeat was my mother's brother. He was your brother's grandson, my lord. You too, Rædwulf, Tatwine, you are also kin to him." He pointed at the two men he had named.

Another man came forward. "Aye, I remember Thurkill well. He was a good man and a good Christian. A king's thegn and a Mercian! His son, also called Thurkill, has lands in Hereford and he was forced to watch his wife raped; his children's throats were cut by Alfgar himself at Hereford."

"What has Hereford got to do with this?" shouted someone else waving his fist. "It was the doing of that Norman fool, Ralph, that got Hereford razed to the ground. He ran from the field, he and his Norman cowards, leaving hundreds of men to die!"

Burghred interjected, "Aye, at the hands of Alfgar and Gruffudd! Come with me and I will promise you justice for those men! And I promise, with me as your earl, I will see to it that your lands will once again belong to Mercia and not Wessex."

Men poured from outside through the doors of the hall. A lad pushed his way through the throng to stand before him. "I will ride with you, Lord Burghred."

Beric looked at Burghred, beaming with enthusiasm at the young man's offer. Burghred sighed. It was men he needed not boys. The youth was no more than sixteen. Hardly worth getting excited about.

A man raised his voice above the chatter. "Listen to me! All of you!" he cried. He was not a young man, though he was agile enough to leap upon a board. From the way he held himself, upright and proud, he was someone of substance. "Have you all lost your wits? Would you betray the father as well as the son for this – this Godwin puppet? We should fight for Alfgar, not this mangy whelp who wants to betray our lord – *his father* – for his own gain. That was what Leofric would have wanted – for us to fight for Alfgar. And he is the only thing we have stopping the Godwins from taking total control of the king and the kingdom!"

"They already have control of the king!" someone called out.

Voices of assent followed.

Wulfgar said, "Neither the Wéalas nor the Norse are our enemies, but Harold Godwinson and his West Seaxan lapdogs are! Inewulf is right; we should be fighting for Alfgar! We must restore our rightful lord! They have taken us from Mercia, but they cannot take Mercia from our hearts! *Hæl* to Mercia, I say!" The scīr-reeve raised his drinking horn.

The crowd raised their mead horns and roared, "*Hæl* to Alfgar! *Hæl* to Mercia!"

A young man stepped forward and coughed before he spoke. "Alfgar was exiled through his own doing. He made treasonable accusations against the king's person. This was not the fault of anyone other than Alfgar himself. If we side with him, then are we not also traitors to our king? Leofric was always loyal to Edward! Godwinson is also a loyal subject of the king, whatever else we might say of the man. If we support Alfgar against Godwinson, we betray Edward and we too will be tainted with treason!"

Heartened by the fire in the young man's eyes, Burghred added, "We will all be damned if we side against the king. I have just come from Rhuddlan and my father not only plans to win his earldom back, he plans to do so with a large army of Norþmenn led by Magnus, Harald Sigurdsson's son. They want to put the Norwægian king, his father, on the throne of Englalond."

"Who is this Harald and why does he not come himself? Why does he send his son?" one of Wulfgar's companions demanded.

"Pah! I happen to know that this Magnus is but a boy!" called out another.

Burghred was ready to answer. "Aye, a boy he is, but he has men, not boys, in his counsel! His father King Harald is greedy and right now he is too busy invading Denmark to add to his empire, so he sends his son to do his dirty work for him. Do we want another foreigner on our throne? A man who has no right to it. A man who will bring strange ways here, heathens who will burn our churches and have no care for our customs and traditions. Do we want this?"

"I don't want to betray Alfgar, but I like treason less," one of the younger men said.

"Nor I," said the youth standing next to him.

"By God, we have had a Dane for a king before, Edward is half Norman, could it be worse to have a Norwægian on the throne?"

"Not just a Norwægian, but a pagan. No man in Englalond would follow a pagan king!"

"I hear this Harald Sigurdsson is a Christian and that he is a good king. A strong king. Edward is but a weakling, one who allows himself to be manipulated by others."

"We should go back to the old days when Mercia was a kingdom in her own right!"

Burghred rounded on the man who had just spoken. "You dare speak such treason? There can be no more pious a king than Edward, our anointed king who holds God's favour. I do not wish to invoke God's wrath by betraying him."

The man who'd spoken a moment ago said, "How do we know this whelp speaks the truth, and that it is not a trick to make us side with him? We should support Alfgar – is what I say. The Godwinsons have wanted rid of Alfgar since before the razing of Hereford. It was they who brought him to exile before! Who is to say that they did not have a hand in it this time?"

"Cuthbeorht is right, we have no proof that Burghred tells the truth. I say we stick with Alfgar and make Mercia great again as she once was."

"That's absurd. Why would I lie? What would be the point?" said Burghred.

"He *could* be lying," Wulfgar said thoughtfully, rubbing his bulbous nose with his forefinger.

"I am *not* lying!" Burghred was exasperated. "Would you throw your lot in with Alfgar and then find you were wrong?"

One of the younger thegns asked, "How do we know Gruffudd won't try to take Scrobbesbyrig? It was once a stronghold of the Wéalas – *Pengwern*, it was called. How do we know Alfgar hasn't promised him our lands if he helps him?"

Other men consulted each other. "Aye, there must be *something* in it for that Wéalas upstart."

"Gruffudd just enjoys killing Mercians."

Exhausted by the debate, Burghred leapt on a bench and called out to them all. "Enough talk – I am done with talking! All those who would follow me, meet me at the eastern gate before sundown. I ride for Tameworth this eve. Use that time to think on what will happen if you do nothing. If you are with me, then be there when I go!"

The sun faded fast and sent out a glorious blaze of pinks and golds and still no one appeared at the arranged time. The two men who manned the gate were the only companions Burghred and Beric had, and they were not exactly friendly. Burghred nervously fiddled with Aries' saddle straps to distract himself. Beric watched him with a sympathetic but irritating expression.

"They're not coming you know," called a guard from the tower. He looked down at them with a mocking grin. "You'll have to face it, lord, you're on your own. *Hæl,* Lord Alfgar!"

Burghred said nothing.

"Lord, we may have better luck elsewhere," Beric said, his toad-like eyes round with innocence.

"Come, he is right, no one is coming. Let's go, Beric. Leave the optimism for another day."

He nodded to the gatehouse boy, who jumped up to lift the locking bar and pull open the gate.

Burghred grabbed Aries' reins and steered him toward the opening. They were outside and well across the earthen ditch when they heard a voice call out to them.

"Lord Burghred!"

He turned in his saddle to see a group of riders, at least forty of them at a guess. *Forty!* Their leader wore the gear of a young thegn, a coat of mail, a polished helm, a sword, a hand axe, and a round shield across his back. He leapt from his mount and drew his sword. Burghred's hand went to his hilt. Then, to Burghred's surprise, the man went down on one knee, his sword held in both hands, offering it to Burghred who glanced in disbelief at Beric. His young servant was as astonished as he.

"Lord Burghred," the youth started to say, his expression humble, "we are not friends of Gruffudd, nor of Harald Sigurdson, and we would have fought for your father had he not betrayed your grandfather's wishes. The elders, they seem to forget Hereford, we do not. We cannot stand by and see the harm that you speak of come to our lands and our families. Nor do we want another Hereford, and for that, I, Ulric, son of Thegn Osric, would offer you my sword and my oath of fealty, and those of my retainers."

Burghred hardly believed this turn of luck. He swung a leg, slid from his horse, and went to the kneeling thegn.

Tears hovered in Burghred's eyes as he took the man's proffered sword. "Ulric, son of Thegn Osric, I accept your oath and that of your men and I accept your sword with thanks and gratitude." He kissed the sword's pommel and returned it to Ulric. "When I am Earl of Mercia, I will see that you are all well rewarded for your loyalty with land and silver. And I swear on oath that I will be a good lord to you and your men." Then he raised his *seax*, for his sword had been confiscated at Rhuddlan. "For God, for King Edward, and for the blood of Mercia!" he cried. "*Vivat Edward, Rex Anglorum! Vivat Mercia!*"

His new followers echoed his cry. Burghred turned to look at Beric. The boy grinned and Burghred's spirits lifted. At last, the tide of fortune might have swung his way.

Chapter Nineteen

Sins of the Father

Evesham, Mid-April 1058

Lady Godgifu stared at her plate with rheumy old eyes, heaving a sigh of regret, for she knew the trouble her loyal cook went to ensuring her food was of the best quality.

Her stewardess asked, "My lady, is it not to your liking this evening?"

"Heavens, Wulfgyth, the meal is well prepared and more than satisfactory. Tell Norbriht he did a fine job with the eels this eve, but of late, I have a weak stomach and so little appetite."

It was a pity, for she needed to feel strong at this time, with her beloved Leofric dead and Alfgar and his young sons in exile, she was the sole ruler of Mercia. If only she were the formidable, canny woman she used to be, with the same strength to face any challenge. Old age had weakened her. And as for Burghred... she had no idea where he'd got to.

After the debacle at Gleawecestre when Alfgar had disgraced himself, Burghred had left quite suddenly, and she had been devastated that he'd sent no word he was safe. He couldn't be in Wales, for he was dead against Alfgar's plans. It was a mystery, and she would most certainly have something to say to him when she saw him again.

Just then doors of the hall were flung open.

"My Lady Godgifu, the Lord Burghred seeks your audience," the door-thegn announced, and was pushed aside by her grandson.

Godgifu was astounded. With the assistance of her maids, she pulled herself on to shaky legs, clutching the edge of the table. Surprised murmurs hummed around the hall as heads turned toward the young man who swaggered down the aisle.

191

Godgifu's eyes narrowed. *Is it really him? Has the prodigal returned?*

He was clean-shaven and well dressed, but his skin was sallow, and he'd lost his stockiness. As he paused before the dais, she gasped at his ruined brow - a nasty, pink zigzag etched on his forehead. His eye sockets were rimmed with dark shadows and his once soft cheek bones were now sharp and hollow. He looked ill.

He gazed expectantly at her, and despite his appearance, there was a confident air about him that evoked both irritation and admiration.

"Greetings, Lady Grandmother. I pray my return finds you in good health and spirit."

Godgifu's eyes widened. *Little upstart!* she thought furiously. *How dare he show his face after he ran off without a word?*

"Mount the dais, my boy," she said, sounding pleased to see him.

She waited for him to make his way around the table, then drew him into a welcome embrace. Tears filled her eyes as she smothered the lad she had raised from a child with her kisses.

"Lord in Heaven, where in God's name have you been?" Godgifu cried, holding him at arms-length and smiling. "Do you know what it has been like here without you to comfort me?"

"Forgive me, Grandmother, I –"

"No matter, for you are home now." Tracing a finger over his scar, she searched his face, then drew back and hit him. He clutched his glowing cheek and staggered off the dais. "You brute! Don't you ever leave me again without my permission!"

A little later that evening, when Grandmother had settled into a better mood, Burghred allowed her to run her hand over the patch of short, bristly hairs that had been his tonsure. "So, you disguised yourself as a monk and escaped out of Wales and into Mercia?" From her crooked smile, Godgifu was either amused or disbelieving.

Burghred nodded and sipped the mead provided for him in the privacy of his grandmother's bower. Beyond the open shutter the twilit sky gave no answer. How had he survived the journey home? "If it were not for the good people of St Asaph's, I would have surely died. I was gravely wounded in a fight against one of the Norwægians Gruffudd had been conspiring with, and if Aldith had not helped me to escape... well, I would have been thrown to the wolves."

She sighed. "Oh Burghred, why were you fighting? That's your father in you, he was always fighting at your age, the degenerate!" His grandmother shook her head, "Honestly, my dear boy, do you want to be like him, forever getting into trouble?"

Burghred ignored the question. He hated her calling him a boy. He was almost twenty for goodness sake! "The fight was concocted to have me killed, only it worked out a little differently than they'd expected." He smiled sheepishly. "I ended up alive and my would-be-killer, dead. Nonetheless he made a good attempt."

"As I can see. But why?"

He bowed his head. "They saw me as a traitor. They didn't trust me after Hereford."

"Stuff and nonsense! Surely your father vouched for you. For heaven's sake, please do not tell me he was part of the plot to –?" She gave a loud gasp.

"I hope he wasn't, Grandmother, though how can I be sure?"

Godgifu sighed. She stroked his hair. "Burghred, did your father have reason to believe you would betray him again?"

He gazed back at her. "I – I could not support him – not when I realised what he wanted to do – the Norse, Harald Sigurdsson…"

"God above," she said, her hand clutched his. "How hard it must have been to be torn between your father and the king."

Burghred glanced up from his cup and gave her a sheepish nod.

"You have done the right thing, in turning your back on Alfgar. Nothing in this world happens that is not the will of God. Your father broke our hearts many a time. Your grandfather did not want the Godwinsons to have so much power, but he would never have condoned what Alfgar is doing now. Leofric would have hated it if he had known that Alfgar had let Aldith fall into the hands of that murderer, Gruffudd…. He died in shame of his son, but you, Burghred, can redeem the House of Leofric so your grandfather can rest in peace."

He put his hand over hers. "Lady Grandmother, I must tell you of my intentions. I seek to gain Mercia for myself, and I have just come from Tameworth, with men, and from Scrobbesbyrig, too."

"They are rallying to your side?" Excitement creased the corners of her old grey eyes.

"Not exactly. I have convinced some, mostly the younger men. I have gathered a retinue of nearly two hundred, but many others were unsure and would not come."

193

"It is a good start, my dear. You may also take fifty of my hearthmen who would go with you of their own free will, with my blessing."

Burghred slipped to his knees before taking her hand to his lips. "I will be forever in your debt, Grandmother. And I promise I *will* come back."

"Oh, no need for all that, boy. I'm coming to Gleawecestre with you. You need your grandmother to keep you out of mischief. No more getting into fights and having to disguise yourself as a monk. No, I shall see to it that you are on your most exemplary behaviour."

Rhuddlan

Alfgar's mood was not much improved by the abundance of mead on offer that evening. Still clutching a flask of the delightful, inebriating liquid, he'd retired to bed in the foulest of tempers. Throughout dinner he'd been forced to listen to Gruffudd's incessant sarcasm in respect to the whereabouts of his treacherous, missing son.

Gruffudd's voice circulated in his mind. "No doubt he has fled as he did last time, back to the Englisc king with his sorry tail between his legs. I should not have listened to you, Alfgar. I suspected all along that he was a spy, and his sudden disappearance proves that I was right."

Before he had fled, Burghred had been bed-ridden for at least two or three days, desperately ill with wound fever. The only people to have seen him were Heulyn and Aldith, who had been tending him, and the man who'd watched his door. The guard denied that he'd fallen asleep, insisting that Heulyn had given him a draft of something that had been drugged. And although the girls refuted any involvement, they were the only obvious suspects.

A servant reported Heulyn riding Burghred's horse out of the palace gates, and so the silly girl was discovered. Alfgar was relieved by her confession for it had not implicated Aldith, even though he was certain his daughter had been party to it. The normally calm and controlled Gruffudd shocked even Alfgar, when enraged, the king lay Heulyn's back naked and publicly flogged her without warning. Later, he'd heard that the girl had been found, knife in hand, her throat slit, evidently unable to live with the shame. *Serves her right. Women were always at the root of trouble.*

He looked across the room at the vacant bed where Burghred and Heulyn used to lie at night. Seeing the empty space fuelled his anger even more and he tossed one of his boots at his son's bed and shouted, "Curse you! You were as ever no use to me! I hope you rot in hell. Better you get there before I see you again!"

He was suddenly aware of a light in the darkness and the sweet smell of a female figure.

"Would you not have fled if what happened to Burghred had happened to you?" His daughter's voice was no more than a murmur. The candle flame flickered around her face, showing a worn expression, fraught with worry. It was her own fault she was troubled – not his.

"What are you doing here? Get out!" he shouted.

"I came to see if my father was in need of some comfort…." Her voice faltered.

"Your father desires to drink himself to sleep so he can forget what has happened. The last thing I need is to listen to your sanctimonious prattle!"

He gulped down a large quantity of the soothing mead. When he looked at her again, she gazed at him with disgust.

"I know it was hard for you this evening. My husband was particularly caustic tonight."

"Your husband, dear daughter, is like that every night."

"Why must you drink yourself to unconsciousness?"

"Ha – because if it hadn't been for that little shit of a brother of yours and that stupid bitch setting him free, I would not be taking his punishment for him!"

"Do you ever think of anyone but yourself? This has been a nightmare. I had to endure being interrogated for hours on end like a prisoner, not allowed any sleep or sustenance. Now I am treated like a leper. If it wasn't for poor Heulyn, then I would have been cast out!" Aldith paced the floor in anger. "Now the Norse are furious that Burghred has evaded their justice and Gruffudd blames *me* for jeopardising the whole enterprise with Magnus."

"But you *did* let him go, didn't you? It was you who helped him." She did not deny it. "You stupid girl! What about the cost to me? I must pay the blood-price for Ivar's death. If Burghred were here, *he* would be the one paying the price. And justifiably!"

"You would let your own son go to his death?"

"It was *his* fault – he need not have started that – that thing with the Norwægian."

"He didn't –" She cut herself short and was looking at him strangely. "You didn't know about it, did you?"

"Know what? What the hell are you talking about?"

For ages, it seemed, they stared at each other until Alfgar broke the silence. "Don't look at me like that."

"Like what?"

"Down your nose at me. Does it disturb you to see your father in his cups? Anyone would think you were a queen with all your airs and graces." He laughed maniacally. "Oh, but you *are* a queen, aren't you? *The* queen... Queen of this worm-hole called Wales!"

"Nay, Father, you do not disturb me, for I have seen many an idiot drinking himself drunk before. You are no exception. But you *do* disgust me. How is it that you can be so full of self-pity when others have suffered more than you?"

"Humph, you would say that, but it is not you who has to face the shame of yet again being deserted by your own son, only to find out that he is a spy and has been feeding information out of Rhuddlan to Harold Godwinson. After all I did to persuade Gruffudd to allow him a place at his hearth. Gruffudd would have had him killed if not for me!"

"Many have been hurt in this. Heulyn was used by Gruffudd to entrap Burghred and took her own life because of it. The Norwægian – he was also used and lost his life. And if Burghred had not been sent here by Harold Godwinson, he would not have –" she paused to gulp back a sob. "Father, if Burghred had not killed Ivar, then it would have been *him* lying on that floor dead."

"Pah. Burghred made his choice. Did you know that one of the spies that lump of a brother of yours was passing information to was caught and forced to confess? Who can blame Gruffudd for wanting Burghred killed," he hawked and spat in the floor rushes, "except Ivar was the one who died." He chuckled at that last. "I would have been proud of Burghred in different circumstances."

"So, you knew about the plot to kill him."

"Of course I didn't, but I know now!" he snapped. "I knew nothing about anything, more's the pity, for I would have happily killed him myself and saved the trouble it's caused had I known what he was up to."

He saw a look of incredulity in her face. "What are you looking at me like that for now?"

"Because with all that you know now, you still blame my brother for this."

"If your brother hadn't come here to spy on us in the first place, then none of this would have happened! So, you see, dear daughter, if you want someone to blame, blame your precious Burghred."

"Perhaps he would have changed his mind if he'd been given the chance! But he was not, was he? In a day or two they would have come for him and they would have wanted his blood, so his only choice was to leave! What would you have him do, lie here and wait for his death?" She covered her face with her hands and sobbed.

"He would have deserved it. Now whose blood will they accept in return?"

"It was Gruffudd who paid the blood-price – not you – and handsomely. At least that appeased them, for now. And what have you done? Nothing – nothing but get drunk every night on my husband's best mead and wine!"

Alfgar tried to get to his feet but his legs were not his own. "If I could stand, I'd whip the hide off you! It was Gruffudd's plot that went wrong, not mine. Serve him right for not telling me about it. This whole mess could have been avoided if Gruffudd had trusted me!"

"Poor Lord Alfgar. Look at you! You cannot even stand before your own daughter. You never want to take responsibility for anything you have done, Father, do you?" Her face was full of vitriol. "Perhaps if you had treated Burghred more like a son rather than an idiot, then he would have been more loyal to you." Aldith cuffed the tears that fell from her eyes. "All his life he tried to get you to love him, to trust him and to listen to him. But all you ever did was shame him, beat him and trample all over his dreams."

"Stop your bullshit, you little bitch! And never speak that *horningsunu's* name to me again. From now on I have only two sons, Edwin and Morcar. Speak no more to me of Burghred. Now, get out and leave me be!"

She retreated toward the door and Alfgar threw his other boot at her, narrowly missing her swollen belly. "Get out of my sight and take your nonsense with you! You know nothing of a man's world! Get out!"

"Yes, Alfgar! I *will* leave you! From now on you are as dead to me as Burghred is to you. You are no longer my father!"

Placing her hand protectively over her unborn child, Aldith fled from the room.

"We will see about that!" he bellowed after her.

Chapter Twenty

The Man Who Wears a Crown

May 1058, Gleawecestre
Edward never missed an opportunity to visit his palace in Kings Holme; and who wouldn't, with the Forest of Dean's lush hunting grounds at their disposal? Because of his kingly duties he'd not been in the saddle recently and would much prefer to be out riding than sitting at a board with his councillors. He imagined the creak and smell of leather and longed for the meeting to finish so he could be out among riders, the hounds barking as they sped alongside the horses; the sound of horns ringing through the trees and the hawks squawking as they flew up into the sky, let loose to hunt their quarry. The muscular effort that one must put into the exercise thrilled one's senses like nothing else could – apart from praying. But here he was, in his dull council chambers, listening to the mundane wittering of the witan. Ha, *wittering witan* was absolutely appropriate, especially when Bishop Ealdred got going. *God's beard that man can witter for the whole of Englalond!*

He sat, hands folded in his lap, bored and desperate to get out into the woods. *To hell with this tiresome warfare matter and the damned blasted Wéalas. And may God ruin Alfgar to his grave; pray it be sooner rather than later!* Why they had to spend all this time *talking* instead of *doing* he had no idea. Why couldn't they just take an army into the bleeding arsehole that was Wales, kill them all and be done with it. Then he could get on with the proper business of being king: hunting, praying, feasting, and indulging in the finer things in life.

And where is Tostig? Harold Godwinson was not as uninteresting as the gaggle of bishops, abbots, and nobles gathered around him, but he was a poor substitute for his brother. Circumstance, it seemed, had dictated that Tostig was better employed in his earldom rather than regaling Edward with his intellectual discourse at this time. Not only was Tostig attractive, fascinatingly handsome, and broadly educated, he was also the most pious of the Godwinsons. No one had as much in common with Edward as did Tostig.

Ah, Tostig... the only person who'd managed to bring light into Edward's life after the exile of his beloved Robert. That spiteful deed had been engineered by Godwin, *pater* of Edward's wife and her brood of brothers. He could see Godwin's face before him even now, smirking as Robert was forced to exile. Thank goodness the sons were not all made like their murderous, conniving father. Oh, how Edward had wept when Robert had been charged with 'ill-advising the king' and had to flee for his life. *Ill-advising indeed!* Robert had always advised him well and it had been *Robert* who had supported him over that Dover business, when Godwin had committed treason. If only I'd listened to Robert and not married into that goddamned family! *The only good thing to come from them is Tostig!*

Edward felt his eyes moisten, hating to think of that time when he'd been compelled to let Robert go. And now, Tostig was away in that dreadful northern wasteland of Northymbralond and had not been to visit him for months. How he wished Harold would spend time with him as Tostig would if he were there. He would have liked the queen's eldest brother as much as Tostig if only Harold would indulge him. But he was always too busy. He thought about ordering Harold to the north and have Tostig in Wessex. That way Tostig would be on hand night and day. But Harold, he knew, would dig his heels in and refuse to go. Refuse his king! *What utter nonsense!*

Edward, as weary as if he'd been on a four hour gallop, sat back in his throne. All that seemed to be happening was talk, talk and more talk. *By all the saints! Why was Tostig not here? He would have brought me Gruffudd's head on a platter!* The inaction of the council rankled with him as did Harold's apparent reluctance to deal with the Wéalas king far more robustly. *Harold should have hung Gruffudd three summers ago, at Billingsley, then that puss-ridden oozing boil on my backside, Alfgar, would have had nowhere to run. I would have seen* him *hung as well, were it not for the respect I had for the man's father.*

Edward checked himself, for he'd begun to mutter and almost spoke aloud as his anger rose with each thought. At least Edith was here. She had plenty to say.

It might have irked him on other days that Edith would speak on his behalf, as though he were incapable of doing so himself, but today he was happy to let her prattle if she must. It made her all the more willing to rub his feet and massage his temples later, an experience he greatly enjoyed, but would never let her know how much. That would not do. In any case, it meant that he could save his energy for more entertaining pursuits like hunting – and after, listening to his favourite minstrels. How he loved minstrels! And perhaps, some dancing. Yes, that would be most pleasant! The music of the West Country was so sweet and invigorating. Just what he would need after an afternoon of this twaddle.

Oh, and now Alfgar's brat turns up with that tiresome grandmother of his. She should have remained at her sewing, that one, instead of encouraging the lad to come here demanding favours. He sighed audibly and heads turned to him. *Oh dear,* had he spoken out loud? He smiled graciously to reassure them he was still awake, and they returned their attention to the day's business.

Edward glared at the Mercian woman and her grandson. *Who do they think they are? As if I would want a son of Alfgar, the insubordinate ogre, in charge of Mercia.*

Edward studied Burghred who was in a fervour about what was happening in Gruffudd's lair. He had a fair face, gentle even, very unlike his father. *He might seem like a decent enough lad, loyal, but bad blood runs through those veins of his, and how could he be trusted if he could turn on his own father so easily?*

The king then focussed on Harold who was studying a map with Burghred. *Well, if Harold has his way, Alfgar will probably be reinstated and Gruffudd will skulk back to his little corner of Wales with a few more lands to his name, and Burghred will probably curse Harold for promising him Mercia, and probably get himself exiled this time instead of Alfgar!* He heaved another deep sigh and once again, speculating faces turned towards him. Again he smiled sweetly. *Oh, who cares anyway? This is not a good day to be king, when the sun is shining and the air outside is warm and sweet and just calling me to a hunt. It's all too tedious for words, that's what it is. Tedious.*

All this talk of fighting the Wéalas and Alfgar left the king feeling sleepy and it was becoming increasingly difficult to keep awake as they blathered on around him. *But wait! What's that? Did someone mention that Harald of Norwæg wants to take my crown?*

Suddenly, Edward was very much awake.

Burghred gazed around the king's council chamber as he and his grandmother were permitted entrance. He felt nervous as he observed the stern faces of the clergy. Archbishops Stigand and Cynsige were there, and so was Ealdred of Worcester amongst others. Edith, the queen, cast her critical gaze over him and Burghred studied her in return. She was resplendent in her exquisite wimple of dyed silk and a flowing gown of several layers, the colour of corn flowers. Next to her, the king was sitting in his own impressive finery, and yet there was something that he lacked. His face was pale, his hands smooth, with long elegant digits. They were soft compared to those of men like Harold and Gyrth, whose hands were manly and large enough to firmly grip a two-handed axe. It was hard to imagine the king wielding an axe or a sword. He wore the garb of a monarch, but the image of a warrior-king who led his men into battle was absent. When he looked at Harold, he saw a king. When he looked at Edward, he saw a man in pretty clothes wearing a crown.

Burghred was permitted to address Edward. All eyes turned towards him. Mostly they seemed curious, but some appeared hostile. Was he being judged? He was, after all, the son of a traitor.

"My Lord King, I wish to speak with you about important matters that concern the realm and your crown; but first I must make my claim to the earldom of Mercia."

Edward sighed. The king's indifference exasperated Burghred. Was it too much for the king to at least acknowledge him respectfully?

Instead it was Harold who spoke. "Burghred, perhaps you can relay to our Lord King Edward the news from Rhuddlan."

Burghred told his tale. He did not go into the events that had led him to flee. He did, however, tell them about Gruffudd and Alfgar's alliance with the Norse. Looking around at the different faces, some looked interested, others appeared indifferent, and some stared at him as though he were nothing but a tiresome child seeking attention.

"Tell us something we don't already know," Lord Gyrth said rather rudely with the lift of an eyebrow that Burghred had previously observed to be a Godwin trait.

All eyes were upon him as he sought to answer appropriately. *What is wrong with them? Is what I have said already not concerning enough for them?*

Frustration rose within him. The West Seaxans amongst them looked down their noses at him. Grandmother smiled encouragingly at him. "Tell them about Magnus, Burghred," she said in her sharp voice.

Burghred told them. At that point, the king burst into life.

"Good God! Lords, we must do battle with these vile heathens! *Oust* me indeed! Who does this Magnus think he is?" Edward exclaimed. The king had lost his previous docile bearing and was now mortified.

The bishops flocked around the king to reassure him. His kinsman, FitzWimarc, offered him words of support, and Edith mopped his brow. All, it seemed, were outraged to hear this news. A disdainful look flashed across Earl Harold's face as he looked at Edward. *He* did not fuss over the distressed king, Burghred noted.

"Magnus is the son of King Harald of Norwæg," Burghred said, once calm returned.

He saw that Gyrth looked at him again with his eyebrow raised. Feeling unnerved, Burghred relayed them the story that Ivar had told the alliance in Rhuddlan.

"Such ridiculous nonsense," Edith said. "A child could make up a more convincing story than that. Speaking of children, that is exactly what this Magnus is. He is no threat. Just a boy of thirteen, not much more."

"Well, lords," coughed the Earl of Wessex. "Let us get to work." Harold unrolled a large piece of vellum and spread it on the table.

"How many are there of these Norse?" Harold asked Burghred, placing weights on the four corners of the map. "We have heard that Harald Sigurdsson is in Denmark, attempting to take it by force and failing."

"Yes, as you all know, lords, Denmark was part of Harthacnut's kingdom, just as this country was, and as the so-called heir to Harthacnut's kingdoms, Sigurdsson believes he has the right to take them both. He is currently very much occupied in Denmark so he cannot come himself, but has sent his son, Magnus, to take the Englisc crown for him." Burghred paused. He licked his dry lips and shifted uncomfortably as sweat ran down his chest inside his tunic. He felt the opportunity of a discussion about Mercia slipping away.

Gyrth repeated his brother's question. "So, how many of them? Surely Harald would have the bulk of his army with him in Denmark?"

"Magnus has his own men. Men that follow him. Yes, I know that he is just a boy, but even so, it seems he is going to be a force to be reckoned with. I am not aware of the numbers he will be providing, but he has ships and crews in the Orkneys and on the Isle of Mann, and allies that can be called upon from Dyfflin, so it is likely to be a substantial amount." Burghred pointed to where he knew Magnus' men to be waiting on the map.

"Then it will be many thousands probably," Gyrth said grimly.

"And there is more than one route they will come," Harold concluded.

Burghred nodded. "They will come by Ceaster, just like they did three years ago. Gruffudd will most likely come through the mouth of the Sæfren and into the Esc here," Burghred laid a finger on the map, "from Caerleon, his southern stronghold. Or – he may venture further, and sail into the River Wæg, here," again pointing on the map, "to wait for orders and then sail into the Sæfren, and up toward Gleawecestre. Their aim is to have the Englisc fyrd surrounded."

"We must stop them," the king said, his voice aquiver. "Once, the Danes came for my father Æthelred's crown - now it seems the Norse are coming for mine!"

Surprisingly, Harold ignored the king and remained focused on the map. "And what of the more north-eastern lands of Mercia, will there be no army coming from there?"

Burghred shook his head. "Possibly, it depends."

"On what?" Harold asked.

"The Mercians. If they heed my father's call, then they will come, mustering in Scrobbesbyrig." Burghred's heart skipped a beat. Mercia would be lost to him unless he was declared earl. "My Lord King!" Burghred cried, turning his whole body to face Edward. "Invest in me the earldom of Mercia, and I will bring those men to *you*!"

There was a pause in which silence prevailed and eyes viewed him starkly. Should he go down on his knees?

Harold spoke, "You have done well coming here today." The touched Burghred's shoulder. "I know it cannot have been easy for you to betray your father, but you have done what is good and right."

"Thank you for your praise, lord; but I would that my actions were rewarded as you promised." Burghred gazed hopefully at Harold, then at the king.

"How many men do you bring with you?" Harold asked.

It was as though Harold was the king's mouthpiece.

"Two hundred and fifty good Mercian warriors, my lord, including thegns from Scrobbesbyrig; though I wish I could tell you that all the men of that burgh are for the king, I cannot. But the ones I have brought with me are those that are loyal."

Harold looked thoughtful, stroking his chin. "So, that is why Wulfgar has not answered my summons." Harold stared at the map, thinking. Then he turned to Burghred and said, "You have proved yourself a true loyal subject to your anointed king in carrying out such a dangerous task, Burghred, and you will be justifiably rewarded. But what of the other men that Mercia can call upon?"

"I only had a few days, I'm sure that if I had more time, and an endorsement from the king, then they could be persuaded. Once some start to follow, the rest will come. I have done as you asked, lord. I have dishonoured my father, endangered my sister, I almost died in the effort. You promised me Mercia would be mine if I did this."

"I would not put it quite that way," Harold said with a smile.

"You need to prove yourself, young man. You cannot expect an earldom just because you betrayed your father," Queen Edith said. Next to her, Edward appeared deep in his own thoughts. His head pressed against his fist, the king muttered inaudibly to himself.

The Story of King Cnut came to Burghred's mind. When Cnut had become king, he executed those who had switched sides to join him. Cnut saw them as breakers of oaths - men who could never be trusted. Is this what they were thinking of *him?*

"I betrayed my father in loyalty to my king, is that not enough? Besides, the blood of Mercian nobles flows through my veins, it is my birthright. Appoint me the earldom and the men must come to me!"

"Not necessarily… but," Harold began, looking thoughtful, "my Lord King, what he says is true. He does have the blood of Mercian nobles, and Alfgar's defection has left a vacancy. What say you, Lord Edward, if Burghred can rally the rest of Mercia to his banner, then he may take the earldom?"

The king held up a hand. "Granted," Edward said, flatly. "I call this council ended," and followed it with a deep yawn.

Harold said. "There, it is done. Go to Mercia and rally the men to their king, before they rally to Alfgar, especially Scrobbesbyrig. We will need Scrobbesbyrig on our side. Take it by force if you have to."

"Thank you, my lord," Burghred said. He was disappointed, but he supposed this was as good as it got for now. It meant that he would have to ride again for Mercia. It was a test. If he could take Scrobbesbyrig he would prove himself worthy.

Burghred gave a light bow and he turned leave.

Harold said to him, "I wish you luck, lad. And I pray that Alfgar does not get there before you."

*

"You two have the faces of men who have just been told to lick the king's balls. What ails the pair of you?" Harold asked his brothers as they walked together to their private quarters.

"You promised that you would help me secure Mercia," Gyrth said. "And now you are dangling the prize in front of Burghred."

Harold looked at Leofwin. "And you?"

Leofwin returned Harold's gaze sheepishly. "Well... I *was* to have East Anglia if Gyrth was elected to Mercia."

Harold stopped abruptly. "Aye, we have talked about it – but it will not be *our* decision. It will be for the king and the witan to decide." He folded his arms. "And we may have to consider that Burghred might also be in the running... as well as Alfgar."

"Alfgar?" Gyrth and Leofwin crowed in unison.

"The devil take him!" Gyrth spat in the grass. "What are you talking about?"

"Mercia may only accept Alfgar." Harold said. "Remember, he is as slippery as Gruffudd. He came back once before, did he not?"

"Aye," Gyrth nodded, "and failed to redeem himself. People have long memories – they will remember Hereford."

"That may be so, but as Leofric's grandson, Burghred has just as good a claim," Harold said.

"I thought you would support your brothers, Harold. After all, it will strengthen our position within the realm," Gyrth said. He sneered. "Tostig said that you wouldn't support me - and he was right. He said that you would be afraid that I would command as much power as yourself and that you would not like it –"

"Is that what you really think?" Harold snapped. "Look at both of you – you are like two crows waiting to pick at dead carcasses."

Leofwin stepped between them, his arms about their shoulders. "Brothers, let's not argue amongst ourselves – especially not here where we can be seen by everyone." He nodded over to where men were being put through their paces on the sward. "Harold is right,

Gyrth. The Mercians are a powerful entity, they will have their way. If they choose Burghred over Alfgar, then perhaps it would be the lesser evil."

Harold had never seen Gyrth looking so grim as he said, "'Tis not about which one is better, father or son, it's about *us* – the sons of Godwin. We are more fit to rule than either of them. Besides, one has only to look at the father to know that the son is not worthy."

Anxious and weary, Harold sighed. The morning's *Witenagemót* had been tiring, and he did not need his brothers bickering. Why was it so hard to keep everyone content? The king had urged him to go hunting and he had promised him that he would, but all he wanted to do was lie down and think of Eadgyth. "Can we not do this now?"

Gyrth, it seemed, was determined to ignore him. "Harold, the Mercians like us not, but with a Godwinson in the post, their minds may change."

"As Tostig has changed the minds of the men of Northymbralond?" Harold asked.

"You know that I have always wanted Mercia," Gyrth grumbled. "If Tostig was here, he would support me."

"Christ on the Cross! I have had a gutful of listening to what Tostig has to say. Tostig is not here, is he? We must be seen to be fair and just. Burghred has a right to prove himself worthy of Mercia and the Mercians have a right to nominate a leader. We already have enemies who say we want to turn Edward into a puppet-king, that we lust for power more than we wish to serve our country. We must tread carefully. We must prove to our doubters that we want what is best for the kingdom, not ourselves. If my brothers want lands and glory, they – and Burghred – must prove themselves – just as I have had to do. That is what Father would have said, and what he would have wanted."

"'Tis nothing for you to say that Harold; you have authority over a land that stretches in the south from west to the east. You pick up earldoms like the rest of us pick up coughs and colds." Gyrth stood, feet apart, his hands formed into fists by his side.

Harold rounded on his brother. "If you think it is that easy to govern an earldom as big as Wessex, I will gladly give you some of it."

"Our brother is right, Gyrth."

"Gah, you always take *his* side." Gyrth jerked his head at Harold and turned to Leofwin. "Harold was younger than all of us when he was invested with East Anglia. Is it not time he supported *you*, just as Father supported *him*?"

"Have you not listened to a word I have said, Gyrth?" Harold intervened. "I would not have it said that I am using our family's reputation to gain favour. There are enough men in this land who already believe we are power hungry, self-seeking, and grasping. I want to see Leofwin flourish as I do all my brothers, but I will not walk over good men to get what we want. We must uphold the laws and traditions of this land."

"Keep your goddamned support to yourself, then!" Gyrth snarled and skulked away, watched by others, grunting various oaths.

"Don't worry about Gyrth, brother, he will get over it," Leofwin said, a hand on Harold's arm.

Harold shook his head. "I hate this fighting, especially in public." Harold nodded at some men staring on the sward. "I fear that our brother has spent too much time with Tostig over the years. Every time we argue it is Tostig I hear coming out of his mouth… Ach, it will pass, you are right, Leofwin. I just wish Gyrth would not be so quick to temper."

Harold rested an arm on his brother's shoulder, and they resumed their walk.

"Do you think that Burghred will do it? Rally Mercia, that is?" Leofwin asked.

"Who knows? I think he would make a good leader, but he is untried yet. And do I think Mercia would choose him over Alfgar? No, I think not. But they might choose him over a Godwin. I do not believe that Mercia will ever have a Godwinson as earl. That is why I think Gyrth would be foolish to hanker after it."

Leofwin looked at him with surprised eyes. "You think Mercia will truly turn against the king and betray their country?"

Harold shrugged. "Where are the Mercians now? Not one thegn, apart from those who came with Burghred, heeded the call to attend the war council. They might be hedging their bets – but I'd wager my horse they are waiting for Alfgar. If Burghred *can* convince them, then with the king's orders to back him, perhaps they might come, though I am not convinced. Now, brother, we shall not worry ourselves with such things, we have more important issues to consider: a king who wants to hunt. Let's leave Mercia's fate to the spinners for the time being."

Chapter Twenty-one

The Wolf Banner Rises

Hechestone, end of May 1058

Freyda squealed with laughter as Æmund tickled her swollen belly. The unborn child responded, its little body moving within her. Æmund, his eyes round like two full moons, gave a cry of delight.

He rested his head on the pregnant mound of her stomach. "Hey, you in there, stop giving your mother trouble. You're keeping her awake at night, not to mention your papa too. We hardly got a wink of sleep." He looked up at her and flashed an endearing smile. "Do you know – I swear I saw his foot just then."

"*His* foot? So, our baby is a boy, is she?"

"What else? I come from a long line of them. My father was a boy, my grandfather was too, and his father, and –"

"I suppose you are going to tell me that your mother and grandmother were boys too?" laughed Freyda, pulling the covers up with a shiver. Though the days grew warmer, early mornings retained their overnight chill, despite the thick curtains that enclosed their sleeping chamber.

Æmund jumped naked from the bed and went to relieve himself. He looked over his shoulder as he splashed into the bucket. "My father always said my mother's face was hairier than his backside. And my grand –"

"Æmund, stop that! I do not care for your tales of hairy-faced women and your father's backside," she threw a pillow at him, then said, as little white goose feathers exploded everywhere, "I need to tell you something."

He rubbed his head as like snowflakes, the feathers fell about him, the corners of his mouth turned down in mock sadness. What is it you want to tell me, *luflic?"*

He was back on the bed, rubbing her knees.

"I want you to take me –"

"What? Now? It's way past sunrise and we must get up. Did you not have your fill of Lord Alfgar last night? We cannot lay abed all day, much as I would like to, but Alfgar, well look at him, he's as lifeless as a side of pig hanging in the rafters!" Æmund illustrated this fact by rising onto his knees, his limpness lying flaccid in his hand.

"Æmund! Put on your braies! And put Lord Alfgar inside them and listen to what I have to say! I want you to take me to –"

"Sweeting, I have told you many a time, fyrd training is no place for the pregnant wife of a thegn."

She touched a finger to his lips. "Can you not keep quiet for a moment? Let me speak, for the sake of the saints!"

"Ladies must not blaspheme, especially when with child. You may corrupt our son before he is even born." He pulled her to him and tried to kiss her and she pushed him away, tutting in frustration.

Picking up her knife from her bedside board, she held it out to him. "Hearken to me now, Æmund Leofnothson, or I am going to cut off your Lord Alfgar and nail it to the porch for all to see!"

"Hell's fire, Freyda, I do believe you would, too!"

"Are you going to listen?"

Æmund bit his bottom lip like a naughty child. Freyda held back a smile and the desire to melt into his arms.

"What is it you want to ask me, *leoftost?* I can resist you nothing."
She hesitated.

He put a reassuring hand on her arm. "You know I will try to provide you with whatever it is you need."

She stroked his face, smiling. "I do not need anything, Æmund. I have everything I need in you and the child, but… I want to go home, I mean, to Horstede. I did not tell you, but a few days ago, a message came from my father. Mother is ill, and my sister and Sigfrith need help around the homestead.

"But you have little more than two months before our baby comes. It will be too much for you."

"I would not go if I did not think my mother was truly unwell. You know my feelings about her, but I cannot expect Winflæd to cope with everything while Father is away with the fyrd. She is barely out of childhood. It is for her sake that I ask this."

"What of Sigrid, or whatever her name is? Can she not take care of things? And what of the troll – the female ogre? Gunnhild? What is *she* doing to help? And your brother, Tovi, surely he can do something?"

Freyda shook her head. "Father said that Sigfrith has also been ill and is still recovering, and as for Tovi, do you not recall that I told you he has been sent to school? Winflæd needs me at Horstede, Æmund. I can have the baby there if needs be. You will be gone for two months. I will be safe there. *We* will be safe, your daughter and I." She smiled faintly.

"*My son*," he said with rare gravity.

"*Yes*, husband," she lowered her gaze to appear submissive, "*your son*."

Æmund lifted her chin and she looked directly into his eyes. She thought he was about to give in to her pleas, but they were both distracted by the sound of a horn. He jumped out of bed and pulled on his trousers, then disappeared through the partition. Freyda sighed. Any chance that she could have convinced him to take her to Horstede was gone. She lay back heavily against the bolster, her hand on the swell of her belly. A moment later he appeared through the curtains scrabbling frantically on the floor.

"What is it?" she asked.

"The fyrd is mustering,"

"I cannot believe that time of year has come already. Seems like only yesterday you got back from court."

He hastily threw his tunic over his head. "No, Freyda, you don't understand, the fyrd is mustering for war. Last year Lord Alfgar, the real one, got himself exiled –"

"Again?"

"Aye," Æmund nodded as he wound his *winningas* about his legs. "And he has gone into Wales to gather an army."

"Oh God in Heaven, Æmund, does this mean…" She heaved herself out of bed to help him with his boots.

"All I know is that the Norþmenn are threatening to invade and Alfgar and Gruffudd are allied with them."

Freyda threw her arms around him and sobbed. She felt him tremble and it scared her. "I might never see you again!"

"Don't fret, *leoftost*. It may not come to war. I shall be back in time for our son to be born." He kissed her before pulling on his boots.

"But I need to go to Horstede," she said.

He gripped her shoulders. "I cannot take you, not now." He released her, turned, and disappeared through the curtains.

She pulled on her under-tunic and hastily covered her hair. As quickly as her encumbered body allowed, she collected some bread and cheese from last night's leftovers. Freyda wrapped it in some linen and dropped it into a pouch with a flask of ale.

Outside, the men were waiting for him. Freyda's heart skipped a beat as he stood in his mail tunic, strapping on his sword. He was very desirable in his war gear. Oh, how she wished she could have taken him back inside and loved him again before he left her.

Leofnoth called to her. "So there you are, my pretty one."

"Father." Freyda greeted Leofnoth with a smile and another for the men that accompanied him.

"*Wæs hæl*, daughter." Leofnoth kissed her cheek.

Her father-in-law grew craggier every time she saw him. How was it that he was still going to muster at his age? "I am well, sir."

"And how fares my grandson?"

"Your granddaughter does well, my lord, as do I. What is so urgent that you take my husband from me when he has only just come home? Is it true about the Norþmenn? What is happening?"

"We go to meet with the fyrd. Alfgar and Gruffudd are stirring up trouble again. It seems they may have allied themselves with Magnus of Norwæg ." Leofnoth's expression worried her, for she rarely saw him so serious.

The Norþmenn. Freyda had heard the terrible stories about the ferocity of such an enemy. She looked over at the men helping Æmund. Seeing all his trappings being loaded on to the wagon, she sighed, for it brought home the fact that she was now a *hlafdige*, the wife of a thegn. And she was pregnant, and her husband was going to war.

"Do you go to meet my father? Can you take me to Horstede?" she asked.

Æmund appeared by her side. "Tell her *no*, Father." He took her arm and looked at her sternly. "She cannot ride in her condition."

Leofnoth shrugged apologetically. "'Tis not possible, Freyda. Besides, we go to meet your father at Fletching, not Horstede. And – Æmund is right, you have the child to think about."

Æmund embraced her and lectured her on the dangers of riding whilst heavily pregnant.

As though he would know.

"Take care of my son, *min leoftost.*" He touched his lips and threw her a kiss.

"I will look after your daughter, do not fear!"

Freyda stood at the gate and waved goodbye with watery eyes, wishing that she could feel his skin against hers one last time. She watched the war party go until they were no more than a glimmer in the sun's rays. He was gone and there had been barely time for her to accept that he might never return. Her child might never meet its father. *And I might never see my own father again.*

The sadness soon turned to weeping and she sat in the grass, consumed by grief. After a while, thoughts of Æmund were replaced by thoughts of her family. For the first time since she'd left Horstede she longed for her mother; for the comforting arms of Sigfrith and the sweet smiles of her sisters. A loud sob burst from her as she thought of Winflæd trying so hard to run the household. In her mind, she was running through the woods, carefree and as full of joy as when she had been a little girl.

If she could not be with Æmund, she wanted to be with her family. She must go home.

*

Horstede

Upon his return home from his courtly duties in Westmynstre, Wulfhere found his wife listless in her bed, refusing to rise, neither eating nor speaking, and Winflæd. running the household. Ealdgytha had lain like that, Winflæd told him, for days and no one knew what troubled her. Sigfrith had suggested sending for Gunnhild, but Wulfhere had been loath to and instead sent word to Freyda. He knew his daughter would be heavily pregnant by now, but thought it better, even in her condition, than to inflict Gunnhild on them all.

The call to arms came swiftly and soon Tigfi came for them.

Wulfhere watched his excited sons readying themselves with mixed emotion, as they polished their weapons and greased their mail. No longer apprentices, boys practicing at war, they would presently march into battle.

Wulfhere thought back to when he had stood before his own father, helm and hauberk polished until the blood had run from his knuckles. He remembered the words he had spoken: "To see a son live to grow to manhood, see him stand shoulder to shoulder with the men of the shieldwall is a moment given to us only by God." It was one of the rare instances that he had seen his father ever show any emotion other than anger. "Remember this moment when your own son joins you in the shieldwall. Granting that God gives you a son and he lives beyond the cradle."

As he reflected on those prophetic words, Wulfric and Wulfwin presented themselves to him, grinning widely, their gear gleaming as they clutched their spears and shields. No longer were they the gangling adolescents of two years ago, all limbs and auburn fluff. Now in their sixteenth year, they were tall and wiry, with clean shaven chins and a handsomeness that would catch any girl's eye. He blinked a tear and wished that their grandfather had lived to see them standing in the ranks of warriors. But even though his heart swelled with pride, there was a sense of foreboding, knowing only too well the frailty of men who went into battle.

It was time to leave and having tried and failed to get a response from Ealdgytha, he'd kissed her expressionless face and left her staring into space. He'd paused before the door just long enough to notice a tear escape from the corner of her eye. The idea he was to blame for her wretchedness touched him fleetingly, then he forced the thought away. He could not let his guilt torture him all his life, could he?

He said a hasty farewell to his daughters and had to pull Gerda giggling from his neck. Folk were saying their farewells to the boys and he watched envious, as Tigfi swept an adoring Sigfrith into his arms and made his customary promise to return and marry her, a promise only Sigfrith seemed optimistic about. Wulfhere yearned to have a wife who would hold him and kiss him lovingly, just as Sigfrith kissed her huscarle. The longing left him with the familiar ache that only a woman could ease.

Wulfhere was the last to mount and as he swung his leg over Hwitegast's saddle, he heard Winflæd calling him. "Wait, Father! Don't go yet!" she cried, running back to the hall, shouting, "I cannot believe that I'd almost forgotten!"

In a few moments, she returned. "Sigfrith helped me fix it for you."

She smiled, breathless as she held something folded in her hand out for him to take. "You can't even see where the joins are."

Wulfhere slipped from the saddle, took the linen, and unfurled it.

"Do you like it?" his daughter asked eagerly as Wulfhere fingered the piece of amber fixed to the image of the wolf. "I thought it would be good for his eye."

Wulfhere felt her gaze on him as he pondered the banner that had once belonged to his father.

"You can take it with you now. 'Tis all done. I wish I could see how it will look when it is held aloft."

"Then you shall, my little one. Yrmenlaf! Give me your spear."

"My lord." Yrmenlaf dismounted and handed his weapon to Wulfhere.

Wulfhere clasped the long shaft between his legs and laced the banner near the spearhead. He raised it aloft, waving it so it the running wolf fluttered above their heads.

"There! The wolf runs into battle again," he proclaimed proudly. "You, Yrmenlaf, shall be my standard bearer."

The lad took the spear from his lord, his excitement obvious by the grin on his face. He looked over at his Uncle Ælfstan who nodded his approval.

Winflæd gasped as she looked up at the banner flapping in the warm summer breeze. Its amber eye shone in the blazing sunshine. Wulfhere recalled that he and his daughter had first found the banner in his mother's old chest, unopened until after her passing. It had been battered and torn, used to march into battle by their forefathers and cast aside in favour of something more Christian. Winflæd had promised to fix it for him so he could once again raise it in honour of his ancestors, the *Wulfsuna*.

Wulfhere placed an arm across her shoulders. "Thank you, little *Fleógenda*," he said and bent down to kiss the top of her head. "It will fly proudly for your father, thegn of Horstede and will protect us in battle as it protected our Wolf fathers."

Waldron

"Where is your lady, good fellow?"

Welan, about to bring the axe blade down onto a log, stopped mid-chop. His eyes were large in his thin weasel face as he stared in surprise at Wulfhere.

"M-my lord, are-are you not heeding the call to arms?" he asked.

"I'm on my way. I wanted to see her before I went. So - Lady Ælfgyva - call her for me, man, will you?"

"My lord, you have not heard?" Welan's expression darkened and

Wulfhere felt his heart quicken, thinking that some dreadful thing had befallen her.

"What? Tell me what has happened!"

Welan leant on his axe. "The Lady Ælfgyva and her daughter have gone from here. She was wed nigh on three months ago, to Lord Hemming. She resides with him in Scheringaham. She has left the homestead to me. I am her tenant now."

Wulfhere's face prickled and his heart contracted as Welan's words hit. Even so, he kept his expression blank, hiding his disappointment. But the feeling only lasted momentarily, recalling the last time he'd seen her, the day she came for the child. She'd changed from the woman she'd once been. It had been over then, and remnants were all that existed now, of a love long dead.

But was that a glimmer of resentment that flashed in the little woodman's eyes? Could it be that the little woodcutter had hoped that Ælfgyva would give herself to him after all these years? Wulfhere understood it if the man felt rejected. After all, Welan's service to Ælfgyva can only have been borne out of love, for he owed her no dues.

"Do not regret her going, Master Welan. She would tempt the moon out of the sky if it had a cock between its legs," Wulfhere said, feeling as though he should have known all along.

"I served her gladly, lord, and wanted nothing in return. There was nothing dishonourable about my regard for her. She was kind to me, that was all. I would have done anything for her... and the lytlings too, and not ask for anything... and I asked her not."

Welan turned away, coolly carried on chopping.

Wulfhere was suddenly filled with a need to explain himself. "I would that things could have been different for her... for us. I would have..."

Welan stopped what he was doing, a reproachful look on his face. Wulfhere went to say more, but thinking better of it, muttered, "Good day to you, woodsman," and left through the gate.

So, she was finally gone. Gone from his life forever. And with her, his daughter, Wulfhild. They belonged to someone else now.

He took Hwitegast's reins; he was free of her at last. Riding hard to catch up with the rest of his men, his heart felt lighter, as if the part of it that was filled with the Lady of Waldron, no longer weighed him down.

Chapter Twenty-two

The Disobedient Wife

June 1058

"He's going to be sorely unhappy with me, Mistress Freyda. His orders were that I was to not let you go anywhere while he was away."

As she came out of the porch, dressed for travel and carrying a rolled bundle of her things, her husband's reeve stood before looking uncomfortable.

"I understand your concern, Ulfer," Freyda said, "but I promise I shall tell my husband it was no fault of yours and that I wilfully disobeyed his orders."

"He said I was to restrain you if you should try to leave, my lady."

The worried look on the reeve's face amused her, and she chuckled. "Goodness! Do you want me to give birth before my time?"

Ulfer backed away shaking his head and muttered, "I don't like it, Mistress, there will be trouble when the lord gets home."

"No doubt there will be, Ulfer, but never you mind. Rymenhild, you can accompany me if you wish, but if not, I shall go alone."

Rymenhild sighed and rolled her eyes. "Well, I best go with you then; my lord Æmund will have my guts for garters if I don't. But if I *am* going, I insist that my Uncle Tatwine come with us as he knows the forest tracks well and will get us there safely. He's handy with a bow and arrow, is my uncle, if needed."

And so, as hazy sunshine bled through the great green canopy of leaves, Freyda and her companions rode at a careful pace along the road that led to Horstede. Rymenhild huffed and puffed for the best part of the journey, making derogatory comments about having to ride on horseback when a cart would have been far more comfortable.

"It would have been much better for you, too, my lady. Better than all this jogging and jigging about on a horse."

"You know why we have to go by saddle, Rymenhild, the wagons were commandeered by the fyrd, so stop your complaining. I didn't force you to come. You're welcome to turn around and go back to Hechestone if you wish."

Midday came. Freyda was anxious to make better time, as they were not even half-way there yet, what with Rymenhild and her uncle riding old nags and struggling to keep up. Her maid had suggested at several points along the way that they stop to rest and partake of some refreshments, but Freyda had pressed them on. Now, however, she was beginning to feel exhausted. Riding to Horstede in her condition was not such a good idea after all. She cushioned the pommel of her saddle to make it more pliable against her belly, but the rocking motion of the horse's gait was causing the baby to press against her innards. Trying to ignore the increasing pain, she continued on until Rymenhild, suspecting something was amiss, grabbed the reins from her, demanding that they stop.

"Nay." Freyda glared at her. "Let go. I told you we will rest when I am satisfied we are making good time."

Rymenhild's mouth was open, ready to argue, when Freyda let out an agonising groan.

"Uncle Tatwine!" called Rymenhild. "We are stopping! The mistress is in pain!"

Freyda fell forward onto the mare's neck, panting. The agony in her abdomen tore over her belly like a thousand burning hot pokers, taking her breath away. She felt nauseous and faint, and something burst within her.

"Dear Jesus and all the saints," cried Rymenhild.

Freyda slid from the saddle and Rymenhild and her uncle gently assisted her.

"God in Heaven!" cried Rymenhild as blood rushed from between Freyda's legs, flooding her clothing.

Freyda cried out, her scream heartrending in her own ears. *Oh God, don't let it be…*

*

Winflæd dabbed at Freyda's forehead as she lay feverish and pale as death. The midwife, Beorhthild, clicked her tongue as she and Sigfrith fought to stop the bleeding, packing Freyda's nether regions with as many linen towels they could find. Her sister had been gushing blood since her arrival in Horstede in the early hours of that morning. She'd been brought there on a makeshift stretcher of willow and hazel branches, and clutched in the arms of the maid was the lifeless body of a boy child, perfectly formed, though underdeveloped, and without the strength to fight for his life.

"She is losing too much blood," Beorhthild said, shaking her head grimly.

"I am going to die," Freyda whispered. With great effort she grasped for Winflæd's hand.

Winflæd held her sister's pale, bloodless hand to her lips and kissed it. "No, dear, sweet Freyda. Just lie still and rest. It will not help you to think of dying."

Freyda turned tear-filled eyes to look at her. Her lids drooped weakly. "I came to look after you... and Mother... and just look at me. It is my fault my son is dead, and now, I am dying...."

Winflæd gave her a sip of water to moisten her chapped lips.

"Hush," she pleaded. "Save your energy."

Freyda tried to sit up. "I deserve to die," she said in a despairing voice and collapsed against the bolster. "I destroyed the life of my child... my son – Æmund's son. He was right, it *was* a little boy." She was so weak, her breaths laboured. "Mother – where is my mother? I would see her one last time before God takes me."

Sigfrith looked up from where she was attempting to stem the flow of blood with soaked, stained linen. "Get her, Winflæd," she ordered.

A sob escaped from Winflæd's throat. "Is she –?"

"Go!" insisted Sigfrith. She waved an arm at her. "Drag her out of her bed if you have to – tell her that her daughter has great need of her!"

Winflæd flew across the yard, through the porch of the longhall, and up the staircase, the wood creaking as her feet pounded on every other step. She ploughed into the bedchamber and thrust open the curtains of the sleeping area. Cuthburga, who sat mending clothes, looked up startled as Winflæd alternated between coaxing, begging, and demanding her mother get up.

The woman on the bed lay unresponsive, her eyes glazed, transfixed on the rafters as if she were in a different world.

In a gentle voice, Cuthburga said, "Little mistress, your mother is weakened by her condition – see, she cannot hear you let alone heed you. You may as well go back to your sister."

Winflæd threw herself across her mother. Sobs wracked her thin frame as she begged. "Please, Mother, Freyda needs you!"

When no sound or movement came, Winflæd grabbed her shoulders and shook her but her eyes remained expressionless, her head flopping. There was never a timelier moment when Aunt Gunnhild's presence wouldn't have gone amiss. If anyone could stir her into life, Gunnhild could.

"Please! Freyda is so sick and calling for you." Winflæd shook her again. "Mother! She has lost her child... she is.... *Mother*, your daughter is dying!"

Cuthburga stood and approached her. Pulling Winflæd close, she said, "Leave her, little mistress, she cannot be roused. She is in a melancholic state. You can do nothing now. It is *you* your sister needs now."

Her cheeks swamped with tears, Winflæd moved to the doorway. She paused, her hand on the latch and turned back.

"You selfish woman!" she yelled. "You lie here, sleeping, never wanting to get out of bed, hoping that you'll just rot and die whilst my sister, who has everything to live for, lies weak unto death, calling for her mother to come comfort her. Why don't you ask God to take *you* instead?"

"Winflæd! You should not speak so to your mother! She is..."

"She is what, ill? Nay, Cuthburga, I think not. 'Tis only the sickness of her soul. The cure for that is to get up and start living again and see to her dying daughter. *She*," waving a hand at Ealdgytha, "has everything to live for yet just waits for death, and Freyda, who cries out to live and has lost her child, is dying!"

Winflæd's sudden outburst jolted some corner of her mother's mind and she sprang up. Then, as if she thought better of it, lay back down again, pulling the covers up under her chin.

Winflæd moved towards her. "All right then, feel sorry for yourself. Stay there and die. But do not expect anyone to weep for you, least of all me. You think you are the only person who has suffered in your life?"

Mother turned stark eyes on her. "No, you're not! Everyone has their sufferings, but life still goes on!"

Cuthburga protested. Winflæd ignored her. Breathing in quick, exhausted breaths, she turned on her heel and strode to leave.

"Winflæd?"

She whirled around. Mother was getting out of bed! "Please, wait for me. I am coming."

Two weeks later
Winflæd watched, her heart heavy, as Freyda knelt at the tiny grave made for her little boy.

Placing flowers by the little wooden cross, Freyda sobbed, saying through her tears, "Æmund will hate me. He couldn't even see him before we put him in the ground. And the poor little mite wasn't even baptised or given a name. He will not go to Heaven."

Ealdgytha crouched down beside her and swathed her with comforting arms. "*Min dohtor.*"

That Mother did not chastise her sister for the loss of her babe was a miracle to Winflæd. Her daughter's plight seemed to have struck a flame within Mother and brought her back to life. And the mere fact Freyda had survived the miscarriage, she knew, was also a miracle. She did not know that day what marvel had caused this to be, but she was certain God's hand was in it.

Heart breaking, Winflæd knelt down on Freyda's other side and her sister clasped her hand and drew her to her so that the three of them were enclosed together, reconciled in their despair.

"We must give him a name," Mother said.

"But Æmund – He is not here to name him. We hadn't even talked about names and now…"

"What would he have wanted to call him?" Winflæd asked. "I don't know…"

"Then why don't we call him for Æmund?" suggested Ealdgytha.

Freyda, her tears abating, was thoughtful for a moment and then said, "Eadric. His grandfather was Eadric. Æmund had talked fondly of him."

Mother said, "Then let us pray for Eadric's soul, that despite not being baptised, God will still take him into his heavenly embrace."

"Aye, Eadric, we shall pray for him." Winflæd clasped her hands together and the two older women followed suit.

God please take this little soul into your arms. It was not his fault he did not make it to be baptised. Perhaps you can see it in your heart to accept him into heaven so his soul shall not be in peril. And I give thanks to you, dear Lord, for saving my sister and healing my mother so that we can once again be a family together in your heavenly light.

Winflæd finished her prayer asking God for his protection over their men folk who were, perhaps, fighting a great battle at that very moment not knowing that their women had overcome a great battle of their own.

Part Three

Battle for A Kingdom

1058

Chapter Twenty-three

Treachery

June 1058, Scrobbesbyrig

It was mid-afternoon on the day after Burghred had ridden out from Gleawecestre, a warlord, leading his warband. The wind cool on his back, and the sun warm on his face as he lifted his gaze to offer a supplication: *Oh, merciful God, hear my prayer that I will be victorious in my quest for Mercia, and that I will be thy dutiful and most obedient servant. Grant me the strength and courage to be a true son of Mercia, righteous and faithful and help me, so that I will perform deeds that will please thee, Oh Lord, and thy servant Jesus, our saviour.*

They reached the bridge over the River Sæfren, south of the indomitable fortress of Scrobbesbyrig. The sun had risen through patches of white cloud to blaze gloriously in the bright blue sky. It was hot and everyone was tired, riding at a fast pace, and stopping only a few hours during the night.

They built their camp by the river, sheltered by trees, their branches creating cover and firewood. Burghred took twelve men and marched to the southern gates. Once there, he paused and drew a deep breath. Beside him, Ulric said, "You look apprehensive, lord."

Burghred looked at his new friend. Since Ulric had joined him, Burghred had become closer to him than any of the others, confiding in him his deepest feelings and his darkest fears. "It's a time of reckoning for me. I must prove myself."

"You have proven yourself already, *Lord* Burghred, and with the amount of praying you have been doing lately, you'll surely have God on your side."

Burghred laughed. "Aye, my knees are somewhat sore…"

Ulric put a hand on his shoulder. "You can do this, Burghred. You *will* win them over."

"You know these men, Ulric. How do I win them over?"

"Confidence – tempered with humility. Not too much though, and not without dignity. We Mercians do not follow those who are devoid of modesty, nor someone who is overly supplicant."

"Hey, I know. I am Mercian myself, remember." Burghred gave his friend a half-hearted smile. It was the men of Scrobbesbyrig he needed first and if he succeeded, others would follow, and if the eastern *scīra* could be swayed, then the western *scīra* would also.

They were given entry through the gates and were escorted through the town's streets.

"Try to look confident, lord," Ulric said.

"I *am* looking confident," Burghred replied through gritted teeth. "If I am not, perhaps it is because I've been here before. What will be different this time?"

"Twelve men, instead of one boy? An army camped outside the gates?" When Burghred said nothing, Ulric continued, "Lord, riders have been sent throughout the earldom with the king's seal two days ago, beseeching the thegns to be true to their king and come to his aid under *your* banner. You also possess the king's emblem. They *have* to listen to you."

"Aye – the king's seal – but will that mean anything to them? Will they listen to me this time? What can I offer them that will sway their judgement? More men? Do I have enough to persuade them? Perhaps it is wits we need, more intellect?"

"You worry too much."

"Time is running out, Ulric, Alfgar is in Ceaster already, and the men there have welcomed him like a saviour. He will be waiting for Magnus, and you know that when Magnus comes with his ships full of Norse warriors, Alfgar will have an army big enough to confront the king's, even without the Mercians. I don't know if we have the balls to face them all. We *need* the Mercians. We need them badly. If they choose Alfgar, all will be lost."

"You're thinking far ahead now, lord. First things first. Let us think about Scrobbesbyrig. They allowed us in, did they not? Considering what happened last time you were here, it's a start."

And it seemed a good omen, but when he entered the meadhall, what Burghred saw hit him like a thunderbolt.

Ragnald.

His father's captain was seated on the dais with Wulfgar as though he were an honoured man among friends. Eyes were on Burghred as he pushed through the throng and his face pricked with unease. Within the crowd were the faces of Alfgar's retainers. *Was he too late?* He turned to his men and touched his nose, signalling to them that there might be trouble.

He approached the dais, and the noise in the hall abated. Men looked at him as though he'd brought plague with him.

"Lord Burghred," Wulfgar welcomed him with insincere warmth. "I did not expect to see you again so soon." He picked up a crust from his table and bit into it. "This time you have a little more company than before," he said, his mouth full. "I also see that my nephew, Ulric, is amongst them and some of our younger men. We wondered where they had all had ridden off to; bewitched by your ideas that are surely above your capabilities."

Burghred's face flushed. "Lord Wulfgar." He gave a curt bow and breathed deeply to steady his nerves, taking comfort that he was not alone with just a sixteen-year-old lad this time. "Alfgar, my traitorous father, forfeited his right to Mercia when he went to bed with the Wéalas – and not only the Wéalas but also with the savages that inhabit the far north. Mercia should fall to me." He turned his head to look directly at Ragnald. "But I see that my father's dog has arrived here before me." Burghred smirked. "Will you join me, Ragnald – fight for *me* and not that faithless father of mine?"

Ragnald scowled. He'd risen from his seat long before Burghred had finished speaking. "My lords of Scrobbesbyrig, this man is the traitor. He was sent as Godwinson's spy to betray his own father, his sister, and all those who fight for Mercia to be kept free from the greed of the Godwinsons! This whelp – this coward – he murdered a man in cold blood and then fled from Rhuddlan. He has no right to steal what is his father's, for he is without honour, a man with no integrity. The Lord Alfgar disowns him!"

Burghred pointed directly at Ragnald. "This man would have us all live under the yoke of the Norse. He and my father have been plotting to overthrow our king and replace him with a heathen and an army of greedy, rapacious savages who will steal our lands and rape our women and enslave our children! We will be like the ghosts that haunt Hereford. Alfgar would have this new king impose upon us a tyranny

228

the like of which these lands have not seen for many decades. Is that what you want?" He paused and there were murmurings of assent. "The Godwinsons may not be your friends, but they are not your enemies. The real enemy is in Ceaster where my father is, plotting against you all!"

"He lies!" cried Ragnald. "He wants you to hear these diabolical falsehoods – Godwinson falsehoods – so that you will turn against Alfgar and join *him* instead! I vouch that Alfgar wants only to be the guardian of Mercia and is loyal to our good King Edward. The Godwinsons are the perpetrators of many crimes against Lord Alfgar, and for that he wishes vengeance. Death to the Godwinsons, I say! Who of you are with *me*?"

"So that is the tactic Alfgar is using, is it?" Burghred raised his voice over the cheers and board banging of those who supported Alfgar. "Good men of Scrobbesbyrig, I beseech you, do not listen to this man's lies. Magnus of Norwæg *is* involved and right now I have no doubt that he raids the northern coasts, his ships full of hardened warriors, ready to land an invasion force –"

"This is not true!" interrupted Ragnald. "He wants only to sully our names to get you on side. Look at him; what does he have to offer you? Where is his army? He comes with a meagre handful of men, all boys – like himself. He is nothing more than putrid waste, shat from his mother's cunt like a dead dog expels maggots from its rotting arse." Ragnald leapt from the dais and stormed toward Burghred, elbowing men out of the way until they stood before each other. "You are no match for your father, *Burghred se Swica*."

Burghred squared up to him, pushing his face forward so that they were almost nose to nose.

A man shouted "*Swica!*"

Voices echoed the insult until the room was filled with chanting, resonating around the hall.

Clenching his jaw, Burghred recalled painfully, the enmity that Ragnald had caused between him and his father over the years.

Ragnald seemed also to remember, for his eyes laughed above the cruel, twisted smile. "You hear that, Burghred? You hear what they are calling you?"

Ulric closed in protectively on Burghred. "Men of Scrobbesbyrig, do not listen to this *scite!* I too am a man of this town, as are Wulfmær, Eadwin, Idwald, and Siward here. You have known us all our lives –

you knew our fathers. Would *we* lie to you?" Ulric turned to the dais. "Uncle Wulfgar, Lord Alfgar is not worthy to step into Earl Leofric's boots – this man here is a thousand times a better man than *he* will ever be. In allying himself with that Wéalas murderer, Gruffudd, Alfgar has gone against his own father and betrayed Earl Leofric. Alfgar causes nothing but disharmony amongst us and his arrogance has made all our lives difficult. He cares not for Mercia – he cares only for himself – and power."

"And the Godwins? Are they not greedy for power either, Nephew?" called Wulfgar from the dais. He remained seated, pensively rubbing the bulb of his nose.

Ulric stepped closer to the dais. "We do not support the Godwinsons, either, but we are here for our anointed king and we know that Mercia will be safe in Burghred's hands. Do we want to go back to the dark days when Englalond was divided and warring amongst herself? If we follow Burghred, we can be sure that a Godwin will not hold sway here!"

"How can we be sure that Burghred won't be another Godwin puppet, like the man who sits on the throne?" argued Wulfgar.

"I will swear for this man," Ulric said, his arm stretched toward Burghred. "He has proved himself to be honourable and has been a good lord to us so far."

Burghred unlocked his eyes from Ragnald's and nodded his appreciation at Ulric before addressing Wulfgar. "Outside these walls, I have some two hundred and fifty men, and more are marching here from the rest of Mercia as we speak," he bluffed. "They will take this burgh, if you do not submit to us."

Ulric put a hand on his arm and said in a low voice, "Lord, wait. There is no need to use forceful words where diplomacy will do."

"If you believe they are flocking to your banner, you will be sadly mistaken." Ragnald sneered. "Lord Wulfgar, let me put this bastard in irons for such treachery!"

Ragnald's men violently leapt upon Burghred. There was a fracas and he and his retainers were overpowered and surrounded.

"Lord Wulfgar!" Ulric cried out, "In the name of all that is good and holy, this is no way to treat this man; he is a noble, grandson of our beloved Lord Leofric. I demand that you intervene!"

Wulfgar stood to his feet. "Ragnald! Stop! I shall not have harm come to anyone in my hall today!"

Ragnald growled and muttered an oath. He let go of Burghred's arm roughly. Burghred straightened his cloak and tunic and ran a hand over his head. The tonsure, now almost as long as the rest of his hair, reminded him of what he had been through to get this far.

Ragnald, it seemed, was not done yet. "Wulfgar, I demand that you allow me to take this man back in irons to Earl Alfgar whom he has betrayed."

"Nay, Lord Ragnald, I am lord here and I will say what happens. You, Burghred," he nodded, "you may leave with your men. I will take counsel here. Tomorrow I will meet with you outside the walls with my answer." When Ragnald went to protest, Wulfgar put his hand up and quietened him. "I will consider both sides, and I and my council will decide for ourselves."

"Go to Lord Alfgar in Ceaster. Inform him of what is afoot here. Tell him to send an army… or come himself," Wulfgar said to Ragnald when Burghred and his men had gone. "If the rest of Mercia is coming as Burghred says, we will need his father's army sooner rather than later – and before the king and Godwinson get here."

Ragnald smiled sarcastically. "Don't be a fool, Wulfgar! Do you really believe the Mercians will support that little leech? That they'd go against Alfgar? You should have let me take him. Why didn't you?"

Wulfgar rounded on Ragnald. "Because he has a sizeable army out there more numerous than ours. Some are the sons of Scrobbesbyrig. I want them back – *alive*. So, for now, I have another plan," Wulfgar leaned closer to him, "and if all goes well, when tomorrow morning comes, we will see the young traitor dead and his men returned to us; lambs to the fold."

"Then I'll go to Ceaster and inform Alfgar of what is happening. In the meantime, you will soon see that Burghred is bluffing and that Mercia still holds faith with the true Lord of Mercia."

"Go, but leave your men here, we may need them."

Wulfgar clapped a hand on the other man's shoulder. Ragnald nodded and returned the gesture. Both smiled.

Later that evening, Wulfgar stood pensively with his deputy, Inewulf, on the ramparts. They gazed at the burning campfires of Burghred's men.

"Do you think there are two hundred and fifty of them as he says?"

asked Wulfgar.

Inewulf nodded. "Aye, judging by my calculations. More than our fighting men. But we have plenty of ceorls that are good with weapons. And plenty of missiles, come to that."

"Did Ragnald get out?"

"Aye, but since then, they've posted men at each gate – archers and spearmen – and there are more bowmen in the trees watching the walls."

"But we have the advantage of being inside the burgh. If they want to get in, they will have to get past our own men first," Wulfgar said.

There was a shared moment of silence before Wulfgar asked, "Why do they follow him?"

Inewulf eyed Wulfgar thoughtfully. "They are young, idealistic and gullible. They do not realise that he is just a Godwin puppet. Do we want to see Mercia carved up any more than it is? If he wins the earldom, Harold will use him, throw him into the snake pit when he is done with him, then replace him with one of his brothers."

"But what if they are right and we are wrong, and Alfgar comes with his Norse to take our lands and put a Norwægian king on the throne?"

"Would a Norwægian king be so bad? If it meant the end of the Godwinsons...."

Wulfgar acknowledged him with a grunt, a nod, and a deep sigh. "I don't know. I was young when we had Cnut on the throne. He was a good king. Edward is many things, but he is pliant. If we could just get rid of the Godwinsons..." Wulfgar paused, thinking, then continued. "If Alfgar's son is half the man that lot seem to think he is, then let him try to take us, if he is not dead before morning."

"What is the plan?" Inewulf asked.

"If we can get rid of him, we might just save ourselves some internal strife."

"What do you mean?"

"Perhaps I should have let Ragnald take him to Ceaster after all."

"And what of *them*?" Inewulf asked, nodding at the encampment.

"If we make him disappear, then they will come back."

"How do we make that happen without killing any of them?"

"That's a chance we are going to have to take. No doubt there will be some casualties, but that will be inevitable."

A quiet time had been spent around the campfires with little said that was merry or jovial. Now, awake still, Burghred lay under an awning wrapped in his cloak. *Was Ulric right to challenge my threat to take the burgh by force?* He'd had to admit to himself that he'd been rash. His men, loath to do battle against their fellow townsmen, had expressed their unease throughout the evening.

Imaginary conversations played out in Burghred's head. How could he convince his men that to fight was the only option? Wulfgar and Inewulf were not going to take his side, that was obvious. But would they have listened to him if Ragnald had not been there? He'd tried to appear confident in front of his followers. Had he succeeded? Their moroseness this evening was worrying. Just what did they think of him? Even Ulric had been sullen.

When the soothing lethargy of approaching sleep did not come, he turned to prayer, beseeching God to bring him an army of Mercian banners, hoping he would drift into slumber.

A dull throbbing in his wounded leg added to his discomfort, but he must have dozed off eventually, for he woke, startled by the dead weight of an unconscious body crushing his chest.

Burghred swore and shoved. "Off you fool! Are you drunk?"

He struggled to breathe. Thick warm liquid tickled the skin of his neck. Panic rose within him. The smell of blood was potent. He touched seeping, sticky wet flesh and realised with horror the man's throat was cut. Before he could react, someone dragged the weight from him.

"Lord…" Beric shook him, crouching beside him. "Are you hurt?"

Dazed, Burghred took a few moments. "What just happened? What's going on?"

There came no answer. Beric was gone. As Burghred sat up, the sound of running feet and panicked voices reverberated around the camp. His eyes slowly adjusted to the night. Shadows were everywhere, moving and darting. Confused voices asked questions that no one answered. More running feet, half-spoken words, and the sudden breaking of loud wailing and shouting.

Burghred grappled for his scabbard and finding it jumped to his feet. "Beric? Ulric? What's happening?" Somewhere, yards away, men were gathering and then came the faint sound of swords clashing.

"Form up! We're being attacked!" shouted someone in the darkness.

Burghred pulled at the hilt of his sword and it slid from its sheath

He ran toward a gathering, hopping over men still asleep and piles

233

of gear.

He spun a young fellow to face him. "What's happening?" Burghred demanded.

"Fighting, lord." The youth looked terrified.

"Who is?"

"I don't know...."

Burghred elbowed his way through the milling confusion and stood on the periphery of the conflict. Ahead of him, twenty yards away, blades shimmered in the moonlight.

"Bloody Ragnald," Burghred whispered. "Damn the whoreson, this is his doing!"

"Lord Ragnald?" Beric was beside him.

Burghred barely turned to look at the youth as he spoke. "It's bloody Ragnald's men!" Nausea rose up in his throat as the sensation of his stomach rolling dizzied him. He could tell his warriors by their lack of armour, some in just their braies. The enemy wore padded jacks and helmets. They'd come ready for a fight, but no mail, perhaps to create stealth and be swift. Burghred's own warriors, no doubt enraged by the cowardly attack on the camp, were giving them hell despite their unreadiness, and driving them back toward the walls of the burgh.

Men yelling, began to disengage the skirmish to run up the sloping green.

"They're retreating!"

"Get the bastards!"

"Kill them, kill them all!" and horrified, Burghred saw that his men began to chase them.

A young man to Burghred's right raised his bow and nocked an arrow. *What the...!* Burghred leapt at him, almost knocking him off his feet.

"You fool! Do you know who you are shooting at? Those are our men out there too. Put your bloody bow down, you idiot!"

"Sorry, my lord," the archer spluttered.

Out across the sloping sward, bodies were strewn over the grass – dead or injured, Burghred could not tell.

He heard a voice from behind call him and turned. Wulfmær, came staggering sleepily toward him, half dressed and wiping slumber from his eyes. "They've ambushed us, the shit-eating bastards."

Burghred rolled his eyes. "I would never have guessed. You took your time, didn't you? Please tell me you didn't sleep through this?"

Wulfmær gazed at the chaos, his eyes widening. "Lord, what shall we do?"

Burghred grabbed Wulfmær, spun him around and shoved the half-dazed warrior back toward the camp. "Round up the men. Call them together!" Then turning from Wulfmær, "*To me*! Form on me, your Lord of Mercia!" His throat seared with the effort. "Light! I need light! You there, bring me a torch. Quickly!"

"Yes, lord." A man hurried away to do his bidding.

The ambushers, pursued by Burghred's men, rushed to the opened gates.

"Should we go after them, Lord Burghred," Idwald asked, ready with his sword.

Burghred shook his head. On the ramparts, torches appeared, blazing against the dark starlit sky. "Look. Bowmen. Up on the walls. I can see their arrows nocked!" And pointing to the chase, he cried, "That lot are about to be shot down." He cupped his hands to his mouth, calling out, "Retreat! Retreat men! To me!"

But it was too late. Men dropped, screaming as the arrows hit them.

At least ten men shot out of the forming shieldwall and ran past him. "Idiots!" Burghred cried as the fools ran onto the field. "Back! Form up on me, your Lord of Mercia!" His voice cracked and he turned, saw Wulfmær. "Do something, Wulfmær! Get them back!"

"Aye, lord!"

"Lord Burghred." He swung around to see two men dragging a captured man between them. One of them, Burghred knew him as Pendric, said, "We found him lying in the camp. He's injured. Not ours, though. Says he knows you."

"Lord, your torch."

Burghred took it and shone it in the captive's face. "Remove his helmet."

Pendric did his bidding and Burghred stood back, sneering.

"No, he is definitely not one of ours. It is Ælred, son of Ragnald. A man I have grown with, trained with and drank with. A man I once called friend."

Ælred, face contorted painfully, was thrown to his knees. He clutched at his stomach, and blood streamed through his fingers.

Burghred walked behind him, spat, and grabbed Ælred's hair and wrenched his head back. "Who sent you to do this, your father?"

Ælred could only whine.

Burghred growled. "Speak! You filthy, cowardly scum!"

Rounding on him, he kicked Ælred in his wounded gut. A cry of pain echoed through the air. Grabbing the captive's throat, Burghred bent, face to face with his former friend and said, "Speak or I'll slice your face off!"

Letting him go, Burghred shoved him. Ælred whimpered. Falling back, he writhed like a frightened adder on the ground.

"You heard your lord," Pendric hauled him upright. "Speak!"

When no answer came, Burghred cuffed him violently with his ringed fingers, ripping open Ælred's lip.

"Talk, you worm-infested anus," Burghred ordered. He lay the flat of his sword against the terrified man's face. "Or you will have another arsehole, right here, instead of your nose."

"It was Wulfgar!" Ælred blurted. He spat blood from his mouth and coughed.

Burghred's heart sank. "It wasn't that *wédehund* of a father of yours, then?"

Ælred, shook his head. "Nay, lord. It was not him."

"I don't believe you," Burghred spat, allowing his blade to split the skin, fascinated by the crimson trickle of blood.

"Nay, lord! Please, I beg you. My father has gone."

"What exactly were your orders?"

"We were supposed to kill you – make you disappear…" Ælred's voice quivered, "then *they*, those men you took from Scrobbesbyrig, would come back."

"Where has Ragnald gone?"

"I don't know."

"To Alfgar?"

"I don't know!"

Burghred thrust the handle of his *seax* into the wound in his stomach and Ælred screamed, fell back and as he was lifted upright once more, he ceded. "Ceaster."

"I knew it." Burghred looked away, then turned back to his prisoner. "How did you expect to know which of these men were me?"

"I thought I would recognise you, but we woke some of your men."

Burghred laughed. "Your mistake was to come with so many. One man – one man to sneak like a wolf amongst sleeping sheep, and you would have succeeded." Burghred bent slightly and spat in his face.

"You foolish scum." Burghred rose up and looked away from the man on his knees. "Cut his throat," he told Pendric and walked a few steps away from him.

"Burghred!" Ælred shouted. "Does our friendship not mean anything to you? I will join you. I'll give my oath to you. Please spare my life!"

Burghred swung round. "What did you do to save mine in Rhuddlan, you snake? You knew what they planned to do to me. What did our friendship mean then, eh?" He walked a few paces.

Ælred called out to him. "Burghred, please! Don't kill me!"

"Kill him!" Burghred roared, shaking with anger.

He turned and faced the other way, shutting his eyes tight. His friend's dying screams rang in his ears until they stopped.

"Is this the way the men of Scrobbesbyrig engage in battle? Through stealth and trickery?" He had been deceived. To be betrayed by Ragnald was expected, but Wulfgar had stooped low.

Along the parapets there was no sign of life, apart from flickering torches, left ensconced. He walked away looking for Ulric. "Ulric! Where is Ulric?"

Wulfmær approached. "Ulric is dead, my lord!" Wulfmær cried.

Behind Wulfmær two men, bloody and exhausted, were carrying the body of a lifeless warrior between them.

Burghred dropped beside the man he had known only for a short while but had come to mean so much to him and held his face in his hands.

Beric said, "He tried to kill them, lord. We all did."

"You bloody fool." Burghred said, in a voice choked with tears. His friend was clad only in undertunic and hose. Burghred looked up at the men gathered round. "Did he not have a sword at least?" Blood leaked out of a chest wound near Ulric's heart, his eyes wide as though surprised by the deathblow.

"I saw him running with just his long knife," Beric said.

"Stupid bloody fools, all of you! As soon as you knew what was happening you should have found me." Burghred closed his friend's eyes and laid the man's head down on the grass gently. "He was the first man who came to me and gave me his sword," he whispered. Tears rolled down his cheeks. He wiped them away with his cuff.

"He was like a brother to me," Wulfmær added.

"Aye, and me," Siward said, joining Burghred and Beric on the cool damp ground.

Idwald, slunk to his knees and touched Ulric's cheek with the back of his hand. "I'd known him all my life," he said.

"We learnt our spear and sword work together; we were born in the same year." Eadwin joined the others kneeling by their brother in arms, each of them voicing what Ulric had meant to them.

After a while, Wulfmær said. "Lord Burghred?"

"Aye?"

"We have lost friends tonight – before the real battle has even begun. I beg that before we fight tomorrow, we bury the dead and that the priest say the words for them."

Burghred looked at Wulfmær and the others. Siward and Idwald were tearful. Eadwin and Wulfmær, angry. "How many have we lost?" asked Burghred.

"By my reckoning at least thirty. Many were relieved of their lives whilst they slept," Beric replied. "And there's at least ten down there," he was looking toward the burgh, "They may be injured, they may be dead."

"Fools," Burghred said. "Why run after armed warriors in nothing but their flesh!"

"It was for you, lord," said Beric.

Burghred gazed at the lifeless heaps of men that had once been his.

"Men. Hearken," he called out. "This night you have shown me your unswerving loyalty. You drove back the enemy who came to destroy me, barely prepared and with little protection. This will not go unrewarded. We will bury our dead in graves befitting warriors and then tomorrow, Scrobbesbyrig will be ours."

Shouts of agreement rang out through the camp. Burghred walked forward. "I'm still alive, you bastards! Look at me! I am still here!" he shouted at the walls. He turned to his men. "Do you mean to still hold off taking Scrobbesbyrig by force?"

"Not I, lord," Wulfmær said.

"Nor I," Siward followed.

"I'm with you, lord," Idwald agreed.

"On the morn, we will do it!" Eadwin said.

"Then let us prepare, for tomorrow, Scrobbesbyrig will be ours, or burn!"

Burghred's closest companions murmured their agreement. With their arms around each other's shoulders, each of them swore the oath of vengeance.

Morning came. The men were gloomy, sitting on whatever they could: fallen logs, grass, tree roots. Burhgred's mass priest had said prayers over the dead and they had finished burying them. The smell of frying hunks of pig meat filled the air, masking the odour of putrefying flesh. Few of them had slept. They had lost twenty at the last count, including the bowmen who had been on watch. Many had their throats cut as the assassins crept amongst them. Others had been killed in the skirmish. Some were injured, most not badly, still able to function.

Burghred told his men to strip the bodies of their attackers and leave them naked, tied to wooden stakes so they could be seen from the towers. One of them was Ælred. Burghred felt no remorse. The death of his only son would break Ragnald. It was a satisfying thought.

Scouts he had sent out to investigate the stockade soon returned.

"The walls appear to be impenetrable, lord," one of them had said. "The scīra have learned the lessons of Hereford. These days, the burghs are maintained regularly, strongly built, with no flaws."

"What of the ditch?" Burghred asked.

"Waterlogged with silt."

Breaching the walls was not going to be easy.

"We should have taken hostages," Pendric said, "and killed them one by one until they let us in."

"We can take this place," Wulfmær said. "But we cannot do it on empty stomachs nor without sleep. We cannot get in through any part of the wall, but they have no more than a hundred trained fighting men. Much less than we."

"You haven't told us *how* we can take it." Idwald sounded sceptical.

"We can," Wulfmær told them.

Eadwin took a swig of his ale then said, "How? The place is impenetrable. They'll pick us off as we come up the hill."

"We have shields; we know how to make the shieldwall and the *foulcon*. We can take it. We just have to think of a good plan."

Burghred wished he shared Wulfmær's confidence.

"What of the messengers you sent to the eastern holdings, my lord?" Pendric asked.

"No word yet. But they have been gone only two days," Burghred replied. He did not feel optimistic.

"If only we could be sure they will come." Siward took the drinking horn from Eadwin, drank from it then passed it on.

Burghred stood up abruptly. "I should have gone myself before going to Gleawecestre to meet with the king." He could have kicked himself, instead he kicked at a stone to relieve the anger he felt.

"What is done is done, lord," Wulfmær said. "We still outnumber them." He nodded toward the burgh.

Burghred knuckled his temples. He had never been involved in a siege before. His father would have known what to do, and that irked him. "Aye, we outnumber them," he agreed, "but they are inside, and we are outside, and we must get in. We cannot wait forever. We need to take it soon, before Alfgar gets here."

"Then we must think about *how* we are going to do it," Wulfmær said.

Burghred sighed and walked to the edge of the encampment to think alone. Leaning against a tree, he gazed up the slope at the burgh's walls. The land outside the burgh was mostly grassy meadow, with pockets of woods. "How can we get through those gates?" he whispered.

Our fate is in thy hands, dear God. Oh, Lord, I beseech thee grant that the spinners will weave victory for me – let it be thy will, dear God.

Just then there was a whooshing sound. He turned to see smoke rising from one of the fires, spreading and blocking his vision. Someone berated a fellow for clumsiness to a chorus of complaints and swearing accompanied by bouts of coughing. What had happened? Probably water from an unsettled pan been tipped over a cooking fire by some ungainly fool, leaving it to smoulder. A veritable screen of smeech-like fog had been created, impeding his sight. Arms flapped like startled bird wings, fanned the firepit, increasing the smog. Burghred watched with interest. *Pour too much water onto a fire and it would put it out. Pour just enough, and it smoulders…*

It suddenly occurred to him that if there was just the right amount of smoke, quite possibly one might not be able to see much at all. A grin spread across his face. "Thank you, Almighty Lord," he said, and gave the quietest of chuckles.

Chapter Twenty-four

Blood and Treachery

Ceaster, end of May 1058

Hunbert Geréfa, reeve of Ceaster, ordered the gates of the burgh to be swung open to admit the outlawed Alfgar and his men. There was much waving and cheering, as though the exiled earl were a saviour come to rid the townsfolk of some terrible tyrant. As Alfgar and his friends rejoiced, Guthlac Geréfa, the king's representative in Ceaster was not so happy about Alfgar's sudden appearance in the town. Flanked by Bishop Leofwin of Lichfield and their personal guards, Guthlac stormed into the meadhall to confront the new arrival.

"Lord Hunbert, this man should be seized!" raged Guthlac. "He is an outlaw! He should be clapped in irons and thrown into a pit, not sat here eating and drinking his fill of the king's provisions!"

Silence descended over the great feasting hall.

Alfgar eyed the king's reeve with a look of malice but did not react. He remained seated and allowed Hunbert to address the uninvited.

"What is the meaning of this, Guthlac?" demanded Hunbert, rising to his feet. Unlike other towns in Mercia, Earl Alfgar was afforded many special privileges in Ceaster, one being that he should have his own reeve to represent him in the town, but Hunbert, who was Alfgar's man, never saw eye to eye with Guthlac, who was the king's..

Guthlac, quivered with rage and continued his tirade. "All men here are duty bound to put this man in chains. He is an outlaw and as thus can be executed without trial!"

"In chains, you say?" replied Hunbert, glancing at Alfgar with a smile. Alfgar nodded.

"Guards! Seize Lord Guthlac and put him in chains," Hunbert said.

"Nay!" Guthlac protested. Armoured men approached him and

Guthlac's own thegns stood back, their hands raised to show that they were not going to intervene.

Bishop Leofwin tried to stop the guards but was forced back.

"Lord Bishop, is it your wish also to be clapped in irons with this man?" Hunbert said.

The bishop stepped back and as Guthlac was dragged away, the bishop turned to Hunbert and said, "You will pay for this outrage. God will damn you for assisting this devil's spawn – this outlaw, oath breaker and destroyer of churches!"

Bishop Leofwin turned to leave. Alfgar waved away the men who went to restrain him, leaving the bishop to sweep out of the hall without impediment.

"Well," sighed Alfgar, "'Tis always difficult for a man of my position to please everyone." He smiled, amused at his own sense of humour.

He and Hunbert laughed as they shared a flask of wine. Celebrations were resumed and Alfgar called one of his men from the mead benches to the dais. "Has there been any word from Lord Ragnald or Wulfgar of Scrobbesbyrig?"

"No, nothing as yet from either, lord," the man informed him.

Alfgar turned to Hunbert. "I am certain that when they hear that Ceaster has welcomed me with open arms, they will be persuaded to support me. It may take some encouragement; after all, though they be Mercians the men of Scrobbesbyrig are traditionally sworn to the king to act as his bodyguards. But if words cannot convince them, then they will be forced."

Hunbert leant in close to him, holding a half-eaten hunk of venison impaled on his eating knife. "It is imperative that Scrobbesbyrig sides with us, my lord; it is the gateway to Herefordscīr."

"I know this, Hunbert. I am sure that Ragnald is using his best powers of persuasion as we speak. He is a good diplomat, is Ragnald. If they do not succumb to his coaxing, he will break some heads!" He roared with laughter, his companions around him joining in. "Yes, he is very persuasive. If anyone can convince them beyond doubt that I have the might of all Mercia behind me, Ragnald will. Besides, Wulfgar is not a stupid man; by my reckoning, he will not go against me. He knows better than that. They all do."

"Then, with both Ceaster and Scrobbesbyrig yielding to you, the rest of Mercia will surely follow." Hunbert took his glass and lifted it in

242

salutation.

Alfgar drank his wine thirstily, then studied the expensive drinking vessel that only a man of great wealth could possess. Hunbert was obviously doing well for himself if he could afford to buy such wares – and good wine to put in it.

"And what of this Norse boy-prince, Magnus?" Hunbert asked.

Alfgar shook his head and hissed through clenched teeth. "If only that whoreson of mine had not bestowed this strife upon me. The little runt has driven a wedge between myself and the Norse, not to mention Gruffudd, damn him, but don't fret, the little turd will be meat for worms when I get my hands on him." Alfgar saw the frown on Hunbert's face and added, "Not Gruffudd, you fool, my son."

Hunbert chuckled. "I wondered, lord. Burghred is conspicuous by his absence. What did he do… this time?"

"He killed the son of one of Magnus' jarls. Magnus demanded that he be handed over for justice to be done."

Hunbert whistled. "*Scite!* What came next?"

"Burghred escaped with the help of some love-smitten bitch, and Magnus withdrew from the alliance," replied Alfgar bitterly.

"Burghred escaped?"

"Aye," nodded Alfgar, rolling his eyes. "God knows where to. Hopefully, he will be lying dead in the Welsh hills somewhere. He has shamed me one too many times… And to think that I trusted him again after the last time he betrayed me."

"So, you have no way of paying this blood debt?"

Alfgar shuddered, remembering the shame. "The Norse wanted blood, as well as the silver. I was not going to give them mine, nor my blood! But no amount of either would bring them back to the table. Anyway, what is done is done. If Harald Sigurdsson wants the Englisc crown, he must needs do business with me or gain nothing." Alfgar spat into the rushes to show what he thought of the Norwægian king. "Sigurdsson's dream of bringing Englalond into his realm can sink along with his goddamn ships for all I care."

"I cannot see Harald Sigurdsson being content with his son's decision to pull out of the alliance," Hunbert declared. "I heard that his fight with Denmark is not progressing well, he will not be pleased to lose Englalond as well."

"To be sure of it. I expect Magnus to come crawling back any day now, but it won't be a happy friendship, not now anyway - thanks to

Burghred."

Alfgar and his companion looked up from their speculations as a commotion could be heard within the hall. Alfgar laughed, welcoming the interlude into the painful issue of his son's duplicity and subsequent disappearance.

Guthlac, now fully shackled, was reeled in through the doors, and whirled from one laughing carouser to the next. The minstrels played, making it seem as though it were some ghastly dance. Encumbered by the manacles, he lost his balance, slamming the floor like a sack of grain amongst the debris of spilled ale, scraps of meat and bones. There was uproar as the reeve was dragged to his feet and spun around the hall. Hilarity reigned as he was spat on, cuffed, punched, and kicked. Alfgar roared with amusement as a squatting, hairy-arsed drunk opened his bowels whilst another, grinning from ear to ear, grabbed a handful of the freshly laid excrement and rubbed it into Guthlac's matted hair. Great shouts of mock disgust and laughter resounded throughout as the beleaguered reeve was pushed to the floor again and pissed on.

The man was stubborn, Alfgar thought, admiring Guthlac's ability to endure the ill-treatment with silent contempt. Bishop Leofwin stepped forward to go to his aid, but Alfgar's threatening glance was enough to dissuade him. Alfgar was not above harming a man of the church.

The doors rattled and Ragnald entered. Alfgar grinned, glad to see him, and space was made for his captain on the dais. Alfgar poured the wine and signalled to a servant to provide more food.

"Is that not Guthlac, the king's reeve?" Ragnald asked, tearing into a hunk of pig and putting a piece of it straight into his mouth.

"Aye," grunted Alfgar before taking a swig of wine.

"What has he done?" A curious half smile presented itself on Ragnald's craggy face.

"It would seem that his lordship was not at his happiest to see me arrive in Ceaster. He suggested that I should be clapped in irons and thrown into a pit and killed; So, I offered him more consideration than he did me." Alfgar watched amused, as a cynical expression crossed Ragnald's face. "I'm letting him live, aren't I? What news of Scrobbesbyrig?"

"My lord, Scrobbesbyrig supports you – but…"

"But? But what?" Alfgar was about to take another mouthful of wine.

"Burghred is there."

Alfgar breathed deeply, flaring his nostrils. He put the glass down without taking a drink and narrowed his eyes. "So, he lives after all?" he muttered and opened and closed his hand around the precious cup. He felt like crushing it within his palm.

Ragnald nodded. "And not only alive, but he was there with an army of Mercians."

Alfgar looked out across the hall at Guthlac being tormented. "How big an army?" He clenched his jaw, grinding his teeth.

"A small army, but big enough to cause trouble. Perhaps two hundred men or so."

"A puny little army, then." Alfgar slammed his glass hard onto the table and spilled his wine. He rubbed the bulb of his nose and in his mind, he brooded. Could he be mistaken about Burghred? Had his son gathered an army and was he bringing it to support him? If only he was wrong – that they were all wrong – and Burghred hadn't betrayed him after all. Nay, it was stupid to think otherwise. He knew the truth of it. "I had thought him dead in the mountains. He'd been wounded in the leg-vein, the one that can kill a man if it is cut."

"How he survived, I do not know." Ragnald shook his head, "but he was there, large as life, hale and whole, in Scrobbesbyrig to rally men to his banner – against you."

Alfgar was silent. He fingered the angry scar that traversed his cheek to the bridge of his nose. Burghred – alive…Burghred in Scrobbesbyrig, there: large as life, hale and whole… rallying men against me… Thoughts of his son had occupied his mind a lot of late. He'd visualised what he'd been hoping for, before it had all gone wrong: he and Burghred united, riding side by side to the rowdy cheers of the people. Father and son, restored in their rightful positions as lords of Mercia.

"We always knew it would come to this," Ragnald said.

"I knew nothing of the sort, Ragnald." Alfgar's palm scraped over his forehead and the crown of his unruly dark hair. "I truly believed he was back in the fold. I was not as good a father to the lad as I should have been, granted, and if I could turn back the tide of fortune that has brought us here… to where we are now, I would. But…"

"Wishful thinking, Lord. Burghred has brought on you the shame of betrayal, not once, but twice, now."

Alfgar was inclined to agree with his friend. The son that had been so hard to love had caused him nothing but torment and hurt. And now, this new treachery. "You are right, Ragnald, there will be no going back. The bastard deserves to die! It should have been him and not Ivar. In God's name, from whose arse did he crawl out of, Edward's or Godwinson's?" spat Alfgar.

"Both, if it were possible."

"May his balls become riddled with the pox if I ever set eyes on him again!"

"Lord, he has proven by his actions that he is a Godwin spy. He has betrayed you – he has betrayed us all! He has no honour and deserves nothing but a traitor's death!"

"Aye, you speak true, Ragnald." Alfgar's head ached. He put his elbows on the table and pushed his knuckles onto his brow, swearing under his breath. "You said he was there to rally men to his banner?"

Ragnald nodded. "He claims the earldom of Mercia, Lord. Your earldom, Lord. He was there to persuade them away from you and to follow –"

"God's Blood!" cried Alfgar. He slammed his fist down onto the solid oaken board, tossing the tableware into chaos. "That he should shame me by betraying me is one thing, but to actively oppose me..."

In an instant, Alfgar's glass flew across the hall, aiming for Guthlac. It missed, exploding on the floor, and Alfgar swore again. Hunbert almost fell out of his chair in shock and the two young boys, Morcar and Edwin, jumped out of their skins. A serving girl cried out as green shards hit her ankle.

Alfgar flung back his head and roared, "Burghred, you traitorous wretch! I should have strangled you at birth when your bitch of a mother spat you from her womb! Why in God's name could he have not been loyal to me? Instead I have a self-serving traitor for a son!"

Alfgar looked at the two boys crouched trembling in their seats. Grabbing each one by their collars, he pulled them to their feet.

"Which of you is firstborn?" he demanded.

"I am, Father," replied Edwin. His eyes met Alfgar's only for a moment before staring at the floor.

"Look at me!"

Edwin's head jerked upwards in obedience. The fear in his son's eyes pleased Alfgar. "How old are you?"

"Eleven, Father. I am eleven." The boy nervously shuffled from one foot to another.

Alfgar grunted and turned to Morcar. The younger boy's bottom lip shook.

"How old are you?" shouted Alfgar. "What are you snivelling for?"

"T-ten, ten – I think, sir," Morcar whimpered.

"Ten, you think? Well, well, well. Stop that blubbing, both of you!" he ordered. "Are you not sons of Alfgar?"

Both boys answered, "Yes, Father."

"Come," he said, "we are going to learn a lesson in how to deal with treachery. Ragnald, make sure my sons witness what is about to happen."

Alfgar jumped down from the dais. "Bring that man outside! I would not have his blood putrefy this place."

"Lord Alfgar! Do you mean to kill him?" Hunbert called after him, an apprehensive note in his voice.

Alfgar turned and observed his reeve, who stood on the dais, his eyes wide with horror. "Any objections, Hunbert?"

The malice in Alfgar's voice was unmistakable.

Hunbert smiled nervously. "No, lord. None at all."

Outside on the cool grass of the sward, Guthlac was forced to kneel. It was a cloudy evening; the light was sparse, and the wind mingled with the trees. Ragnald corralled the boys to the front of the crowd.

Alfgar loomed over the doomed reeve with a great axe in his hands. Guthlac sobbed piteously; but he was proud, Guthlac, and he begged no mercy and Alfgar gave him none. This was how a man should die.

As Alfgar raised the blade high, clasping the shaft with both hands, he called to Ragnald.

"Make sure my sons are watching. Make sure they know that this is how we deal with treachery!"

The axe glinted momentarily in the pale sunshine. A few heartbeats later, it descended upon its target. No last words for the condemned man, just a sickening thud as his head was discharged from his body on to the grass. Another moment and a blizzard of blood spurted from the stump.

The deed was done and the gasps that resonated from the watching crowd, trailed off into a stunned silence as the headless torso slumped forward. Alfgar turned to face the crowd, the odour of blood and the smell of fear flayed his nostrils.

The bishop came running forward, pale, and sweaty, his eyes wide

247

with terror and his mouth gaping. He pushed past the onlookers and sank to his knees by the mutilated body, making the sign of the cross. Stuttering words of prayer, he drew his hands to his chest and laced his fingers around his crucifix.

"Your words cannot comfort him now, priest!"

Alfgar still gripped the axe-shaft as the perspiration glistened in his dark sideburns. He looked toward his sons and smiled. Their emotionless faces were splattered with a mixture of red streaks and tiny red spots. Picking up the hideous, disembodied head by the hair, matted with excrement and other detritus, he held it before him, his eyes fixed on his boys. "This is what I, Alfgar of Mercia, will do to any man who betrays my loyalty, my honour, and his oath to me – son or no!"

He slung the head, and laughed as it rolled along the ground, painting streaks of red in the grass as it approached the terrified Morcar and Edwin. They flinched as it came to rest by their feet. Edwin vomited and Morcar cried out, spewing forth sobs and tears.

Then Alfgar, Earl of Mercia, turned to Hunbert. The reeve's eyes fluttered as he rubbed his hands agitatedly. "Get rid of this thing before the sight of blood leaves me wanting more!" Alfgar stormed with his bloodied axe, back toward the hall, feeling invigorated and wholly satisfied.

Chapter Twenty-five

Fears and Nightmares.

Kings Holme, Gleawecestre

A great resounding belch disrupted the activity of everyone as all heads turned in both amusement and revulsion. Even the servers carrying platters of food stopped in their tracks.

"You slovenly pig!" Wulfhere muttered, slapping down a freshly torn hunk of bread in disgust. He was ravenous, having recently arrived back at Kings Holme after a scouting foray to the south and Leofnoth's poor table manners had well and truly put him off. The old warrior was reclining against the wall, his thick fingers tapping his swollen gut in satisfaction. Wulfhere returned his friend's grin with a scowl.

Cana, one of Wulfhere's other companions, laughed. "I would have been proud of that myself." Cana was even older than Leofnoth and had been part of their hundred unit for as long as Wulfhere could remember, having known him for what seemed like all of his life.

"That was damned good cooking!" Leofnoth said, a toothless grimace pre-empting a loud fart. "I'm full to the brim."

Wulfhere pushed away his food as Leofnoth expelled more wind. "How in God's name are we to eat with you giving off a worse stench than a prize pig? My meat is fouled for certain!"

Leofnoth simply smiled and patted his stomach with apparent contentment. "What are you complaining about, Wulfhere? You can blow up a thunderstorm yourself when you have a mind to. You've never been this delicate before. I remember the night you –"

Wulfhere thumped his ale horn down on the table so hard it cracked, the contents beginning to leak. "I just want to eat my supper in peace, without breathing in the smell of your arse."

"Humph, it seems that some of us are not happy this evening," Leofnoth muttered. "I don't know what's got into you lately, Wulfhere, but there was a time you'd have laughed along with the rest of them."

It was true, Wulfhere knew he was not as cheerful as everyone else seemed to be. The meadhall was a noisy, boisterous place, filled with the proverbial banter of warriors and their dubious behaviours. Mead and ale were readily consumed and the only women who dared enter this masculine environment were those with few virtues, happy to open their legs for a coin or two.

He looked over to where his sons and Yrmenlaf joined in with the raucous banter. Wulfhere was pleased that Æmund, being slightly older, had taken them under his wing, introducing them to his gang of young companions. His heart warmed to see them forge new friendships just as he had done in his day, but on the other hand, the cold steel of fear crept through his bones, knowing what those bonds meant.

Leofnoth elbowed him, jolting him out of his thinking.

"So what is it that ails you, Wulfhere?" his friend asked. "If a man could kill with one look, you would have murdered a thousand men already. What are you chewing over in that thought hoard of yours?"

Wulfhere looked up sheepishly. "I'm sorry, Leofnoth, I know not what is wrong with me. These times spent with my shieldwall companions… they used to be the happiest…. But now, it is dread that seems to dominate my every waking moment."

"We all get this at one time or another in our lives. Death is always around the corner, and the closer we get to it, the more we think about it."

"'Tis not just that. Does it never concern you that this battle might be your last – or that it may be the one where your son dies? Do you never fear that you will not see your grandchild? Or that the child may never see its father? When we were young, these things did not matter, because they did not exist, but –"

"Do you think you are the only one who has these fears? What can we do? The norns spin our fates as we speak. It matters not that we die; what matters is the manner of our living and that we die well. Dying in battle – now there's a death for every man to dream of. What is a straw death to a glorious end on a field of blood, eh?"

"Would it surprise you to hear me say that I pray God for a peaceful death, in my bed, with my children and grandchildren around me? Do you not fear that this may be the last time you see Æmund standing in the shieldwall – that he will die before you do?"

"Of course, but what can I do? He has his path – I have mine. I cannot change what happens. As to dying in my own bed, I would prefer it was with some comely young maid."

Wulfhere ignored Leofnoth's efforts to elicit an amused response from him. "I worry for my sons. I want to protect them."

"Look at them, they are just as you were when you first marched with the fyrd. Let them be. Let them find their way. You cannot always watch over them. What happens will be the will of God, not yours."

"I had a nightmare last night that I was standing on the battlefield and I couldn't find them. I kept looking out for them. I was fighting for my life, but I had this feeling they were dead. Other times I have dreamt they die right in front of me, their heads cleft in two and there is blood everywhere."

"It's just dreams, Wulfhere. Many men suffer them."

"Do you?"

"Occasionally. I try not to dwell on them."

"Ever since Dunsinane I have had them."

"You have never been the same since Dunsinane. All of those who survived that thing have been touched by it. But you – you are scarred by it."

"But how do I forget, when it is always with me?"

Leofnoth squeezed his shoulder. "Make every day you live as if it was your last. Be joyous. Give thanks to those who died that they did so that you could live – and that you lived to come back to your loved ones."

Over by the hearth, a scop was reciting a great battle poem. The scop's wordhoard drifted up to them on tendrils of hearth smoke as they sat on raised benches around the hall. The poem was familiar to Wulfhere: The Wanderer. Wulfhere silently mouthed the words he knew so well but had never felt so much affinity with until now.

Oft ic Sceolde ana uhtna gewylce
mine ceare cwiþan. Nis nu cwicra nan
þe ic him modsefan minne durre
sweotule asecgan
Ic to soþe wat þæt biþ in eorle
indryhten þeaw, þæt he his ferðlocan

fæste binde, healde his hordcofan,
hycge swa he wille.
Ne mæg werig mod wyrde wiðstondan,
ne se hreo hyge helpe gefremman.

Often, I am alone to speak of my trouble
each morning before dawn.
There is none now living
to whom I dare clearly speak
of my innermost thoughts.
I know it truly, that it is in men
a noble custom, that one should keep secure
his deepest feelings guarded like treasure in his mind
to think as he wishes.
The weary spirit cannot withstand fate
Nor does a troubled or sorrowful mind.

"Wulfhere!"

He looked up and saw the hulking form of Helghi across the hall with his ubiquitous band of kinsmen, those who followed him everywhere.

"God damn him," Wulfhere grunted.

"God damn who?"

"Over there." Wulfhere waved his hand, "Helghi and his pondlife."

Leofnoth looked aghast. "Why is this ceorl permitted to be here? He has no right to be in the warriors' hall."

"He is a five-hide man," Wulfhere replied with a sneer, "But he doesn't have five hides, as far as I know. Though I swear he would have mine if he could."

"Wulfhere!" Helghi raised a horn in salutation.

"What do you want, Helghi?" Wulfhere called out.

Helghi stepped down from the benches and ambled around the hearth to stand before them.

"Share a drink with me," Helghi said with exaggerated cordiality. "Let us talk about the dowry for your little daughter, soon to be my son's wife. How old is she now? Thirteen, fourteen? She must have flowered by now, eh? Just ripe enough for the picking."

"There will be no marriage between my daughter and your son, Helghi. If you remember, he was outlawed. So, if I were you, I would

252

shut your mouth and keep out of my sight if you know what's good for you. Besides, after what Edgar did, he is lucky to be alive, let alone marry my daughter."

Helghi laughed. "You are forgetting, Wulfhere, I have another son." Helghi glanced behind him at his son Eadnoth who saluted, drinking horn in hand. He appeared pleased with himself.

Wulfhere instinctively reached for his sword at his hip. He forgot that it was with the door-thegn for safe-keeping as was the protocol when entering the meadhall. He longed to feel Hildbana's sharp tip sink into Helghi's windpipe, shutting him up for good.

"Ignore him," Leofnoth said.

Looking at his friend, Wulfhere said as though it were a revelation, "He has another son. He has - another - son."

"That spot-faced ugly spawn of Grendl's mother, what's his name? Ead - something…" Leofnoth said pensively.

Wulfhere's eyes narrowed. Mildrith's earnest words floated in his swirling mind, *Heed this warning, lord. Helghi still believes that Winflæd will marry his son, not Edgar now, but the other one, Eadnoth. He will come for her soon, so keep her safe. They want her…* He saw her face before him. *Accidents happen, my lord. It is not uncommon for young lads to die in a drunken brawl, or a sporting event, or whilst out hunting…*

Wulfhere growled. Leofnoth's arm went across him and Wulfhere flung it aside. He sprang down the benches, two at a time. Seax drawn, he launched himself at a surprised Helghi, pinned him to the floor with one hand closed over his throat, and poised the blade at his neck.

"Just give me one good reason not to kill you, you foul maggot-infested piece of dog shite."

Wulfhere willed Helghi to give him an excuse to unleash the wild anger within him. Hands pulled at him, fists battered and punched, but none could break the hold. Voices remonstrated with him and he ignored them. He was buffeted, stamped, and jostled but would not be moved.

Nose to nose with his enemy, he growled, "You'll die before I let my daughter marry your *earsling sunu!*"

"This will not get you anywhere, Wulfhere!" It was Leofnoth who spoke, and Wulfhere was hauled from his victim.

Looking about him at the faces of his friends, he caught his breath.

"Bastards!" He scowled, wiping spittle from his chin.

Helghi was helped to his feet and Wulfhere's hackles stood on end.
Helghi reached for his seax and Leofnoth was between them in an
instant.

"Don't you move!" he said to Wulfhere, holding up a warning hand.
Turning to Helghi and his cronies, Leofnoth cautioned, "Hold your
man back! And you, Helghi, stay, or I swear I will stand aside and let
my friend take his piece of you."

Wulfhere stood, hands clenching and unclenching, growling.

"Hold him back, lads!" Leofnoth bellowed, and when Wulfhere
thrust them away like pups, shouted, "Hold him, I said - idiots!"

Wulfhere, now surrounded, felt them seize him, his arms held
behind him. The bloodlust fury roared through his veins and through
a mist of anger, a crazed wolf tore into Helghi as he lay on the ground.
Razor-sharp fangs ripped the flesh and gizzards from his bloody
carcass. The animal, at once both graceful and terrifying, turned its
head to stare at him with huge blue eyes. Blood dripping from its jaws
and salivating, it licked its lips. The staring eyes – the wolf – it was
himself.

He shut his mind to the vision and his temper began to dispel.
Helghi, no longer a deadly vision of blood and gore, was speaking,
"…if Lord Wulfhere is not happy with the first choice of husband for
his daughter, I have another… here."

Helghi calmly presented his son – the pock-faced Eadnoth.

A blur of gangling flailing arms, fists, and kicking feet, flew at the
unsuspecting son of Helghi who rolled on the floor, clutching his
privates. "See what my sister can do with your balls in your guts – you
verminous slime!"

Wulfhere saw that it was Wulfwin and he stood rigid behind the
defensive wall his friends had built around him, unable to intervene.
Helghi lunged and grabbed Wulfwin's long hair, smashing the boy's
face onto his knee. Blood splashed before Wulfhere's eyes, and he
sprang into action forcing his way through the human palisade like an
almighty boulder bounding down a mountain, sending the men this
way and that. He was about to throw his seax when a gloved hand
wrenched his wrist and grabbed the weapon. Wulfhere whirled and
swung a fist. His assailant moved swiftly aside and Wulfhere missed,
punching the air.

"I suggest you don't do that," Alfwold, the local scīr-reeve said, as
he caught Wulfhere's stray fist, "unless you want to be reduced to

latrine duty with the ceorls."

*

Wulfric paced the floor, his face angry and red as his hair. "Father, do we really have to let Winflæd marry that piece of scite?"

Wulfhere wiped the blood from Wulfwin's injured nose. "Not if I have anything to do with it. Christ on the Cross, it will be over my dead body."

Wulfwin was fingering his bruised and bloodied nose gingerly.

Leofnoth said, "It's not broken – you still look pretty."

"Are you sure? It feels like it." Wulfwin groaned.

"That you're still pretty? I wouldn't go anywhere near the girls just yet, but your beauty will return to its former glory," Leofnoth reassured him.

The others laughed, but Wulfhere didn't. Helghi had gone too far this time. "If that swine comes near me or mine again, they'll be mopping his blood from the floor with his gizzards!"

Wulfric, still pacing, paused to mutter, "What are we going to do about this? You cannot mean to send our sister to live with that maggot-infested *horningsunu?*"

Wulfhere turned tiredly to stare at his son. "Now is not the time to do anything about that. Here is not the place. You heard Alfwold, if he catches us fighting with Helghi again, he will report it to the earl, and Harold will not be as lenient with me as he has been in this matter before."

Wulfric gave an arrogant toss of his head. "Then I will go to the earl and speak with him myself," he said.

"Nay, you will not." Wulfhere clipped his son around the ear. "Trust me, going to the earl now, when we are about to go to war, will not help our cause. We wait – we wait for the right time."

"And when will that time be, Father?" Wulfric asked, folding his arms.

Wulfhere rounded on him. "Not now."

"Leave it, Wulfric," Wulfwin said, removing the compress from his nose to speak. "Father is right. It's is not the time. We can take care of Helghi once and for all without the earl being any wiser. In battle, none would be able to tell what had happened."

"You're right, battle is a good place to do it. No one will know."

Wulfric looked at Wulfhere as though he had stumbled upon something remarkable.

"What kind of madness has removed both of your brains from their rightful place in your heads and inserted them up your arses? Don't you think that during battle we will have bigger enemies to kill?"

"Shush – keep your voices down," interjected Leofnoth. "We don't want anyone to hear this, do we? You lads, your father is right – there will be better times to deal with Helghi and his minions. This is not one of them."

Wulfhere sat in silence and reflected on the idea of killing Helghi in battle. For a moment, ashamedly, he wondered if his sons might be right, he could kill Helghi in the confusion of battle, given a chance. But what worried him most was if he was to die himself. Who then would protect his family?

Later, in their quarters, he sat alone with Leofnoth.

"I have never seen you so crazed as you were tonight. You were like a wolf, growling, snarling, and I swear you were frothing at the mouth."

"Since you have made that observation, I will confess - I thought I was one."

"Christ's wounds, Wulfhere, I believe you are a berserker!"

Wulfhere shook his head and laughed grimly. "What in Hell's name am I going to do about Helghi?"

"I don't know. Kill him?"

"I like that idea. You cannot know how close I came to that today."

"Oh, yes I do."

"But I am better than that, I am not a murderer."

"Nay, but for some reason, it is he who seems to be committing all kinds of wrongs against you, falling into scite and coming up smelling of flowers. Whereas you, my friend, are falling into scite and coming up smelling like a pig's arse."

"I have thought of killing him in battle, but it is the coward's way." He shook his head. "If I am going to kill him, it should be out in the open, I want him to see me coming. I want him to know it was I who took his last breath away from him."

"The trouble with you, my friend, is that you are too principled. Me? I wouldn't think twice about it. In fact, if you want, I'll do it."

"Nay, I beg that you do not. One day, I will get my chance, so don't take it away from me."

Leofnoth put his palms up. "Aye, if that's how you want it, then so it shall be."

Chapter Twenty-six

A Man Worth Following

Scrobbesbyrig

Burghred knew they could not stay outside Scrobbesbyrig forever. It was midday and they had been taking it in turns to get some sleep, but Burghred could rest no longer and roused his comrades. He told Beric to pick up the standard, then gathered his closest companions and together they approached the gates of the walled town. There were grimaces and hands went over mouths so as not to gag as they walked past the rotting corpses that were tied to the stakes.

Burghred stopped a few feet away from them, not enough to be rid of the mouldering stench, but any further forward, and they would have been within arrowshot of the walls.

"Lay down your weapons, men. Beric hold that standard upright, let them see it," he ordered. Then facing the parapet, he cried out, "Wulfgar, I come to negotiate!"

Holed up in one of the towers, Wulfgar came out on the bulwark. "There is nothing to negotiate, Burghred. We stay loyal to Alfgar, the true Lord of Mercia, not you – the whelp, the runt of the litter!" he shouted. "Mercia will never be yours. Come any closer and you will see what loyal Mercians do to traitors!"

Bowmen appeared along the ramparts; arrows nocked. Burghred ordered his men to pick up their weapons and they began to stealthily withdraw.

Burghred called out to Wulfgar, stretching out an arm to the bloodied, maggot infested carcasses as they passed them. "See what *we* do to traitors? This is what awaits you when we take the burgh! It is you who are guilty of treason, Wulfgar – to your king and your people. When the burgh is ours, you will meet a traitor's death, be sure of it."

Wulfgar cupped his hands to his mouth and roared his message, "Men of Mercia, leave this Godwin puppet and return to the fold. Alfgar will forgive those who come back to us now. If you do not, then these fields will be awash with your blood. But the Lord Burghred, we will take alive for his father to do to him as he wishes, and my guess is it won't be pretty."

"My men will not surrender to those who kill like thieves in the night!"

"Then you will all die. Like lambs eaten by wolves!"

Burghred returned to his men and sat with his closest companions, thrashing out ideas for their next move: how to get into Scrobbesbyrig. Most of his army were men in their early twenties, idealists who'd elected to follow the younger lord rather than the older Alfgar. But they were inexperienced, unlike the seasoned warriors inside the burgh, who had served Leofric and grown up alongside Alfgar. The youths had little understanding of war. The most fighting they'd seen was in the meadhall when their bellies were full of ale and their minds addled. But what they lacked in experience, they made up for with fresh blood. Their recently trained muscles were strong; their bones unscarred; their abilities honed.

But as his companions discussed and dismissed various ways into the burgh, Burghred's mind was elsewhere. What if his messengers had his son gatherrwere beaten to the eastern scīra by Alfgar's? He didn't dare voice his doubts aloud and jeopardise his leadership, but if his father was on the move, he could be gathering forces right at that very moment.

A remark by Pendric brought him back to the now. "I say we go back to Gleawecestre; we can bring the king's forces here to meet Alfgar's."

Burghred's cheeks flushed. "Nay! We will not run back to Gleawecestre like cowards. We stay here and fight, or we die."

"Why should we die if we can save ourselves and fight another day?" said Pendric, his tone reasonable.

"And what if the men from the east come and we are not here? How foolish will that make us look?" Burghred stood and began pacing.

"What if they don't come at all, lord?" Siward asked. "What if Alfgar comes, and we are sitting out here, undefended, ready to be slaughtered. None of our own messengers have yet returned."

"It has been but a few days since we sent them out. We need to be patient," Burghred reminded them. "Give them time."

"The men of Stafford should be on their way by now," Idwald added. "Stafford is no more than a day's ride."

Burghred's rounded on them. "Shall we run, then? Is that what you are asking me to do?"

Wulfmær approached him tentatively, "Lord, we need to devise a plan, urgently. It is not safe for us to be in this place like this."

"What do you propose we do, Wulfmær?"

When Wulfmær did not reply, Burghred turned and walked away out of earshot.

Wulfmær followed and caught up with him. "I understand that you feel you cannot go back, lord. All your hopes are on this – but the men do not understand that."

"They do not need to understand," Burghred replied. "All they need to remember is that they gave their oath to me; to follow and fight with me."

"And they do." Wulfmær's gaze was supportive.

Burghred stopped in the shade of an old oak. "Then they need not gainsay me – we will stay put, wait for word to come, and when it does, we will decide our next move."

"And what if word does not come, lord?"

"You are not helping me. Ulric would have been more positive," Burghred said, a hand sweeping through his hair in frustration.

"Men are not exactly rushing to your banner, are they, lord?"

There had been no heat in Wulfmær's voice, nonetheless Burghred had not liked what he'd said. "You dare to say this to me? Am I not a man worth following?" For a moment he thought his bitterness had unnerved his young retainer, but the steady eyes, never left his own and the calm voice continued.

"Aye, lord, you are. None of us would be with you now if you were not. But not everyone knows you as we do, and we have to accept that the men we are trying to convince may not be for turning." Wulfmær put a hand on Burghred's shoulder. "Let us go back to Gleawecestre, where we can warn the king. We can march with the fyrd, meet with Alfgar with a larger force."

Burghred pulled away from him. "I will not give up this chance to win the earldom!"

"What use is a dead lord to an earldom?"

Burghred barely heard Wulfmær's last remark.

The sound of cantering hooves caught his attention and his gaze drifted to the river. A single rider was coming across the long grass. The youth, Wolfram, hardly out of his adolescence, leapt off his steed and ran to them.

The lad addressed him, puffing from his recent exertion. "Good news! They are coming. The lords of Mercia have agreed to join us. The men of Stafford are on their way. The rest have promised to follow."

Burghred beamed and punched the air with a whoop of delight. He reeled Wolfram to face the men in the camp. "Tell them, boy!"

Wolfram repeated his message, the excitement in his voice clear. Men grabbed one another and a great roar rose from them, and Burghred sprinted towards the gates of the burgh.

"You hear that? They are coming, Wulfgar! Soon this place will be surrounded with Mercians, *my* Mercians. I'm going to hang you, Wulfgar! Your evil infested rotting carcass will be swaying in the wind for the crows to peck at your eyes and feast on your decaying cock!"

Beric panting, reached him with his shield to cover him from any arrow attack, but Wulfgar called out of the tower. "You can try, whelp, you should know by now that Scrobbesbyrig is not for taking. The walls are impregnable." The Reeve of Scrobbesbyrig went on to shout more but his voice no longer carried over the yells and cheers of Burghred's men.

Burghred, relieved, sighed. He could afford to wait now, and for the next hour or two, the men shared insults across the fields. The morning sun that had been shining so brightly earlier was now shrouded by the gathering clouds, and a warm breeze was now picking up. He sent out men to forage for supplies, taking food from nearby settlement who had no choice but to give it.

As Burghred and his men sat around in groups, drinking, and entertaining themselves by thinking up the best insults for their foes, the sound of hooves could be heard. Burghred turned his head to the path along the river, his heart quickening. It had to be the thegns of Stafford.

But there was no sign of the promised army. Instead six riders, wearing helms and hauberks, galloped into the camp.The horsemen sped straight past him through the camp, sending men reeling. The fluttering of anxiety rose from his stomach to his throat as he recognised Alfgar's banner, the charging boar.

Each rider swung something that rolled and bounced like a thrown ball made of pig bladders. Around him men recoiled in horror and the sky instantly darkened as if to give credence to this evil portent.

Burghred drew his sword and the riders halted in a circular formation, rump to rump, bows drawn, warning them not to come closer.

One of them lifted his helm and exposed his face.

Ragnald!

"I bring you your men, Lord Burghred, regrettably just the heads. As you can see, their mission was not successful. Your father is on his way with an army ten times bigger than this little gathering here. And the men you thought were coming to *your* aid... they march to meet him."

Burghred looked to where the putrefying faces of his messengers lay on the ground. He could smell them, and his stomach roiled. In a matter of minutes, his exhilaration had been ripped out of him and was now a humiliating defeat. He glanced at young Wolfram, who stood rigid, disbelieving, with gaping mouth and eyes.

"M-my lord – it – it must be a-a trick!" the boy cried.

"Not a trick," Ragnald replied. "The thegns were easily swayed. They know who best to throw in their lot with."

A roar went up and a hand axe spun through the air, embedding itself in one of the riders' thighs. Immediately, the injured man loosed his arrow and it caught the assailant through skull and bone sinking him to his knees. Before anyone could avenge him, the rider had another arrow nocked, showing no discomfort despite the blade embedded in his leg.

Ragnald smirked. "We are not weak like you and your boys here."

Angry heat rose within Burghred. "Bastard!" he spat, pushing forward. His men held him, cautioning him with anxious voices.

"Aye, hold the little *scite*." Ragnald wore a look of malicious triumph, his spear only a finger's width away from Burghred's chest. "Come near me, *Swica,* and I'll run you through. It would be a shame not to meet you in battle, or should I say, 'your slaughter'? Best you scurry back to Uncle Godwinson, if you want to live."

Ragnald's words stung Burghred and he felt a storm of fury welling within him. "You better hurry back to Alfgar, then, and tell him to get a move on." Burghred spoke evenly, though shaking. "I am not going anywhere."

Ragnald gave an ominous laugh. The man with the axe in his leg removed it with a defiant gesture, backhanding it so that it bounced along the ground leaving a bloody trail. Ragnald heeled his horse and he and his followers, cloaks fluttering behind them, turned their horses and galloped toward the burgh.

Burghred stood at the edge of the camp and watched, his jaw muscles grinding, as his father's captain halted by the corpses and circled his horse around the bodies. Ragnald looked back and even from that distance Burghred could sense the malice. He watched as Ragnald reached down to run his blade through the rope securing his son, hefted the body over the front of his saddle and rode away. He left Burghred nothing: no cry of anger, no declaration of vengeance, no tears, no sentiments of any kind, just the knowledge that he'd been dealt a heavy blow.

Rounding on his men with a towering rage, Burghred shouted at them, "We should have dragged them from their horses and killed them, sent their fucking heads back to my father! Don't you, any of you," he roared, pointing his sword at them all, "ever put your hands on me again!" He thrust his face at Wulfmær's. "Why did you stop me?"

"We were not prepared, lord," Wulfmær said.

"There were just six of them!" Burghred scrubbed his hair in frustration. He was so angry.

"Six mounted men with spears and arrows aimed at us all," Wulfmær told him. Unlike Burghred, he was calm.

Burghred sank to his knees in dismay. How could he be a good leader when even his own men went against him? Not for the first time, he felt the effects of his inexperience.

It was then, as he prayed for God's guidance, that the spilled pot of water and the smoke came to his mind. It was a sign. God would not have sent him the idea if it were for nought. He must fight! There was no going back. He had no choice.

Chapter Twenty-seven

"For God and Mercia!"

Wulfgar watched the advancing wedge from his high point on the parapet.

Before him was a sea of polished steel; glinting spearheads cutting the air as they trooped up the sloping field in close formation. He calculated they came in ten lines of twenty. Burghred, recognisable by the green cross on his shield, positioned himself in the front line, commands rasping as they marched. An eagle flapped above the heads of his warriors on his pennant, giving the impression it followed them into battle. The booming of metal as weapons thrashed against shields and the roaring of voices responding to their leader's exhortations rang out thunderously: "For God, king, and Mercia!" and "Death to traitors!"

They were impressive, but Wulfgar sneered at this boastful display. The heat was dwindling. He sniffed the air. "The wind is in their favour."

"They might have the wind in their favour, but they will need more than wind to get past these walls," Inewulf said.

"Fools," said Ragnald as he grasped the edge of the parapet, his knuckles white. "When Alfgar gets here, they will not be shouting with such self-assurance."

"Alfgar will tear Burghred apart," said Inewulf.

"Not if I get to him first," Ragnald growled. "I will kill two birds with one stone this day. I will avenge my lord's honour *and* my son's death. When this is over, my sword shall be dripping with the bastard's blood and entrails – they'll be left for the wolves and ravens." Ragnald's eyes were as cold as steel. "To think that my son and that *earsling* drank from the same ale horn and shared the same

264

hearth space before they were old enough to hold a spear in their hands. Alfgar was foster-father to my son – he will not begrudge me my vengeance."

"I wouldn't be so sure," Wulfgar said shaking his head. "Justice belongs to Alfgar by right of blood."

But Ragnald was defiant. "I know Lord Alfgar better than either of you. I have served him for nigh on thirty years – loyally, and with honour. His son killed mine, and vengeance for this bloodletting is mine by right. Alfgar will not deny me. He will have Burghred's head and he can give it to Magnus."

Wulfgar let him be. He knew Ragnald well enough to know he must always say the last word. Turning to Inewulf, Wulfgar spoke quietly so that Ragnald could not hear, "If I had a son who had betrayed me as Burghred betrayed Alfgar, I would not suffer any man to take my right to decide his fate. See that Ragnald does not get near him, even if you have to kill him – Ragnald that is. Burghred must be taken alive."

"Last night, you wanted Burghred dead."

"That was last night. This is now."

Inewulf grunted and Wulfgar turned his attention to the enemy coming into range. He commanded his archers to nock their arrows, then shouted for the draw. "Loose!"

An answering cry went up and Burghred's men leapt into action to form a *foulcon*, locking their shields together in a tight protective shell.

Wulfgar swore.

As the arrows thudded to the ground uselessly falling short, shouts of *"Steppan!"* reverberated up to the parapet, and the formation moved forward, one step at a time.

"They can't hide behind their shields forever," Ragnald said.

Wulfgar was irritated. "They can hide behind them until we run out of arrows, then they can use them to attack us."

"We judged wrongly. They are not in range. Wait until they get closer. There will be more chance of breaching the shieldwall," Inewulf said. "Bring up the javelins, Wulfgar. When the rabble are near enough, it will have more of an impact on them, breaching the shell, leaving openings for the arrows to break through."

Wulfgar had to agree. Inewulf was right. Less waste of good arrows and missiles.

As the *foulcon* marched decisively toward them, Wulfgar gave orders to pull men from other sides of the stockade, leaving smaller units to guard the other areas. If the action was going to be concentrated here on the south side of the palisade, he saw no sense in having warriors inactive elsewhere.

"Wulfgar!" cried Ragnald. He pointed at a unit of six on the enemy's left flank breaking away from the shieldwall. They moved, crablike, sheltered by some crude makeshift contraption. "What in God's name are the fools trying to do?" He laughed loudly. "They'll never make it!"

Wulfgar shouted to the archers on his right, "Shoot at *those* bastards!"

Undaunted, the little group of Burghred's men sallied forth, skirting the field in an arc, tightly enclosed behind their protective casing.

"Inewulf, take command of the archers over there. The stupid idiots haven't seen what's coming their way." Wulfgar pointed to the other side of the gated entrance. "See that they aim at those crazy whoresons in the moving shieldwall."

Inewulf nodded and leapt down off the parapet to carry out Wulfgar's orders.

Wulfgar turned next to the men nearest him. "You lot, ready the javelins, as many as you've got, and any other missiles, stones in slings – anything that can be thrown."

"Very well, lord!"

"Archers!" Wulfgar shouted, "Prepare to aim! And nock! Draw... loose!"

Arrows flew into the *foulcon*, briefly halting Burghred's army, only to stick harmlessly in the shields.

We need to break through that shell. Wulfgar started to sweat. "Hurry up with those javelins and missiles! Come on! Where are they?!"

Three ceorls came up with bundles clutched in their arms. "Here, lord!" one of them cried, throwing them on the wooden deck. Men started grabbing them. Wulfgar snatched up one himself.

The barrage was relentless as the weapons crashed into the foe, going on for several rounds with alternating bouts of arrows and javelins. Wulfgar punched the air with satisfaction, hearing the screams that came from the enemy lines. Inewulf had been right: the bombardment had forced gaps amongst the shields, allowing the

266

missiles to penetrate the body of men within the shell.

Wulfgar glanced to where Inewulf's archers were following his commands readying their arrows for the next round. Shouts of warning rang through the air as three of Burghred's warriors appeared from behind the mantlet to release a volley, hitting their targets before Inewulf's men could discharge their own. Cries of delight could be heard from the enemy as their tips thwacked into exposed torsos.

Wulfgar clenched his fists. "Kill them!"

A sudden chaos erupted in the shieldwall below. A column of men was retreating down the slope to a wooded area to the left of the burgh. Wulfgar called out to Inewulf, "Do you see them running?" he cried.

Inewulf turned to watch. More seemed to be joining the escaping troops as they ran from the onslaught of arrows. Insults were flung at the fleeing enemy. At least half of Burghred's army was deserting him.

Burghred appeared to be desperately ordering them to stop and failing. The young leader was pleading with them, calling them cowards and *niðinga*, men of no honour.

"Draw!" called out Wulfgar. "Loose!"

The arrows flew into the disorder and Burghred's warriors went down screaming. Wulfgar smiled and said under his breath, "I've done you a favour, *Swica*, and stopped them for you!"

*

After the first hail of arrows, Burghred ordered his men to move forward once more. Their battle cries flooded the air. "Why aren't they shooting at us now, lord?" asked Beric.

"They want us closer – that last volley went nowhere," Burghred said.

As they manoeuvred nearer to the burgh, Burghred prepared to accept another barrage of arrows. When the cry to draw came, he called out to the men to ready themselves, and when the order came to release, he raised his shield over his head, shouting, "Reform!" and his men leapt into their positions in the *foulcon*.

An arrow shot through his shield, strumming as it caught there. Down on a knee, he swore, thankful that he was quicker than the enemy.

"Stay down, men! Do not move until you hear my order!"

Burghred's instructions were echoed by his commanders throughout the lines. Screaming and the jarring thuds of javelins could be heard all around as the *foulcon* cracked like an egg.

"Close those gaps!" Burghred bellowed from under the protective casing of the shields. "I can still see blue sky! Close them, damn you!"

Shields crashed together, as they covered the breeches made by the fallen. Nearby, a cry of pain went up from a warrior who had been struck. Burghred flinched. He felt a shuddering and realised it was Beric trembling beside him. It was the boy's first battle, possibly his last, and Burghred felt responsible. But he had a plan, and it was time for that plan to come to fruition.

He turned to Pendric behind him and whispered, "Feign retreat," trusting that Pendric would send the order back through the lines. He turned to Beric, "Ready, lad?"

Beric's voice quivered as he asked, "Now, lord?"

"Yes, now, Beric."

"B-but the arrows, lord?"

"It's unlikely they will be hit running away from them. You have everything?"

"Aye, lord."

"Then get going. Get your men and go! Now!"

"Now, lord?"

"Yes, now! Now is the time!"

"But we are more than a hundred yards away, lord. You said a hundred yards."

"*Now, Beric!* I don't care what I said earlier. The thing needs to be done, and it needs to be done now! Our only chance of getting in is to get them out, and that's your job!"

"Yes, lord, as you say, lord." Beric moved out of the line and shields closed in and readjusted.

Burghred heaved a sigh as a drop of sweat from underneath his helm slid off his nose. The warrior with the javelin in his chest was crying and a comrade was trying to comfort him.

"Leave that man!" shouted Burghred, "Cover that hole or I'll make you one of your own!"

At last the barrage stopped. Crouching, Burghred peeped from under cover to look behind him. As he'd hoped, the men were carrying out orders dutifully, feigning retreat, running into the woods where Wulfmær and a score of others were already hiding with the horses.

He leapt up from his haunches and shouted to the runners that they were vile cowards, calling them all *niðingas*. Some of them were shot down by Wulfgar's bowmen and his heart lurched for his warriors. *The bastard will pay!*

Wulfgar called out from the palisade. "Your army is deserting you. See how they run? They know you cannot win. There is no way in, Burghred. Run with your men. Soon your father will be here, with warriors by the thousands – and there will be a great slaughter – yours – so run, run back to Harold Godwinson with your tail between your legs, you useless barrow of maggot infested crap! The worms will crawl up every hole in your body, whelp!"

Devastated at the loss of those men shot down, Burghred turned, hoping that Beric and his small contingent had made it to the gates. He saw the mantlet they had used for cover. Behind it they lit the fires quickly and Burghred allowed himself a smile.

"Pendric, gather your men and go!" he yelled.

Whilst Pendric and a unit of archers rushed to the gates to protect Beric and the fire-starters, Burghred took stock around him. Men were still running out of the formation into the woods, others were trying to form up in the confusion. He scrubbed at the rivulets of sweat that trickled out of his helm with the back of his hand. Not even the wind provided any relief from the hellish heat bubbling within his armour. His confidence wavered at the shouted insults from the rampart. His stomach roiled; his bowels contracted. *God give me victory this day and that Wulfgar swallows his words with his pride when I am through those gates!*

"Men of Mercia! Form up on me!" Burghred coughed, his voice cracking as he repeated the order again and again until men sprang as if from nowhere around him. One of his men caught an arrow with his shield and another arrow thuncked into the ground before him. *They must run out of missiles soon!* he thought gleefully as fewer and fewer were loosed at them.

The cries of the injured rang across the field as men were doing their best to move their wounded comrades out of danger. The stench of burning grass wafted through the air and Burghred turned toward Beric's unit to see that several small fires were now lit. Missiles and arrows were raining down on them but were being deflected by the bowmen sent to cover them. A man on the palisade screamed as a returning javelin slammed into his chest.

Burghred felt a sense of pride. They were *his* men, oathsworn, and they were risking their lives for him. He was Burghred, Lord of

Mercia, and if he died today, at least he would do so in the truth that men believed in him.

Instinctively, he looked toward the parapet. He'd felt Ragnald's hateful glare boring into him before he even saw it. Burghred sneered, certain that Ragnald was, like him, determining where he would sink his blade when the time came for them to face each other. Burghred shivered involuntarily. Either he or Ragnald would die today and Burghred prayed that it would be his hand alone that killed his father's captain.

At the sizzling sound of water on flames, Burghred's head swivelled. A man on the parapet was looking over the side, holding an empty bucket as Beric and his comrades worked to keep the fires smouldering with dampened dried grass. It had not been enough to put them out, but the fool could not have known it was just enough to reduce them to smoking embers which was what Burghred had intended.

Siward beside him shouted above the din, "Lord, there is smoke! It is working – just as you planned." The young man was excited, and he lifted the eagle penon high, punching the air with it.

Burghred smiled. The smoke rose thinly at first but was growing thicker. It *was* working. The dampened grass and leaves that the fire-starters had doused the fires with were turning it into blinding smoke.

He looked down each side along the row of his men as he stood in their centre.

"Lock shields!" he cried. His shoulders lifted. His warriors stood determined and steadfast, their armour and helms polished, their spears clutched in their hands and looking every bit worthy of fighting men. They were a smaller unit now, but all that had to happen was for the enemy inside to open the gates to face and fight them.

*

"We need to get to the gates, before they burn them down!" Wulfgar shouted.

Ragnald was grumbling. "We should have had oil, bloody boiling oil!"

"Never mind the oil, half his army has run away. Now we can fight them outside the burgh. We will kill them all!" Wulfgar gave Ragnald a sidelong glance of warning. "But not Burghred. I want him alive."

Leaving archers on the parapet to continue their onslaught, Wulfgar shouted to his commanders to form their squad of a hundred men before the gates. Banging their shields and sounding their horns, they shouted, "Alfgar! Alfgar!"

Wulfgar waited for the signal from the parapet that meant it was safe to open the gates. A cacophony of shouting filled the air along with the heat and odour of scorched wood. His hands shook as he readied his spear and when the horn sounded three times, he gave the order to unlock the gate.

*

"They don't appear to be coming yet!" Siward said, looking behind him.

"Don't worry, they will," Burghred said. "Just stand fast and don't worry!"

Smoke billowed around them, good and thick now. A sound of wood being pulled through brackets could be heard.

"They're opening the gate, lord!" a man shouted.

"Ready the javelins!" Burghred shouted. The excitement of impending battle filled his senses. "Now! Throw!"

The javelins whooshed across the sward and Burghred called to his men to ready the spears. The great fog that had moments before hampered Burghred's vision had diminished to spiralling tendrils. Wulfgar's men could be seen dropping, hit by the steel points of the missiles. Burghred wondered if they realised it was their own that they had thrown previously at their enemies that were now killing them.

There was a muffled sound of a distant horn. The ground trembled. Wulfmær was coming. *Thank God!* Burghred grinned and he shouted. "Come on lads! Get ready to shatter their spirits!" He tried to moisten his lips, but his mouth was barren. "Stand hard men! Spears ready!"

Horns blared again, louder this time and the growling earth vibrated stronger. Burghred looked over his shoulder. The mounted unit was behind them, charging from the rear. They were a magnificent sight. "*Foreweard gengan!* Forward advance!"

Moving forward with cries of *"Ut! Ut!"* the smoke billowed across them and through holes in the fog, Wulfgar's men were seen recovering from the onslaught of missiles. Beric and his men bravely engaged them inside the gateway, pushing them back, keeping them busy so they could not shut the gates.

"Attack!" Burghred shouted as the horses thundered behind him, closer now.

He ran forth, his men running with him.

Horses appeared on their flanks either side of them, their riders cutting down any enemy who attempted to run out of the burgh to escape by slashing through Beric's men.

Burghred laughed, hardly concealing his pleasure at the success of his plan unfurling like the smoke that swirled above the smouldering fires.

"God is with us!" he shouted. Raising his spear he thrust it into the first man who got in his way.

*

As the gates opened, Wulfgar and his men rushed forward. His vision was obscured.

"Fuck! Where's the smoke coming from?" Wulfgar shouted. His eyes stung; a trail of snot seeped from his nostrils.

"*They're* creating the smoke!" Inewulf shouted.

"Of course they bloody are! Tell me something I don't know!" Wulfgar cursed, folding an arm across his eyes to protect them.

Men around him were being hit by javelins. Wulfgar brought his shield up to defend himself.

"We have to withdraw back inside - shut the gates!" Inewulf cried, his voice muffled by the sounds of ominous roars.

Wulfgar began shouting for his men to draw back inside, but they were confused and, stuck in a narrow space.

"Close the gates! Close the gates!" someone shouted.

Horns were blowing. Men cried out in rage and agony, the clash of weapons resounding in the disorder.

Then came men on horseback, an earth-shattering explosion of splintered wood as they charged through the open space. The gates, already flung wide open, burst from their hinges and horses trampled over the screaming wounded.

The blades carving into squelching flesh brought the bile up in Wulfgar's throat as men were hacked to the ground.

He found himself being pushed back, tripping over the fallen left to die in their blood and innards. He lost his spear as he tried to keep on his feet but found space to draw his sword and began slashing at any man on foot who came near him. Chaos. He must kill or be killed himself.

Chapter Twenty-eight

Blood of a Traitor

Scrobbesbyrig

Burghred's men burst from the smoke and in through the smouldering gates of Scrobbesbyrig, roaring war cries accompanied by the shattering of shields, armour, and bones. The beautiful music of battle.

Wulfgar's defenders broke under the onslaught of the rider's charge, reeling back into the burgh in disarray. Leaving his spear in the heart of a squirming enemy, Burghred drew his sword and slashed at the dazed men before him, stabbing one in the throat, then another in his mouth. The blood lust on him, Burghred had achieved what had earlier seemed impossible. The siege was broken.

Screams of victory exploded all around him. His warriors fought like demons as though they had caught his battle fever. Wulfmær's riders shouted and jeered, their horse's hooves clipping the cobbled pathways. Blades hacked at limbs and torsos as men mown down or butchered by infantry cried out for mercy. Fountains of blood spurted everywhere and whoops of delight rang in Burghred's ears.

When the fighting was over, Wulfgar, Inewulf, and Ragnald were nowhere to be seen. Wulfgar's thegns, their spirits broken, threw down their weapons and yielded, though some died still battling to the end, drawing their last breaths.

A search was carried out and a weary, beleaguered Wulfgar was found, hidden in a pigsty, disarmed and manacled, and brought before Burghred. He wore no helmet and his face, blackened by the smoke, was bruised, bloody, and beaten, his eyes still defiant.

"Kneel, Wulfgar, kneel to your victor. Did I not tell you it would be so?" Burghred felt pity for the man, seeing him reduced to such a state – stinking of pig-shit.

"I will not kneel to you, *fæderswica.*"

Burghred was not surprised by his insult. He'd heard it more than once that day, but the pity he'd felt vanished and he struck Wulfgar with the handle of his *seax*, splitting the man's mouth. "Kneel! Kneel or I will cut your knees, so you have no choice!"

A mouthful of bloodied spittle was Wulfgar's reply. Burghred cuffed it from his face then shouted to the men with spears. "Make him kneel!"

Wulfgar's legs were smacked at the back with the shaft of a spear and he groaned as he buckled, and he was forced down onto his knees.

"Now swear your fealty to me as your new lord, Wulfgar. And swear that you will be a good and loyal subject of your king, Edward!"

Wulfgar remained silent.

"Lord." Beric approached. "We have rounded up the townsfolk and stray fighters; the rest of the men have locked themselves within the church."

"Then burn them out," Burghred said.

"Lord, it is a church, a place of worship," Beric replied, his eyes wide with dismay. "Besides, there are women and children there too."

"Well, then warn them first, I'm sure they'd rather not burn. If they don't submit, then at least they had their chance!"

His young servant tried to protest but scuttled away at Burghred's seething look.

Turning back to Wulfgar, staring at him with hateful eyes, Burghred demanded, "Do you still deny me and your king?"

"I already serve the king. Such has been the duty of this burgh for generations."

"And yet you are on your knees, a traitor."

"I am also loyal servant to the *true* earl of Mercia, your father, Alfgar. You remember him, don't you? I will not bow down to a hand-puppet of the Godwinsons!"

"My father is a traitor. He is not *for* the king, but against him. Do you not understand that he wants to put Harald of Norwæg on the throne?" Burghred looked around. "*Where* is Ragnald? Ask *him*!"

"You lie," said Wulfgar. "Alfgar only wants what is rightfully his, and Mercia desires that he remains our lord. The very idea that he would put a Norwægian on the throne is preposterous!"

"You're a fool if you believe that, Wulfgar," replied Burghred. "I was there when they planned it."

"Alfgar may be many things, but he is a true Mercian. He wants what is good for the people of this land," Wulfgar said.

"Then why were the Norwægians in Rhuddlan making an alliance with Alfgar and Gruffudd? Is it so hard for you to believe that the man you all seem to value above any other might not be the man you think he is?"

Wulfgar's eyes brimmed with moisture, his resolve wavering. Burghred forced back the pity as he studied this proud man brought on his knees and broken before his gloating captors.

Burghred hunkered down on his haunches. He spoke softly, "Wulfgar, my father has only ever had his own interests at heart. He thinks that if he helps this Norwægian Harald take the throne, he will gain favour with the new king. That he will have more than he had from Edward. Your lands will be given to the Norþmenn – your children made slaves; your wife will be no more than their whore. How else do you think Alfgar is going to pay them? With Mercian lives and lands – that's how!"

Wulfgar lifted his head; shook it in denial. "It is *you* who are the false one, Burghred. And soon your father will be here, and he will burn you out and you will squeal like a rat!"

Burghred sighed and returned to his feet. "Alfgar is not the only one who is coming," he said looking down at his captive. "So is the king – with an even greater army – and you will be hung as a traitor along with my father – dishonourably – like the piece of *scite* that you are!" He turned to his men. "Now take him and sling him back with the pigs where he belongs!"

They poured out of the church at the first sign of smoke when, as a warning, a fire-arrow hit the roof. The odour of burning thatch stank in the air as they surrendered, accepting Burghred as their new lord. Ragnald and Inewulf were still in the church, refusing to surrender and determined to hold out with a handful of stubborn men who also had no wish to yield.

Burghred shook his head as he watched them attempt to defend their religious fortress from the belfry. The priest leant out of the loft hatch shouting his defiance at them and bombarded them with arrows and javelins.

"Look at those fools," Burghred said to his men. "They must know that this is futile."

Despite what he'd said to Beric earlier, he'd no desire to burn in hell. The thought of innocent children dying in there unnerved him.

"Wulfmær, take men, go into the church and bring them out or kill them, but not Ragnald, I want the bastard alive."

Some of the men would not give up the fight until they were dead, among them Inewulf whom Burghred felt regret that he had not been able to win that noble man over.

Ragnald was found and dragged, struggling, before his conqueror, stripped of his armour and in irons. Burghred ordered that Wulfgar also be brought to him.

They were forced to bend to him and Burghred gazed at the two men. In Wulfgar, he saw only resignation. Ragnald, on the other hand, mocking. Burghred refused to give anything of himself away, his expression rigid. He did not want to bring bad *wyrd* upon himself by revelling in the blood he'd shed that day, risking God's wrath.

Blood trickled from a deep gash on Ragnald's temple, but he showed no discomfort. A battle-hardened man, hard in body and hard in heart.

It irritated Burghred that he should stand there so bold in the face of capture. "Tell him, Ragnald…" Burghred tossed a nod at Wulfgar. "Tell him the truth about my father and his plans."

Ragnald laughed. "You think it will matter, now? What good will it do? Alfgar will soon be here, and when he is, all men will show their obedience to him."

Wulfgar, his face like stone, looked at the man beside him.

"'Tis true, is it not Ragnald," Burghred said, his voice laced with irony, "that Alfgar's plan is to replace Edward with Harald of Norwæg? You've lied to Wulfgar all along. Haven't you?"

Ragnald laughed. The truth dawned in Wulfgar's weary eyes, and screaming a curse, he slammed his forehead into Ragnald's face.

Blood poured from a split between Ragnald's brows as the guards dragged him from Wulfgar's reach.

Burghred smiled with satisfaction. "So, you *are* a liar as well as a traitor?"

Ragnald flicked his tongue at the bright scarlet liquid that dripped down his nose and into his mouth. "Who are you to accuse *me* of betrayal?"

"My loyalty has always been to God and my anointed king, Edward."

"Loyalty," growled Ragnald, "is owed to the lord who feeds you, nurtures you, gives you succour, and pays you in gold, silver and land. The man who gave you your life, more than once!"

The heat rose in Burghred's cheeks. "That man was my grandfather, Leofric. *He* was everything to me when I was growing into manhood – not my father."

"Alfgar taught you the ways of a warrior," Ragnald went on, "He taught you how to fight and to kill. You used those skills to betray him and shame him."

"I would not have done what I did if you had not turned him on the wrong path. It was *you* who goaded him into exile. *You* who led him to Gruffudd, wasn't it?"

"Alfgar thinks for himself."

Burghred's heart pumped and the urge to pace was overwhelming. "You have always sought to usurp me from my father's side," he growled at the man he hated, "You resented me. I was Alfgar's son., and you wanted to be close to him, so you could counsel him in ways that would gain you favours before anybody else. Before even me!"

"I have always loved Alfgar. I have been loyal to him for years. But everything he has given me I have earned. You were always the jealous son, jealous of his regard for me."

"Oh yes, you love my father – not as a son loves a father or a brother loves a brother. You love him only for the reputation it gives you. You wanted me out of the way because I am what stood between you and he."

Burghred halted his pacing, the hatred in his heart raw. He had spent all his adolescent years failing to impress his father and Ragnald had always been there to gloat in the background like a snake, urging Alfgar to ridicule him.

Burghred returned to his agitated pacing, an incident long ago but not forgotten plaguing his mind. A prank that Ragnald had engineered, sending him on a wild goose chase for something that had never gone missing in the first place. Burghred saw his fifteen-year-old self, red-faced, humiliated, the subject of much hilarity as his father's retainers made fun of him. There were many such memories, painful and haunting, and they flashed before Burghred's eyes one after another.

He looked back at his prisoner, and a feeling that he was somehow detached from what was going on came over him. Ragnald's lips moved, but Burghred's reality was what was happening in his head, in his mind… as though he were somewhere else in another time and place.

One day his father made him fight Ragnald in a hand-to-hand combat tournament. Burghred had been just sixteen, small in stature, but wiry for his age, but inexperienced. Ragnald, twenty years older, had been Alfgar's strongest and most skilled warrior. Alfgar had wanted Ragnald to toughen Burghred up. It was his opinion that Burghred was cossetted by his grandparents and a weakling because of it. Ragnald had beaten him to a pulp; flung him around as if he were a pup.

A shudder went through him as the images in his mind took on a greater life. Ragnald had not stopped the beating, even when Burghred had yielded. He recalled again the terror that he was going to die as blow after blow devastated his face, his head, his body, until he finally passed into merciful unconsciousness.

Afterwards, when he learned that his father had done nothing to stop it, had refused to punish Ragnald for his over-zealousness, a deep depression followed. Alfgar accused Burghred of oversensitivity, and worse than that, he broke him.

That was the day he learned the secret about his mother.

"She was not your real mother. Your *real* mother was the daughter of a traitor. She betrayed me. Your blood is tainted. I wanted Ragnald to beat it out of you, though much good it had done."

So, the woman whom he had only ever called his mother was not, after all, the soft gentle lady his father had married, but a daughter of a murderous traitor. Pleas to tell him who that traitor was went unanswered. And to this day he still did not know.

Burghred had cut himself that day, watching the blood from his arm seeping onto the floor rushes. He saw it now, as vivid as it had been then. The blood of a traitor. Had he turned against his father because he was destined to?

Burghred shook his head in disbelief. He was not to blame. There, in front of him, was the man who had caused this.

"You!" shouted Burghred, storming toward Ragnald and drawing his seax. "You brought the hatred between my father and I!"

"You did that yourself, you ingrate!" Ragnald retorted.

"You told my father my blood was tainted!"

"I did not have to tell him that. If you want anyone to blame, blame your mother," Ragnald hissed. "She was the one with the traitor's blood, and now it is yours."

Burghred lunged. He'd intended to slash Ragnald's throat, but Ragnald's words stayed him.

"Coward!" Ragnald jeered. "Kill me while I am down on my knees with my hands in irons? Is that how you killed Ælred? Is that how you killed my son? Show everyone – all your followers – how much of a man their lord is and unshackle me. Fight me with a weapon and shield in my hands!"

"Beric!"

"Lord?"

Burghred's gaze never left Ragnald's steely stare. "Get me my shield and bring this man his sword and shield also."

Burghred indicated for his men to unshackle the prisoner. Burghred bent forward, calling to Beric to help him out of his chainmail.

"What are you doing, lord?" Beric asked him.

"I will not have it said that I killed a man wearing armour while he did not."

Out of his mail, he paced the yard like an enraged bull. "You sent your son to kill me and instead *I killed him*! You should have learned from Ivar, no one can kill me! You want revenge, Ragnald?"

Ragnald stood rubbing his sore wrists. He did not answer. Instead he muttered some oath under his breath and spat in Burghred's direction.

Burghred drew his sword and clasped the shield that Beric had given him. He prepared his stance and lifted his weapon. "You want revenge, dog? Then come take it!"

Ragnald took his shield and sword. He roared his war cry and stormed toward Burghred.

"Wait, lord!" Beric cried. "You must let the priest absolve you both first!"

Beric's words came too late, for Ragnald laid into Burghred with frightening energy, pushing him back, his sword strokes fast and fierce. Burghred swung his shield to parry them, bringing his weapon into play, stepping forward, slashing high and low, trying to find a way to break open the other man's shield.

Ragnald slipped. But Burghred let go this opportunity to better his enemy to catch his breath. Pain and blood flowed from an injury to his sword arm, and the day's fighting weighed heavily on his muscles.

Ragnald was back on his feet. They stood facing each other again. Ragnald was panting, struggling to breathe.

"Come on old man, you're losing your touch," Burghred taunted. "Look at you, you're worn out already. You've not had as much as I've had to do all day. It was I who had to march up that hill, all you've done is stand on the palisade and watch."

Still trying to get his breath back, Ragnald continued to pant.

"Kill me, then, dog! What are you waiting for? I killed your son. He died crying, like a frightened piggy squealing for its mother. He cried out for her, like a *bearn*, wailing as I cut his throat!"

A rasping, terrifying scream emanated from Ragnald as he rushed forward, weapon raised. Burghred's reactions were quicker and sharper this time. He averted the blow and immediately moved towards him, countering Ragnald, blocking all his well-aimed shots. As quickly as Ragnald defended himself, Burghred was looking for his next hits. He lowered his sword arm and swiped to his right, finding his way to the back of Ragnald's knee. The blade tore into a meaty calf, and the squelch as Burghred withdrew it was sickening.

Ragnald cried out, stumbled out of Burghred's reach, haemorrhaging profusely from the wound. He let out his war cry once more and lurched forward, clumsily, crashing his shield into Burghred's face.

On his back, and stunned, Burghred tasted blood as hundreds of sparks burst around his head like a hammer banging an anvil. Voices called him to get up and he grasped for his shield, rolled to one side, and leapt to his feet just as Ragnald brought his weapon down, missing him closely. The numbness in his nose and lips palpitated, as he stood recovering. Blood dripped down the back of his throat, making him gag and cough out the blood which dribbled down his front.

Before he was ready, Ragnald came at him again and Burghred quickly pulled himself together, wielding his sword left and right, pushing his opponent back. Weary with the effort, he dropped his guard, and Ragnald cut him once more, and he staggered, losing strength. Burghred waited for the breath to return to his lungs. The old cur had worn himself out. Through bloodied lips, he gave Ragnald a wry smile. "Just a little taste of what is to come."

Ragnald lifted his blade again, weakly this time. Burghred was surprised the man still stood. His *winningas* were stained red and yet the man still came, feigning shots and dragging his feet half-heartedly.

Burghred's must have been more affected by the blow to his face than he'd thought, for he sensed a slowing in his own movements.

A piercing sting sliced him just below his collar bone and he swatted Ragnald's weapon away and stumbled. But where had Ragnald gone to?

A slashing jolt across Burghred's back crashed him onto his knees. The crowd urged him to get up, Beric's voice the loudest, anxious, and pleading.

Winded and in pain, Burghred remained down. *Scite!* He breathed heavily, waiting for the finishing blow and when it didn't come, he surged up and turned to face the man he'd hated all his life.

Bent double and panting, swathed in sweat, his father's captain clasped his shaking knees. He looked as though he'd had enough. Burghred summoned his reserves. It was now or never. He booted Ragnald in the face with such force that the man went to the ground like a door kicked off its hinges. He lay there, sprawled like a starfish beached in the sand.

Snatching the sword from Ragnald's feeble grasp, Burghred flung the weapon out of his reach and stood over the beaten warrior whose eyes followed it in despair. Burghred pressed the tip of his blade into his vanquished opponent's throat with just enough pressure, causing a tiny stream of scarlet to glisten as it trickled down Ragnald's neck.

"Kill me then, if you have the balls," Ragnald growled through gritted teeth, his breast rising and falling rapidly.

"I want to know why – why you have reviled me all these years?"

"You know why – *Swica!* You betrayed us."

"No," Burghred shook his head, still breathing hard, "your hatred for me… it has burned like fire all my life – why? You did everything you could to make my father hate me… drove a wedge between us… counselled him against me, gainsaid me in everything… everything I advised." He wiped the blood from his top lip before continuing. "You whispered poison in his ears, caused him to reject me at every turn. I swear if it were not for you, my father would have not led us to this. Because of you, your son, who was my friend, is dead and now you are about to die."

"If you plan to kill me, then you better hurry because you have repairs to do. Soon *he* will be here and then your dreams of an earldom will be shattered beyond reparation. You will be *níðing, Swica!* A man without a lord or a home. You will be the *Wanderer* in the songs of of the *scop*s. You... will be like the walking dead."

"Before I kill you, tell me – tell me what it was that made you burn with hatred for me?"

Burghred pushed the point and Ragnald's throat began to gurgle. He heard the rip of flesh. Blood was seeping where the blade had cut. Ragnald smiled, an evil grimace. "Ask – your – mother," he spluttered, making a choking sound.

"Kill the bastard and get on with it," Wulfmær said, coming to his side. "We need to be rid of this scum and look to the defence of this burgh - and you are wounded, lord."

Burghred ignored Wulfmær. Ragnald's answer had not been the one he'd wanted. There was something more, something that Ragnald was withholding, most likely out of spite.

"Tell me!" Burghred demanded, restraining himself from pushing the sword tip deeper into the man's throat.

"Ask your mother," Ragnald rasped.

"My mother is dead!" Burghred screamed at him.

"Then ask your father, if he doesn't kill you first."

Ragnald was still smiling. Resigned, Burghred pushed the tip of his weapon deep into Ragnald's flesh. Blood gushed out of the wound and a terrible wail emanated from the dying man.

Burghred pulled the blade out, staring at the open, glassy eyes of the man he had just killed. Placing Ragnald's sword in his hand, Burghred's own weapon slipped from his grip as he crossed himself and he slunk down on his knees and prayed for forgiveness.

Chapter Twenty-nine

The Curse of Sabrina

Mynstreworth

Jarl Ótryggr stood proud at the helm of his favourite vessel, *Ægir Skorpiónn,* The Sea Scorpion, so named for its high-speed agility on the water. He'd heard of the killing of Ivar with a great fury and cursing. Even the silver, the blood price paid, had done nothing to satisfy his need for revenge. Ótryggr had sworn to Magnus he would have the life of the man who'd taken his son from him. If not, there would a such a *maelstrom* waiting for those who had not seen that justice had been served.

As he watched the coastline coming into view, Ótryggr reflected on the encounter at Ceaster where he'd enjoyed watching Lord Alfgar squirm before him. The man was a worm wriggling at his feet, begging for his forgiveness with disingenuous sorrow. But after Ótryggr was promised gold and revenge by Alfgar, Magnus, who'd threatened to withdraw from the alliance, surprised Alfgar by sailing into the Dee at Ceaster. In return for his aid in the expedition, Ótryggr would be given the head of the man who'd killed his son to add to his rewards.

Ótryggr's magnificent monster-headed prows and decorated sails were not spotted by the coastal guards, for he came with stealth, and at night, at the head of his fleet, when it was damp and misty. He was excited about the raid. It meant more gold and silver to be had. Ordering that his fleet of fourteen ships beach their painted keels along the river called Sæfren, they crept ashore before the first spark of dawn illuminated the sky.

His hordes overran the sleeping village. The inhabitants had no idea what number of hells had descended upon them as the invaders looted and despoiled the buildings, slaughtering any who got in their way.

The little minster was stripped of its possessions, and the priest slain when he tried to stop the carnage. Weslac Gerefa, left in charge while the thegn had been summoned to the king's war council, was dragged before Ótryggr, and forced to provide food, board, and livestock. Women were raped, though some gave themselves willingly, and little children rounded up to be taken as slaves. The bloodbath went on until the only thing the survivors could do was capitulate.

Though Ótryggr's orders from Magnus had not included a raiding stop along the way, he wanted more than what could be had in the small settlement along the River Sæfren. Two days were spent allowing his warriors, numbering at least one thousand, to slaughter and eat their fill of the livestock before they went on stolen horses to Berclea. This was a manor belonging to Earl Harold, as the townsfolk told him before he slit their throats. The slave women of Berclea were pretty and the manor furnished with many comforts. With most of the village overwhelmed, there was little to thwart the pirates. They took what they wanted, leaving the hall destroyed.

Ótryggr enjoyed watching his warriors as they helped themselves to what they desired in the Englisc countryside. In fact, Ótryggr enjoyed himself so much that he forgot about his mission to advance on Gleawecestre as part of the north-south attack on the Englisc fyrd. Rather, Ótryggr chose to dally along the rich and bountiful regions, where there was plenty of booty to be had as well as mead, wine, and women to enjoy.

A decision soon to prove fateful.

*

Ótryggr left his son, Harald, and daughter, Astrid, in charge of his mercenaries to continue their raids whilst he returned to Mynstreworth in the evening with his hearthmen. He hated to be away from his boats too long. His ships were as precious to him as his children, if not more so. After checking on them, he called to his other son, Karli.

As the boy hurried to him, Ótryggr's pride in his youngest offspring swelled. He'd loved Ivar more than the others, but this one was special, for he was the son of his second wife who was more beloved than his first.

"Yes, Father?" the boy asked, his eyes round and eager.

Ótryggr took Karli's ample fourteen-year-old shoulders in his hands and said, "I'm leaving you in charge of the boats, boy. There is a wind coming, see that they are secure, get the men to help you."

"Aye, Father," Karli answered, eagerly throwing his shoulders back to stand tall.

Ótryggr smiled to see the promise in this last-born son, ready to be given such an important task. Satisfied, Ótryggr made his way up the furrowed track to enjoy the enforced hospitality of their hosts.

Later, as Karli struggled to keep his eyelids from closing, he sat cross-legged by the crackling embers of a fire. This was his first trip with his father. He felt sluggish. He did not hold his ale well and the men, who he'd asked to help him check the boats moorings, had persuaded him to sit with them and partake in their drinking games.

The sound of those around him snoring grew fainter as his head drooped. The wind had quietened a little. An hour ago, it had been blowing a fierce gale and the river danced rhythmically. Its guests, Ótryggr's longships, swept up and over the swelling water, propelled against each other with the force of the rolling waves. Karli had been concerned that an immense storm was coming in, but when calm returned, he relaxed.

Thinking of the young sweetheart left behind in Dyfflin, his eyes grew heavier when, unexpectedly, he was punched by a giant fist of water. It drenched him, filling his baggy trousers and braies – even his seafarers' boots. He shook himself alert, tasting salt on his wet lips. Unscrambling his legs, he leapt up to stare at the river. The previous, quiet swell of the tide was now a rampant wave several feet high, gushing its way upriver, pulling the boats from their moorings. They crashed against the bank and each other, some about to overturn. The rain came down hard, punishing his face, impeding his vision.

In the sky, it seemed the gods were trying to extinguish a great fire with a howling wind. Helplessly he watched as the colourful tents were torn from the ground and carried through the air on ferocious, whirling gusts.

Exposed, half-naked men woke, startled from their slumbers by the raging gods wreaking their havoc. Karli ran here and there, shouting in a despairing voice as it took some time for the men to make sense of the devastation and scramble out of their sleeping bags. Karli stumbled forward, pushed by the storm. As he opened his mouth to cry out, a great gush of water filled it and another huge wave swamped the embankment and knocked him off his feet. As he lay dazed and nauseous, looking up at the outstretched branches of a swaying tree, he caught a glimpse of a flying tent, the last thing he saw before something heavy smashed down on his face.

Ótryggr stumbled down the path from the village to the riverbank, alerted by the gale that beat against the walls of the longhall. A branch whipped his forehead and blood oozed from the wound, sending rivulets into his eye. Like a blind man, he staggered down the precarious slope to the camp. The air was filled with panic-stricken cries and shouting. Debris flew past his him and a heavy sheet of rain bombarded him, startling him into slipping, landing in the mire on his back in a muddy rut.

"Give me your hand, lord!" An arm extended down to him. It was Eirik, one of his stalwarts. He took it and the two men struggled to stay on their feet as Ótryggr heaved himself out of the cloying mud.

"My-my-ships..." Ótryggr's voice trailed on the wind and the rain. Sodden strands of hair flicked in his eyes. He held onto Eirik's arm and they walked toward the shore, blown this way and that, tripping each other up. He slipped again, and it seemed to Ótryggr that Eirik had left him briefly, his words, barely audible, buffeted in the squall.

Then Eirik was back. "Lord! The ships' moorings are broken..." Eirik's voice vanished into the storm.

"What?" Ótryggr cried. The two men staggered a few paces forward and back before they steadied themselves again.

"The ships!" bellowed Eirik. "I think we have lost some of them!"

"We cannot lose them! Get the men - save them! Save my ships!"

"Lord, we will lose the men if we do, some have already gone into the water trying!"

The wind howled, its eerie pitch a woman's screams as it lashed against their bodies.

"No!" the jarl protested, sinking to his knees. He cursed Thor, the god of thunder, and ripped the hammer amulet from his neck. Then he cursed the nailed Christ on the Cross and did the same to the silver crucifix. *Damn the gods to hell!* He rarely shed tears, not even when they'd told him Ivar was gone. But he did that night.

Sabrina, goddess of the Sæfren, had inflicted her vengeance on the intruders.

Chapter Thirty

"Sometimes the Enemy is Closer Than You Think"

Kings Holme, Gleawecestre

Harold opened his eyes to the sound of urgent knocking. Rubbing sleep from his eyes, he leant on an elbow and yawned. Leofwin's shadow leapt from his cot and pulled aside the curtain of the sleeping chamber. Harold sat up, grabbed his tunic, and searched for the neck hole. The door scraped across the wooden floor as his brother drew it open, letting in pale morning sunlight.

"What is it?" Harold asked, struggling to get his head into the tunic in his drowsiness.

"A rider from Scrobbesbyrig – from Burghred," came Leofwin's reply.

Harold jumped out of bed in anticipation. "And so?"

"Burghred and his men have besieged the burgh and Alfgar is on his way from Ceaster with the whole of Mercia marching to join him."

"Christ's wounds – the whole of Mercia?"

"Aye. He said Alfgar will be upon Scrobbesbyrig soon if he isn't there already."

Harold and Leofwin stared at each other. "And Gruffudd?" Harold asked.

"He makes no mention of Gruffudd," Leofwin replied. "But he said if we didn't leave soon, Burghred and his men will soon be carrion for wolves and ravens."

"Burghred…" Harold whispered. A feeling of guilt flushed through him. "Where has the rider gone now?"

"I sent him to tell the king."

"I hope the king sleeps lightly these days," Harold said, wishing that he had not imbibed so much mead the night before. A headache was emerging, and he felt a terrible thirst. He scrubbed his head and looked for his blowing horn, found it and tossed it to his brother. "Get dressed and summon the commanders."

*

Mid-morning and the day already promised to be scorching. Daylight came early in June and by the time the priests were saying tierce around the makeshift altar, a golden glow began to disperse the clouds to make way for a shimmering blue sky. The encampment was a hive of activity. Wulfhere, supervising the carting of the war-gear, turned when a voice called him. A young man approached, coming down the pathway from the direction of Edward's palace of Kings Holme.

Wulfhere squinted and shielded his sun-sensitive eyes. "Tigfi."

The huscarle greeted him, clasping his hand. "Tell your men to stop packing. 'Tis not likely we will need the tents."

"What? I thought –"

"I know, Wulfhere, and the bulk of the fyrd is going to Scrobbesbyrig, but you and I, plus the Súþ Seaxan fyrd, are not."

"We are to garrison Kings Holme? Why not the men of Gleawecestre?"

As if Tigfi had read Wulfhere's mind, he shook his head. "Nay my friend, not to defend Kings Holme. Some Norse have moored along the Sæfren – several ships are beached on the shore of Mynstreworth. Lord Harold has entrusted his brother, Leofwin, with commanding a task force to engage them. The invaders have already raided the area along the coastal regions, killing any local militia that got in their way, and taking slaves. We believe their plan is to anchor their ships and march on Gleawecestre, hoping to catch us unawares. Except, we will not be."

"And Gyrth?" Wulfhere asked, "Does he go with Lord Harold?"

Tigfi shook his head. "Gone to East Anglia to safeguard the coasts there. Tostig has been busy chasing raiders along the north-western coast. There is a danger that Harald Sigurdsson will invade from Denmark once Magnus and Alfgar have defeated our army and removed the crown from Edward's head."

Wulfhere looked aghast. "In God's name, what…"

"Aye, Sigurdsson wants to add Englalond to his collection!" Tigfi gave a wry smile. "See that the men of Súþ Seaxa are rounded up."

Wulfhere nodded and called Yrmenlaf to him, tasking him with carrying the news amongst the camp. "And be quick about it," he ordered, smiling as he watched Yrmenlaf dash off.

Later, when he returned, Yrmenlaf asked, "Are we to await the Norþmenn here, lord?"

Wulfhere saw the excitement in the boy's eyes and shook his head. "Our orders have not yet been confirmed. Our best recourse would be to surprise them as they mean to surprise us."

"But why not use the protection of Kings Holme – or Gleawecestre and defend our position here?"

Yrmenlaf wore the armour that had once belonged to Esegar. Ælfstan had made some adjustments, for his new five-hide man was much smaller than Esegar had been, having not yet filled into his man-size.

Large inquisitive eyes looked out from under the oversized helmet, and Wulfhere felt a knot developing in his stomach. *So young – just eighteen summers; too young to die.* "We should strike while the iron is hot," he replied. "Destroy the Wícinga army before they have time to meet up with Gruffudd's."

"I'm afraid Wulfhere is right. I hate it when that happens, but it does sometimes." Leofnoth, held his sword before him, examining it with the same loving care a mother would give her child. "A pre-emptive strike: divide the fyrd into three armies, one to march south, one to march north. The rest will defend Kings Holme and the king."

Leofnoth nudged Æmund, who was sitting at a work bench quietly working his spear head with a whetstone. Æmund sighed, rolled his eyes, and vacated it so his father could take the seat.

"We have no choice," Wulfhere said, "Dividing the fyrd will make us more vulnerable, but we are in our homeland and most of them are not. They want us to be divided –hoping to catch us off guard. But we are on guard, thanks to the scouts."

Nearby, the laughter from the younger lads as they wrestled each other brought a lump to Wulfhere's throat. He saw the twins among them and was touched by both fear and happiness that they were passing to manhood.

"What does Alfgar hope to gain by attacking his king?" Æmund asked.

"He has been outlawed, he has no king, though it is not going to win him a lot of friends." Wulfhere shrugged. "Besides, he desires revenge on the Godwinsons for standing in his way of advancement."

"He's a bloodthirsty cur!" Leofnoth hawked and spat in the dirt. "A nasty piece of work. Even as a lad growing up, he and his gang would run around terrorising people, out of their minds on mead, causing trouble! *And* getting away with it, as I recall, more often than not."

Wulfhere said, "Aye, that he used to, though not anymore. This is the second outlawing he has had in the space of a few years. And I'd wager he believes that by putting Harald of Norwæg on the throne he will be able to control him, like a puppet, and Hardrada will do his bidding."

"So, he would have us exchange one puppet king for another?" Æmund asked cynically.

"From what I've heard, Harald Sigurdsson is a hard man and not one to dance to anyone else's tune," Wulfhere replied.

The twins came to stand with them, listening intently.

"Alfgar likes to have various options to choose from as suits the situation, you can never trust what you think you know about him. Usually it's the option you haven't thought of," Leofnoth said.

"Then we will kill the Wícinga scum, Harald of Norwæg, and Alfgar the Norse-loving bastard," Wulfwin said.

"What will you do, strong man?" Æmund laughed at him.

"I'll rip out their guts and feed them to the man who steps into his place!" Wulfwin snatched up Æmund's spear and jabbed an invisible opponent.

Wulfric added in a loud voice, "*I* will kill many Wícinga, not just one!" Grabbing the spear from his brother, he went on to fell several unseen men of his own. "Let them come and they will see what it feels like to have their hearts cut out of their breasts, their veins torn open, and their cowardly blood spilled over Englisc soil. I will darken the earth with their entrails! I shall make them meat for the worms!"

The two of them fought on, killing their imaginary army to loud cheering from their friends. But Wulfhere did not see the humour in it.

"Idiots!" he snapped at the boys so that they jumped like frightened hares. "You think you have suddenly become men now because you clutch real weapons instead of the playthings you've only just thrown away?"

He grabbed the spear from Wulfric and threw it to the ground and, wiping a thumb across his son's lips, he said, "Look at you, your mother's milk still dribbles from your lips! Christ on the Cross, neither of you know where a man's heart is let alone cut one from his body! Do you know what it is to fight until your breath is forced from your lungs because your heart feels like it's about to burst? Have either of you stood in the shieldwall with your friend's bloodied corpse wedged so tightly between you because if he wasn't, the enemy might just get through and then *you'd* be as dead as he is?"

Wulfhere paused for breath. "God's teeth, just look at you! No more than children – boys playing at being warriors. This is not a game. Those sacks of hay you stuck your spears in earlier this morning, they're *not* the real thing! Soon we march and this time there won't be any sacks of hay waiting for us. There will be men. Big men. They say the Norþmenn are over six feet tall and just as wide, with muscles the size of Leofnoth's arse." Wulfhere grabbed Wulfric's cheeks, fingers digging like claws, so that the boy's lips puckered. "Are you so brave now, lad?"

Something guttural emanated from Wulfric's throat as he tried to respond.

"Take my advice – you had better be afraid," Wulfhere continued, "because a man who is not afraid is a fool in battle. He thinks he is invincible, but his misbegotten hubris will bare his flesh like a skinned dear, primed and ready for slaughter – and no amount of armour or weapons will save him!" His raised, angry tone alerted others nearby, and they began massing around him to listen to his sermon.

He freed Wulfric to rub his cheeks and test his jaw and looked from face to face in the crowd. In his periphery, he caught sight of a blurry, but familiar shape some yards away in another part of the camp. He shivered, and as his vision cleared, he saw that the figure was Helghi. He was there with his kinsmen as though he was a lord, and they his retainers. And Helghi's gaze was directed at him.

Wulfhere grimaced and turned away, disgusted at the sight of them. He focussed on the growing crowd and took in the young faces. So many youngsters, barely men.

Breathing deeply, he said, "All of you young whelps who think you are brave men, listen to one who knows. Courage is good, but courage alone will not keep you alive. Fear is what stops you from thinking you are invincible when you are not. None of us are. Many of you here have never fought in such a battle as we may soon face. Do you know what it is to be outnumbered by a thousand men or more? Have you slipped in the blood of your shield-companions, their gore drenching you in the putrid smell of death?"

Wulfhere paused, his throat dry and scorched. Some of the older men nodded while the younger battle virgins stared with horror-filled eyes.

"Do you know what it is to have your blood run cold, every inch of your skin oozing with the sweat of terror tearing at your belly with its monstrous talons, stilling you, seizing your mind in a vice-like grip. That is fear. *Fear*! It makes your heart pump, fills your veins with the strength to survive, and when it does, you will use every means known to you to fight, kill – stay alive. Courage without fear makes you stupid – and stupid men will die. It will keep you alive... Forget your mail, your shield or your spear. They won't protect you if you are not afraid... So be brave when you dance with *Déaþscufa* and let your courage, and your fear, be your armour!"

Wulfhere drew his sword and held it aloft. He bellowed, "Men of Súþ Seaxa, are you afraid?"

A great roar went up amongst them. *"Ut!"* they cried drawing their weapons and thrusting them upward in unison with their war cry.

"Good! Now you are ready to face your worst nightmare!"

As if to reinforce this message, a war horn blew time to muster. The men began to disperse amidst a hubbub of excitement.

The twins looked downcast; their spirits crushed. Wulfhere dared them with his eyes to defy him. "You boys, are you afraid?"

"Yes, Father," both said.

"We don't need idiots like you two letting us down. Get yourselves ready."

They hurried away and Leofnoth came to stand beside him. "Well, if that doesn't scare them, nothing will. Let's hope they don't all act like jellyfish floundering on a beach when the time comes, my friend," he said with a wry smile.

"They needed to know," Wulfhere told him, fixing Hildbana back into her sheath. "You and I are still here, not because the enemy was easy to kill and not because we are skilled warriors –"

"Hmph. Speak for yourself."

"…but by sheer luck. It is better to prepare them for the worst out there, for if they go into battle like children at play, what use will they be for the rest of us?"

"The boys were just excited, and why should they not be? Think how you were first time out with the fyrd. I remember you couldn't wait to get yourself and your spear in the front line. I had to drag you to the back."

A hint of a smile formed briefly on Wulfhere's lips. "And I remember you pulling me aside, giving me a lecture too... Ah, Leofnoth, I fear for them. They are but sixteen, seventeen summers. I could not bear it if anything happened to them. Any of them. I want to make sure they all get home to their mothers."

"Father," Wulfwin said, flicking his eyes in the direction of a group of men. "He is here."

"I know," replied Wulfhere. He shaded his eyes as looked to where Helghi stood staring at him, purposefully at him. "He is here with his *wyrmlicin*. They follow him like flies round a turd."

Inside his head, Mildrith's warning floated. He turned to his son, put a hand on the boy's shoulder. "Listen to me, Wulfwin, make sure that you and your brother steer clear of that scum at all times. Do you hear me?"

Wulfwin looked bemused. "I am not afraid of them –"

Wulfhere rolled his eyes. "Have you not listened to anything I just said?" He grasped the boy and spun him to meet his eyes. "Stay away from them, do you hear me? Stay with me, or Leofnoth, Ælmer, Wulfward, or any of the others. And make sure Wulfric does too. We may have more than one enemy to fight this day, and Helghi could be one of them. *Stay away from him!"*

"Y-yes, Father."

"Good, now get Wulfric and make ready!"

"Is there something I should know, Father?"

Wulfhere went to answer then faltered. "Just be on your guard, boy. Sometimes the enemy is closer to home than you think – and I don't trust that scum."

Wulfhere followed his boy's eyes to where Helghi and his men were. They laughed amongst themselves as if they were sharing a joke at their expense.

"You men!" Wulfhere called to them, his voice hostile. "Make ready, we march within the hour."

Helghi took a swig from a flask. "Aye, *sir!*" Helghi called back to him, raising the flask to him in salute. He wiped the froth from his mouth, revealing a malicious grin in his hand's wake.

"Come, son, it is time," Wulfhere said, turning to go as the horn resounded.

*

293

Wulfwin began to follow his father, but something made him turn back to look at the men of Gorde. They were still laughing amongst themselves. Helghi caught him looking and returned the look ominously with staring dark eyes. There was something portentous in his gaze. It wafted across the air as if it were something tangible. In Helghi's hand was a hunting knife and he drew it across his throat.

A hand gripped his shoulder, startling him.

"Christ on the Cross, Wulfwin, you look as though you've seen a ghost."

"Did you see that Wulfric?"

"What?"

"There... Helghi."

"Where?"

"I swear he was there a moment ago. He wants to kill me." Wulfwin faced his brother. "He was staring at me with a knife in his hand and he did this…" Wulfwin drew a finger across his throat."

"Brother, you know him. He would cut all our throats if he could. Come, we have another enemy to be more fearful of."

Wulfwin was not so sure. As he turned to follow his brother, he remembered his father's warning...

"Sometimes the enemy is closer than you think."

Chapter Thirty-one

Reputation is All

A light breeze made gentle ripples in the river, quiet and calm now that the storm had abated. The sun, gloriously golden, reflected its morning glow over the previous night's devastation. Ótryggr stared through disbelieving eyes to where his ships had once been moored along the inlet in all their splendour, hardly grasping what had happened. Three months ago, he'd had four sons, now there were only two. Yesterday morning he'd fourteen ships; now only five were afloat, possibly damaged and ready to submerge.

He stood amongst the wreckage washed upon the bank; three of the ships had taken on water and capsized. The missing six must have been pushed upriver by the bore. His beautiful ships, with their scarlet dragon heads gracefully perched on the prow, would fly in the wind no more.

He'd counted twenty crumpled bodies, some with their skulls broken, bloated on the embankment. How many others had drowned trying to save the boats, he did not know. The body of his youngest son with his face smashed lay only a few feet away. He'd cradled him all through the night, quietly sobbing, lost in grief for what seemed like hours.

His other son and daughter were somewhere out there in the place that was called Sumorsǣte, probably sleeping off the night's mead, for even his daughter, Astrid, ate, drank, and fought like a man. He was bereft of emotion. Everything he'd built: his honour and prestige – gone in one night of storm.

He turned to walk up the embankment. As he trod through the debris, he saw a leather horn-case with his son's name worked in runes above two entwined serpents. It had been given to Karli by his mother,

Ótryggr's second wife, Lind, just one of the gifts given their son for his first journey beyond home. Bending down, Ótryggr picked it up and pulled the horn from its sheath. Karli had loved that thing. It made him feel important. The boy had used it for everything: for hunting, for summoning, or warning of danger.

Ótryggr felt a sense of detachment, as if watching someone who looked like him, walked like him but was not him. Feeling the smoothness of the horn against the skin of his fingers, he stared at it, bewildered. Then, intuitively, the horn went to his lips. The first blow was insufficient, and it croaked a mournful note. Sucking in a great breath, Ótryggr blew it again and again until the sound rang out clear and loud. Summon the men…

He needed his warriors and with every breath and sound, Ótryggr began to feel more alive.

*

Eirik lay dreaming, burrowed cosily next to the woman whose house and body he'd appropriated for his own use. Eadwena nudged him, and he ignored her attempts to wake him, muttering for her to leave him alone, but she didn't. She jabbered away in a half-understood language. It was the horn, though, that made him sit up abruptly.

Eirik leapt out of bed and searched for his clothes. Found only his breeches. He pulled them on in a state of panic and hopped on one foot to get the other leg in, trying not stamp on his fellows asleep on the floor. Shouting for them to rouse themselves, Eirik ran out of the house in a groggy daze, horrified at the damage. Surveying the mess, he remembered he'd left his lord huddled over the body of his son the night before, unable to move him. Eirik had returned to Eadwena's, leaving Ótryggr to grieve alone.

Shock rendered him fully awake and he let out a loud yell, "To the ships!"

Repeating the cry, Eirik ran through the storm-wrecked village, heading for the grisly scene on the shore.

Men came out from the buildings, half dressed, bewildered, rubbing the sleep from their eyes.

Eirik shouted at them, "Get moving, you donkeys!"

He called out to Ótryggr, "I am coming, lord!" and dashed past the little stone church and the damaged wooden houses gathered around it. He dodged scattered fragments of timber, danced over puddles and piles of rubble, and slipped in the mud, losing a boot as he pulled his foot free. He trampled through broken hurdles, cursing the missing boot, until he was the first to reach the master.

Ótryggr fell into Eirik's arms, his eyes wide as moons, an axeblade buried in his back. "My ships..." the jarl said and sank to the ground, his blood oozing warm in Eirik's hands.

Eirik looked up and gasped. Ahead was a large group of mounted warriors. At the centre, their leader sat proud and upright in his saddle, richly armoured and cloaked in scarlet, wearing a helmet of silver and gold. Beside him his pennon, a black raven on a red background, impressive as it fluttered in the breeze was proudly held by his standard bearer. Behind these two, hundreds of riders were assembling.

Eirik's legs quivered, and he let the limp body of Ótryggr fall to the mud. A sword was his only weapon, sheathed and looped through the leather belt hastily strapped. Having no armour was to feel vulnerable, and he estimated that little more than a tenth of his lord's forces were available. Like him, they were poorly dressed and carried few weapons. No one had expected to be met with a full-scale army geared up for war.

His friend Yngvr joined him, a sturdy veteran of the seas as he was himself. Yngvr, out of breath from running from the village, gasped as he took in the situation.

"Fuck!" Yngvr cried. He gazed unbelievingly at his lord dead at Eirik's feet. Then he saw the Englisc gathered along the shore path. "Fuck!"

"Double fuck," said Eirik.

*

"Where are the rest of your men?" Leofwin called to the Norþmann. He remained in his saddle, watching the invaders thrown into chaos at the sight of so many Englisc come to kill them.

This Norþmann was not running around like a frightened chicken. He stood his ground and spoke Englisc with a tongue of steel, "You killed our jarl. Ótryggr Sea Serpent." Then he spoke louder, this time in Norse which Leofwin had some grasp. "*Þú eiga killed okkarr lord.*"

Pacing, clenching his fists, the distressed man whined like a wounded boar. "Cowards!" he shouted. He drew his sword, pointed it at Leofwin, and reverted to Englisc. "Who are you?"

"I am Leofwin Godwinson. Forgive me, I am sorry for your lord. One of my men was a little over eager. They have been waiting a long time to test their skills and now they have the chance, there are less than a hundred of you. Where are the rest of your men?"

Behind the Norþmann, his men made a meagre line of defence. The spokesman bent down to withdraw the blade from his lord's back. "Then... you may have this!" he snarled, grunting as he let the axe fly.

It whirled across the space between them and thudded into Leofwin's shield causing his horse to prance. The Norse chieftain's blood mingled with the blue woad paint. Leofwin pulled the axe free of it, was handed another shield and threw the ruined one to the ground.

"Tigfi!" Leofwin called to the yellow-haired huscarle.

"Aye, lord."

"I want forty riders. Lead the left, I'll take the right! Let's show these Norse *horningsuna* some Englisc steel." To the leader of the Norþmenn he said, "What are you called, so I may know the name of the man I am about to kill?"

"I am called Eirik, Eirik the Avenger, and I will see you in Valhalla, Godwinson!"

Leofwin gathered his reins in one hand and drew his sword aloft. "Kill them!" he roared, spurring his horse forward. Behind him, he heard his captain bellow at their men,

"You heard your lord! Forty of you, now! Let's kill the bastards!"

Most of the Norpmenn were cut down as Leofwin and his riders gave them neither chance nor mercy.

Leofwin surveyed the mangled bodies of the dying and dead, as his men looted the corpses. A horn sounded, and a great chant filled the air. Shading his eyes, Leofwin looked out across the tree-lined meadows to see as many as a thousand Norse had amassed into a shieldwall. The rest of the Norse army.

As Tigfi restored order amongst the men, Leofwin viewed the invaders with anticipation. Mowing down a mere hundred poorly armed warriors had left no satisfaction. This better matched encounter was a chance to prove his skill as a leader.

They were banging their weapons, goading, and Leofwin felt a wave of exhilaration. This must be the rest of Ótryggr's forces. The new enemy formed their lines. Leofwin knew they were being challenged. Excited, Leofwin smiled. His older brothers had earldoms and he was about to get one for himself. A sudden doubt crawled into Leofwin's mind and he checked the urge to engage the screaming mob. These were the feared Norþmenn – known for their viciousness in battle. They were not farmers, who, for two months a year, practiced their fyrd skills. These were professional warriors. Fighting was their trade; it was in their blood. This would be no easy battle, no easy kill. He must think of a plan.

*

"So, a woman leads this army," Tigfi said as a tall female, with hair so fair it glistened like snow in sunlight, approached them.

"I am Astrid Ótryggrsdottir." Her husky accented Englisc was delivered with what seemed like genuine warmth. Hands on her hips, she spoke with an air of authority. "Indeed, a woman does lead this army." She turned and surveyed the mass of men gathered in lines behind her. "My father made me his second-in-command. I have carried a sword all my life. I fight as well as any man, better than my brothers. And I swive as well as any man."

Wulfhere was stunned by her. His gaze raked over her, trying not to make it obvious. She was mature, perhaps late twenties. The light scarring that distorted her top lip failed to mar her striking features. Rather, it added to her enigma. She was somewhat manly in her stance, her height adding to the illusion. Dark leather boots met the edge of her grass coloured tunic hemmed just below her knees and decorated with red stitching. Her long hair, bound in two thick braids, draped down the front of her chest and meeting her eyes, he drew breath, for they glittered like shattered green glass. She was equipped with a sword belted on her hip, and he was called to mind of the legendary *wælcyrian*; women warriors, riding the maelstrom, swords aloft, cloaks swirling, invoking Odin.

She tossed her head provocatively, perhaps looking for a reaction of some kind.

Tigfi did not rise to the bait. "We have killed your father," he told her.

The smile did not leave her face. "I know."

It was strange that she was so calm.

"So, you want to swive me and in return we will go away and leave you to carry on ravaging our land?" Tigfi said.

Wulfhere rolled his eyes. The other four men accompanying Tigfi all sniggered. Astrid's men looked affronted and drew closer to her. It was typical of Tigfi to be thinking with his cock at a time like this.

Yet it didn't seem to bother Astrid. "The pleasure, I can assure you would be all yours – however I only fuck men I find manly and you are definitely not... manly." Her eyes drifted over the huscarle. "You look like a girl."

Tigfi threw back his head and laughed heartily. "For such an insult so pleasantly given I cannot be offended, my lady."

She gave the smallest of bows with a gracious grin.

A white fluffy veil drifted across the sky. With no breeze to lift them, Leofwin's raven and Ótryggr's sea serpent clung limply to their shafts. It was warm; the faint aroma of summer rain hung in the air as each side's protectors stood around their leaders, sweat pouring down their faces despite the shrouded sun.

"So, what is there for you now? Your ships are all but destroyed. Your father is dead –"

"I have my brother, Harald." She cocked her head at one of her bodyguards and the resemblance was immediate, though he was less attractive. He had the same glittering green eyes and white hair, an ugly protruding brow, and a magnificent scar that zigzagged down the right side of his face. He stared at them ominously, sizing them up, lingered too long over them for Wulfhere's comfort.

"My Lord Leofwin urges you to surrender, give back the booty and people you have stolen, and you may leave in whatever ships you can piece together as long as you leave these shores, and never come back. We will require hostages, of course."

Her laughter sounded unusually light for one in her position. She swept her arm wide to encompass the lines of men behind her. "I think not," she said. "I have eight – maybe nine hundred men. We can fight."

Tigfi said, "Go with as many of you that can fit into whatever ships you have left and those you wish to leave can remain to whatever the gods decide will be their fate... Oh, and in addition, your brother as hostage."

She looked Tigfi up and down. Her lips hovered between a smile and a sneer.

"After you have let me fuck you, of course," Tigfi added.

Astrid stared at him. "I said we will fight."

Tigfi was still willing to bargain with her. "We outnumber you by a quarter and more of your bedraggled troops. You will lose... Or you can surrender and take what my lord has offered you."

Astrid muttered something in her own tongue as if cursing to herself, then turned to her men. When she had finished speaking, her brother, Harald, burst with anger and tried to force his way forward. He wasn't coming to shake Tigfi's hand, that was certain. Wulfhere and his comrades closed in on their spokesman protectively.

Astrid stood in her brother's way, a hand on his strongly built chest. She spoke mildly to him, as if placating a skittish horse. He replied to her, his anger evident. Whatever she had said to him, he had not liked, but her soothing stayed him.

Astrid turned to Tigfi again., her expression steady. "These are my terms. My brother will fight any man that your lord chooses. If he wins, then we will accept payment to buy more ships and we will leave with our booty and slaves. If your lord's man wins, the terms you offered us by him will prevail - except *your* offer to me, Englisc," this she directed at Tigfi, " My men would kill you before that happens, but I have assured them that there would be no need, for I will kill you myself."

Tigfi ignored the threat. "Why don't *you* fight; why your brother?" Tigfi asked, his tone mocking. "After all, you say you fight as well as any man."

"Would you expect *your* lord to fight?"

Tigfi laughed and nodded. "I will speak with my Lord Leofwin and let him know your terms." He gave a curt bow and turned to leave, Wulfhere and the others following.

"Wait, you did not tell me who you are," she called to Tigfi.

Each man turned and looked back at her as their spokesman said, "Tigfi. Tigfi the Yellow."

Her audacious expression gone, Astrid Ótryggrsdottir swung round to join her men, and, with a confident swagger, she accompanied them to their army.

Wulfhere glanced at her brother before walking away. Harald Ótryggrson shot him a look of deep contempt that made him shiver. If Lord Leofwin chose to agree her terms, he did not envy the man who would have to fight him.

Back at the Englisc lines, Wulfhere stood with Tigfi as the huscarle relayed Astrid's terms to their commander. "Their leader is a woman?" Leofwin laughed.

"I can assure you, she *is* a woman, but doesn't act like it," Tigfi replied.

"How many of them are there?"

"She says eight or nine hundred. We overwhelm them but we are well matched. These men are all seasoned fighters."

Wulfhere stood quietly as they spoke and glanced at the arrayed shieldwall. He was aware that his unit was close by and could see his Running Wolf banner above the heads of the warriors. He felt more at ease than he had done the whole time they'd been on campaign. This time, he would be on the side that numbered more. But it did not mean the victory would be theirs today. It all depended on whose side was the strongest, whose commander was the better, and how the ground lay – and what the fates were spinning. War was fickle and so was *wyrd*; one could never know which way the tide would turn.

"What do you think, Wulfhere?" Leofwin asked him.

"My lord?"

"I was contemplating their terms. Should I ignore it and attack, or should I accept?"

Wulfhere knew that Leofwin and the men were eager to fight, having been holed up at Gleawecestre for weeks. And Leofwin was eager to prove himself and get his earldom. If they were to lose the champion fight, then the rewards would be much better for the Norse than they would be for them.

"Lord, we have the upper hand. They must be heartsore after losing their leader and their ships and perhaps a hundred or so of their men. I think that it is you who might call the terms here, not them," Wulfhere replied.

"That is so," agreed Leofwin. "Would you fight their man, Wulfhere?"

"Me, my lord? I –" Wulfhere was surprised that Leofwin would choose such an option. He met Leofwin's eyes. He was a lot like his brother, the Earl of Wessex: convincing, persuasive, charming.

"Would you fight their man for me?"

"But if I lose...."

"Think not of losing, Wulfhere, I know of your bravery, what you did at Hereford. Your courage has been talked about much since then. And you are skilled in many weapons. They say that few can beat you in a fight."

Wulfhere stared blankly at Leofwin, hardly knowing how to respond. He was flattered. But could he refuse the request, even if he wanted to? And he wanted to. Then there was this reputation that Leofwin spoke of. Men may think him brave because of what he had done at Hereford, taking leadership after the Normans had run from the field. But within him beat the heart of a coward.

"Lord, if Wulfhere does not wish to fight this man, then I will," interrupted Tigfi with a look of disdain at Wulfhere.

"No!" Wulfhere said, pushing Tigfi aside. "I will fight him, my lord."

"Good," Leofwin nodded. "Then, our terms will be thus: if Wulfhere beats their man, then we will give them battle and they have the chance to be victorious. If their man beats ours, then we will give them half a day's head start to meet their allies before we go after them, and we will keep their booty and all the ships that are salvageable."

"Or we could just fight them anyway," Tigfi said.

"No, I am a man of my word and I would give them this chance," Leofwin said firmly. "Tigfi and you men, go with him." Leofwin looked at Wulfhere, adding, "May God and the Fates go with you, Lord Wulfhere."

"Lord, are you sure this is the right thing to do?" a huscarle said to Leofwin as they watched Wulfhere walk away to meet with Astrid and her brother – and possibly his death. "Would it have not been best to just fight them now? What if Wulfhere loses?"

"He won't lose," Leofwin answered him. "But if he does, then we will fight them anyway, later."

Chapter Thirty-two

A Pleasant Day to Die

Wulfhere was tall amongst his companions, but this Harald was taller – and broader, armed with a dangerous axe. As he warmed up, the Norþmann swung the weapon with effortless agility, as though it were a child's plaything. The blade's span was at least a foot and Wulfhere shuddered, remembering that at Hereford he'd witnessed smaller axes than Harald's cutting into horses' necks with frightening ease.

Amidst the cacophony of jeering and cheering, a soft wind blew and with it, the essence of meadowsweet and sun on damp grass. Ironic that there he was, waiting to be slaughtered by this massive brute, nature infused the air with the beauty of nature.

Such a pleasant day to die.

Leofwin's priest gave him the battlefield blessing, though it was little comfort in the face of possible death, to know his sins were absolved. His sons – they would be watching – and he wanted them to witness that if he lost today, it would be gloriously. He mouthed the words of the paternoster, and readied himself, his spear high, shield gripped across his torso.

Then it began.

Wulfhere's stomach muscles tensed as Harald stormed towards him, raising the terrifying axe. The great blade danced before him, undulating the air above Harald's head as he swung the weapon, his muscular arms warming up. Wulfhere's heart quickened. Bile rose in his throat and he breathed deeply to steady his shaking limbs. Studying his opponent, he made a mental note of the exposed parts of Harald's body with every swing.

Harald closed in on him. The blade, glinting in the glow of the sun, descended, aimed at the unprotected part of Wulfhere's neck. He leapt clear of the blow and Harald stumbled, an ungainly oaf.

Wulfhere rounded on him and thrust low into his enemy's inner thigh. The sensation of torn linen, skin, and tissue vibrated along the spear shaft.

Harald gave a weak cry as though merely stung by a wasp. Wulfhere tugged the blade free, wondering if the hulking Norþmann had even felt it. A bright shade of crimson dripped down along the ash as Wulfhere retreated out of Harald's reach. The big man drew himself up, shaking his head like a hound out of water. Raising his mighty bearded axe, he scowled, his ugly face even more so as it contorted with rage.

Wulfhere shrugged an apology. "Oh, have I hurt you? I am sorry."

The Norse shouted encouragement, as Harald repeated his display, swinging the axe around his head, showing his lithe dexterity.

Wulfhere watched, unblinking. In the glassy eyes of his enemy, a thousand Dunsinanes and Herefords were reflected. Wulfhere's fear settled. The anger of those battles, long hidden within him, were brought to the surface. Starting deep in his chest, a growl rumbled and like a weir breaking, it rushed to his throat.

"I am not going to die today!" he roared.

The axeblade gathered momentum. Wulfhere's gaze went to his opponent's midriff to avoid being blinded by the blur. Focusing on the deadly movement of his opponent's arms, he counted: one, when the arms went up; two, they came down. The timing must be right. In crab-like movements, he sought to creep around Harald – turning to the right and to the left. He tried a swipe at the monster's side and had to snatch the spear away as Harald's axe blade threatened to carve the shaft in two. Whichever way he went, the giant moved with him and he could not get his spear into the devil.

Harald lunged, the air buzzing with the whooshing of his axe at Wulfhere's head. Wulfhere, crouched under the blade's terrifying descent and flung up his shield, the wooden planks taking the brunt. An excruciating jarring pulsated from shoulder to wrist. He was down, kneeling, not badly injured, but his shield was wrecked. The crowd chanted, urging him to rise.

Someone called out, "For Hereford! For Hereford!"

Wulfhere was immediately transported to another time, riding amongst the carnage of that battle. Great gore-stained broad-axes flashed and cut into the beautiful necks of the war horses. Blood rained on Wulfhere's face and splattered into his mouth and eyes.

The air was full of tortured screams, of beasts and of men also. The maiming of such beautiful creatures had made him angry then, and he was angry now!

Men dying was one thing, but Christ on the Cross – not the horses!

Struggling to his feet, his shield arm a dead weight, he took up his position, waiting for Harald to start the deadly routine once more.

One, the arms went up, two – they came down – three, up – four, down – five – and Wulfhere screamed, rushed forward and thrust his spear tip through the mail-rings, just below the armpit. He drew back, blood streaming onto the shaft. Harald twisted and groaned, pushed a fist into the wounded area, his face contorted. Wulfhere swore. His aim had fallen short of the heart. Harald, recovered, brought his axe down again and Wulfhere danced out of the way.

The cries of the Englisc threatened to drown Harald's ringing curses. Wulfhere backed away as far as he could and prepared himself, his spear couched in the crook of his elbow as he caught his breath. Harald stood, nonplussed, felt under his arm and examined the red, sticky substance. The giant's vicious glare was terrifying. There was a dangerous fire in the man's eyes, and Wulfhere trembled.

Harald grabbed the axe shaft in both hands, roaring and shaking his head like some visceral creature. A colossal swing of his arms raised the weapon, picking up impetus as he approached. When Harald raised his arms again, exposing his torso, Wulfhere flipped the shaft, drew it back and propelled it – like a javelin – straight at his opponent's bulk.

The spear buried itself in Harald's chest followed by Englisc roars of delight and dismayed groans from the Norþmenn.

The great axe, slid from Harald's hands as yet unbloodied, with a thump as the blade lay flat on the grass. The big man clutched his midriff, bewildered as he looked down at the protruding weapon then sank to his knees, mouth gaping wordlessly.

Wulfhere let out a long sigh. It was over. He tore Hildbana from her scabbard and sprinted toward the dying man. Men swirled around him. Someone called his name. He ignored them.

Wulfhere pulled at the spear-shaft and Harald hung on to it, snarling like a dog guarding its food. Wulfhere tugged hard at the shaft, grunting.

Still Harald would not let him retrieve it. It was the only weapon he had to get to Valhalla. Wulfhere was not going to let him.

He threw Hildbana to the blood-soaked ground and tugged at the shaft with both hands. Blood showed black as thick tar between Harald's teeth, and his scream filled the air as he pushed himself on to the spear, a deathly act of defiance. Wulfhere grabbed up his sword, stepped behind Harald and was about to take his head when the bastard slumped forward. Wulfhere stared at the gaping hole right between the dead man's shoulder blades as the sharp tip forced its way through, exposing a mess of blood, sinew, and splintered bone. It was done.

Chapter Thirty-three

The Battle Lust

Suddenly all seemed chaos on the field. The white-haired woman raged with fury, and Yrmenlaf's heart leapt with fear for Wulfhere, as clusters of Norse broke out of their lines heading for his lord and his defeated opponent. A sudden swell in the shieldwall jostled him. The men of his unit surged as his fellow Súþseaxan rushed to help their comrade. As Yrmenlaf threw all his strength into carving his way into the ranks to join them, he lost his grip on his lord's banner, Running Wolf. There was no time to stop and retrieve it, for right that moment, his lord needed him more.

Yrmenlaf sped across the ground between the two armies, his blood rushing to spur him on. The woman's ear-piercing wails filled the air and the terrifying shrieks of men clashed with the ring and thud of weapons. Warriors from his unit were already there, engaged in fighting the enemy as others tried to prise Wulfhere away from the grotesque scene. Yrmenlaf forced himself through the crowd to reach his thegn and saw him, eyes glazed, refusing to let go of the spear that was embedded in his lifeless adversary. The dead man was slumped to his knees like a ghoulish stone carving, determined even in death to best his vanquisher.

"Lord, you have to leave. It's over!" Yrmenlaf cried.

One of the men, Wulfward, tugged at Wulfhere, crying out, "Let's get him away from this lot before they tear us limb from limb."

"My spear..."

"Forget your bloody spear, man! Let's get out of here." Wulfward dragged him, and the lord of Horstede allowed his comrades to carry him between them, arms around their shoulders.

Yrmenlaf picked up Hildbana and followed them through the noise of horns sounding; weapons clashing; men screaming; grunting, yelling, and roaring.

"Are you hurt, lord?" Yrmenlaf queried as Wulfhere stumbled and fell on one knee at the Englisc lines, struggling for breath.

all the commotion, Leofwin could be heard shouting at his warriors. "Did I tell you to leave your positions? You undisciplined bastards! Get back to your lines - now!"

Yrmenlaf felt the heat pulse from his lord. Sweat dripped like a shower of rain down Wulfhere's face and neck as he removed his helmet.

"I... I'm... all right," Wulfhere puffed.

The twins appeared through the crowd gathered around them. Wulfwin thrust a flask at his father and he drank deeply.

Wulfward gave him a new spear, and Yrmenlaf shrugged off his shield and placed it before his lord. "Here, your shield is useless now, lord, take mine – I'll not need it." He held out his hand to assist him to his feet.

"Where is the banner?" Wulfhere asked, his eyes darting here and there anxiously.

"I left it in the lines, lord. I –"

Wulfhere looked worried. "Go back and find it, boy."

"Aye, lord!"

Yrmenlaf turned to run, but Wulfhere stopped him, his hand shaking on Yrmenlaf's arm. "Do not let go of it. Guard it with your life, and stay safe during the battle, you understand? Don't – let – that banner – go!"

Yrmenlaf nodded vigorously, the oversized helmet wobbling over his eyes. "Aye, lord, I will guard it with my life."

"You're a good lad, Yrmenlaf. Tighten that helm, boy."

"Back to your lines!" shouted Leofwin. "Now! We have a battle to fight!"

Yrmenlaf's pride swelled as the Godwinson lord slung an arm around Wulfhere's shoulders and walked him back to the shieldwall. "Wulfhere, you fought bravely, man. You can be assured that the king and my brother shall know of this."

*

Horns sounded on both sides of the field. Commanders were shouting orders down the lines trying to regain some control amongst the ranks. Wulfhere, standing centre of the front line with Leofwin to his right, watched as Tigfi went to meet with the Wícinga woman and her bodyguards once more. This time it was a heated discussion with snarling, waving of arms, and raised voices. Wulfhere turned his head again and glimpsed his boys to the rear of him, their faces tight with expectation.

Directly behind him the Running Wolf snapped in the wind, clutched in Yrmenlaf's grasp. At last Tigfi and his group returned. Words were exchanged between the yellow-haired huscarle and Lord Leofwin and they rejoined the lines.

"Gengan forþ!" Leofwin cried, and the wall moved forward. Wulfhere braced himself. His legs wobbled, heart raced, and stomach churned. Bile rushed to his throat as he was slammed against the shields of the enemy and crushed by those of his own. With no room to manoeuvre his spear and pushed from behind and in front, he let it drop. Damn! There was no way to release his seax let alone draw Hildbana from her scabbard! Nose to nose with the warrior facing him, he tasted the man's breath, the hot stench of it on his cheeks, and he heard every grunt, every murmur, every oath, and every wheeze the man made as he, too, fought to play his weapon.

All they could do was push, shield to shield. Voices were yelling, but the overwhelming cacophony was so immense it was impossible to decipher the words.

Battle-horns. He listened intently to decode the signal. A voice, no doubt Leofwin's, screamed out, *"Onbæc! Steppa Onbæc!"*

As the Englisc began to respond to the command, the Norse jeered at them, calling them cowards for retreating.

When there was at least fifty feet between the two armies, Leofwin and his guards moved into the space between the lines, his standard flying. Astrid and her men joined them once more to talk. Yrmenlaf leaned forward from behind Wulfhere to whisper in his ear. "Lord, why do they talk so much?"

"Leofwin is offering new terms."

"Why? Why don't we just get on with it and fight?"

"He wants to win. He needs this victory, but he wants to slaughter the Wícinga without spilling the blood of his own warriors. A bloodless victory keeps an army intact to fight another battle if needed. These Wícinga are seasoned warriors, they fight all year round, they are thieves, pirates, and they love to fight.

Most of our army are no match for these men, so, if he can get them to agree terms, then it would be much better than winning a battle that leaves him with many dead."

"But you won your fight against the troll with the big axe – surely 'tis a sign God is on our side and we will –"

"That was luck," Wulfhere cut in. "Just luck." Wulfhere lifted his helmet enough to wipe the sweat from his brow. The afternoon was still bright, and the heat beat down from above.

"We have more men, lord. We outnumber them."

"Aye, we do. That doesn't mean that we will win."

Leofwin and his men returned to their lines and from their faces it appeared there was no conclusion. They stood locked in a huddle.

"What's happening now?" Yrmenlaf asked.

"They're deciding what to do next," Wulfhere replied.

There was a nodding of heads and then a mutual clasping of hands as the commanders hurried back to their positions. Leofwin squeezed into the line next to Wulfhere.

"You know what a *fleóswin* is, Wulfhere?" Leofwin asked, staring ahead as he spoke without looking at him.

"Aye, lord."

"Good."

"You want us to form the snout?" Wulfhere asked.

Leofwin's eyes remained on the enemy lines. Astrid was striding up and down, speaking to her own commanders and organising her warriors.

"No. *They* are." Leofwin pointed his sword at the Norse. "If not now, then at some point in the battle," Leofwin replied. Now he turned to look Wulfhere in the face and said, "We are not going to resist it."

"We're not?"

"No, we are not. We are going to open the lines. It will start when I give the order. The rear-guard will make way for the lines in front to open up like double gates – you and I are the brackets that hold the locking bar, Wulfhere. The right and left flanks will arc round to surround and enclose them. Those in the middle ground will kill them as they come through." Leofwin used his hands to explain the movement.

"That will be us," Wulfhere said.

Leofwin nodded. "Yes, that will be us."

"How do you know they will give the snout?" Wulfhere asked, wondering if this outrageous plan would work.

"I don't, but I think they will. The Norse always give the *fleóswín*. The *swinfylking,* they call it. They couldn't break us just now, so they will try it, of that I am certain." Leofwin smiled broadly. "And they are less than us, so they will need to make a big impact on our lines if they are going to breach us."

"If they do, lord," Wulfhere said, "it won't be the first time that you have been right." Leofwin eyed him curiously. Wulfhere continued, "You said I'd defeat their troll in the *Cheampa feoht.*"

"I did and you beat him... you, are the champion, Wulfhere."

"Aye, I did and I am." Wulfhere's injured shield-arm throbbed to remind him. "Lord, if they don't make the *fleóswín*, do you have another plan?"

"No."

Wulfhere nodded and turned his attention to the advancing enemy troops. The Englisc stood their ground, creating a tight formation; their overlapping shields locked in place. Banging their shields, they shouted, *"Ut! Ut! Ut!"* and Astrid's army marched toward them in a square, filling the air with their battle thunder. A terrifying, menacing rhythm boomed as their weapons and shields crashed together. It was as though the ground had opened and Hell had spat out its evil. At the helm of this devil's ship was the woman, Astrid. And she was formidable.

Out of the mouths of the men that stood shoulder to shoulder with Wulfhere came a collection of vile obscenities.

"What kind of men allow a woman to lead them in battle? She'll be roasted before she has time to draw her sword!"

"Just let her come my way, I'll swive her with my *seax*, see how she likes   that!"

"I'll give her a battle or two between her legs!"

"She can suck my *pintel* before I shove my sword in her!"

"She won't know her arse from her cunt by the time I'm done humping her!"

Their booming comments, designed to humiliate, did nothing to undo the woman's confidence. She was magnificent; silver-white braids hanging from under a gold-plated helm. She strode gracefully at the head of her army, self-assured in a shirt of mail, carrying spear and shield. As she grew closer to them, her ferocity glowed, the red streaks smearing her face, undoubtedly her brother's blood.

Wulfhere shivered at the sight of her, certain she was coming for him; a *Wælcyrie*, whose task it was to collect the dead for Odin. He thought he heard her voice - *I am coming for you.*

Leofwin was shouting orders, but Wulfhere's gaze focussed on the onslaught about to arrive. The enemy's feet pounded in his ears and he prayed his boys would be safe as he waited.

Oh God. He was back again – that day in October - three years before – facing the Wícinga at Hereford. *Don't think about it! Don't!* He shook his head, trying to clear his mind.

Leofwin's cry to ready the archers was echoed by his commanders.

Arrows and javelins flew from behind over Wulfhere's head at the enemy lines. Men collapsed as they were hit, but the wedge kept coming. Over the injured they stormed and closed the gaps. Astrid raised her spear. Her voice boomed across the battlefield, deep and resonant like a man's. *"Swínfylking!"* she cried.

"Did I not tell you, Wulfhere?" Leofwin laughed as Astrid's men swamped her like flies would around meat. "I knew they would make the *fleóswín.*"

God, they were well-disciplined, these warriors.

With the boarsnout almost upon them, Wulfhere prayed they would get the timing right because if they didn't, the whole battle could be lost. "We should move now, lord!" Wulfhere shouted. *Christ!* He felt the crush upon him already as the ground rumbled.

In a steady voice, Leofwin said, "We are about to release the locking bar, Wulfhere." A horn blew. Leofwin roared above the battle din. *"Áwæcnan!* Prepare to open!" And then, with moments to spare, "Open the lines!"

The shieldwall loosened and the ranks behind him unfolded as the lines moved back.

Leofwin screamed again, "Men behind, *Onbæc!* "Men in front, stand your ground! *Nimath weapnan!"* Spears were thrust forward accompanied by a warrior's grunt. *"Onbæc!* Open the lines!"

It was chaos. The boarsnout crashed through the gateway they'd made and Wulfhere and his fellow shoulder-companions, attacked the nose of the boar as it came roaring through. They stabbed, jabbed, and brought the bloody battle death to the stunned Wícinga.

"Kill them! Kill them all!" Leofwin shrieked and his cries urging his men to make the slaughter was taken up all around them. The Norþmenn's own chants did not help them. They were butchered line after line, after line, as they fell into the trap made by their enemy. Flanked and surrounded by Englisc warriors, confusion reigned among them as more of their comrades rushed through, only to be faced with a wall of Englisc spears and the dead bodies of their own troops.

Wulfhere, locked in the shieldwall with his companions, moved forward to Leofwin's cries of *"Steppan! Steppan!"* treading over the dying and dead to slaughter the next group of Norþmenn coming through.

The enemy fought back ferociously, close, and fierce. The Englisc flanks were circling them, trapping them, leaving no escape.

The boiling bloodlust gave life to Wulfhere's weary body. There was no time to think about his sons; only time to plunge his spear into the next man who appeared before him. Both sides were packed in tightly now. Wulfhere threw down his spear to draw Hildbana from her resting place and brought her down on the neck of a raging fighter, and as he struck another opponent with the metal boss of his shield. The wounded warrior caught at the gash, blood leaking through his fingers as he squirmed, crying out. Wulfhere kicked him and he slumped to the ground and then Hildbana found her way into his spine. In one ferocious movement Wulfhere dragged her out and turned to plunge the deadly blade into the warrior he'd parried with his shield.

The man's hands went up and he shouted, "Wulfhere! 'Tis I, Wulfward!"

Wulfhere hissed, "Out of my way! Stupid bastard!" *Christ on the Cross, it is impossible to know who I fight!*

He swung round, sweat flying off his face. *Where are the enemy shields? Look for enemy shields.* A warrior whirled into his path, blocking Wulfhere's aimed blow with a savage parry. His flank, exposed, Wulfhere twisted, brought his shield down to protect himself and thrust forward, hurling his body weight behind it. The enemy was knocked off his feet and Wulfhere spun, twisted again, and brought Hildbana slashing down on another Wícinga's back. Blood rained; splashing over him as he sliced Hildbana into the enemy's throat and the head flew off, leaving a bloody stump.

Wulfhere caught his breath. The ether was foul with the stench of heat, gore, and battle. *Cannot stop. Must keep going.* If he stopped, his legs would collapse, and he would expunge his guts. He ploughed on, slashing high and low at exposed parts of bodies, shield smashing into

scowling faces, hacking into muscle and veins. It was relentless, for as soon as he put a man down another stepped in his place. The ground was sodden; blood, innards, and lumps of hacked flesh, some still in its mail, hindered his path. Blood gushed from mutilated torsos, seeped over ground already covered in filth and carnage. At times, he was fighting multiple warriors, spinning in circles, his blade slicing, legs kicking, men on him from all sides. The sounds of steel upon wood, wood upon steel and steel upon steel clashed around him.

The impact of opening the lines had reduced the power of the *fleóswin*. The enemy was surrounded. But like a trapped animal, its bite was deadly.

Finding a moment to catch his breath, Wulfhere looked around and saw Tigfi, fighting around Leofwin's raven standard. He was yelling for men to rally to Leofwin's banner. "Form up on me!" he cried, his voice breaking.

Wulfhere leapt and dodged the debris, a slip here and a trip there, but blessedly staying on his feet. He paused to catch his breath, exhausted. He wanted to vomit and prayed for someone to fight with so he would not. He was in luck, for he was offered a giant Norþmann with a bloodied face.

The man was snarling, killing any who came in his path. He was almost a pleasure to watch, graceful, elegant.

Suddenly, the warrior's glazed eyes locked with Wulfhere's.

"Come on, *horningsunu!*" Wulfhere called to him.

The man was heads above them all, his ample frame covered in mail from head to toe. White spittle gathered in the corners of his mouth as he employed his deadly weapon with merciless ease.

A *berserker*. Wulfhere shuddered. Legend told of these men who became crazed in battle; something about the sight, sound, and smell of war, transformed them into battle demons. Not even iron or fire could destroy them. The man made for him, an insuperable creature, swatting mailed warriors like mere flies. Transfixed, Wulfhere watched as the wild-eyed *berserker* fought his way through the heaving mass of men. Coming for him.

Glancing around, Wulfhere realised there was no clear path to Leofwin's banner. He faced the berserker, resigning himself to the onslaught. The axe blade crashed down. As he raised his shield, a brutal thud shattered it and his already damaged arm. He staggered back, shield slipping from his jarred fingers. Instinctively, he caught at his arm. Falling back against a cluster of fighting men, he slid to the grass, the agonising pain radiating along the injured limb.

An ominous shadow cast itself over him as he scrabbled desperately in the gore for his sword. The *berserker's* blade loomed. He rolled to his left as it descended, slicing into a man directly behind him. A glance at the victim told him he bore the colours of a Súþseaxan warband. The man was on his knees, screaming, the gaping hole in his mail laying bare his splintered spine.

Wulfhere leapt to his feet, his shield arm useless. He swung his sword at the axeman catching the brute's side, a blow that made little impact. The man was solid, like rock. For a few moments, he and Wulfhere danced the warriors' dance, encircling each other with slow, measured steps, the berserker's axe poised. Wulfhere readied his sword. Whatever happened next, it would end in his death. He could do no more but wait.

There was a moment's hesitation and his opponent's eyes widened; the weapon slipped inexplicably from the *berserker's* hands. He looked dumbfounded before staring down at his abdomen. He roared. Blood gushed as the iron tip of a huge, footlong spearhead forced its way through him. He gave a bloody grimace, fell to his knees and onto his face.

To Wulfhere's astonishment, Leofnoth appeared, tugging at the spear shaft.

"I'll take that back, you bastard!" Leofnoth growled, his boot on the man's back as he tugged. He looked up at Wulfhere with an almost toothless grin and quipped, "Too old for the front line, eh?"

Wulfhere was panting. "What the devil took you so long! Have you seen our boys?"

"Aye, I saw them. They were around Yrmenlaf and the standard. And where else would I go, my friend?" Leofnoth grinned. "You need me to keep you out of trouble."

Leofnoth discarded his spear and unhooked his axe from his belt. "You ready?" he asked Wulfhere.

Together they formed their two-man shieldwall, Leofnoth using his axe to hook open shields so Wulfhere could kill their owners with his sword. A Norþmann came for them, with another huge broadaxe.

Wulfhere swiped his sword down low and caught his new assailant across the legs where there was no protection. The blow took the man off his feet and he sprawled in the mud, hamstrung.

Leofnoth grabbed his spear from the ground and pushed the tip through his throat, finishing him off.

The battle raged on around them for what seemed like hours. It was as if it was just the two of them against a thousand Wícinga. They stood their ground, their senses heightened by the need to survive. Gradually others joined them and soon they were fighting in an ever-growing shieldwall.

Chapter Thirty-four

Wolf Cry

Wulfwin fell. His line pushed back by the men in front, he landed, sprawled in the grass, holding fast onto his spear. Men tripped and stamped over him, and he gaped and cried out as one of them fell straight onto the blade of his weapon, screaming as the spearhead impaled deeply within the man's back. Wulfwin, his chest crushed under the injured warrior's heavily mailed body, lay helpless, struggling to breathe. Another body thudded across his legs, and he was completely trapped.

For what seemed like an eternity, he was unable to move, as men fell and tripped over them. He screamed and shouted, "Get off me! Help!" Then hands grabbed the collar of his hauberk and kept heaving him until he was pulled free.

"Bastards!" he cried as he was brought to stand. He turned, grateful to see it was someone he knew, but whose name he didn't remember.

"You're Wulfhere of Horstede's son? Pick up your weapon and stay with me," the man urged.

"It broke," Wulfwin moaned. The ruined shaft of his beloved first spear lay splintered over the grass, the head of which was now stuck in the idiot who'd fallen over him.

"Take mine," the man said, thrusting his spear in his hand before he quickly unsheathed his sword.

With this new weapon, its blade already bloodied, Wulfwin followed his saviour, hoping that his brother was safe.

*

Wulfric thrust his hand axe forward, hooked it over the shield rim of the warrior that faced him, forcing it aside and his shoulder-companion speared the man's exposed gut. He resisted the urge to

318

glance down the line to see if Wulfwin was there and kept his eyes on the man he fought as he had been told to. A moment's distraction could cost him or his fellows dear.

What had happened to Wulfwin? The front lines had opened, the formation had fallen into disarray and Wulfric had been swept away with those that had regrouped, but of his brother, he saw nothing. As the Wícingas stumbled through the opening into the trap, he and his companions took the stunned enemy down before they knew what had hit them. Exhilaration filled him each time he caused death. Every drop of Norse blood that rained down on him added to his jubilation. He thrust his shield forward, pushed aside a Norþmann's spear and rammed his axe into the young warrior's neck. He tasted the blood on his lips – blood of the foe, blood that he had wrought – and it pumped him full of the battle lust and the sense that he was invincible.

Another adversary appeared before him. Hunger blazed in this older man's eyes. The fear that his father had talked about shot through him; fear that would keep him alive.

"My sword is going to drink your blood, *lyttle Englander!*" the warrior growled.

"Get his shield!" shouted the spearman to Wulfric's left.

Wulfric swung his axe, caught the rim and pulled it open. *"Stinga him! Kill him!"* he called out. When nothing happened, he looked round to see that his shoulder-companion had been speared, leaving Wulfric with his axeblade still caught in the shield.

The Wícinga tugged it back and Wulfric stumbled into a random sword blow that hit his helmet. He regained his balance and stunned wits, and the bastard who had been about to kill him fell on the bloodied ground, his guts spilling out onto red-stained grass. Wulfric kissed the cross around his neck and rejoined the fray.

*

Yrmenlaf stayed his ground, blood splashing over him as the men around him battled through puddles of slaughter. He clutched the Running Wolf banner tightly, hand cramped with the effort. *Guard it with your life,* his lord had said.

Embattled soldiers fell against him in their death throes. A stray sword-blow landed on his shield. A large globule of gore splattered into his open craw and was promptly expelled along with undigested fragments of his last meal.

He hid behind his shield and shut his eyes tight, only opening them now and then to peer at the horrific scene. Hearing a familiar voice, he looked up. A huscarle holding a bloodstained broadaxe, called to him.

"Rally the men to you, lad!" Tigfi was saturated in scarlet and only recognisable by the wisps of sun-yellow fringe, untouched by battle escaping from his helm. "Rally the men! Call them to you!"

Yrmenlaf breathed in and raised his voice, "Form up on me!" he shouted. "Men of Horstede, men of Súþ Seaxa, form up – form up on me!"

He leant the shaft of the standard into the crook of his arm, swung his horn to his lips and blew. The note faltered, and he was startled by a clap on his shoulder. He turned to see Wulfwin, his blue eyes glinting in the sun, his face, pitted with crimson droplets. He laughed as he said, "Let's kill the bastards!"

*

Wulfhere slashed, parried, and smashed his way through the heaving morass of fighting men. He had not survived Harald's evil broadaxe only to be killed in this! Battle had heightened his senses so that even the ripping of armour rings, the tearing of flesh and the cracking of bones could be heard.

He felt no pain, just the innate rush of blood that drove a man into the fight.

The enemy came relentlessly, one after the other. Wulfhere roared with every blow he administered, growling with animalistic ferocity sparked by angry memories.

As he fought on, a faint but discernible wail entered his mind. He finished the next adversary, slashing at him until the fellow's legs buckled under the stress of yet another killing strike. *There it was again.* Anguish tore at him and nausea swirled in his stomach. He paused; towered over the man he'd just beaten to the ground. The wailing – it was faint, as though it were a distant, faraway echo. And yet instinctively, it was close, somewhere within him. *A warning.*

Bewildered, he stared about him, panting, motionless. The battle circled him. He listened, hearing nothing but the sounds of fighting. He glimpsed the Running Wolf banner flailing in the wind, a whirling mass of men clashing around it. He froze. *There, again, a wolf cry.*

His ears were muffled. Only the howling resonated with any clarity before a voice called, *Father! Father come...*

Then his cheek ripped, and a stinging sensation seared through him as the skin on his face flapped. He hunkered down and raised his shield. A blade bit into his right side, followed by a vicious thump to the back. Winded, he fell forward, unable to move, the air sucked out of him. He attempted to lift his head, pain encompassing him. There was nothing to do but wait for the death blow as within him a raging storm surged.

*

Leofwin paused amid the battle. The fighting was diminishing. He'd fought like a maddened boar and was now exhausted, breathless – heart pounding in his chest. The elite unit of Norse berserkers were hard to beat but not indestructible. Frenzied, they'd lost their sense of organisation and strategy to be cut down by Leofwin's triumphant warriors, surrounded, overcome – with nowhere to run.

Unexpectedly, a battle-horn echoed around him. He looked towards the expanse of fields and saw banners flying. The *fyrds* of Sumorsǣte and Defnascīr were riding to their aid, encircling the fighting, too late to be of any real use. What was left of the Norse had lost heart. Those who were of a mind to live, immediately surrendered as the mounted militia rode onto the field and mopped up any resistance.

Beaten at last, the few surviving Norþmenn were brought before Leofwin and his victorious troops.

"Where is the woman?" Leofwin called to his men rounding up the defeated.

"I have her!" She was kicking and growling as Tigfi, her long braids in his hand, dragged her by the hair through the carnage. "I caught her running away."

Leofwin shook his head at Tigfi disapprovingly.

"What?" Tigfi retorted, panting. "I had nothing to tie the bitch with, she was refusing to come nicely, so I used whatever means to bring her."

Tigfi threw her down like a carcass of meat. Leofwin laughed. "It wouldn't be the first time you had to drag a woman against her will I'd wager."

Tigfi grimaced, rubbing his hand. "The she-wolf bit me."

Astrid, her chest heaving, sprawled before them. She made to stand and Tigfi, pushed her back down with a boot. She tried again, and he did the same. She turned jaded eyes to her surviving warriors, on their knees, heads bowed.

A wry smile faintly touched her lips. "I will not kneel to you, Englisc." She rose unsteadily to her feet again. "Astrid Ótryggrsdottir does not kneel to Englisc dogs."

Leofwin nodded at Tigfi who struck her in the mouth. She staggered, spat blood, and narrowed her eyes at them.

"What? You think I wouldn't harm a woman?" Leofwin snarled. "If you want to fight with men, expect to be beaten like one."

"I would expect no special favours just because I am a woman."

Leofwin was in her face. "Then I ask that you kneel to me or I will give you to my men. Some of them are just waiting to have their way with you, and I am all that is standing between you and them."

Astrid folded her arms over her chest and refused to do as she was bid.

"You want my men to take you?" he asked.

She shifted. "You wouldn't dare. I have many kin who would avenge me. So, if you want to bring the wrath of more *Vikingr* upon you, then... do it!"

"Tigfi, give her to them," Leofwin said coldly, turning away.

Tigfi nodded to a fellow huscarle and grabbed the woman's arms. She squirmed, crying out, "Wait!"

Leofwin turned, signalled to the huscarles to let her go. "Look around you, Astrid – what do you see? You are defeated. You have lost. What choice do you have?"

She gazed at her remaining warriors and bowed her head.

Leofwin looked her over. Even scarred and blood-splattered, she was an attractive woman. "Strewn across this meadow, your warriors are dead, dying, or wounded. Their blood soaks the grass. Your army has been decimated. Your father and brother are dead. Your ships, all but destroyed, their magnificent beauty sunk into the swollen waters of the Saefren. With no way home, Astrid Ótryggrsdottir, you have no choice but to submit to my mercy."

Sullenly, Astrid sank to her knees and listened to Leofwin's terms. Then she was permitted to speak with her warriors.

"Would you have really given her to the men?" Tigfi asked him.

Leofwin breathed deeply and crossed his arms. "Do you think I would have?"

Tigfi shrugged. "Maybe, but it would not perhaps be a story to be proud of."

"No, but it was a chance I had to take."

"It seems that your *wyrd* has been good to you today, lord."

"Aye, it has," nodded Leofwin.

"What do we do with them now?"

Leofwin followed Tigfi's gaze as Astrid stood in discussion with her remaining men.

"I have offered them places in my household," Leofwin said. "I will need men such as these in the earldom I hope my brother and the king will make for me."

"What about *her*? Would you allow a woman in your household?"

Leofwin smiled. "I have other uses for her, perhaps."

*

Wulfhere, wind returned, dragged himself to stand. Horns blared and riders were on the field. Englisc militia. The fight was over. He touched his face, flinching, the skin flapping over the wound. His breathing, laboured and painful, indicated badly bruised ribs. One leg was bleeding. On one side, a gash burned like the fires of Hell, blood pooling at the site. He reached for Hildbana and pain wracked his body, but he was glad, for it meant he was alive.

With difficulty, he straightened, sheathing Hildbana without cleaning her. Looking round he saw the Running Wolf flying in the wind, stuck in the ground around twenty yards away. As he made towards it, he saw that Yrmenlaf sat in its shadow, his knees beneath him, head bowed, shoulders heaving. He cradled something in his lap. A helmet...? Or a head.

Chapter Thirty-five

"Vengeance Will Be Mine!"

Wulfhere froze. Something was wrong. He hurried, limping, through the morass of mangled bodies, and reaching him, dropped to his knees beside the boy. Yrmenlaf, a hand over the bloody torrent gushing from Wulfwin's throat, looked up through misty eyes and said, "He kept me safe, lord. They were trying to get Running Wolf, but he saved me. He saved my life."

The lad began to sob. Wulfhere, speechless, pressed his own hand over Yrmenlaf's to help him, knowing that there was nothing that could be done now. But he did it anyway. The blood flowed between their fingers and Wulfwin's mail appeared as though it had been forged with red links of steel. There was so much blood.

"Your father is here" Wulfhere choked on the words. "Wulfwin, I am here."

The dying eyes searched. Lips, tinged blue, moved mutely, and from the wound came a strange sucking sound of air. He drew a last breath.

Wulfhere's tears flowed. He gathered Wulfwin to him. "Nay! Nay! Not my boy! Not – my – son!" Gently he removed Wulfwin's helm, kissed his head and stroked the auburn hair. "It should have been me, not you."

At a shout, Wulfhere looked up and saw his other son with Leofnoth and Æmund. "I have to see him, let me see him!" Wulfric cried.

"Wait, there is something you should know." Æmund, his arms around his distressed brother-in-law, tried to stop him.

Wulfhere gently let go of Wulfwin. With nothing to be done for the son now dead, he stood and went to give comfort to the son that lived.

Wulfhere moved Æmund aside and took his weeping son in his arms.

324

"I have to see him, he is calling me!" Wulfric fought against his father. "Please let me see him!"

"He is gone," Wulfhere said, gripping Wulfric's arms.

"Nay, he is not! He calls to me. I can still feel him," Wulfric put a hand over his heart. "He is still..."

"He is gone, Wulfric, gone," Wulfhere said.

His son gave in and pushed his body against him, tightening his grip on him. As Wulfhere held him close to his breast, soaked in the grief of one son and the blood of another, he saw them across the battle ground. He felt the rush of suspicion. Helghi, Hengest, and the youth, Eadnoth, watched them like malevolent figures from the shadows, a sly smile and an air of triumph on each face. Wulfhere imagined he heard Helghi's voice: a *son of Wulfhere, dead....* Another victim of the feud between them has been claimed. But always the loss was Wulfhere's – never Helghi's.

Wulfhere closed his eyes and held fast onto Wulfric. His other son had not lost his life to a Norþmann's blade, of that he was certain. A nice sheer, clean cut across the throat was not the usual mark of battle, but more the mark of an assassin. If Wulfwin was attacked from behind, or if he'd been put out of his misery as he lay amongst the dying, it might have been credible... It might have...If he had not recalled Mildrith's warning: *"Accidents happen..."*

He tensed.

Wulfric sensed it and withdrew, turning to follow Wulfhere's gaze. He whispered, "Helghi..." Wulfric turned back, eyes bright with insight as he said, "Something is wrong Father, isn't it?"

Wulfhere clasped his son's shoulders. "Your brother is dead, Wulfric, that is what is wrong."

"Helghi has done something, hasn't he? Was it his throat? It was, wasn't it?"

Wulfhere did not speak. Wulfric turned again and called out, "Helghi, you bastard! You killed him, didn't you?" Then he put a hand on Hildbana's hilt at his father's hip, pulled her from her scabbard and raged toward Helghi, brandishing the blade, still bloody from battle. "You cut his throat, didn't you? You piece of filth!"

"Wulfric! God, boy! Stop this!" Staggering, Wulfhere failed to stop him. He called out to those nearby, "Help me, please. Don't let me lose another son!"

Æmund and the others rushed to encircle Wulfric, and Wulfhere, catching up with them, grabbed Hildbana from his son's grasp. "What in Hell's name are you going to do?"

"*He* did this, Father! You know he did!"

"And you want to kill him – here? – for all to see? I have lost one son today; I do not want to lose another!"

"So, we just let him get away with it?"

"God knows that if I could butcher him like a pig, right here, right now, I would. I would tear him in two, but I have too much to lose. *We* have too much to lose. It will not happen here, do you understand? Not here!... Not like this! *And not – by – you!*"

"Wulfhere!"

He swung around. Helghi was leering, his hand on the pommel of his sword. Wulfhere felt the hackles rise on his neck. It was too much. Shoving Wulfric behind him, he stepped forward, trembling to contain the rage he must suppress. *The bastard was smiling!*

"You lost a son, Wulfhere, I sympathise. I know how that feels. I lost mine also. But you know that, don't you? Now you know what that does to a man."

In his mind, Wulfhere saw a scene splattered with blood, and the pain in his leg forgotten, he strode toward his enemy -the mocking voice drawing him on.

"*My son*, Wulfhere. The one you broke your oath to. The one you crippled – the one who was outlawed – because of *you* and your whoring daughter!"

Wulfhere thundered through those who got in his way, rage dispelling caution. A javelin stood lodged in the sludge and he snatched it up, and sent it whipping toward his enemy.

Helghi, face contorted, dived out of harm's way and the missile landed harmlessly in the earth. Wulfhere, vengeance denied, rushed toward his enemy, *seax* drawn.

Leofwin's huscarles rushed forward and brought him to the ground.

Wulfhere, despite being restrained, lifted himself off the ground, and knelt on one knee. The men fought to hold him, and he strained against them. Leofwin called for more reinforcements and an arm tightened around Wulfhere's neck.

"Jesus Christ, man!" Leofwin bellowed. "What's got into you? We have just fought and won a battle against hundreds of madmen and now you have become one of them. What has this man done to you that you attack him?"

"That foul, black-hearted son of a pig killed my son!"

Helghi held his hands in supplication, like a priest reading Mass. "The man is grief-stricken. He doesn't know what he is saying!"

Leofnoth stepped forward. "My lord, Wulfhere is bereaved, his son is dead. During the battle, Wulfwin was felled, and his throat cut. He was nowhere near the enemy."

"And what has this to do with this man?" Leofwin, gesticulating toward Helghi who was behaving like an aggrieved victim. "What is your name?"

"He tried to kill me, lord."

"Your name?" Leofwin repeated.

"I am Helghi of Gorde, lord."

"Did anyone see this man kill Wulfhere's son?"

Heads shook.

"Yrmenlaf, he saw it – ask him, my fyrdsman. It was he who found my son."

Leofwin indicated to his men to let Wulfhere go.

"Perhaps then it was this Yrmenlaf who killed his son." It was Hengest, Helghi's kinsman who spoke. "If he found this Yrmenlaf with his son, why is he not accusing *him*?"

Leofnoth huffed, rolling his eyes.

"Yrmenlaf?" Wulfhere laughed joylessly. "He would not kill my son. The boys have grown up together. They are friends."

Yrmenlaf was brought, still carrying the standard, red-eyed, tearstained, and frightened. "Come lad, speak to our lord. Tell them what happened to Wulfwin," Wulfhere encouraged.

Leofwin gently touched the lad's shoulder. "Yrmenlaf, lad, did you see what happened to your young friend?"

Yrmenlaf shook his head, "I am sorry, lord, I just found him... like that," he said, sobbing. "He stood by my side until the end of the fighting and kept the enemy away from me – I-I wish I had seen, but I saw nothing. One minute he was there with me, the next he was grabbing me – his hands holding his throat – and..."

"Did you see this man, Helghi, nearby, Yrmenlaf?" Leofwin asked.

Yrmenlaf looked across at Helghi and said, almost indiscernibly,

"Nay, lord."

Wulfhere groaned.

"I'm sorry, lord. Please don't be angry with me. Father Paul says I must tell the truth, always, and it is a sin to lie. I will go to hell if I do!"

Wulfhere turned away from him, holding his forehead. He felt drained. Helghi had got away with it again!

"Wulfhere, you cannot attack this man without proof!" Leofwin said. There was anger in his voice.

"You know me to be an honest man, Lord Leofwin. I have known you for years. My father served yours faithfully, and your brother Harold, as do I –"

"As did *my* father also!" Helghi bellowed. He was walking toward them across the gore-infested field, his shoes squelching. "*My* father, who died at *your* father's hands!"

Wulfhere looked at Helghi, stunned by his words. There was nary a drop of blood, nor a cut, nor even a bruise on him. He was wearing his old mail shirt, polished to perfection. Once he'd grown too large for it, but now fitted him flawlessly. He was stronger than ever, just as he had when Wulfhere knew him as a young man. He had been a good fighter back then.

"Look at him," Wulfhere said. "There is not a stain of battle on him. How is it he has come out of the fight so unscathed? He has followers here – they must have hidden themselves, kept out of the heart of the battle – waiting for my boys to be helpless."

Leofwin regarded Helghi. He seemed to be considering what Wulfhere had said.

It was Leofnoth who broke in, "Lord, first he blames Wulfhere for crippling his son, now Helghi claims *his* father died because of Wulfhere's father. Is it pure coincidence that Wulfhere's son ends up dead on a battlefield with his throat cut nice and cleanly as though from behind, and without any other injuries?"

"Did you kill this man's son, Helghi?" Leofwin asked.

"Nay, I did not! But it is true that there has been enmity between our families for years. I have been victimised like–"

Leofnoth rounded on Helghi, "Your father died, because he drank himself to death! Your son was crippled because the horse you insisted on buying was too wild for a seven-year-old. Wulfhere tried to dissuade you, but you would not heed him. None of these things were Wulfhere's fault. Wulfhere's father was my friend. He was not responsible for your father's death."

"This man does not know anything, lord. They were drinking together one night – when we awoke, Wulfhere's father was alive –

and mine, he was dead!"

"That means nothing!" shouted Wulfhere at Helghi.

"It means *everything*!"

"Shut your mouth!" Leofwin shouted. He turned to Wulfhere and put a hand on his heaving shoulder. "Wulfhere, I *do* know you. I know you served my father and my brother well. Why do you think this man has anything to do with your son's death? Did we not just fight a battle here? A death such as this during battle cannot be proven otherwise where there are no witnesses."

Wulfric came forward, his face furrowed in anguish. "Lord, Wulfwin was my brother, this man is my father. Before we went to battle, my brother told me that Helghi made this sign." He drew his hand across his throat. "He meant to kill him."

"He is lying! Why would I do such a thing?" Helghi roared. "Wulfhere wants me dishonoured so that his daughter does not have to wed my son, which your lord brother, the earl, has sanctioned."

Leofwin looked thoughtful at this new information.

Æmund came forward, speaking for the first time. "Those who know this man well will know that Helghi is not known for telling truths. They will see it in his lying eyes and the smirk he hides behind the affronted expression. Aye everyone will know what has occurred on this day."

There were nods of assent from amongst Wulfhere's associates.

"They are all lying!" Helghi pointed at Æmund. "This whelp here, is the husband of Wulfhere's daughter, the one that my son was ordered to wed by your brother, Lord Harold."

Wulfhere lurched forward. "*Horningsunu*! You know you did it! I will not rest until Wulfwin is avenged. The slain will not lie still!"

"Wulfhere, do not stain your hands with his blood, he is not worth it," Wulfward said, stepping before Wulfhere, his hands on Wulfhere's shoulders. "Think of your family."

"Listen to your friend. He is right. One thing my brother will not tolerate is conflict amongst the fyrd. You will have to take this up with him. For now, no one has witnessed your son's death, for which I am sorry. I am sure he died fighting bravely. And you, Helghi, get you out of here,!" Leofwin ordered, waving his arm at the man. "As for you, Wulfhere, if you disobey my orders, I will clap you in irons and hand you over to Harold! Now tend to your sons, for they both have great need of you. That is all I will say on the matter!"

Wulfhere turned his eyes upon Leofwin. "When the time is right, I *will* kill him," he said. His strength was waning. He felt clammy, breathless, and slurred his words.

"Come, Wulfhere, let us do what we can for Wulfwin."

"I won't let him get away with this, Leofnoth." Wulfhere was swaying; beads of sweat were prickling his forehead.

"I know, but for now... for Wulfric's sake, let's do what needs to be done. Helghi can wait. We can do this thing properly at the right time." Then Leofnoth, his arm about his friend, drew Wulfhere away, their companions following.

Wulfhere's feet suddenly twisted and he lost his footing. His arms were around Leofnoth and Wulfric as they took him between them. His head began to loll, and he sank to his knees.

"Father!" cried Wulfric. "He's bleeding!"

Wulfhere felt cool grass beneath him and Leofnoth's hands searching through his mail, examining him.

"I thought this was Wulfwin's blood, but it is not," Leofnoth said.

Gravely wounded, exhausted and overcome with grief, Wulfhere succumbed to unconsciousness.

Chapter Thirty-six

"Too Tedious to Tell"

When Harold arrived in Scrobbesbyrig, Burghred's men had not long broken the siege and were busy clearing up the damage. Harold was surveying the scene as Burghred approached him.

"You've done well here, Burghred. Scrobbesbyrig is known for being impenetrable. How did you do it?" Harold gave the young lord a friendly backhand in his midriff. "Never mind, we must leave the story for another day. What happened to him?" Harold indicated to a corpse lying alone in the courtyard instead of piled up with the rest of the dead.

"Ragnald? My father's captain. I had an old score to settle with him." Burghred spoke wryly.

"I know the man. Your father will not be pleased. I hope you have the wergild." Harold smiled at him with a raised eyebrow and then looked around at the men who were hurriedly repairing the damaged gates, sounds of sawing and hammering filling the air. "Well, I must go. I have duties to attend. I'll leave you to finish this...."

"Earl Harold, when will I know?"

"Know?"

"If I have done enough to win my earldom."

Harold felt the guilt rise within him. Burghred was bloodied, exhausted, and broken. "I hardly know what it is going to happen with your father yet. Outside the gates he is camped with an army big enough to overwhelm us. Now is not the right time to be talking about this."

"Of course, lord. I will wait. Excuse me, lord, I must see to things here."

Harold nodded and went to leave, then turned back and said, "I meant it when I said you did well. Oh, and you had better see to those injuries, lad."

Harold made his way to Edward's camp, a rich sight of colourful banners, vibrantly painted tents, and carts laden with weapons and war gear. Collecting Skalpi, Gauti, and his brother Leofwin, they made their way through the bustling, hive of activity to the king's tent. As he entered with Leofwin, leaving Skalpi and Gauti outside, Edward's face lit up with a disingenuous smile.

"Ah, my lord Harold, so good of you to join us at last."

Edward was seated comfortably in his high-backed cushioned chair. Edith sat delicately on a pile of furs, massaging his feet as she often did. It always seemed a peculiar sight to Harold that she would do this even when Edward was holding court.

Beside Edward stood Wulfstan, abbot of the newly consecrated minster of Gleawecestre, standing in for Bishop Ealdred who was on one of his adventures abroad. Behind them, waiting on the king, was the royal cupbearer, Wigod, and the unfortunate chamberlain, Hugolin, whom Alfgar had taken hostage last Christmas and left bruised and bleeding by the wayside.

Harold and Leofwin made their obeisance and rose when permitted. "Lord king, I would have been here sooner, but I stopped to inspect the young Lord Burghred's work in the town. He did well, taking into account how impenetrable the walls are."

"Yes, yes, I have heard all about it already," Edward said waving his hand. Boredom showed in his pained expression. "He needn't have gone to all that trouble. After all, we are here now, and Scrobbesbyrig would have capitulated to us anyway. The whole thing was pointless if you ask me. A lot of bluster and damage done for nought."

On the floor, Edith looked up at Edward, her face and eyes crinkled with adoration, her head tilting from side to side; then she turned from him to Harold, her lips now pursed into a smug smile.

Harold sighed inwardly. It was going to be a long night.

Messengers went between the two camps well into evening and by the time midnight had come, Harold settled in his bed for the night. An intoxicated Leofwin snored gently on his pallet next to him. There had been no settlement. It was not looking easy for Alfgar. Not this time, unlike in '55 when he'd ravaged Hereford only to be reinstated as Earl of East Anglia. Negotiations had provided no conclusions other than if they could not come to a satisfactory agreement on the morrow, there would be battle.

Harold lay back on his pallet, wishing he'd drunk as much wine as Leofwin. Damn it he wished he could sleep. But his mind just couldn't stop pondering ways of avoiding conflict.

Some were surprised that there was no sign of Gruffudd, but not Harold. He'd be holed up somewhere in one of his impressive strongholds. Gruffudd rarely put himself where he did not feel safe. Instead, the coward had sent his half-brothers, Bleddyn and Rhiwallon, leading a large contingent of Welsh soldiers to augment Alfgar's Anglo-Norse troops.

The next day, negotiations resumed. Thegns from across Wessex had been arriving even in the early hours of the morning. The king's tent was crammed. And despite not having slept well, Harold was up at daybreak to ensure that the talks started at a timely hour.

It was clear that the Mercians had rallied willingly to Alfgar. Burghred, sadly had failed the challenge to claim the earldom for himself. Harold felt sorry for him, but Alfgar was still a force to be reckoned with. Despite all Alfgar's misdeeds, the Mercians remained loyal to him, and with the Norse king's eyes on the crown, the kingdom could not afford to risk such division. Preferring diplomacy over war, Harold managed to win over the opinions of those who mattered most and advised King Edward against battle if it could be avoided.

Edward looked displeased as he glared at his councillors, furious that they had agreed with Harold that they should seek peace rather than do battle.

"So be it," the irritated king said. "But his position in Mercia must be negotiated. I will not brook him as Earl, Lord Harold. I shall not! He needs to be punished this time!"

Harold made his way to meet with Alfgar, knowing that the king's demands would be difficult to carry out. With Bishop Wulfstan and Leofwin walking beside him, and Skalpi and Gauti behind, Harold said, "Alfgar will not accept anything other than the earldom of Mercia. He would not be here with the thousands of men he has if he were willing settle for less."

It seemed that his companions were in accord with him, for they did not argue. No one but the king saw sense in encouraging a civil war.

Harold and the others met with Alfgar's party in an open space between the two camps.

Alfgar was there, arms crossed, a nonchalant expression on his scarred face. His own bodyguards flanked him, and a priest stood behind them. Alfgar's standard bearer held his banner of the fighting boar, proudly flapping in the wind.

There was a brief moment of silence initially. Harold studied Alfgar. His cheeks and chin were newly shaven, his moustache neatly trimmed, but his dark hair was still bushy and wild. The smile that graced the Mercian's lips made it seem as though he was scowling and there appeared to be an air of victory about him. Or was it arrogance that Harold saw?

"I thank you, Lord Alfgar for agreeing to speak with me, since you bring such large numbers with you."

Alfgar snorted. "I knew what I would be facing," he replied. The annoying crooked upturn of his lips was still there as he spoke.

"What is it you want, Alfgar? I take it you mean to resume your position in Mercia?"

"What else? Or were you hoping to give my lands to Burghred?"

"Your son? He was loyal to his king, that is all." Harold sighed inwardly; he didn't want to get into a discussion with the man about Burghred.

Alfgar sniggered. "Perhaps one day, Lord Harold, you will know, what it is to be betrayed by a son."

Harold averted his eyes momentarily, then looked back at Alfgar with a nod of acceptance. "And where is Gruffudd? It seems he is too much a coward to come here himself but sends his men without him."

"I have an army of his men loaned to me. The Wéalas king is my son-in-law and has been of service to me." Alfgar inclined his head as he spoke as if he agreed with him.

"He was right not to have come. I am sure there are many here today who would like to see him swing from the gallows."

"Including yourself, Lord Harold."

Harold found himself nodding involuntarily. He wanted to wipe that stupid smile from Alfgar's face. "It seems we are forever putting out fires where Gruffudd is concerned, only to find another one kindled. And every time we have a peace deal, the man breaks it, and you go running off to him whenever you find yourself in trouble. And why should you bring, Gruffudd, when you have your Norse army and a boy to lead them."

"As I said, Lord Harold, I knew what I would be facing. And you yourself know what it is to be exiled unjustly."

"Unjustly you say?" Harold laughed. "Did you really think Edward would allow you to get away with marrying your daughter to Gruffudd without his permission? Or to insult his person, kidnap and assault his chamberlain?" Harold mentally kicked and checked himself. It did not bode well to show feelings to an adversary.

"You Godwinsons are so self-righteous! You have Wessex and have taken lands that once belonged to Mercia. Tostig is lord in the north and East Anglia went to your brother, Gyrth, when it should have gone to my son!"

"East Anglia was not Burghred's hereditary right."

Alfgar sneered. "As it was not Gyrth's either. Why should there be three Godwinsons in power and just one Leofricson? It should have gone to Burghred!"

"Burghred, the son you hate?"

Alfgar's eyes burned and his face flushed scarlet with fury as he clenched his fists, shuddering as if to contain himself.

"You are responsible for that, Lord Harold – you!"

"Nay, Alfgar. That was *your* doing! Why do you think he came to me? He was ashamed of you!"

Growling, the enraged Mercian gave Harold an almighty shove and was about to ram a fist into his face when it was blocked and Harold flung Alfgar away from him. Their guards intervened and Harold stood back as Alfgar regained his feet, his men calming him.

"We are not here to fight amongst ourselves, Alfgar," Harold panted. "If you want to get Mercia back, then so be it, but let us leave our personal grievances out of this."

"Aye. But one day, you will fall, I swear it."

"All right, Alfgar." Harold stood for a moment, brushing off Leofwin's concerns for his wellbeing. "Now, what are your terms, and what are you going to do with Magnus?"

Harold returned with his men to report back to the king. It had been a hard negotiation. Alfgar's hostility toward him had been prevalent throughout the meeting. It left him with a sour taste in his mouth and a tinge of regret they would not meet in battle after all.

"I still can't believe that Alfgar did not want to fight," Leofwin said as he walked side by side with Harold. "Why bring Norse and Wéalas troops all the way here at great cost if he is not going to deploy them?"

"I don't think Alfgar was ever going to go through with the plan to put Harald Sigurdson on the throne." Harold replied as they walked back through the damp grassy meadow, negotiating the path through the tents and campfires through the darkness. "He wanted to make us think he was going to – but I doubt he ever would. Even his own men would never have gone along with that."

"They soon rallied round though," Leofwin replied.

"Pah, I don't think they ever believed it, but I'm glad we don't have to find out." Harold sniffed the air. There were no clouds that evening, and the temperature was cold.

"Yet if he had wanted to, he could have. He had a sizeable enough army." Leofwin bent down to pick something up off the ground and threw it away when he realised it was just a piece of scrap.

"Ah yes, but despite Alfgar not being the cleverest player on the board, he knows that Edward still has others to play in the shape of Tostig and Gyrth. Alfgar was only interested in getting his lands back. The presence of so many troops was just a show of strength."

"And what if Magnus does not accept the terms?"

"Magnus needs Alfgar on board. Without him, he would never succeed. He is just a boy after all. What can he do, Leofwin? It is not as if he is going home with nothing, is it?" Harold was disgusted that he'd been forced to add the silver to the concessions to pay off the Norse. Another price to pay for averting the war.

"What of Gruffudd?" It was Wulfstan who asked the question.

"Aye, Brother, why does he not show himself?"

"Yes, what of bloody Gruffudd." Harold stroked his chin. "Gruffudd is not stupid. He hides away in his mountain fortresses because he knows that if he came here himself, he'd be swinging. He is the one we need gone. He hates us, wants to divide us so he can sweep into the chaos to gain more lands. And so he sends his brothers, for in a land where men would kill their own kin if it served their purpose, it is better his brothers lose their liberty than he his life. But I tell you one thing – the day will come when I will have Gruffudd's neck in a noose."

"And Alfgar is his father-in-law and he can carry on raiding now with impunity and there will be nothing that can be done, because Alfgar will protect him," added Wulfstan.

The men continued to walk in silence until Leofwin asked, "What do think Edward will do when he knows Alfgar and Gruffudd have got away with it again?"

Harold shrugged. "What he always does. Have an apoplectic fit."

So it was that Alfgar had won back his earldom with no blood shed. An agreement had been made for the leaders to meet a week later in Gleawecestre to finalise the peace treaty, but to ensure the two men, Alfgar and Gruffudd, behaved with honour, Harold had insisted that they give hostages. Alfgar's young sons, Morcar and Edwin, were to be handed over, as were Gruffudd's half-brothers, Bleddyn and Rhiwallon. The Wéalas ruler was given a promise of safe conduct should he come as was required of him. After all, he was Edward's 'under-king' and as such it was expected. Or it would be treason.

Harold was right. It seemed it was beyond the king's capability to recognise that there was no benefit to the kingdom to cause a civil war, leaving the country vulnerable to external invasions. He stamped his feet and threw his cup of wine at an unfortunate servant.

"I wanted the heads of Gruffudd and Alfgar!" he shouted. "Once again, Harold, you have disappointed me. Tostig would not have allowed this to happen."

"Lord King, I regret that you should be so disappointed in me, but I must remind you of the threat that was placed upon your crown, and what happened when last Englalond was invaded by Danes who usurped your father's throne. If we allow Alfgar and his allies to divide Englalond, then the same will happen again, which is what has brought us to this point."

It was enough for Edward to withdraw the complaint, though reluctantly, muttering something about Harold's father colluding with Cnut.

Relieved, Harold had retired to his own tent for some well-earned rest. As he lay on his bed, he reflected that the whole mountainous event had been whittled away to a mole hill. The threats, the boasting, the money spent, and the bombastic demands of both sides had all come to a tiresome conclusion.

And as Harold quipped to his men at the mead board that evening, one could almost hear the monks sighing, sat in their cold, wind rattled scriptoriums, quills gripped in their frozen, ink-stained hands, writing all they could be bothered to say of that time in Englalond's saga: 'It is too tedious to tell'.

Chapter Thirty-seven

The Slain Will Not Lie Still

Dawn had long been stirred by a glorious sun when Leofwin's army set out for Gleawecestre. Wulfhere rode in silence, enshrouded in a pall of gloom. He was not alone in his grief, for they had lost around two hundred men to the Norse, and amongst those revelling in glory were those who grieved for the friends and comrades that would never again join them in the warriors' meadhall.

Wulfhere refused to be carried on a stretcher or in a cart like the other injured. "There are those worse than I," he said after being hastily patched up by the healers. When the men referred to the gash on his face, he'd not laughed at their jests about his good looks being ruined; not because he was vain, but because how can a man laugh with one of his sons dead? His bruised ribs chafed as his armour rubbed against them, the hole in his mail testament to where the enemy sword had pierced it. He bit down on his lip at the throbbing of his injured leg. Not even the poultice applied to it seemed to help.

Wulfric had not strayed from his side, as though he feared losing his father as well as his brother. Luckily, except for a few cuts and bruises, the lad was unscathed. He too, Wulfhere knew, would suffer the deeper wounds of battle. Wounds not seen by the naked eye.

"It wasn't supposed to have ended like this, was it?" Wulfric murmured. "We were supposed to have returned together, *all of us.*" He stifled a sob. "Half of me has died, Father."

"I know..." Wulfhere replied, not knowing what else to say. "I know."

"Father?"

"Aye?"

"I wish we could have brought him with us. Do you think he will

339

hate us for leaving him?"

"Hush, Wulfric. He will understand. Besides, he will not be alone."

"He wants vengeance. I feel it."

"He will have it, I promise you."

Wulfhere's eyes locked with his son's and there, reflected, was his own pain. The death of Wulfwin might have been less wretched if he'd not died at the hands of Helghi.

"How, Father? How will we avenge him? *When* we will avenge him?"

"We will bide our time, Wulfric."

"I don't want to bide my time, I want to kill him now," Wulfric muttered bitterly.

Wulfhere looked away, too weary to argue or agree.

Kings Holme, Gleawecestre

They'd been back for only a matter of hours when Wulfhere received summons to meet with Harold in his lodgings.

"Stay here," he advised Wulfric as he was permitted entry into the earl's antechamber. His hand shook as he clasped the wrought iron latch and twisted it open.

Harold sat with Leofwin, a game of *hnefatafl* and a flask of refreshment between them.

"Wulfhere, my friend, come, come in," Harold beckoned. He rested an arm nonchalantly on the board, his long legs outstretched before him. Beeswax candles in iron holders illuminated the faltering light that fell across the earl's amiable features. "Come, take a stool and sit with us."

Wulfhere pulled over a seat and the earl continued, "Please accept my sincere condolences. I heard that your son lost his life in the battle. I would that he had not. So many young lives... it is so regrettable." Harold shook his head forlornly. "I will have prayers said at tomorrow's mass for him and all the men who were slaughtered. I recall the twins were good lads. How does your other son fare?"

Wulfhere, fixated on the floor, shrugged. He couldn't understand why he felt so sluggish. "He does as badly as one would expect." Even to his own ears, his speech sounded slow.

"Have some mead," Harold offered, passing a horn to him.

Wulfhere took a swig. He felt unkempt compared to the well-groomed brothers. He was ashamed of his overgrown moustache and matted hair; his boots, caked in the grime of battle and he smelled like something found in a cesspit, a creature with grubby hands and bloodstained nails.

"My lord, I am not fit to be in your presence."

Harold's gaze was kind. "Of course you are, Wulfhere. Leofwin has told me how you fought the *cheampa feoht*. He tells me you defeated a giant Norþmann; that you fought with the courage of a boar and with the prowess of a wolf. I wish I had been there to see it."

If the brothers were repelled by him, neither of them showed it.

Wulfhere's hands shook as he took the mead horn once again and held it in his hand, afraid to drink lest he spill it.

"Wulfhere, I wanted you to know that we appreciate what you did, the *scops* are already singing of your skills. I am proud to have you in my service." As if sensing Wulfhere's disquiet, the earl laid a hand on Wulfhere's shoulder momentarily, then took a purse from a pouch and held it out for him to take. "Please have this for your son's wergild."

"Wulfwin's wergild is not yours to pay, my lord. The responsibility belongs to the one who murdered him. Helghi."

Harold put the purse on the table, pushed it in front of Wulfhere and sighed.

"We have been through this, Wulfhere. Your son was killed in battle," Leofwin said.

"He was not," Wulfhere replied. He shook his head. "That is what you think, but I know differently."

"There is no way that anyone can prove it was Helghi, Wulfhere. And why, why would he do such a thing?" Leofwin asked.

Wulfhere looked straight at Harold. "My lord, you know my story, the hostility between myself and Helghi –"

"Wulfhere," Harold interjected, his voice sympathetic, "We have been here before, have we not? You must let go of this thing you have with Helghi. A feud like this could tear Súþ Seaxa apart. I have seen it in the north; in my brother Tostig's earldom. I do not wish to see it in mine."

"My lord," Wulfhere said, leaning forward in earnest, "I know… I know from a reliable source that what he wants is revenge…. He wants to take everything I have. My land, my children, everything."

Harold smiled faintly. "Revenge for what, Wulfhere?"

"It is a long story… lord."

"Who is this source?" Harold asked. "Let them come before us so that we can hear what they have to say. If what you are telling me is true, then give me the proof and I will see to it that Helghi is stopped."

Wulfhere went to say her name but thought better of it. He could not betray Mildrith. Helghi would kill her. He sighed. No, she had brought his daughter back to him. He owed it to her to stay silent and not put her life at risk.

They sat in awkward silence for a moment. Harold breathed deeply and said, "Wulfhere, your daughter, Freyda, she was promised to Helghi's eldest son, I recall, but now she is married to Leofnoth's?"

"Aye, my lord, but –"

"And the last time we spoke about this, you gave your word that your youngest daughter would be wed to Helghi's son to compensate for the broken oath?"

"Lord, he was outlawed… for kidnapping Freyda," Wulfhere replied.

"That was a heinous crime, but I understand that Helghi has another son and you still have your youngest daughter unwed I hope?"

"Lord, I cannot allow a daughter of mine to enter into such an alliance. Do not force this upon me, I implore you."

"Wulfhere, I am not a hard man, I know that you want the best for your daughters." Harold paused, stroking his chin. "This can be discussed at a later time – in the shire moot. If you bring proof of what Helghi's intentions are, then we will call an end to this contract of proposed marriage, and Helghi will pay the price for murder."

Wulfhere stood, feeling his legs shake, trying to mouth words that would not come. His strength left him. The drinking horn tumbled from his trembling hands, spilling its contents over his boots. His heart beat feverishly as he swayed, forehead prickling with perspiration. Arms reached out to steady him; muffled voices spoke words he couldn't rightly hear. The floor came up to meet him and he found himself on all fours, expelling the contents of his stomach.

He continued to heave even when there was nothing left to get rid of. Men called his name, and he felt himself lifted. Doors were thrust open, and white-plastered walls flashed by him as he was hurried along a lane. He heard Wulfric's voice imploring, "Stay with me, Father."

Everything spun and his body seared with the heat of immense pain. Closing his eyes to avoid more vomiting, they stayed shut until he slipped into blessed unconsciousness.

"Lay 'im down 'ere, lads," the *herelæch* ordered in his strong country burr. He indicated a board, stained red from previous occupants, and Wulfhere was laid gently upon it.

"Get 'is shirt off, lads." He immersed his bloodstained hands in a bucket of the water, brought by a young apprentice.

Wulfric, too stunned to help, watched them pull at his father's disgusting tunic. He gasped as it stuck fast to the wound and no longer unconscious, Father screamed as the material was yanked away. Wulfric gagged on the fetid smell as blood and puss oozed from the gaping wound.

The *herelæch* sucked in a breath, puffed out his cheeks, and shook his head. "Has this not been treated?" he asked, staring at Wulfric.

Wulfric could not speak for retching and looked to Tigfi to answer for him.

"It was, sir, but Wulfhere is a stubborn man and refused to let them touch it again once he'd been stitched."

"Well, whatever's been happenin' since, them stitches t'aint 'oldin' now. What was the weapon?"

"Sw-ord," said Wulfric, coughing, but recovered enough to speak.

"Why didn't the fool get this seen to afore? This will not do, senseless idiot."

Wulfric studied the man's expression anxiously. "Can you treat him?"

"Well, I'll try. See 'ow the skin is discoloured here, very dark, almost black and is stinkin' like a smoked herrin'. T'will need to be cut away, it will."

"But he will live?" Wulfric swallowed a wave of bile.

"Can't promise anything, lad, I never promises anything, but I do try."

Wulfric felt his head spin and his stomach roll. He clutched the side of the board to steady himself.

"First time yee've seen anything like this, lad?"

Wulfric nodded.

"Well, it won't be yer last. Yee'll be all right lad, just have some of this afore I give it to yer father, not too much, mind, 'e'll need it mor'an you."

Wulfric downed almost all the mead before he promptly spewed the lot up and the flask was snatched from him by the angry *herelæch* who exclaimed, "Bloody waste of good mead that was!"

Chapter Thirty-eight

Burghred

One Week later
Kings Holme, Gleawecestre
Burghred found a quiet place by the wharf where he could sit alone with his anger. The recent overbearing heat had now evaporated into mildness, though had done nothing to cool the tension of his current position, now that the conflict was over. Having tried several times unsuccessfully to catch Earl Harold in Scrobbesbyrig, he'd been told to be patient and wait. That his time would come. And now in Kings Holme, he had been seething for over a week.

He stared blankly across the river at his serene surroundings, so at odds with his troubled mind. The wind-blown redolence of wildflowers and the peaceful bleating of newly shorn sheep and their lambs, should have relaxed and calmed him, but it had not.

The reasons for his anger were many: Gruffudd, Alfgar, Magnus… All his efforts to bring them to justice had been fruitless. And as for the so-called invasion, all it had been was bluster and burning air; threats hanging meaninglessly between the two camps until eventually the hostility disintegrated into indifference.

Earlier in the warriors' meadhall, songs praising Leofwin's achievement had echoed around the hall and it had been more than Burghred could bear to stay there and listen. But he had not left until he had drunk more than his fill.

"Lord?"

Burghred swivelled and saw that Beric stood behind him, a linen drawstring bag in one hand.

"I brought you something to eat. And mead, too."

"Oh, I thought they'd sent you for me," Burghred said, "Well, never mind, one more day will not make much difference, I suppose. Come,

345

sit here with me." Beric's eyes settled on the tell-tale sign of an empty flask that lay on the grass nearby. "You eat the food, Beric. I'll take the mead."

"Perhaps it was not such a good idea to bring you more."

"What are you talking about? Sit down and give that mead here, I have a terrible thirst in this heat.... What on earth is ailing you? Come here immediately!"

"'Tis no longer hot, lord. The weather has cooled. And I don't like to see you drunk, lord."

"Why the hell not?

"Because it makes you maudlin, lord."

"Nonsense, it's sweltering, and I am *not* maudlin. Sit down."

Beric did so and held out some bread and cheese which Burghred declined, snatching the bag. He rummaged inside and pulled out the mead.

"Tell me what's happening. What have you heard?"

"Not much, lord."

"Humph. I do not believe you, Beric. What are they saying? Are they singing about me as they are Leofwin Godwinson?" Burghred smiled falsely and took the stopper off the mead, sniffing its contents before swigging it back. When he'd taken a good few gulps, he said, "No need to reply, lad, I can see it in your face that they aren't. Oh well, better luck for me next time, eh?"

He sat quietly for a moment, toying with the rim of the flask before continuing, "So, the earl's brother, has he received an accolade?"

The boy, his eyes downcast, did not answer.

"Beric? Tell me, lad."

"He is to receive an earldom, lord."

"The bloody *earsling!* Damn the bloody Godwins! Where is this earldom, then?" He leant back on the lush grass, supporting himself on an elbow, the flask in one hand, his jaw clenched tightly.

"It is to be created for him in the south-eastern scīra," Beric replied.

"The pig-shagging, arse-licking *horningsunas!* And no tribute for me despite what I did! No praise, not even a 'well done' for bringing Scrobbesbyrig to heel!"

Beric winced. "Lord, do not give up hope –"

"Hope?!" Burghred leapt to his feet. "What hope is there for me?" he asked bitterly. "My father has once again fallen into a midden pit and dragged himself out of it as clean as my grandmother's fresh linen.

I never stood a chance of leading Mercia. Right from the start, I have been used, Beric. Used." He downed the rest of the sweet tasting liquid, flung the flask at a group of ducks and roared: "God!" The creatures flapped their wings and squawked in fright. "Why do you always forsake me?"

"Lord, please, you must calm yourself."

"Why?"

"You may come to harm, lord. And you are drunk."

"What of it? Have you never seen a drunk lord before? I mean, I know that you were brought up religiously, but... have you never seen Father Rodric sup the communal wine, or any of the other priests pissed after compline?" Burghred laughed, gasped, and cupped a hand over his mouth. "'Tis because I blasphemed that you are upset, is it? I'm so ss-sorry, lad, I didn't mean to... forgive me!

"Lord, please, this is not you. This is not how you are."

"And how am I?"

"Lord, I –"

"Come on, tell me. What sort of man am I? You know a lot more about me than I do."

"You are a man of honour, lord, a man whom many looked up to. You keep your temper when it is needed, and when it is warranted, you let it go, but now, lord, you are behaving like a sullen child."

"A sullen child... Ah. I see. First, I am a drunk, *then* I am a child." Burghred swayed as he turned to face his young servant. "I suppose it's all *my* fault?" He looked away and said to the air, "This is what I get for taking on someone with an education." He turned back. "Now, tell me, what should the man you just described do now in this childish drunk's shoes, because clearly, I am not me?" He hiccupped.

"He would fight for what was his. He would stand up to them, demand to be listened to. He would earn their respect."

Burghred stared, unconvinced. "So, that is what he would do?"

"Aye, sir."

"The one thing about you I dislike so much, boy, is that you have the ability to tell me how stupid I am, whilst retaining that humble look on that obtuse face of yours!"

"Where are you going?"

"To do what you just told me to."

Beric ran after him. "No, lord, not now, not like this and not in this state!"

Through the haze of his drunkenness, Burghred thought if he focussed on the blood red doors of the great hall, he would somehow find his way there safely. What happened between the wharf and the steps leading to those doors, he'd no idea. It was as if he'd winged across the sward, and when he landed before the guards at the top of the steps, their spears blocked his path.

"I would speak with the king 'mediately!" he demanded, swaying in a fog of mead. "I have waited long enough, and I have been *re-re-rebuffed* enough times now! This is most unjust!"

"The king's council is currently in session," one of the guards said. "Only members of the witan may enter, or those with special permission."

"Do you not know who I am? I demand that you tell the witan that Burghred of Mercia wishes to speak with the king - now!"

"We've had no word that Burghred of Mercia is to be given audience!"

"Let me through, man, or it will go badly for you!"

"I will not – I have my orders – whoever you are."

Beric was breathlessly puffing at the bottom of the steps. "Lord, please, do not do this!"

Burghred looked over his shoulder. His servant was clutching the handrail, his face crumpled with angst. He turned back and said to the thegn, "He *will* see me... he will see me now!"

"Or what?"

Burghred removed his *seax* from its sheath. His voice, thickly inebriated, said, "I *haff* - risked my life for the king – and the Earl of *Wezzex* and I will not be *g'nored*,"

"You little bastard! You dare to threaten a huscarle of the king's own guard?"

The blunt end of the guard's spear prodded Burghred's midriff. Clumsily, he danced down a few steps and up again, brandishing his *seax*. The guard flicked the blade out of Burghred's precarious grip with his spear and then slammed the shaft sideways at Burghred's chest sending him stumbling down a few steps into Beric. At least he thought it was Beric.

His *seax* clattered down the steps and he reached blindly for the hilt of his sword.

"No, lord!"

348

Before he could draw it, his arms were forced back. One of the guards sniffed. "You're drunk," the man said.

"Not quite, but I intend to be – later." Burghred's mirth was short lived, and they removed his sword belt. "Tha's right, take the last thing a man has apart from his *digniddy*. Leave me with nothing! You might as well take my clothes and leave me naked!" He made for the doors, and when they grabbed him again, he lashed out, recklessly aiming blows indiscriminately, some hitting the air.

"Just let me see the king!" Burghred demanded. "I am owed a *bet* of honour, don't you understand?"

"A *bet* of honour, my lord?" It was a new face arrived. Burghred wondered where they all came from.

"Come on, man, where's your *digniddy*?" a mimicking voice said, as a face was pushed closely into his. "Wait, I know you, you're the son of that low-life, Alfgar. What kind of self-seeking bastard betrays their own father, then has the audacity to come crawling to the king, begging his honour?"

The rage of a thousand insults burst through Burghred's veins and the man's nose cracked beneath his forehead.

"Christ on the Cross!" The guard yelled. Blood and mucous poured through his hand.

"It wasn't me!" cried Burghred as he was swiftly pounced on, his wrists locked behind him. His hair was grabbed and the flat of a sword blade stung the back of his calves. His knees buckled, and he was slammed onto his face. He bucked and kicked, smelt the tang of leather as a boot pinned his head, pushing his cheek against the harsh wooden deck. He fought for breath, tasting blood as his chest was crushed. Iron encircled his feet as someone held his legs together. He couldn't move.

"Ooof!" A knee pressed down on his back between his shoulder blades and the air inside his lungs was compressed. "Please…" he squeaked.

"You still want to see the king" asked a contemptuous voice. "You might just get your wish, but it will be in manacles. You will pay for this, mark my words, scum of Mercia!"

The doors unlocked and swung open. Burghred, spitting blood and dust, turned his face, his nose scraping the deck as the foot continued to press down on his head. He saw the expensive red leather boots of a noble.

"I can't… b… breathe." His rasping words were barely audible.

"Let him up, Guthrum. Let him go."

"Lord Harold, this *cur* was attempting to force himself on the king, perhaps to endanger his life."

"Aye, lord," said another voice, "he threatened to use a blade, and assaulted these fellows, too."

"He's broken my nose!"

"Let him up for Christ's sake! Can you not see he can't breathe!"

"But lord."

"Let – him – up! Before you crush the life out of him!" Harold was in no mood to be gainsaid by the sound of it.

The man growled and Burghred was hauled to his feet. Earl Harold's eyes wafted before him, a look that was half sympathy and half disgust.

"Good God, man, that's a bloody nice shiner you're getting there."

*

Harold bent to have a closer look at Burghred's injuries. One eye was swollen shut; a red sore grazed the bridge of his prominent straight nose and across his forehead; his mouth was cut, so far as Harold could see, in at least two places along the top and bottom lips. An older injury above his brow looked to have reopened. To add insult to his list, Harold noticed the poor state of his apparel which was torn and covered in dust.

Harold released him from his manacles and whisked him down the stairs.

"Where are you taking me? I want to see the king!"

"Somewhere private."

"I said I want to see the king."

"Haven't you made fool enough of yourself?"

Harold took hold of Burghred by his tunic and yanked him, stumbling, to his own quarters. The young servant who'd valiantly tried to protect his lord from a beating, followed them.

Inside, Harold set about cleansing the injuries as the young lord perched precariously on a board.

"I tried to tell him, lord. That it was not a good idea, not with him having had so much mead," the boy said.

"Aye, well, you tried. What is your name, son?"

"Beric, lord."

"In the chest over there, there should be some linen. Pass it to me, then fetch that jug of water from the board by that bed and open the shutters so I can see."

"Yes, my lord."

"Thank you, Beric," Harold said as the boy set down the water and linen by him. "Your master owes you a debt. Are you all right? It looks like you took a blow for him."

Beric looked confused.

"Your face," Harold said.

"Oh," Beric said, touching his cheek.

Harold turned the boy's head this way and that. "I think you'll live. But you might want to stand further away next time your master gets into trouble."

The beating had not done anything to sober the young Mercian. Slurring as the blood was being wiped from his forehead, Burghred said to the boy, "'Tis nothing to worry about, *Rebic*...." He paused as though forgetting what he wanted to say. "'Tis no more than a little mis-misunderstanding... Nothing more."

Harold steadied him as he almost slipped off the board.

Beric addressed Harold with a look of anguish. "I was trying to stop him –"

"S-stop me?" the Mercian interrupted, "From what? Demanding my rights or demanding that the k-king – oh and L-Lord H-Harold – keep their word, which is *zactly* what you *avised* me to do, boy." He muttered something under his breath, cursing his servant.

"Perhaps you should keep a tighter rein on your master," Harold quipped, dabbing at the bleeding wound with a sponge. "Looks like this could do with a stitch but I've no needles or twine to hand."

"I can fetch some, lord. And do the stitching."

"Aye, lad, if you would," Harold said. With a short bow, Beric left.

Burghred swayed. "I got that killing a *Wicinga*, you know? He was trying to kill me, all part of a plot between Gruffudd and my father – or maybe it was Ragnald – *yessh*, Ragnald. Did you know I nearly died that night – did you? Did you?! Spying for *you*. No of course you didn't. It nearly wrecked the whole alliance with Magnus. Ha! I killed one of his favourite warriors, you see." His leg slipped, and he steadied himself. "I nearly died for it. They were going to kill me."

"I do know, Burghred. You have told me the story before." Harold stood back to examine his handy work. "It seems your loyal servant is looking out for you, but he needs to give you better advice. Or *you* must take better heed of *him*." Harold wiped his hands on a linen towel.

"I w-want to see the king. I will not go… until I see him and put my *face* to him." He hiccupped. "Those men, they treated me no better than a dog –"

"Well, you were no doubt behaving no better than one," Harold replied.

"I am no lowborn peasant to be trod into the ground. I am a son and grandson of earls! They dared to *mandandle* me…"

Harold tried to supress a smile but couldn't.

"Is this how the mighty *honnable* Lord Harold, Earl of Wessex, *Dux – Dux something*, treats men who are loyal to him? Even when that loyalty could have cost a man his life? You are not the *honnable* man I thought you were, *Lord* Harold. I should have known you would betray me. I should have listened to the men of Scrobbesbr – Scrobber – Scrobbsbur –" Burghred put a hand to his forehead. He looked pale.

Harold, his good humour toward the young Mercian beginning to fade, said, "I regret that things have not turned out as we hoped, but I feel your accusation of betrayal is somewhat unfair. That was not my intention."

Burghred slipped off the board to his feet and stood unsteadily. An accusatory finger pointed at Harold. You – gave – me – your – word… It was all for naught. All for naught… in the end."

"I promised you nothing," Harold replied evenly, feeling somewhat indignant. "I told you that you needed to prove your worth, and you had a chance to win the Mercians over and hold them. You failed. It was beyond my control to refuse Alfgar his demands. It was clear that if he did not get his lands back, then thousands of men would have died fighting fellow Englisc men and Gruffudd would forever be a thorn in our sides. Even the men you came with have gone back to Alfgar – yes, they have – because they know that he is the stronger of you. I am sorry, Burghred, but this is how it has to be."

Harold realised by the look on the lad's face he was unaware that his men had gone.

"My men have deserted me?"

"They have, and do you know what? Looking at you now, the way you have been behaving, I am not surprised."

Harold saw that his words hit home, for suddenly, the younger man lost the haughty expression his damaged features wore. His one good eye blinked a tear away and he hung his head as though ashamed.

"I had them…" Burghred cupped his hands, gazing at them as though something precious were inside. "Right here…I had them… in my hands. *Mercia*. They'd all agreed. The thegns, all of them. They were coming – coming to me at *Scrobbabrig*. Then *he* got to them – Alfgar. He got to them and forced them back to his side with – with…"

"With his ability to command men to his banner?"

Burghred looked up. "With force and threats! He lied about Magnus. He lied. They would not have gone to him otherwise."

"You're right, lad, that would never have happened. Alfgar is not stupid. Your father cleverly used the Norwægians – and the Mercians… hedging his bets. God knows he probably used Gruffudd too."

"Just as you used me."

Burghred put out a hand to steady himself. Harold caught him as he fell forward, holding the young Mercian to him.

"I have nothing to give you. I am sorry," Harold whispered as the young lord, his head on Harold's chest, sobbed.

"Then create an earldom for him as you have done for Leofwin."

Harold had not heard or seen Lady Godgifu enter his bower. She was standing in the open doorway, regal in a scarlet gown of the finest linen, and a pale silk veil. She stepped inside and behind her appeared Beric.

"Lady Godgifu." Harold went to her and took her hand, leaving Burghred to Beric, now in possession of a needle and thread.

"Grandmother, Lord Harold and I were just talking about that very matter –"

"Oh, shut up, Burghred. Is it not bad enough that I have a truculent ignoramus for a son and a drunken dolt as my grandson?" She looked at Harold with cold eyes. "So, is this where we do the king's business now? Never mind," she said with a wave of her hand as Harold opened his mouth to offer an apology. "We can discuss the matter with the king – but you, young man," she said, turning to Burghred, "need desperately to clean yourself up. Just look at you. Been fighting, have we? You are just like your father used to be. Drunk and pugnacious."

Her grandson took her hand and Godgifu withdrew it swiftly, causing Burghred to kiss the air. "Grandmother, I –"

"Don't bother trying to explain. What a dreadful state to be in. Go get yourself washed! Can you walk straight? I shall find you and talk to you later – *when* you are sober."

Later, after the Witenagemót was ended, Harold agreed to a private meeting with Lady Godgifu. The king had already dug in his heels and was not going to give in where Burghred was concerned. There were already enough Alfgars in the world, he'd said, and he was not going to give another a position of power and wealth. Edith was very much on Edward's side about that. Then the king had gone hunting and it was left to Harold to placate Lady Godgifu.

"I am sorry for your grandson, but I made no promises. He had to prove himself. Unfortunately, he failed to win the Mercians over."

Seated together in a quiet part of the hall, Godgifu observed him like she would a naughty child she was taking to task. "And Scrobbesbyrig? Was that not proving himself?"

Harold looked at her sheepishly and said nothing.

"You could have done more to support him. You sent him into Wales to spy for you on his own father, instead of going to Mercia and rallying the thegns. It would have been an opportune time for him, whilst Alfgar was doing business with the enemy. You dangled the promise of Mercia before him like a plaything you would promise one of your children. *You* wanted him to do your dirty work – but Mercia was not yours to dangle, Harold, was it? If it is anybody's – it is mine. You are an assuming man, just like your father was –"

"Madam, my father was my father. I am not he," Harold cut in wearily.

"My apologies – you are right. Even Godwin would not have used someone like you used Burghred then throw him to the wolves. If I'd known what danger you were sending him into, then I would have stopped him."

"Lady Godgifu, your grandson is his own man, and he did well for us. Without his knowledge, we may not have been able to avert a war. If he *had* won the Mercian nobles over, I would have supported him wholeheartedly. However, the Mercians, it seems, are of a different opinion and preferred Alfgar."

"They might have preferred Burghred if instead of sending him into the lion's den in Wales, you'd sent him to Mercia with a bigger force to support him. If he'd had longer to gather the thegns to him…. Instead, you played into Alfgar's hands."

"Alfgar was Leofric's heir and whatever Alfgar has done, he was Leofric's choice. Plus, the men wanted a strong leader; Burghred is young and inexperienced. His efforts at Scrobbesbyrig, duly a credit to him, are unfortunately not enough."

"That may be so, but Burghred's association with you has not done him any favours. Burghred did not come to you, it was *you* who drew him into your employ. The men of Mercia view him as being in your pay and, with Tostig in the north, they wanted a buffer to stop your family from rising further. They see Alfgar, sadly, and I say so even though he is my own flesh and blood, as that man. So, I *do* blame you for my grandson's predicament."

Harold opened his mouth to defend himself, but Godgifu had barely paused for a moment before continuing. "You should have supported his claim to Mercia from the outset, then things might have been very different for him. Now he is nothing. Edward refuses to acknowledge him. God knows the king never loved Alfgar and –" she paused, looking sadly at him. He saw her old eyes glisten with tears, and he felt sorry for her. "You saw him today, Harold; he is bereft of any dignity. He is utterly devastated."

"So, what is it that I can do? You saw how Edward was. He will not have a piece of it. Nor will Alfgar, I'm sure, when he finds out."

She leant closer to him with the light of determination shining in her eyes. "Offer him a place in your household. He has a few lands in the east, but nothing of great note. A place in your household and some land, is that too much to ask for all that he did for you? There has always been bad blood between Burghred and his father, he was not born of Ælfgifu's womb. His real mother let Alfgar down badly, perhaps you know the story, gossip travels far."

"If there was talk, I have never been party to it," Harold told her.

"All you need to know is that Alfgar will never forgive him. Not this time. And for a son to be torn asunder from his father's love is a sad situation and one that *you* put upon them both. At least with you he can have a new life and a position that may give him some standing."

Later that evening during supper, the king having retired for the night with a stress-headache, left Harold at the head of the royal table, surrounded by courtiers and some of his own retainers in the great hall.

Lady Godgifu approached the dais and asked Harold, the highest in ranks, for permission to speak. Harold granted it.

"My lord, I would ask that you make that offer to my grandson –

now."

Harold wiped his mouth on a linen towel and summoned a servant to call Burghred to the dais. The young Mercian approached the high table somewhat gingerly.

"My lord, you wish to speak with me?" Burghred asked. He was no longer drunk but in his battered face, echoes of his earlier defiance remained.

"The king owes you a debt, Lord Burghred, as indeed do we all. I fear that there cannot be an earldom now, but one day, the time will come, and until then I would offer you a place in my household and some land. I would be honoured to have you join my hearthmen."

Burghred let out a grim laugh, his expression mirthless. "Small recompense for a promised earldom; I want nothing from you, *Earl Harold*, not now, nor in the future."

"Take the offer," Godgifu said, touching her grandson on the shoulder.

"Nay, Grandmother. There is nothing here for me. I shall depart on the morrow." He turned on his heel and made his way past the diners, calling to Beric to follow.

"Wherever you go, Burghred?" asked Harold, calling out to him. "My offer will always stand should you change your mind."

The young lord stopped a few yards away from the doors. The hall was silent, heads swivelled, ears pricked. As Burghred slowly turned, it was clear by the look on his face he was angry at this humiliation in front of all. "I changed my mind once before, lord, and look where that got me."

Chapter Thirty-nine

Beautiful Medusa

The next morning, Burghred's anger was still raw, even after breakfasting in the pleasant sunshine outside his tent. As the haze of inebriation began to clear, embarrassing glimpses from the day before came to his mind. At first, he was flushed with humility, and he buried his head in his hands. And then, the anger grew. Anger because he had been used and lied to.

Beric caught him cursing the earl and said, "You have only yourself to blame, my lord."

"Of all the maggot ridden turds I had to be landed with..." He swivelled to glare at his outspoken servant. "Could you not be a little more loyal, Beric? Or understanding at least?"

"Nobody held you down, lord, and forced that mead down your throat."

"If I had not been so ill-used, I would not have needed to drink to excess, would I?" Burghred drained his mug of ale and thumped the board with it. Beric's berating and forthrightness was infuriating.

Burghred jumped up toppling the bench and began to pace. "Harold's promises were just empty words, Beric," he fumed, "Empty words thrown into the air and blown away by the wind, as if they'd never existed. I risked my life going into Gruffudd's lair. I came *that close,*" he used his thumb and forefinger to demonstrate, sticking his face in Beric's, "*that close* – to being dead – and for what? So that Alfgar could return from exile and take what should have been mine. What *I*, in fact, deserve!"

He stormed down to the river where once again it was peaceful. He'd intended to leave that morning, though had no idea where he'd go, but now, all he wanted to do was sit alone and wallow in his resentments as they whirled around his head. Maybe he would have another cup or two of mead a little later, but not overdo it. He did not want a repeat of yesterday.

Soon his peace was disrupted. Officials and servants were milling around along the bank, waiting for something or someone. He was sure they were staring, talking about him, sniggering as though he were an object of scorn.

He walked up-river, found a quieter place, and sat down, letting his legs dangle over the edge of the wharf. Taking out his whetstone, he proceeded to sharpen his *seax*. Flinching, he caught a finger as he tested the blade. He watched, transfixed as the beads of blood trickled down his palm, tracing the lines on his hand, igniting a memory. He rolled up a sleeve, drew the blade, cutting into the smooth, fleshy underside of his forearm. He squeezed the incision, and it flowed, drop by drop into the river. He let the sting wash over him and relief came like a soft breeze to soothe his tortured soul and pumping heart. Using his *seax*, he sliced a piece of his under-tunic to wrap the wound and dipped the blade in the water before drying it on his cloak and returning it to its sheath. *If only Harold had sent me south instead of Leofwin, things might have been different.*

He sat with his head resting on bent knees, hands clasped around them. What now for him? He wanted to go away – somewhere – anywhere. He did not want the place in Harold's household. Neither could he bear the shame of having failed. He'd betrayed his father for nothing. Even his own men had turned their backs on him, the oaths made to him, meaningless. Not one of them had the stomach to face him, nor given him an explanation, at least. How could he ever trust anyone again?

He stared at the water, still cloudy with his blood. Tears pricked his eyes and he felt sick to the core. There was a heaviness in his chest as though someone had left their boot there, and the thought that he would be better off dead seized him. He drew his *seax* again, let it hover over the veins in his wrist. The water rippled, signalling movement from upriver. A commotion: horns sounding; voices calling; the plunge of oars in water.

He turned and saw the dragon-head of the first vessel coming into view as two more followed. The familiar wild hair of his father blew in the breeze as he stood at the prow, supporting himself on the neck of the dragon, head high and haughty. His appearance spoke of victory

358

He was back – Lord Alfgar, Earl of Mercia – and this time, for good.

Soon the wharf was swamped with men lining the riverbank. Burghred stood amongst the crowd with his hood drawn up so not to be recognised. He watched the proceedings silently, a tear in his eye, as he caught sight of Aldith and his young brothers. *They shouldn't see me like this.*

His sister alighted gracefully from the boat with the aid of her father. Her face was pale, and she looked drawn and tired. She would have given birth by now and he wondered if it had been the little girl she'd been so certain of having. Not surprisingly, there was no sign of Gruffudd.

Burghred smiled knowing that Ragnald would not be among Alfgar's retinue. He hoped the loss of his captain caused his father as much pain as he had caused him in his life.

Wanting to get a better look at his sister and brothers, he pushed his way to the front of the onlookers, keeping his cowl pulled as far over his face as possible. A sudden, forceful breeze caught the hood and whipped it off. Morcar recognised him first, stopping to stare at him. "Look, Father!" he proclaimed with a grin, "'Tis our brother, Burghred!"

The air went silent. The sound of chattering and humming of voices diminished in awkward anticipation.

"You!" Alfgar declared as Morcar and Edwin ran to Burghred and hugged him. "You dare to show your face to me?"

Burghred gave a curt nod of his head. "Lord Alfgar," he acknowledged politely.

The boys withdrew. The sadness in their eyes turned Burghred's stomach. Then Aldith came, holding a hand to him. Burghred thought her magnificent, dressed in a lichen-dyed woollen cloak, signifying her queenship. The red robe underneath was braided at the edges with threads of woven gold and open from the waist down, belted by twisted silken strands to reveal layers of the purest white linen. A bleached wimple cascaded in folds about her shoulders and down to her waist in a curve. It gaped at her neck, allowing just a glimpse of her coppery-brown braids and gold necklace. She looked every inch a queen, and he was proud of her, his beautiful sister.

Behind her a well-attired maid stood, cradling a swaddled babe.

"I am glad that you are safe and well," Aldith said. He took her hand and kissed her fingers.

"Come away from him, daughter! I order you – *now*!" Alfgar snarled. "I will not have you sully yourself with a traitor and a murderer!"

Burghred stepped forward. "'Tis not I who is the traitor here, Alfgar! I am loyal to my king!"

"You are no more than a puss-ridden *wyrmlic,* shedding your skin for another when you think the rewards will be better. Who gave you the swollen eye? I should give him a bag of gold. Just remember, after this, there will be no place for you amongst my honourable men in Mercia!"

"If I am the *wyrmlic,* then you are the *wyrm – Father!*" Burghred clenched his fists. He wanted to hurt him, humiliate him, as *he* had been.

Aldith drew her arm across Burghred's midriff, gently urging him to stay calm. Addressing Alfgar, she said, "Father, we have come here to do business with King Edward, not fight with Burghred. What is done between you is done. Conserve your energy for what truly matters."

Alfgar scowled at her. Burghred detected some strain between them.

"Do not worry, dear brother, I no longer need him as much as he needs me," she whispered, her lips curving into a confident smile.

Alfgar's gaze lingered only a moment before he turned away, barking at Morcar and Edwin to follow. Burghred hurried them on, promising that he would see them later; then he turned to his sister.

"Why are you here without Gruffudd?" he asked her. "Or should I say, why are you here instead of Gruffudd? Does Father know he is doing the Wéalas king's dirty work for him?"

She smiled wryly. "Do you think that my husband would be welcomed here?"

"Why not?" Burghred smiled. "Alfgar is."

Aldith acknowledged what he'd said with a graceful smile. "My lord husband sends me here as his emissary. He has the ague and cannot attend himself."

Burghred noted the glint of amusement in her eye. He bent toward her and whispered, "Do not worry, sister. If I were he, I would rather send my pretty wife than come myself. Alfgar might not have endeared himself here, but at least he is Englisc. Gruffudd, on the other hand…well, his life might have been in danger, *if* he had chosen to attend. Better he stays at home with the ague. I hear Edward was demanding his head again and not answering the summons could be seen as treason." He winked at her. She returned the smile with a nod of her head, but with little humour, so he thought.

She lifted her hand to cup his cheek, ran a finger across the sticky wound on his eyebrow, and sighed. "You have been fighting again, Burghred. Will you never learn?"

He looked away, shamed by her scrutiny. "These are scars of war," he said, gravely.

"Do not lie to me, brother, that bruise on your eye is fresh, and so is that cut above your eye, not to mention your split lips."

They began to walk together toward the great hall. "I am sorry I missed the birth of your..."

"Daughter," she said. "I told you I would give birth to a girl child. I named her –"

"Nest."

"You remember?"

"Of course. How does Gruffudd feel about you presenting him with a daughter and not a son?"

"He minds not, for he has already sons aplenty. He dotes on her. Women have far more respect in the lands of the Wéalas than they have in Englalond – why, I could divorce my dear husband just for his bad breath if I wanted to." She laughed.

"And does he have bad breath?

"No."

He paused and turned to the maid who followed and asked of Aldith, "May I see her?"

"Of course," his sister replied.

The maid, a pretty girl of his sister's age, presented the tiny creature to him so he could view her little face.

"She is a beauty, like her mother," Burghred said.

"She has Gruffudd's hair colour."

"But she has your beautiful eyes." Burghred sniffed away a tear.

They reached the doors of the great hall. Alfgar had already gone through them. The door thegns stood with their hands ready on the bars to allow her entrance. Burghred held her back for a moment. "Is there word from Heulyn?"

She suddenly blanched. "I am sorry..."

He caught her by the shoulders. "Tell me."

"She was found out..."

361

"What did Gruffudd do to her?"

"She killed herself. She could not live with the shame," Aldith withdrew from him then, her young face suddenly lined with sadness, and went in but he did not follow. *She killed herself...* Her words were like a sword plunging inside him stirring up the bile that rushed to his throat.

After that, he had no stomach to hear Alfgar wheedle his way back into favour, nor did he desire to meet the flames of hatred in his father's eyes for a second time that day. If they ever met alone again, one of them would be dead. He walked away from the hall. Heulyn had died because of him... and because of Gruffudd. He found a quiet place behind a hut and vomited. *I promise I will avenge you, sweet girl.*

Harold threw his head back in laughter at a joke of Skalpi's. Leofwin elbowed him in the ribs and said, "Harold..." nodding to his left.

Harold turned and glanced at the reason for Leofwin's interruption.

A girl, elegantly dressed, was standing nearby, cold eyes staring fiercely at him. A finely plucked eyebrow raised above her right eye gave the impression that she thought him a creation of rare interest.

"Can I help you, my lady?" Harold asked, smiling his most charming of smiles.

"Perhaps. Perhaps not. I just came to see what manner of man you are, Lord Harold," she replied. Her voice was sleek, like a songstress.

The courtyard was busy with servants carrying food from the kitchens to the king's great hall. People were milling about in the still warmth of the summer's evening, awaiting the call for supper, and sharing opinions with each other regarding the day's proceedings.

Harold studied this confident looking girl with interest. *God, she is beautiful.* For a moment, Harold felt as though his whole being shuddered as a sensation of lust rose within him.

He'd seen her for the first time that day at the council meeting. She'd been sitting with her father, soberly watching and listening to the proceedings. There to represent her husband, Gruffudd, she had put forward his demands with the eloquence of a stateswoman. She was very handsome, this Queen of Wales. This daughter of Alfgar.

"My lady." He smiled. He stepped away from his friends, their amused faces in the periphery of his vision. He took her hand and pressed it to his lips. "Forgive me, I had not realised with whom I was speaking."

Aldith withdrew her hand sharply. Her unimpressed expression displayed her hostility. A purposeful cough made him glance in the direction of Lady Godgifu, waiting for her granddaughter a few feet away, arms folded. He saw then how very alike the two women were.

"So, now you have seen me, what manner of man am I?" Harold asked in a pleasant voice.

"I was wondering what manner of man rewards the men who have done his bidding by having them beaten and abused, made lordless, and without *Cýþþ* or *Cýnn*. I was wondering if a man who would do such a thing had any honour himself, and if he did, where was it now?"

Harold opened his mouth to defend himself but thought better of it. Although he had not personally inflicted those wounds on Burghred, he felt responsible.

He pursed his lips. From the look on the young queen's face, he knew he was in danger of losing this battle of wits. He needed to salvage his self-respect or lose it altogether. He thought of Burghred; the injuries he'd sustained in yesterday's scuffle were unpleasant. *It should not have come to that.*

Aldith was right. His honour, which was everything to him, was nothing if he did not at least try to make amends.

"My lady," Harold said solemnly, "I offered him a place within my household. He refused it. If you could persuade him to accept, then I would happily have him in my retinue."

Aldith said nothing. She did not have to. Harold could see the loathing in her eyes. Too little, too late, perhaps. Or not enough.

"Good day, Lord Harold," she said with a curt bow of her head. As she turned to leave, she glanced back at him, a strange look on her face that caused a shiver of unease within him.

"Thor's beard!" exclaimed Skalpi. "That one could turn a man to shingle in less than no time. If she had looked at you for any longer with that stony face, we'd have had to take a hammer and chisel to you."

"So, that's why Gruffudd is not here," laughed Gauti. "He is nothing but a stone statue! I wonder if he knows he is married to Medusa."

The companions roared with laughter. "Aye," remarked Harold, smiling. "She could turn me to stone any day, I wouldn't mind."

Chapter Forty

Unexpected Arrival

February 1059, Horstede

Wulfric sat naked wondering whether it was a need to relieve himself of last night's ale, or a need to swive the girl that had made his manhood swell like a cow's udder. He felt nothing for her. It was just a normal reaction to a normal situation, but in his mind, he was bereft of any emotion.

He stood from the bed, stepped over his sleeping dog, Brun, and pissed into the urine bucket. The air was so cold that steam rose, and the brazen smell hit him starkly in the nostrils.

"Are you not going to perform your husbandly duty, Wulfric?" The girl stretched her lithe, youthful body, gazing invitingly at him through eyes of startling green.

God, couldn't his parents have found him a wife with a less irritating voice? In fact, everything about her, except for that between her legs, irritated him. Handpicked for him by his mother and father, she was the daughter of a local thegn. They'd thought that a pretty young wife, and the possibility of a child, would ease the loss of his twin brother. But Wulfric had not wanted a wife, nor a screaming brat to keep him company. What he wanted was Wulfwin back, to fight and hunt with, ride out to ale houses with, and to go a whoring with. Without Wulfwin, there was nothing to live for and in the absence of his usual spirit, he'd not the energy to protest either way. So, he had gone along with the wedding ceremony, merely to appease his parents and stop the nagging.

What would be the point in resisting, anyway? Whatever Mother decided or wanted, went; that was the way of it. Father was as useless as a dead dormouse, excused of court duties, sending Ælfstan in his place. Mother, on the other hand, was remarkably calm. Wulfric swore that she'd not shed one tear over Wulfwin. Oh, she'd said all the right words and showed a respectable amount of sorrow, yet there was something different about her... *She has changed,* he told Wulfwin in his nightly conversations with him, *there is a coldness about her; it's as if she is dead and a wraith walks in her stead.* Father had done that to her, with that stupid idea of his to deceive her with that child of his mistress.

"Wulfric?" the girl called to him again.

Her name was Cynethryth. She was older than he by at least a couple of years, skilled in lovemaking, so he'd discovered on their first night. She was as loose as the sleeve on a noble lady's gown, but he cared not. As long as Wulfwin was not there, what was to care about? He smirked, thinking that he and Wulfwin had shared everything. Perhaps they would have shared her too. It wouldn't have been the first time they'd shared a girl.

He turned after shaking the last drops from his rapidly deteriorating erection and gave her an unflattering grimace. She was not unattractive, in fact, she was quite pretty, some would say beautiful, with the greenest of eyes as big as a cow's, and plump lips that reminded him of wild strawberries. But he was unable to see further than her physical assets, which were of no use to him once swiven.

His cock was flaccid now. *Must have been the piss after all.* He climbed back into bed and turned his back on her, wanting to sleep. She moved closer to him and he shifted his body, stiffening at her touch. The Goddamned woman! He'd humped her last night, hadn't he? Was not that enough for the bitch? He elbowed her, catching one of her breasts.

She cried out, "Pig!" He felt a punch to his spine. "What is wrong with you? Are women not to your liking?"

He tried to ignore her and closed his eyes.

"Mayhap you like boys? Or dogs even!" She was behind him, digging her nails in the flesh of his back. "Perhaps you hump your dog every night?" Her hand slipped around him, touching his crotch and she laughed at its softness. "Perhaps you're not up to it! Lord, it is as soft as a —"

Wulfric swung round and hit her, interrupting her intended insult.

She gasped, cupped a hand to her lip and caught the trickle of blood from a corner of her mouth. Wulfric rose to his knees, expecting her to run sobbing to his parents. Instead, she dabbed at the cut with her finger, then licked it.

He hardened at the sight of her tongue flicking at the edge of her injured lip. His eyes roamed her voluptuous body, eventually resting on her large, hardened nipples. He lunged at her, taking her breasts one in each hand and kneaded the soft flesh between his fingers, squeezing them hard so that she squealed like a cat. Her nails ripped into his face and he clutched the injury, falling back against the bolster. The hound, skulked into a corner, whimpering.

His wife was on her haunches, scowling, cornering her prey. Something base stirred within him, a mix of pain and intense pleasure. His already risen cock was stiff as a brick. Desire filled him like he'd never experienced before. She was a witch, a temptress, this girl, with waves of dark red hair tumbling like silk around her shoulders.

Green eyes devoured him as he leaned forward, grabbing her fiery red mane and pulling her close to him. Feeling her skin hot against his trembling body, his lips sought hers and she responded with savage intensity before they fell into each other's arms, legs entwining, joined together in a primal act of instinctive need.

*

Wulfhere blew onto his hands to warm them. He was pruning the fruit trees in his orchard with the help of Winflæd and Father Paul. The priest infused his kind Christian philosophy into the whole purpose of the task as he intoned, "The skilful pruning of branches demonstrates a man's ability to create a profitable relationship with God's gifts to us: his trees, bushes, vines, and his bees - let's not forget the bees."

Father Paul had been a huge source of emotional and spiritual succour for Wulfhere in the months since he'd returned home without Wulfwin. Most of Wulfhere's time in those early days of mourning had been taken up with consoling both his wife and Wulfric, the latter having fallen into dark, melancholy mood. The boy had taken to his bed and not emerged for some days, and when he finally did, he barely spoke to anyone but the ghost of Wulfwin. Seeking out Father Paul for advice on what to do, the gentle priest had counselled to allow his son to grieve in his own way. The boy, the priest told him, found comfort in talking to his dead brother, and this would help his spiritual healing.

*

Wulfhere climbed the ladder to reach the higher branches. He did not envy those who were out in the fields right now, clearing them in readiness for the coming tilling. It was freezing, despite the presence of the late winter sun. The cold temperatures lingered longer than was usual this year. Tomorrow it would be *Candelmæsse* and there would be the traditional rituals. Father Paul would bless the candles, and everyone would proceed around the whole village and out into the fields as the priest sprinkled holy water and granted blessings to the earth sprites and the plough.

Father Paul's songs of elves, pixies, and other woodland spirits, filled Wulfhere with a sense of contentment and he smiled, feeling his soul warm, if not his hands. He was looking forward to the procession later when some of the sol cakes, now baking in the large Horstede clay oven, would be scattered in places around the fields and meadows to thank the elves in advance for not ruining the coming harvest, and the rest would be eaten by everyone. These were the times he loved most, being at home with his people and his family.

Wulfhere indicated to Winflæd to hand him his *serp,* the long, flat iron blade he was using to slash at the thinner branches of the apple tree. As he reached down to take it, the ladder wobbled.

"Father! Let me hold this before you fall and break your neck!" his daughter reproved him. "You've only just got over your wounds. I do not want you getting more injuries. The new year has only just started!"

"Work needs to be done, daughter," he responded, throwing down the cuttings.

"Father, there are others that can do this! It need not be you! Your wounds still give you trouble, and do not deny it. I've seen you limping when you think no one is looking."

Just then, a harassed voice asked, "Winflæd, where is your father?"

"Up there."

"Lord?"

Wulfhere looked down and Winflæd gasped as the ladder shook. His daughter tutted as she steadied it.

"Aye, what is it Sigfrith? Can you not see I am busy?" Wulfhere said impatiently.

"My lord, Tigfi – and some men – they are outside the gates. Ælfstan is refusing to let them in."

"Why on earth not?" he said, descending the ladder without care, the *serp* clenched in his hand.

"Because, my lord, they have Helghi of Gorde with them, and that spot-faced idiot son of his."

"Edgar?" Winflæd's voice was bright.

"No, not him, the other one; the one with those horrible lecherous eyes like his father's." Sigfrith shuddered.

"What in Hell is that murdering scum doing at my gate? And what is Tigfi thinking – bringing him here to my manor?"

He strode purposely, despite his bad leg, toward the hall. He paused when he saw Ealdgytha coming toward him, a steely resolve in her eyes.

"You are not going to let them in, are you?"

Wulfhere gritted his teeth. He ignored her and carried on walking.

"Damn you, Wulfhere!" Ealdgytha shouted after him.

He went inside through the back door, and then out through the front after picking up his sword and a spear.

When he reached the gatehouse, Ælfstan stood on the rampart, waving his hammer ferociously over the fence. "I'll not open this gate unless my lord commands it!" Ælfstan shouted.

Wulfhere thought about leaping up the palisade but knew that his injured leg meant those days were over. Instead, he used the steps and joined the irate smith on the deck.

"Ælfstan? What is going on here?"

Ælfstan turned an angry soot-blackened face to him. "Tigfi. He brings Helghi of Gorde."

Tigfi's response floated over the palisade, "Ah, Lord Wulfhere, let us in, man. 'Tis freezing out here."

"Father, what is happening?"

Wulfhere swivelled, saw his daughter about to step onto the palisade, and was irritated by her presence. "Go inside, Winflæd. This is not any business of yours." He leant over the wooden stakes and called down to Tigfi, "What brings you here? And for what reason do you bring *that* murdering scum?" he demanded, tossing his head at Helghi and his kinsmen. He saw the lad, Eadnoth, and the woman, cloaked against the bitter cold. Mildrith, he supposed. "I would have thought that you at least, Tigfi, would know better than to come here with that garbage in tow."

"Justice, Wulfhere, the king's justice is what brings me here." Tigfi produced a rolled parchment and held it up for Wulfhere to see. "I have here a writ from the *scīr* court that you must attend to."

Wulfhere glanced at Helghi. He seemed to be looking better than he had done for years. There was a fresh look about him. His clothes were clean and had been sewn anew. He'd shaved his beard, trimmed his moustache, and combed his thick greying hair into something that resembled a well-groomed man. He'd lost most of the paunch that encircled his girth and he looked remarkably younger.

"And what business is it that would bring this dark evil to my house?"

Helghi smiled at him, or rather he sneered.

Tigfi sighed. "I have a writ here requesting that you hand over your daughter, Winflæd, for marriage to Helghi's son, Eadnoth of Gorde."

Wulfhere's jaw dropped. "In whose name has this writ been issued?" he asked.

Tigfi looked uncomfortable. "Wulfhere, you have not attended the hundred moot when summoned over this matter for three times now." He sighed impatiently. "I warned you what would happen if you did not attend the last time."

Wulfhere's eyes shifted from Helghi to the reeve. "You know my reasons for that, Tigfi. We have discussed this many a time – I thought you, of all people, understood."

"Wulfhere, you know the law. You know that I must uphold any decisions that are made by the earl or the scīrgerefa. This matter has now gone before the shire moot and –"

"What?" Wulfhere demanded.

Helghi raised his fist. "It is my right!" His companions agreed with him. "You are not above the law, Wulfhere, thegn though you be."

"Wulfhere, let us in so that we can discuss this business in a more comfortable manner and as custom demands. Standing outside a man's gate in the freezing cold is not the way to do such things. We should be sitting around your hearth, sharing a horn of peace and welcome, not shouting at each other across a barricade. Let us cross the ford and enter your gates peaceably, otherwise I shall have to return with more men to break down your gate. That is *not* something I wish to do."

"And what about *my* right to contest this suit?"

"As I said before, you have ignored the summons to the hundred moot three times already. Now Helghi has appealed to the shire, as is his right, and they have upheld it. I understand that you were to provide proof of Helghi's wrong doings and, it seems, you have not. We can discuss *your* right to appeal if you open the gate."

"Aye, I will open the gate!" Wulfhere shouted. He was like a wolf defending its territory, pacing up and down. "I'll open them over my dead body!"

"Father! Open the gate!"

"I told you to go inside! Do not come up here, Winflæd, this is men's business!"

"Father! If you do not open the gate, Sigfrith and *I* will!"

Wulfhere looked down. Winflæd was standing with her hand resting on the locking-bar. Sigfrith merely shrugged.

"Winflæd, you do not know what you are doing!"

"Yes, I do, Father! You think because I am no more than twelve that I don't know what has been going on? We need to settle this matter - finally. You heard Tigfi, he will break down our gates if we don't."

"Winflæd! Get away from those gates!" Ealdgytha's slight form came striding up the path. "Don't you dare open that gate!" she raged. "Do you know what will happen? They will take you away and that will be the end of you."

"Argh! Let go of me, Mother, you're hurting me. No one is going to take me anywhere without I give my consent. Freyda told me that the law says that no maiden shall be forced to marry unless they wish it."

"Stupid girl! The law means nothing when high men have ordained a thing. Now come."

Winflæd pursed her lips and stood her ground. "We shall see," she told her mother.

She pulled the bar out of its lock; Ealdgytha, her face puckered with determination, tried to stop her. Wulfhere hurried down off the rampart and separated them. "She is right, Ealdgytha. Sooner or later, this *will* have to be sorted out," he said. "Tigfi means business."

Ealdgytha looked at him aghast. "You mean to allow this to happen? Our daughter to wed into a family whose father murdered her brother?"

"We know this, Ealdgytha, but they say we have no proof. Without proof, we cannot bring a charge!"

"We do not need proof! We know he did it! All they need is our word. *Our word against his!* Wulfhere, if you let them in – if-if you allow them to take our daughter, I will –"

"I would die first before I let them take her!"

"Then you better mean it because if you don't save her, I will kill you myself!" She turned on her heel, and marched back toward the hall, her disgust hanging in the air like a cloud of smoke.

Touching his arm, Winflæd said, "Open it, Father. Whatever comes,

I will always love you."

Wulfhere turned to her and took her face in his hands. "Goddamn! This is all the fault of that wanton sister of yours, she started all of this. And now it is *you* who has to suffer. I will not let them take you, *min Fleo.*"

She threw herself into his arms. "Don't blame Freyda. She could not have known the trouble she would bring."

He held her close to his chest and kissed her wimple-clad head. It suddenly occurred to him that she now wore one. He'd not noticed before. "I will not let them take you. I did not let them take Freyda and I will not let them take you."

"So, let them in and let them try. If they do, I'll spear their guts, like you showed me."

She laughed, her blue eyes sparkling. It seemed she had floated through her years, no longer the little snip of a thing who once sat on his lap at hearth-time, listening to tales of wolven forbears. Now she was graceful and tall. *When had she become this fine young lady?*

She withdrew from his arms, whispering that all would be well, took his hand and placed it on the locking bar. Together they lifted it across and taking a gate each, opened them.

Chapter Forty-one

Peacemaker

Once inside the courtyard of her father's hall, Winflæd caught up with them all.

Helghi was speaking in a voice that was loud and demanding. "We had an agreement. The earl commanded that my son should wed your daughter."

"The agreement was not for this spot-faced prick," Wulfhere said, indicating the object of his scorn.

Eadnoth glared indignantly.

Winflæd put her hand on Father's arm. "Why don't we go inside and discuss this civilly?"

"What a good thought, Lady Winflæd," Tigfi said. "Besides, I am certain it will be warmer by your hearth than out here."

Without even acknowledging her, Father pulled Tigfi aside. Winflæd edged closer to them to hear what they were saying.

"Have you gone mad? This man killed my son! You want me to let him sit by my fire, drink my ale and talk *civilly* about marriage with my daughter?"

Tigfi snapped, "Satan's bollocks, Wulfhere. Why didn't you answer the summons?"

"God knows I should have… and got him for murdering my son. I would not be standing here now, in my own yard, trying to argue my way out of this damned predicament, now would I!"

"And that's the rub, isn't it? You didn't." Tigfi looked weary, as though he were thoroughly tired of the situation.

Father, too, was affected, looking ill. Winflæd stepped forward and said in a gentle voice, "Tigfi, you know that my father was grieving for my brother and had been seriously wounded in battle. He needed time to recover on both counts."

"He could have sent someone on his behalf," Tigfi argued.

"He was inconsolable, lying in his sick bed. How would he have remembered?"

"I can speak for myself, Daughter." Wulfhere turned to Tigfi, "You could have come here in person and fetched me. Surely you know how ill I have been."

"You think I have not better things to do than making sure men answer their lord when they are summoned? Nay, Wulfhere, this is not my fault."

"And it is not my fault that *he* killed my son!" shouted Wulfhere, flinging out an arm in Helghi's direction.

"*Killed your son?*" Helghi broke in. He took a few slow steps toward them and said pointing at Wulfhere, "It was *I* who lost *my* son at *your* doing – twice! The first when he was but a child, crippling him with that damned horse you sold me, rendering him useless to me. The second time because you reneged on your oath, then had the audacity to make *him* the lowest of scoundrels, causing him to be *nithing*. And now, you blame *me* for the death of *your* son which is in fact, no more than God's justice for your sins against me and mine!"

"Helghi! You lie and you know it!" Wulfric burst from the hall, his face contorted with rage.

Winflæd hurried toward her brother as he lunged forward, his *seax* raised. She was roughly pushed aside as Tigfi got there first, knocking the seax out of Wulfric's hand. "Oh no you don't!" The hundred reeve grabbed him in a bear hug.

Wulfric was still raging at Helghi as Tigfi dragged him away. "My brother told me you threatened him, like this!" He drew the side of his hand across his throat like a knife.

"Ælfstan, contain this boy on pain of death should he move."

"Aye, lord," Ælfstan agreed.

"Wulfric, if you do that again I'll have my men clap the fetters on you. Stay there with Ælfstan – do not move!"

Straightening her wimple, Winflæd picked up the *seax* from the ground where it had fallen. She pointed it at her glowering brother. "Don't worry, I'll make sure he doesn't move."

Tigfi then turned to her Father. "I know this is difficult, Wulfhere, but it could get worse. Is there nothing we can do here? I know that Helghi is an *earsling*, but the boy may not be so bad–"

"Worse? They couldn't get worse! Helghi killed my son and now you want me to hand my daughter to them. You have known me for, how long? You have seen my boys grow up. Look at Mildrith. Once she was pretty, now look at her, she is an empty shell. They all treat her like dung, Helghi and his filth. What do you think they will do to Winflæd?"

As if she'd heard him, a tear rolled down Mildrith's cheek. Winflaed felt sorry for her as the woman's haunted eyes briefly met Father's before looking away again. If she had not known better, Winflæd would have thought that something might have passed between them, but it couldn't have, could it?

She watched them closely. Father continued, lowering his voice, perhaps so Mildrith could not hear, "In a few years, my daughter, too, will be looking at me like that, asking me why I let her go. You know what manner of man Helghi is or have you forgotten that night when he tried to rape Sigfrith? Look at the son. What do you see? I see another Helghi."

Winflæd heard every word. She realised that she had finally entered the world of men and women. She was no longer a child. Her innocence gone. So this was what it was to be grown. The hatred between men that spilled into the lives of those around them. It had to stop.

She looked at Eadnoth picking at a spot on his nose as he stared at her in a way that made her skin crawl. His eyes devoured her as though she were a fine morsel of meat. Her stomach turned. Could she really marry *him*?

"What can I do, Wulfhere?" Tigfi said. "I have been charged by the shire with resolving this feud. And if the earl were here now..."

"I know what he would say," her father replied, hardly disguising his bitterness. "I thought him a friend once. Now I know he is only friend to those who do his bidding – even if they don't want to. Even if it causes harm to their family. So, what is in this for you? There must be something."

Winflæd's mind was whirling. *Even if it causes harm to their family.*

Her thoughts rushed around her head. She barely heard everything that was said, only catching words here and there. Something about Lord Harold wanting an end to the feud, and that Father had failed to prove that Helghi had killed her brother. When her mind settled, her father was jabbing a finger in Eadnoth's direction, "*He* is not getting

374

my daughter!" He turned to look at his enemy. "Helghi!"

Tigfi pulled on his arm. "What are you doing?"

"You wanted a solution, I have one." Father's eyes were filled with burning hatred.... "Helghi!"

"What?"

"We fight. You. Me. If you can get me to submit, then you may have her."

Winflæd gasped. "Father! Do not do this! You are still not well."

"Winflæd, go – in – side!" He pushed her toward the hall.

"Don't do this, Father. Please?"

Tigfi taking her arm, said, "Go, Winflæd. This is not the place for you to be right now." He led her to the porch.

"Tigfi, he is not fit. You can see how ill he is? He is weak as a kitten."

"Why don't you just tell him how he will pound me into the ground?" Father's words, laced with sarcasm, were like a punch to her guts. She was just trying to protect him.

Helghi smirked, looked Father up and down as though he were measuring his chances.

"All right." The smirk on Helghi's face stretched to a wide grin which showed his discoloured teeth and Winflæd cringed, imagining his foul breath.

Wulfhere nodded. "When you lose, you never darken my door again."

Wulfric interjected. "Father, Winflæd is right. Let *me* fight. I will fight Eadnoth. If I win, then Winflæd goes free." He glared at Eadnoth. *"And I will win."*

A cacophony of male voices busied the air. Various ideas for settling the situation violently went back and forth. In the middle of it all, Winflæd screeched, "Stop, all of you! Have you not had enough of fighting?"

Everyone went quiet. Father went to rebuke her, and she held up a hand to him and said, "No one is going to fight anybody. Father? Wulfric? Is it not enough that we have already lost Wulfwin, Esegar, and Uncle Leofric?" Catching her breath, she continued, "It is time to put an end to this, or the bloodletting will just go on and on."

"That is what we are about to do, little girl." Helghi gestured at Wulfhere and himself. "Your father and I will fight it out and your fate will be decided."

"Don't, Father." Winflæd went to him and laid her head against his chest.

"I'd sooner wed you to Edgar than this godforsaken *wyrmlicin.*"

Winflæd looked up at him sharply. "Then it shall be done."

"What?" exclaimed Tigfi.

Her hands resting on Wulfhere's chest, she half turned and looked around at everyone. "The law says that a maid shall not be forced to wed unless she has given her consent."

"Thanks be to God." Wulfhere sighed in relief.

"And so, I *do not* give my consent to marry *him*," she flashed a disdainful look at Eadnoth, "but I *will* consent to marry Edgar."

Amongst the astonished gasps of the others, Father groaned, rubbing his forehead. "Oh no…"

"That is not the bargain here, and besides," Helghi interjected, crossing his arms, "Edgar is outlawed."

"I will not allow it, Winflæd. You will not–"

"Father, enough! You have spoken, so now it is my turn, after all, it is *I* who am the subject of this dispute. I will marry Edgar, and," she put her hand up to silence him once more, "if you try to stop me, I will leave right now and go to Gorde myself, and you will never see me again."

Wulfhere stood back and shook his head.

"If I may speak, lords," Mildrith said. She came forward, her eyes down cast.

"No!" Helghi snarled at his young wife. "You may not speak."

"You may, Lady Mildrith, as long as it is helpful to this discussion," Tigfi said.

"Lord Wulfhere once gave his word that Edgar would have nothing to fear from him; that he would rescind the charges against him."

"When did he say that?" Helghi stared at her with eyebrows drawn.

Looking directly at Wulfhere, Mildrith continued, "Edgar saved the life of Lord Wulfhere's daughter." Her gaze shifted to Winflæd momentarily before it fell on Tigfi. "She was gravely injured… Edgar found her unconscious and ill in the forest. He cared for her, and when she was recovered enough, he brought her home."

"It is true." Winflæd took Wulfhere's hand. "Father, you know I would have died if it had not been for him. Tell them what you said. That Edgar need no longer live as an outlaw because of you."

"Is this true, Wulfhere?" Tigfi asked, sounding optimistic.

"Father? Tell them."

"Wulfhere?" Tigfi asked again.

"I said he no longer had anything to fear from me, but –"

"Then it is settled. I will marry Edgar, and this will bring peace between our families." Winflæd smiled and looked around at them all.

Wulfhere rounded on her. "Stop it, do you hear me? You are *not* going to marry Edgar."

"But you said that you would rather I married Edgar than Eadnoth – so I will."

"You did say it, Wulfhere," Tigfi said, crossing his arms.

"I didn't mean it – by all the saints – you would really marry Edgar?"

"I will only agree if she weds Eadnoth!" Helghi shouted.

"If you do this thing, you will no longer be my sister!" Wulfric shouted in Winflæd's face and turned to Wulfhere, "And *you* will no longer be my Father!"

"Since when do you have the right to speak about who I should marry?"

"You little conceited bitch! *I* am your brother and have every right to speak about this matter. Tell her, Father." Wulfric grew redder than his hair.

"Come, Winflæd," Sigfrith took her arm, glancing at Tigfi with disdain. "I think you should go inside, you are confused, cold, and tired. All this nonsense has addled you. I think you need to lie down."

Winflæd shook her off and said, "Father, I am going to marry Edgar. I have wanted to ever since he brought me home from the forest." It was worth the lie if it convinced him. "He was gentle... and – and kind to me. He is not at all like Helghi."

"Have you taken leave of your senses, girl?" Father stared at her aghast.

"No, I want this to end. So, I will go with them."

"Hell will freeze over before I would see you married to a son of that evil bastard! And where is Edgar? Is he to be found anywhere?"

"He is," Mildrith said, squeezing her hands together. "I know where Edgar's place is in the woods."

"Well! That is a relief." Tigfi heaved a sigh and raised his eyes. "That's that, then. Let us go and find this Edgar and get this marriage done."

"*This Edgar* is an outlaw!" Helghi cried.

"Well I have just *unoutlawed* him." said Tigfi. "I'll have it written.

377

I am the earl's representative here, therefore I am the law."

"This is not right!" Helghi shouted. "What about Eadnoth?"

"Eadnoth can go to hell," Tigfi replied, he slung an arm around Helghi's shoulders. "What are you complaining about? You will have a daughter-in-law, your eldest son is no longer outlawed, and he gets a wife, too. I bet you never imagined that would happen today, did you? Getting your son back. God is good, right?"

"So, what do *I* get?"

Tigfi looked at Helghi's youngest son. "A new sister." And when the lad scowled, "Nephews, nieces?" Eadnoth skulked off toward the gates. "Helghi? Do you agree for Winflæd, daughter of Wulfhere, to wed your son, Edgar?"

Helghi did not answer.

After some moments, Tigfi said, "I once nearly unmanned you Helghi, do you want me to do it this time?"

Helghi threw up his hands. "I agree."

"Wulfhere, do you agree? Good. Father Paul, would you be so kind as to fetch ink and vellum?"

Tigfi was clearly relieved at the resolution and so was Winflæd. The arguing would be over, and father would not need to fight.

"It just so happens, sir, that I have just the very thing here," Father Paul said in his amiable fashion. I always carry some on my person."

"Good, we will need three copies."

"Father, are you are going ahead with this madness?" Wulfric asked. And when Wulfhere looked away, saying nothing, "God, you are!"

The priest went to the work bench that Father used for his wood smithing and retrieved the writing tools from inside his pouch.

Father allowed Winflæd to guide him to where the little priest had vellum and ink at the ready. She saw him glance fearfully at Mildrith and he stopped and said, "I cannot… I cannot do this."

"Father sign, *please*," Winflæd implored him.

"Never will I sign this thing!" He drew her into the crook of his arm, brought her close to him, and tightened his grip on her neck so that it almost choked her. "If all of you do not leave my land now, I shall cut her throat and then no one will have her. Come, Winflæd, Wulfric, Ælfstan, Yrmenlaf. And you, too, Father Paul. Inside."

Winflæd had no choice but to be dragged along in Father's grasp, her hands holding on to the forearm that held her captive. But they did not get far when Tigfi called out. She looked back as Father turned and saw the huscarle waving the skins with the contract written on them.

"Wulfhere, we shall be back on the morrow, if your daughter is not handed over then, you may not have any land to order us off!"

There was a pause. She could feel her father's body, stiffen, and she knew, without even seeing him, that he had gone white with anger.

Moments later, he said, "How could you of all people do this?"

Father struggled with the words. His speech devastated by sobs. Her chest tightened and she felt an ache in her stomach. Why did this have to be so painful?

Tigfi stepped cautiously toward him. "Wulfhere, I was charged with this mission –"

"To hell with your mission – to hell with the earl. What did he offer you – gold, land?"

Father spat, then releasing Winflæd, limped to snatch the contracts.

"You know me better than that, lord," Tigfi said as Wulfhere leant on the bench and put his signature on the contracts.

"There will be no marriage celebration." Wulfhere told them, "No, merry-making, or dancing – or feasting…" He looked sourly at Father Paul. "Let the priest say the words over them – but not here, not in my home. I will not be witness to it."

Scowling, Father signed his name on all three copies. He stood up, turned without looking at Winflæd and headed for the hall, shuffling his feet like one who was utterly beaten.

She remained watching him, doing her best to hold back her tears.

Something wet splashed on her cheek. Rain, perhaps. Her fingers went to the spot and she saw that it was not rain.

"You little bitch!" her brother cried.

Sigfrith went for him, and he scuttled up the steps, making for the hall. "If you do such a thing to my lady again, I'll set your arse on fire, you red-headed beast!" Sigfrith sobbed. "I just don't know what has happened to this family," she said tearfully, as she wiped the spittle off Winflæd's face with the corner of her apron. "He is one half of a devil, that one. God forgive me but thank the Lord, there's only one of them, now."

Winflæd stayed Sigfrith's hand, feeling as though she would wipe the skin from her cheek if she let her. She looked at Tigfi. "Will you send Helghi and his men home please, Tigfi? Please, you stay, though, I want you to take me to Gorde when I am ready."

"This evening, little one?"

"'Tis best I go as soon as possible," Winflæd said. "Who knows what might happen if we wait until tomorrow." She shuddered at the thought that Father had threatened to cut her throat, even though she did not think that he really meant it.

"As you wish my lady."

"Good. I will go get my things together."

"At least let them find Edgar first?" Sigfrith turned watery eyes to her. "I cannot believe you would wed yourself to that family. He's not good enough for the likes of you, little lady. They say he's been living wild in the forest!"

"I owe him my life, Sigfrith, and he doesn't deserve to be living like that. If I marry him, he can come home."

"Have you forgotten that Edgar killed poor Esegar, leaving his wife and children without a husband and a father? Then there's the matter of your brother's death…"

"Edgar had nothing to do with that. I have made up my mind, men will always kill one another. It is for women to be peacemakers and that is what I aim to do, bring peace to our families."

Tears ran down Sigfrith's cheeks as she stood watching her little mistress enter the hall. Tigfi put his arms around her and kissed her neck.

"She is not yet a woman. I've known her since she was born and now, she is leaving me. First Freyda and now her. What am I going to do?"

Tigfi turned her to face him, lightly brushed her forehead with his lips, then took her face in his hands. "You still have me, my love."

He went to kiss her. Sigfrith pushed him away. "Don't you dare!" She slapped his face so hard he staggered, rubbing his cheek.

"What was that for?"

"For coming here and causing this misery!"

Chapter Forty-two

The Bird Flies

Winflæd eased herself quietly into the hall. Suspended in a large cauldron over the hearth, the supper bubbled loudly, a stab in her heart that she would never again hear the familiar sounds and smells of home. She closed the door as softly as the latch would allow.

Mother was stirring the supper more vigorously than it needed, her irritation on show for all to see in her grim, knotted features. Shadows of the helpers reflected the firelit walls as the old green foliage was replaced in preparation for the coming festivity. Somewhere within, she heard Father and Wulfric's raised voices as they exchanged heated words.

Swiftly she set about gathering her possessions, trying not to draw attention to herself. Mother, who never missed a thing, called out to her, "Winflæd?"

She paused, what she was doing. "Mother?"

"Ah, there you are girl, what are you up to? I need you to help with supper."

Winflæd sighed. Typically, Mother was carrying on as usual, choosing to ignore all the disorder that reigned around her.

"I can't – have you seen my silver brooch? The one with the dark stone that Grandmother left me?"

Mother looked up from her stirring. "What do you mean, 'you can't'?"

A loud oath and a clattering filled if someone had tipped over a stool in anger, filled the room.

Wulfhere stormed across the hall. "Winflæd is getting married. *He*," Wulfric jerked his thumb at Wulfhere, "signed the contract, didn't you, Father?"

"You agreed to the marriage?"

Father said nothing.

Wulfric's eyes focussed on him. "He did. He agreed that Winflæd should wed Edgar —"

"Edgar?" Mother looked aghast, her eyes wide.

Furious at her brother's interfering, Winflæd said, "He had no choice. The idea was mine."

Ealdgytha half-turned from the pot. "But Edgar is—"

"Outlawed? Apparently not anymore. Father agreed to forgive him for what he did to Freyda." Wulfric's tone was harsh and spiked with sarcasm and Winflæd screwed her face up at him and shook her head.

Looking to where Father stood, his head bowed, Mother said, her teeth gritted, "Oh, he did, did he?"

Father turned away and faced the lime plastered wall with its elegant hangings.

"*I* chose Edgar, Mother. He saved me when I was lost in the woods. I would have died if not for him. Better he than that horrible, Eadnoth!"

"Say no more, daughter, I cannot bear to hear it. And you agreed to this, Wulfhere?"

Father turned to face her. "Do you think I am happy about this, Woman?" In the fading light from the high window, his face reflected was pale and clammy, a warning that his temper was on the rise.

"You said that you would die first!"

Wulfhere took a step toward Mother, his thick yellow brows furrowed, and mouth open, ready for a fight. Winflæd gasped, afraid of what he might do.

"My lady…" Winflaed turned. Tigfi entered the hall with Sigfrith, her eyes swollen with tears. "Lord Wulfhere's hand has been forced. He must obey the shire court," he said.

It was the huscarle's turn to face Mother's wrath. "You could have turned a blind eye." Her hand trembled as she waved the dripping ladle at him. "I shall forever hold you complicit in this injustice."

"This is *not* my doing, lady," Tigfi replied. "The judgement comes from the court and it is my duty to see that it is done."

Mother stepped forward as she spoke. "For more than three years you have been coming here; you have sat by our hearth, drank our mead, dined on our meat, and dishonoured our maid…"

Sigfrith spun around with a moan of anguish. The door opened and clattered shut behind her as she flew outside weeping loudly.

Everyone stood quietly and when Sigfrith could be heard no more, Ealdgytha continued, "We have cared for your son, seen that he is fed and clothed and done this without complaint or much recompense from you. How is it you can come here and take my daughter away from me? How, sir?"

Whilst Mother berated the huscarle, Winflæd put on her mantle and hood, pinned her cloak at the shoulder with Grandmother's brooch, then, with all her possessions in a drawstring-bag went to the reeve and touched his arm. "Tigfi, I am ready."

"Have you gone completely mad, girl?" Ealdgytha said, then to her husband, "Have you nothing to say, Wulfhere?"

Once more, Father just stared blankly, and Mother huffed in exasperation.

Wulfric pushed past them and grabbed Winflæd by her bad arm, "You're not going anywhere, sister!"

Winflæd screamed as he tried to drag her away from the doors.

"Father, we should tie her up or something!"

Then Mother, throwing down her ladle and leaving the cooking pot, grabbed Winflæd's other arm to help him.

"Father - make them let me go!" she cried. "They hurt me! Father…" His inaction was gut-wrenching as he made no attempt to come to her aid. A sob caught in her throat as tears rolled down her cheeks.

"Tigfi?"

Mother tightened her grip and her brother's fingers dug into her arm like claws. *"Ow!"* Winflæd cried. She aimed a kick at Wulfric's groin, feeling his balls squidge under her boot. Before Winflæd knew anything else, her face smarted with the sting of a mighty slap. She teetered on her feet, holding a hand over her throbbing cheek whilst Mother just stared at her.

Wulfric yelled, rolling on the floor in agony, "Bitch! Whore! I'll kill you!"

"You'd have to get off the floor first, *eosol!*" she cried and hid behind Tigfi. "Let us go - *now!*" she urged, pulling on the reeve's arm.

Ealdgytha cried, "Winflæd, stop! Do something, Wulfhere!"

Wulfhere suddenly lurched into action and pulled Wulfric violently to his feet, tossing him out of the way as though he were no more than a pile of hay.

"Nay, Father. Mother, *please* – just let me go," Winflæd pleaded as Father moved toward her, a murderous look on his face. She shut her eyes, holding on to Tigfi's cloak. The material was wrenched from her grasp and when she looked, Father had Tigfi by the throat against a pillar. His teeth were clenched, and his face was contorted. "Take her, you bastard, and if any of that scum harm a hair on her head, I will hold *you* responsible. And you can tell Helghi, that spawn of Satan, that if anything happens to my daughter, I will hang them all – and I'll hang you too for that matter!"

Tigfi nodded subserviently. "I'll even give you the rope, lord."

Father let go of Tigfi and backed away, refusing Winflæd's offer of an embrace. Mother wailed and collapsed; her hands closed over her face as she burst into sobs. The sound was like that of a wounded animal and to Winflæd it was just another blow to her guts. She turned to Tigfi – the pain of leaving them like this heavy in her heart. "Come," she said, "let's hurry."

Neither of them said a word as they stepped out into the darkening afternoon. Holding his hand, she felt Tigfi tremble as they hurried across the courtyard. She looked up at the reeve, seeing his eyes moist. He was devastated.

She squeezed his hand for reassurance. He sniffed and wiped his nose with his other hand but did not look at her. The mist was coming down and the dampness enveloped them as they approached the gates where Tigfi's men awaited.

Wulfric shouted and cursed from the porch. It wasn't just anger she heard, but distress, too. What had she done?

"We need to get away quickly before my brother does something stupid."

"As you wish, my lady."

"Let me ride with you, Tigfi."

"What of your horse, Lady?"

"She is not ready. There is no time, we must go."

As Tigfi lifted her into his saddle she heard her name, and her heart sank when she saw her father hastening to them. He called to her again, "Winflæd!"

She turned. "Father," she said, softly, hoping for no more anguish.

He limped to her. Pain was etched on his once strong features now hollow and sad. She wondered what had become of the handsome man

384

always so upright and without fear.

"Wait," he said, coming to stop a few feet away. "I cannot let you leave without saying this: I know that you are doing this because you think it will make things all right between Helghi and I, but it will not. This is too great a sacrifice. If you want to change your mind, we can—"

"Father, I am duty bound now, but... I do this because I believe it to be right... and I want to."

"You want to?" His once bright blue eyes seemed clouded with grey.

"I owe Edgar my life. He was kind to me when I was with him. He is a good man... what happened with Freyda was as much her fault as it was his, she promised herself to him then broke his heart."

Father's voice was bitter. "He abducted and tried to rape her!"

"He was mad with grief. He had lost her and... *please*, Father, let us have no more talk of the past. The future is what matters now."

"Then go, *min fleógenda*, my little bird." He blinked, his voice full of such sorrow that a sob rose in her throat as he continued, "But I cannot – will not – come to a wedding, you know that."

"Please, Father..."

"Do not ask that of me – or your mother."

"She hates me now."

"Nay, she does not. She wanted better for you, as do I."

"You will not come?"

He shook his head. "I cannot. I will never set foot in that place - never."

He came to her, and tears gathered in her eyes as she bent down to kiss him. She let them trail down her cheeks, before wiping them with the ends of her wimple.

"Please do not be angry with me," she sobbed.

"Not with you... I am angry that I could not protect you."

"It is best I go now –" she glanced over at Ælfstan, Sigfrith, and Yrmenlaf. They all stood with the grief of her going upon their faces. Even her brother looked sorrowful. She imagined Tovi was there and wondered if he would have fought like Wulfric to make her stay. She pushed away the thought of him as a tide of grief threatened to overwhelm her. She had enough unhappiness to deal with at that moment without thinking about the loss of her beloved brother.

Her father, his hand on Tigfi's arm said, "Make sure that Edgar is found. Do not let her marry the other one. If it *has* to be one of them, I'd rather it was him."

"Aye, lord," Tigfi nodded. "I have sent men with Mildrith to find him." Taking the reins of the horse, he leapt upon his horse behind her. "Come, Lady Winflæd. Let us be off now." Tigfi gently nudged his horse's flanks.

"Winflæd!" She turned and saw her mother running breathlessly along the pathway. "Wait! At least let me say farewell!"

Mother was sobbing, her arms beckoning her. Wulfhere lifted her down and Winflæd allowed her mother to embrace her.

"God be with you, Mother, Father," Winflæd said, "I shall come back and see you, after all we are not so far away. Kiss Gerda goodbye for me. Tell her I shall come back one day."

"I will miss you, my daughter – my lovely, beautiful daughter," Ealdgytha cried.

Sigfrith also said her farewell and then led Mother away, both women heaving with tears as if their hearts had broken.

As the party rode through the gates, Winflæd look behind her one last time to see Father standing on the rampart. He saw her and waved. She waved too, waved until her neck hurt. And her tears did not stop until she reached Gorde.

Chapter Forty-three

Wulfsuna

She was gone. A cold wind blew, and in the darkened ether, clouds of frost emanated from his breath. As he stood watching them go until they disappeared into the winter mist, it seemed to him that God had reached down with a hand of ice, touched his heart and left it there. Wulfhere hopped down off the rampart, legs carrying him as though they were made of lead.

Wulfric waited for him, blocking the way, so white with ire, it blanched even the freckles on his face, contrasting starkly against the bright red of his hair. "Why did you let her go?" The boy asked in a voice that trembled with emotion.

"Leave it, Son. I do not wish to quarrel with you… not now."

"The hell I will leave it!" Wulfric said, mirroring him as he tried to move out of his way, obstructing his path. "Come on, Father. Tell me. Why did you let him win?"

Wulfhere stood still, hands on hips, head bowed. Wulfric pushed him and he staggered. "Don't," he said.

"What's wrong with you? Are you turning coward? There was a time when you would have torn Helghi limb from limb rather than let him win this thing."

"I do not have to justify myself to you. Men do not always think of consequences when they do violence. A sixteen-year-old thinks even less of them." He moved to pass him, but again Wulfric refused to let him.

"I say you have lost your nerve." Wulfric spat. With his hands balled into fists, he thumped Wulfhere's chest, causing him to stumble.

Wulfhere pushed him again. "You *are* a coward. What kind of a man allows his daughter to be carried off by the murderer of his brother, his friend, *and* his son?"

Wulfhere's blood rose, but he did not retaliate. He knew what it was he saw in the boy's eyes because he felt it himself. Loathing, and hunger for vengeance.

"Don't you think I want the same as you? I want revenge, I want to see Helghi dangling on the end of a rope. To see his eyes bulge and the stain of shit soiling his trousers as he cries for mercy!"

"Spare me the sermon, Father. I've heard it before, remember? In Kings Holme?"

Wulfric turned to walk away and Wulfhere caught his arm. "It will come, Wulfric, I swear it."

"When?"

"That, I cannot say. But it will."

"When Wulfwin and I were little, we sometimes used to comfort each other when we feared the dark. He used to say to me, 'Do not fear, brother, Father will protect us from the *nihtgenga*.' I wonder what he thinks of you now," a sob seemed to catch in his throat, "to see the weakling you have become. He asks me every night, Father, 'Where is my vengeance, Brother?' And every night I must tell him I do not know."

Wulfhere stood boiling as Wulfric's words ripped through him. There was no quelling the rage now it had been roused beyond its seether. He threw his son to the ground and crouched down by him, holding him there by his throat as the boy's hands clasped Wulfhere's wrist.

"Do you think it was easy to let her go? To *him*, knowing he killed my son. Knowing that because of him my brother died – that Esegar died – and there is nothing I can do about it? Do you think it has not torn my heart out? You know nothing of what I have just been through in my head. Fighting is easy! I could swat you like a fly – just like that, I could crush the life out of you, but–" He felt his hands tighten around Wulfric's neck, the boy's eyes watering, as he tried to extricate himself from the choke-hold. "Coward, am I? It takes more courage to walk away than to fight – aye! It takes more courage than you will ever know, to see your daughter stolen from you and not be able to do anything about it."

As Wulfric's face began to redden, Wulfhere let him go, and rising to his feet, stepped over the boy, and strode, his leg paining him, back toward the hall.

"Father!" Wulfric caught up with him. "You have fought many battles. You fought and won the *cheampa*. Men sang your praises in the warrior's hall – and now you speak words of cowardice, not courage."

Wulfhere halted, turned to face his son, his forehead so close to Wulfric's he could feel the heat of the boy's anger. "Do not even think to talk to me of the things you know nothing of. You will regret your words to me one day – by God, you will! Aye, you will learn in the fullness of time, if you get there." He walked on.

Wulfric hurrying alongside him, continued to harry him. "You have lost your mind. We are warriors. *Wulfsuna* – a bloodline that stretches back through our family since the first sons of the wolf came to this land."

"Aye, we are warriors. But there are many kinds of battles to fight other than the ones you fight in the fields. As you go through life, you will find out what they are! Now, get out of my way, *lyttel mana!*"

Wulfhere returned to the warmth of the hall. Wulfric slumped in after him, head bowed and went to his mother who was sobbing in Sigfrith's arms and said a farewell, kissing her cheek.

"Where do you go, my son?" she asked him as he collected his things. "Am I to lose all my children?"

"I go to Leofnoth. I'd rather eat pig shite for the rest of my life than stay here," Wulfric said, venomously.

"What about me?" Cynethryth hurried to his side.

"You may come, if you wish," Wulfric said joylessly. He went through the doors, carrying his shield strapped over his shoulder and his spear in his right hand. Cynethryth grabbed her cloak and hood and ran after him.

"Don't let him go, Wulfhere!"

"He will come back in his own time."

"Just as Winflæd will come back, I suppose," Ealdgytha retorted.

Her words were a stab to his heart.

Later that evening, when all had gone to their beds, he was alone in the hall, drinking by himself and staring into the flames, listening absently to the unmelodic snoring and wheezing of the men asleep in their bed spaces. Once, the hall had been filled with children. Now there was just Gerda, and Sigfrith's little one. His wife had turned her back on him long ago, and he'd never felt so alone. He missed Esegar. They'd often spend late nights by the hearth, sharing their thoughts and problems. Talking to Esegar had always made him feel better. *If only he hadn't died...*

His thoughts floated to happier times: he and Esegar, the children, a game of warriors, wooden sticks for swords, and laughter. There'd been such joy in those days, when the children were little. He saw a young boy laughing, with gleaming blue eyes and a sweeping fringe of golden hair that flopped wildly across his brow. Tears stung Wulfhere's eyes and a pang of longing overwhelmed him.

Tovi. It was the third winter since the boy left for Waltham. Banished like an exile. He'd not once heard word from him. Even though gifts had been sent to his son, in return came nothing. Perhaps Tovi should come home. He was never the scholarly type, often hiding in the village or in the forest from Father Paul and his lessons. He would never make a good priest. It had always been Ealdgytha's idea, not his. She would have sent him to a monastery at seven if he had not put his foot down.

He must have passed out, inebriated. When he woke lying on the floorboards, the fire was almost out, and it was cold... so cold.

He staggered to his feet, tripping over the contents of a half empty jug of mead. His head throbbed. God's teeth, not even liquor could ease the noise in his head or help him sleep soundly. But then he could hardly expect to be comfortable on a cold floor instead of a nice, feather mattress with the warm flesh of a beautiful woman next to him. And she was still beautiful, his wife – aye, she was. He shivered and his teeth chattered. He put some wood on the fire and stoked it, searched for a taper, found one, and ignited it in what was left of the flames.

Shuffling across the dimly lit hall, his damaged leg almost gave way with the pain. He must have been lying awkwardly. Damn! When would this thing heal properly? He was tired of pretending it did not hurt. He looked about for the space where he had been sleeping of late. Ealdgytha had frozen him out since Ælfgyva had come to take the bearn. But that night he was desperate not to be alone. He needed her.

"What are you doing here?" she exclaimed as he stood at the foot of her bed, holding the taper, and staring at her.

"I want to talk with you," he whispered.

She pulled herself up on her elbows. A brazier was still burning in the corner of the room. It felt warmer there, unlike the hall downstairs.

"Now? At this time of night? What can there be said between us which cannot wait till the morning?" Her breath came in clouds in the cold air.

"I cannot live this way anymore, Ealdgytha, not without love or affection, or a sense of... of unity. We are always at odds with each other... it-it is destroying my soul." He sat down on the end of the bed holding on to one of the carved posts to steady himself.

"Your soul was destroyed long ago, Wulfhere."

He sighed. "I do not want to go to that place again. Much has happened since then."

She looked anywhere but at him.

"She got married you know."

"I know."

"So you sought her out, yet again." She sounded cynical rather than angry.

"She has my child."

"Ah yes, the little bastard that you passed off so cleverly as a foundling; such cunning surpasses that of the wiliest of wolves. And I fell for the ruse, didn't I?" Moments passed before either of them spoke again, and then she said, "I know what you are thinking...."

"Of course you do; you will be thinking: he wishes I was more like *her*. That's what you will be thinking, but it is not true."

"How very perceptive of you."

"I know you well."

"As I do you."

She shifted, turning sideways to sink back down under the covers, shivering. "Then you will know that I am only your wife in name. Now leave my chamber. I wish to sleep. Nothing has changed."

He lay down by her side. She stiffened, turning her back to him.

"Don't," he said, leaning on his side, his lips close to her slender neck. "I am frozen by the ice in your heart."

He entwined his legs and arms around her. She struggled, but only half-heartedly. "If I am cold, it is because you have made me so. Now leave me be, Wulfhere. I am yours no longer."

"Nay, Ealdgytha, I love you..." he whispered, pushing aside the golden braid to kiss her. "I need you, *min leoftost*. We need each other."

He rubbed himself against her buttocks. She resisted for a moment, but only a moment.

He undid the ties on his trousers and entered from behind, her moistness allowing him to slide in easily. She gave a little moan of pleasure as he penetrated her. "See, you are not so impervious to me after all," he said, as they moved together.

She said nothing. He felt her arousal as his hands brushed her soft breasts through her shift. Her loins were moist and pulsating. He reached down to her mound and she gasped as he stimulated her with his fingers. Reaching up, she wound an arm about his neck, tilting her face to seek out his lips. His tongue probed inside her mouth and his hands reached under her night garment to caress and squeeze the taut nipples.

He slid himself out from between her legs and she turned onto her back, spreading her legs, waiting for him to re-enter. He pulled off his tunic, and lifted her shift to expose her smooth skin, wanting to feel his flesh against hers. His arousal grew, but it was not Ealdgytha's face he saw on the bed below him as he re-entered. "Ælfgȳva," he whispered.

Not noticing the tears streaming down her cheeks until he climaxed, the look on her face told him what he'd done. Still inside, he collapsed, breathing heavily from the exertion. Ealdgytha turned away as he went to kiss her.

"I am sorry…" He removed himself from within her and breathlessly sat, his head in his hands. "She has enchanted me; witch, that she is."

Ealdgytha sat up abruptly. "Everything you do is marred and tainted by that woman. Aye, you are indeed bewitched, and you will never be – nay, *we*, will never be free of her!"

Ealdgytha sat, her back to his, on the edge of the bed just as he did. Her voice as she spoke was filled with bitterness. "You think you are the only one to know the sinful luxury of adultery, but I too had a lover, once."

It took a moment for him to comprehend the meaning of what she said. Slowly, he turned towards her and was met with the slenderness of her back. "I don't believe you would do such a thing."

She stood from the bed and swung to face him, tossing her braid over her shoulder; face twisted in a deep anger of her own. "Do you not? Why? Do you think it impossible for me to want someone else? Or that another man would want me? Did you think that I would always remain faithful to a faithless husband?" A smile hovered over the victorious lips. "Aye, Wulfhere, women have needs too. Just as you sought comfort and pleasure in *her,* so I sought comfort for myself."

"You're lying. Tell me it isn't true."

"Oh, but it is." She laughed. "Now you know how it feels, don't you, to be betrayed?"

He was on his feet. "Who was it? When?"

"His name was Thierry. He came with Ranulf. He'd not long gone through the gate, you must have just missed them, the day you came home from court and Tovi–"

"Tovi slapped you."

She nodded.

"It was when the Francs were here. So it was a Franc?"

"Aye. Young and handsome."

"And Tovi, he knew?"

At this she looked ashamed but said nothing.

"No wonder you wanted him to go away!"

Wulfhere leapt across the bed and grabbing her braid, swung her down onto the mattress. He pinned her with his body, face close to hers. "Tell me it is not true!"

She laughed. "Nay, for that would be a lie. And that would be another sin to atone for on the day of reckoning."

Wulfhere felt his hands go to her throat. They squeezed. She was coughing, eyes rolling. *My God, what the hell am I doing?*

He pulled away, releasing her, shocked by his violent reaction. As she recovered, coughing and spluttering, he felt ashamed. *What has she done that I have not, but a hundred times over?* Still gasping, Ealdgytha staggered to where a jug of mead had been left on a trestle.

Watching her pour the liquid into her, Wulfhere said in a voice choked with sadness, "What have I done to you?"

Now he understood something of what she must have felt every time he went to be with his lover. Not even when he learned that Ælfgyva had taken a husband did such jealousy as this find him. But his wife was not to blame, she had been driven to it… by him. No wonder she'd taken to her bed in a melancholy state all those weeks. She would have been riddled with guilt at what she had done.

"No more than I deserve…" she sobbed.

He shook his head. "I've hurt you for years." Mucous had gathered with his tears and he sniffed hard, wiping under his nose with his arm

"You were always the light of my life and I should have known it... I should have..."

"You should have," she muttered.

He went to embrace her, but she pushed him away. "It's too late. On the morrow, I will go to the nunnery at Wilton. I will take Gerda with me. She will never find a husband, not with her condition. She will be looked after there when we are dead and gone. I hear the nuns are educated and kind. It is where the queen grew up and a good many more noble ladies have sought comfort there. You will be free, of course, to take another woman. I absolve you of your husbandly duty toward me, other than what you owe me regarding my comfort and wellbeing."

"You say this as if there is nothing between us – and as if there never has been."

"I have been thinking about it for some time. It is for the best."

"Nay Ealdgytha... I could not bear for you to leave me."

"We will kill each other if I do not."

"I would rather we took our chances, than you left."

"Wulfhere, I have nothing left to give. Living with you has turned me into the worst kind of woman. I have betrayed my children... I've been dreadful to them. Freyda... and now Winflæd has gone. And Wulfric, too. I drove Tovi away. God forgive me what I did to that boy. The awful things I said to him... And you... you are a strong man in so many ways and yet... you are so weak," she put a hand to her heart and choked back a sob, her voice barely audible, "in here."

"I will make things right..."

"Nothing will ever change. We cannot go back to the past. You would never forgive me, and I could not expect you to. Now all I ask is that you to take your leave of me."

"I do not care what you have done. We have both done wrong, I more times than you. Let us wipe the slate clean and forget the past. Start again.... Look at me, Ealdgytha... my wife...."

"I can't, Wulfhere. If I look at you, I will stay, and I can't. I want to be as I once was, not this harridan that you have turned me into. Please go."

He shrank away into the darkness and returned to his place in the hall, his heart heavy. So, this was what the spinners had been spinning all along, that he would ruin everything he touched: his marriage, his children...

She held back the temptation to give in to him. If she didn't, her soul would be like the snow melting in the warmth of the sun until there was nothing left of it. Her back was turned, and she prayed silently for him to leave, though she hoped he would not. When she finally plucked up the courage to turn, he was gone. Wrapping both arms around herself, she let the tears go. A heart can only be fixed so many times and hers had been broken a hundred-fold and now, there was nothing left to break.

Epilogue

March 1059

Tovi's heart thumped anxiously as he rode in through the gates. He was home at last. Grendl nodded his head, as his hooves clopped over the familiar wooden boards of the old ford. It was as if the horse, too, was glad to be home.

Tovi wondered what to say to his parents, after all, he had been gone three winters now.

Yrmenlaf greeted him, opening the gates with a joyful grin. The old stable boy had changed so much Tovi almost hadn't recognised him. As the older lad took Grendl to the stables, Tovi hurried up the path to the hall, past Ælfstan's forge where the old blacksmith was busy hammering away.

"Tovi? Is that you?" He stopped and turned to see Sigfrith. He recognised the little boy that was now grown beyond toddling as Leofweard. "It *is* you!" she cried, dropped her hand cart and came running toward him, the little boy too. "What are you doing here, Master Tovi?"

She embraced him, pulling down his hood as if to make sure of him.

"Winflæd's letter, about Wulfwin. I didn't receive it until recently. It said that Mother and Father might have need of me, but I don't suppose..."

She didn't seem to be listening to him, looking him up and down, grinning like a loon. "Master Tovi, just look at you, why, you are almost a man now!"

He laughed and took the cart for her. "How is Mother?" he asked.

Sigfrith's face darkened. "She has gone."

"Gone?" He halted, thinking she had died.

"Left, with Gerda, to a nunnery, somewhere I know not."

Tovi smiled in disbelief.

Good God, he thought, *so she finally plucked up the courage to leave him.* "And Father?"

"He is not good," Sigfrith replied. "But he manages day to day."

They approached the hall and Sigfrith's father, Herewulf, who was baking bread in the yard, called out, "Why, just look who is here! What a sight for these old eyes. What brings you home, Master Tovi?"

Tovi was engulfed in Herewulf's welcome embrace and was about to reply when he heard a voice call to him. "Who is here, Herewulf?"

He turned and saw his father emerge onto the porch from within the hall. He came down the steps like a confused, weakened old man, walking with a stick. His hair, still blonde in places, was greying, long and unkempt, his beard, a soft shade of auburn, wild and bushy. Once, Father had been proud of his finely groomed, warrior's moustache, but now it was almost indistinct from his beard. His eyes were lined, and dark circles shaded his lower lids. He looked leaner, and a scar that curved in a horseshoe on his cheek was livid.

"Father?" Tovi whispered, stepping toward him, hardly believing it was him. "Father, 'tis me, Tovi."

"Tovi." A smile crept over Wulfhere's face. "It *is* you. You came! God has answered me. I have been praying that you would come."

"Aye, Father, I have come."

Father threw down the stick as if embarrassed by it and limped toward him. Tovi drew closer.

Father smiled, and in a voice that was barely audible, said simply and with a sigh of joy, "Tovi."

In the warm embrace the two of them shared, the son and the father, Tovi's bitterness melted.

"Yes Father, I am home."

397

HISTORICAL NOTE

One of my aims when writing this series, is to be as true to the period as possible, in terms of how my characters lived, what everyday trials they faced, such as lice, illnesses, the everyday drudgery, working the land, the times they enjoyed, feasting, how the Old English loved to feast and make merry, and still do! Life was hard in comparison today, but they still found time to laugh, love and have fun. You can see this in their poetry and sagas, and their riddles, too, which shows their earthy sense of humour. Even the lower classes were afforded some medieval time out. There were so many holy feast days in the Anglo-Saxon calendar, and generally a feast, though preceded by a fast, was celebrated to the max.

As with *The Wolf Banner* and *Sons of the Wolf*, the feasts take place in the lord's hall, or the meadhall. The hall was the centre of their lives, for it was there that they felt at home, protected, and a sense of who they were. They would make their way to the hall on feast days, invited by their lord and lady, perhaps bringing honey, cheeses, ales, and bread for the privilege. They would spend the next three days in merriment and nonstop drinking and eating. No wonder they looked forward to these days.

Battles were another thing. We often get the image that these were bloody times, with bloodthirsty people, excitedly awaiting their next chance to stand in the glorious midst of a battle, their swords raised, their voices roaring. By the time *Sons* and *Banner* is set, the old ideology of the Teutonic warrior, who lived his life just to fight, was fading. The concept was most likely to have started diminishing with the advent of Christianity when warriors no longer went to Valhalla upon death, but to heaven. Although it was still honourable to die in battle, clasping one's sword, it was no longer a requisite, and men passed on their weapons and other warrior trappings to their sons for use in this life rather than being buried with them. However, I am sure that the ideology was still there in the mindsets of the youths as they marched to their first battle. Songs of a warrior's bravery – think of Byrhtnoth – were still being sung by the *scops*, so the thought was there, if not the belief.

Those young warriors who survived their first time on the field of blood, may have had their illusions squashed, just as young Wulfric's were after the Battle of Mynstreworth. I am sure that throughout the ages, many men suffered the torments of the battle madness, as they referred to PTSD in those days – just as we have seen soldiers today – experience the trauma stress of combat.

Many things have been said about Edward's sexuality; that he was gay, asexual or a woman hater, that he and Edith had never consummated their wedding. When Edith was cast out into a nunnery, during the Godwins crisis of 1051, Edward's Norman friends were coercing him to put Edith aside and perhaps consider marrying one of Duke William's relations. Edward had plenty of time to do this before the Godwins returned from exile, but he didn't. He could have used the excuse that they had not consummated the marriage, he didn't. Personally, whether he and Edith had consummated the marriage or not, I think he came to enjoy her in the same way a father would enjoy his children. He allowed her to fuss over him and was content for her to dress him in splendour, from her own purse. He does refer to her, fondly in his deathbed speech in the *Edwardi vita* as his 'daughter', though we must remember who the *Life* was commissioned by – Edith herself.

The conflict of 1058 was probably the most difficult part of the book to write about because evidence is scarce. The Worcester Manuscript of the *Anglo-Saxon Chronicle* (ASC) states that Alfgar was expelled in 1058,

> '...but he soon came back again with violence and the help of Gruffudd. And there came a raiding ship army from Norway...'

Then it follows with that infamous line:

> '...it is tedious to tell how it happened.'

It goes on to discuss the various ecclesiastical events such as bishops being ordained etc., things that were probably not so tedious to the monk who was writing, as a full-scale invasion of England might have been. But the Canterbury version of the ASC, says even less. In fact, it mentions nothing about Alfgar's exile, and nothing about the fleet from Norway. Nor do the Peterborough and the Abingdon versions say anything about Alfgar's invasion with Gruffudd and the Norwægians. And yet, an invading fleet from Norway sounds more exciting than something that was 'too tedious to tell'. According to the Welsh chronicle, the *Annales Cambriae*, this Norwægian fleet was a largescale invasion by Magnus, the adolescent son of Harald Hardrada, and aided by Gruffudd ap Llewelyn. It came to support Alfgar in his return to England by force. But if this is so, why do the English chronicles, bar one, omit it from their entries for that year? Why does the only English chronicle to mention it, say it is too tedious to tell, as if it was some event that came to nothing, rather than a full-on war? Perhaps this is because it did come to nothing. Perhaps it promised to come to something but fizzled to nothing. Perhaps this is why that monk in his scriptorium couldn't be bothered to mention the whys and wherefores because just like Alfgar and Gruffudd's other incursions, this one ended up the same: with the English ceding more land to the Welsh, and Gruffudd and Alfgar, having to swear to behave themselves before the king. My story of Harald Hardrada making a bid by proxy for the English throne, is not at all unfeasible; however, it is my interpretation only, and I hope I have explained it satisfactorily.

The lack of assistance from the sources to help me unpick what happened, provided me with one of the biggest headaches as author of this book, to fill in the gaps. Many historical authors might rub their hands in glee at having a free rein to fill in the cavities of history, however in this instance, it was to prove somewhat more difficult than I expected. Somehow, I had to create something out of very little and all I had to go on was that Alfgar was exiled once more, just as he had been in 1055; but he returned, by force, with the aid of Magnus Haraldson and Gruffudd ap Llewellyn. So, to work out what, when, where and why, was my first port of call in creating this part of the story, then how to absorb my characters' narratives into my interpretation.

It was important to me that I was able craft plausible threads for each of the main characters involved; Wulfhere, Burghred, Alfgar and Harold. It was clear that something of note had happened, but why had the English chronicles been so quiet on the subject is something we can only conjecture. Still, having worked hard to create a narrative that fits, I can rest easy in my bed at night on the understanding that whatever it was that Alfgar and his allies had in mind, was resolved with the diplomatic skills of the king's leading earl, Harold Godwinson.

I was going to skip 1058 out of the story, or at least the story of the 'invasion', but I felt that this would be a cop out and it needed to stay in. After all, it was a perfect device to create more havoc in the lives of my people, as I have come to think of my characters – especially poor Wulfhere and Burghred.

Burghred, son of Alfgar of Mercia, is one of those shadowy characters, who gets little more than a mention in the chronicles of the time and that is only to mention his death and that his father had endowed a church for his soul. It made sense that Burghred was the eldest of Alfgar's sons. He makes his first appearance in the series, in Book One, *Sons of the Wolf.* I had only ever intended to give Burghred a small part, but when writing *The Wolf Banner*, he took the story and ran with it, leaving me powerless to stop him. He obviously had his part to play, and not even I, the author, could change that. He was as useful to me, as much as he was to Harold Godwinson, because I could cast him in a dual role, the betrayer, and the spy.

The battle of Mynstreworth was also entirely my invention, as was the siege of Scrobbesbyrig – both part of my mission to create the something that eventually came to nothing. Both Burghred and Wulfhere were crying out to have a battle, and if Burghred was going to have his, then Wulfhere was not going to let me rest, especially since he is the central character. I have always wanted to include the Severn Bore in the book somewhere, so I went on location, so to speak, and found Minsterworth, a little village mentioned in the Domesday Book, a sleepy little Hamlet along the Severn, in Gloucestershire. The characters of Ótryggr and his friends were fun to write, but they are totally of my imagination.

Alfgar was reinstated as Earl of Mercia; this is fact. It seemed sensible to send Magnus home with his coffers filled, and this was not unknown in this era. Alfgar's son-in-law Gruffudd's position as his ally was now reinforced, and the Welsh king would continue to be a thorn in the side of the English for more years to come.

If you have got this far, I do hope that you have enjoyed my book, and that the imagined events of 1058 make some sense. I hope that you will join Wulfhere and his friends as we go into Book Three, *Wolf's Bane*. If you would like to read a longer version of this historical note, please check out my website, 1066:The Road to Hastings and Other Stories.

The Author would like to thank you all for reading and hope that you will join us for the next instalment of Sons of the Wolf– *Wolf's Bane* –

Coming in 2021

Please email her with any comments or questions at

sonsofthewolf1066@googlemail.com

Printed in Great Britain
by Amazon

83092523R00246